THE PARIS PROTECTION

———◦◖✳◗◦———

BRYAN DEVORE

Printed in the United States of America.

ISBN-10: 0-9852413-5-7
ISBN-13: 978-0-9852413-5-3

Also available as an e-book.

I do the very best I know how—the very best I can;
and I mean to keep on doing so until the end.
—Abraham Lincoln

1

MAXIMILIAN WOLFF CRACKED open the silver locket in his palm and gazed at the little oval photos of his wife and son. As he thought of them, he vaguely heard the rustling of the two hundred men standing below him on the floor of a big, old Parisian warehouse. He tried to look inside the two innocent faces in the tiny pictures: Naomi's radiant eyes and long, dark hair; his little Eli's wide, happy smile. Recalling the joy that had once been in his life, he felt a brimming tear and blinked it away. This was perhaps the last time he would see their faces before the world erupted in fire. He took a moment longer, then closed the locket and tucked it back under his shirt. Then he stepped out onto the platform, raised his fists in the air, and yelled, "In less than an hour, we will kill the president of the United States!"

The room exploded in cheers. In their black tactical clothing, some of the men raised their Heckler & Koch MP5 submachine guns in the air like championship trophies. The surge of violent energy helped Maximilian move past the bittersweet memories and focus on the rhetoric of his battle cry. This would likely be the last night of his life, and he was determined to live every minute with the courage and control of the paramilitary general he had become over the past decade.

Patting the air with both hands, he quieted the men enough to continue.

"For too long, America has poisoned the world. For too long, they have plundered its natural resources so that they may live in wealth and luxury while so many others suffer in poverty and sickness and starvation and war." He raised his arm. "But in less than an hour, we will sever the head of the demonic nation." He swiped his hand through the air as if delivering a death blow.

More cheers erupted from the floor.

"We will wound their people as never before. Their corrupt society shall witness our moment of triumph! We will rise up from below this city like resurrected warriors and descend on the American president like a tidal wave."

More fervent cheering.

"For we are that tidal wave of change!" Maximilian yelled. "To bring the world back closer to equality and end the imperialism that strong, corrupt nations impose on the vulnerable and weak."

As he fired up his men, he saw that they had already grouped together in their units. The two in the demolition team stood next to the engineer with the packed diamond-toothed industrial chainsaw. Beside them stood four other men with large tanks strapped to their backs. His advanced elite made up most of the group, with early first-wave pawns behind them. The dozen dark-skinned men from his personal guard were closest to the platform. And Kazim Aslan, his second in command, stood to the right with his elite dozen warriors waiting patiently for the start of the assault.

"What we do in the next hour, we do for all those whom America has harmed!" he continued. "We do it for those who cannot claim their revenge in person! And we do it for our children, so they have some hope for a future without America trying to control the world that God has given us all!"

The men yelled like berserkers spoiling for a fight.

Maximilian paced slowly back and forward on the steel platform as the hardened faces stared up at him.

"Men," he continued in a deep, gravelly voice, "let there be no doubt, this will be a Herculean task. To attack such a powerful enemy will cost us many lives tonight. But we must remember the importance of our task: one that will be chronicled in history for thousands of years after tonight. We are not the first to face impossible odds in conquering our enemy. More than two thousand years ago, Rome had defeated Carthage in the First Punic War. Afterward, a great Carthaginian general from that war raised a son named Hannibal Barca, who would grow to become perhaps the greatest military general of antiquity, matched only by Alexander the Great."

Maximilian stopped and looked down on his men with pride. He had been planning this moment for three years, and he felt more alive in this moment than at any other time since his wife and son were taken from him. He had taken a long, dark path, abandoning his nation and his faith to arrive at this point in his life. But the energy he felt right now only confirmed that he was exactly where he needed to be, exactly on course to meet his destiny.

Again he spoke to the men. "Hannibal would eventually lead the next generation's Carthaginian army into Roman territory, fighting the Romans in their own lands, conquering Roman legions on Italian soil, burning Roman cities that would not join his alliance, and striking fear into the hearts of Roman citizens for the first time in centuries. His army was always outnumbered on the battlefield, but through courage, clever deception, and brilliant strategic maneuvering, he won battle after battle. History remembers them all."

He turned to Kazim, standing slightly below him, beside the metal platform. His second in command, a tall Turk with a mop of black shoulder-length hair, had heard him give speeches like this many times over the past few years. But there was now a look of concern on Kazim's face, as if he had something to say.

Turning back to the men, Maximilian continued. "But before Hannibal ever fought a single battle on Italian soil, he achieved what is still considered one of the greatest feats of any army in history. He crossed the rugged, snowy Alps with an army of nearly forty thousand men and a few hundred elephants. No one thought it possible. Even Scipio, leader of the Roman army dispatched to intercept him in Spain and Gaul, never imagined that Hannibal would take his army through the high mountains instead of the lower coastal lands. But the Carthaginian had planned his invasion of northern Italy with careful calculations and a bold strategy. For fifteen long, cold days, he marched his army through the treacherous mountains. Many of his men froze. Others fell to their deaths. Before he reached the foothills leading down to the plains of northern Italy, he had lost nearly half his men and most of his elephants. But this secret crossing of the Alps had allowed his army to arrive in Italy—to the Romans' horrified amazement—with a remaining army much stronger than if he had battled Scipio all along the coastal lands."

He paused and listened to the silence in the vast room.

"And just as he used the snowy Alps to surprise Rome, we will use the Paris catacombs to surprise the president of the United States."

The men gave a loud, savage roar. To Maximilian's ears, it sounded like the barbarians from ancient tribes—Goths and Huns and Vandals—whose anger at all dominant powers had been faithfully passed, whether through genes or through spoken lore, down the centuries to the present.

After allowing the men to build their energy with their battle cries, he raised his hands to speak again. When the roaring at last subsided, he recited the words he had memorized from the historian Theodore Ayrault Dodge's writings on Hannibal after crossing the Alps into Italy.

"Hannibal had reached his goal. He had with him a force of twenty-six thousand men . . . What was the purpose of this reckless army? To attack on its own soil a people capable of raising three quarters of a million of men; a people which, in the last conflict, but a generation since, had utterly overthrown—all but exterminated—the Carthaginian power and nationality . . . To dare this and any other danger for the chance of bringing to his feet the cruel, rapacious power of Rome, which had inflicted such injustice and degradation on his beloved country . . . The man whose courage cannot be daunted, whose mind and body are incapable of fatigue, whose soul burns with the divine spark of genius, may always confront the impossible. And Hannibal had faced all this with a full knowledge of what he was about to do. To him there was no impossible. To him, with his honest cause and unconquerable purpose, there must be a way. It is, indeed, when such a hero looks the all but impossible in the face that he is at his greatest. It is here that he shines forth, clad in all his virtue. Be it that the palm of the victor awaits him, be it that he is destined to sink beneath the weight of his herculean task, at such a time he is no longer man. He is a demigod!"

The men roared in wild jubilation.

"So follow me, men! Follow me into the darkness under this city so that we may rise up and free the world of this evil. And afterwards, as we are all taken into the brilliant light of eternity, as servants to God and proud patriots of our native lands, I shall forever know each of you as my brother! For tonight, we will achieve a victory that history will never forget!"

Maximilian's eyes shone, reflecting the excitement he had stirred within the men. Turning to Kazim, he said, "Is everything ready?"

Kazim nodded. "The equipment is packed and waiting at the entrance to the tunnels . . . But there is a small matter you need to know about."

"We don't have time! We have to go now!"

Kazim leaned in and whispered, "Julian arrived with some men a few minutes ago."

A wave of fury washed over Maximilian. "Right before we leave!" he snarled. "How did he know our schedule?"

"Someone from the syndicates informed him, I suppose."

"You think they're changing their plans?" Maximilian asked his trusted friend and adviser.

"They could be hedging. They have billions of euros riding on tonight."

"It's ironic," Maximilian said.

"What is?"

"History—people like to say it repeats itself. Do you know why it often repeats itself?"

"Why?" Kazim said. He flexed his neck as if impatient to get moving.

"Because human nature is the same in every time. Passion, loyalty, love, honor, pride, ambition, stupidity, fear, hatred, betrayal, shame . . . Human nature seems the only thing in nature that doesn't know how to evolve. Do you know the main reason Hannibal ultimately failed to destroy Rome?"

"No."

"It was because the Carthaginian senate failed to support him at a critical time during his campaign in Italy. He had just beaten the Roman army at Cannae, in the single greatest defeat the empire ever suffered in its entire eight-hundred-year existence, before or after that single day. But the politicians of Carthage— the country Hannibal was fighting for—were too foolish and fearful in their senate chamber to send the support he needed to win the war in Rome. They failed him, and it eventually cost him—and Carthage—everything."

Maximilian paused before continuing.

"We will not let Julian and the syndicates fail us. We will not let their cowardice stop us. We will not let that species of flaw in human nature once again allow history to repeat itself. Dominik Kalmár has entrusted us with this operation, and we will triumph for him as well as for ourselves. Tonight, we will do what Hannibal ultimately failed to do: we will succeed in our decapitation strike against our greatest enemy."

Moving away from the platform, he clomped down the grated metal steps, with Kazim in tow. They must leave the warehouse soon. He had little time to deal with Julian.

2

REBECCA REID SWUNG the pillow as hard as she could, catching the side of his head and knocking him off the bed. Twisting her body sideways, she pulled the ruffled beige sheet up to cover her naked body. The man, having recovered from the fall to the hardwood floor, scrambled back to the side of the bed, where he stayed on his knees as if to pray or ask for clemency.

"I'm sorry," he said.

"Too late," she replied. "I don't care."

"Forgive me."

"Never," Rebecca said. "You just made the biggest mistake of your life."

David Stone smiled. It was a big, happy smile that lit up his eyes, temporarily relieving his habitually serious demeanor. Rebecca was the only one in the United States Secret Service who ever saw this side of him. It was one of the reasons she had let him break down her usually strong defenses and—against her better judgment—risk her reputation on his decency as a man. But she was smart enough never to reveal her vulnerability to him.

David walked his elbows a few inches forward on the bed, leaning closer. His dress clothes and hers were strewn in a crooked line from the door. His pale, muscular chest pressed against the rumpled sheets, his arms reaching out toward her.

She swung the pillow at him again. This time, he blocked it and sprang off the floor to pounce on the bed. But as he leaned in to kiss her neck, he made the mistake of keeping his weight forward. She threw an arm up under his right arm while twisting her hips and knocking his left arm out from under him, throwing him off balance as his momentum carried him across the bed and down to the floor on the other side.

She laughed as he tumbled back to the floor.

"This is ridiculous," he groaned, sitting up. "We don't have much time."

"You're *out* of time, buster. POTUS will be here soon, and you need to save your energy."

"Oh, I have plenty."

"No way," she said, grinning as she slipped out of bed. "I'm going to take a really fast shower and dash downstairs."

"Perfect! I'll join you."

"You'd better get back to your own room and clean up before she gets here." She motioned with her eyes toward the nightstand. "And don't forget your gun."

"You really don't want it?" he asked. "It was an expensive gift."

Rebecca pointed at the small nickel-plated subcompact semiautomatic, still in the wooden box on the bed, near the nightstand. The box was surrounded by torn red wrapping paper. The box's purple felt lining seemed to accentuate the fine craftsmanship of the pistol, which was only slightly larger than the palm of her hand.

"It's a prostitute's gun."

"No, it's not."

"It's a Model Fifty-two Special, right? That's for prostitutes."

"No."

"Yes! Look, it even came with a harness that straps high on the leg and can attach to a garter belt."

"No—I mean yes, but no. That's not what I meant."

"You're supposed to get a woman chocolates or roses or diamonds, not a gun—and especially not a gun favored by ladies of the evening. That's how you think of me? As your prostitute? Is that it?"

"No, of course not! I just thought . . . I like guns and saw it at a trade show in Philly last month, and my instincts told me to buy it for you. I don't know why. Maybe it's stupid, but I've been looking forward to the right moment to give it to you. I've never bought anything this expensive for anyone before. And honestly, if you reject it, it'll feel like you're rejecting my instincts towards *you*."

She thought about what her father and three older brothers would think of this. "I'm sorry, but I just can't accept it."

"Becky . . ."

She shook her head. "Nope, sorry. I can't."

She walked naked across the wood floor, past the palatial white curtains and into the bathroom. Closing the door, she pulled the thick towel off the hook and slung it over the shower rod.

From the other side of the door came David's muffled voice. "I'm sorry."

She ignored him and stepped into the shower. Just before she turned it on, she heard "I love you," accompanied by soft scratching on the door.

She picked up the hotel's complimentary bathroom slippers and tossed them hard against the door. "You'd better hurry," she said. "You don't want to be late for the shift change."

She heard a muttered *"Damn."* She unhooked the Parisian-style hose nozzle from the shower to avoid getting her hair wet. The hotel room's door thudded shut—David had left.

Two minutes later, she jumped out, dried and dressed, brushed her hair, and put on her array of weapons and equipment: collapsible baton, loaded P229 with two extra magazines, belt with plastic hand ties, mace, and a flash-bang grenade for emergency crowd control. She attached her Thales P25 Digital Encryption radio to the back of her belt, ran the wire up inside her suit jacket and down the sleeve, and clipped the microphone to her wrist, and the earpiece up the back of her neck and over and into her ear.

She had so rushed when getting ready that it wasn't until she moved around the bed that she saw the box still resting on the stand. She sighed. Why hadn't he taken it, as she asked? Opening the box, she looked at the diminutive weapon, gleaming in the room's sharp canned lighting. It did look nice. But she couldn't accept it. The only daughter of a Colorado sheriff, and the baby sister of three Denver police detectives, she had spent her entire life fighting to prove that women could be just as strong in law enforcement as men. Being accepted into the Secret Service was still one of the proudest days of her life. And she just couldn't play into the roles that women had historically been forced to tolerate. A small gun would have been bad enough, but the make and style used by prostitutes of the early twentieth century—that was unacceptable.

Then she thought of David's final plea to accept the gift as nothing more than a good-faith gesture. It was sweet that he had thought of her and planned to give her this gift for over a month. She hadn't even realized he was thinking of her for that long. And she did like him a lot—maybe more than just *liked* him. She certainly didn't want to discourage him.

She would return it to his room. It was only a gift. It wouldn't change anything if she returned it. She hoped it wouldn't, but look how long it had taken to get him to open up to her.

What kind of fool felt an "instinct" to buy a girl a gun like this?

Perhaps *her* fool.

She stared at the gun, knowing she didn't want to risk losing him over something so small. Maybe she could keep it. If she did, it would be wise to keep it a secret from her family and anyone else who asked.

She picked it up, held it in her hand, and thought of David. It was a sweet gesture, even if it had been a miscalculation on his part. Perhaps he just might be the thoughtful, silly fool she had been looking for all these years.

3

MAXIMILIAN AND KAZIM walked along the concrete shipping platform, where the two hundred men were distributing cases of weapons. Maximilian grabbed a Heckler & Koch MP5 submachine gun from one of the men, checked that the safety was on, and released the magazine. Seeing the full double stack of nine-millimeter rounds, he pulled the bolt back and locked it, reinserted the magazine and felt the two clicks, and vigorously slapped the cocking handle out of the indent. Then he opened up the collapsible stock and flipped the safety selector to full automatic, raised the MP5 to his shoulder as if to fire, and lowered it, switching the selector back to the safe position.

"You need to grab anything?" Maximilian gestured at the case.

Kazim took one of the MP5s.

"How many men does he have?" Maximilian said.

"Five here with him, but he also has the cartels behind him."

"An hour from now, that won't matter."

They kept walking until they reached the metal staircase leading to the basement below the abandoned factory.

Approaching the large windowed foreman's office on the underground level, Maximilian saw Julian with five burly bodyguards inside. When the men made eye contact with him, Kazim took a quick step forward and fired the submachine gun. The windows shattered as bullets punched through the glass and riddled the falling, sprawling bodyguards.

Julian fell back in his chair. Looking wide-eyed at Maximilian, his shocked expression hinted at a question he seemed desperate to ask if only he weren't so terrified.

Maximilian stepped through the shattered glass doorway, his boots crunching the shards scattered along the concrete floor. Kazim followed and stood a few steps behind him.

"Why did you do that!" Julian yelled, as if he were in charge.

But Maximilian saw sweat building on the pudgy Frenchman's pale skin. "Why have you come here tonight?" Maximilian asked. "You should be far away from this place by now."

"It has been my responsibility to make sure you have everything you need. Have I not supplied you with everything you requested during these past two months? Have I ever failed you?"

"You failed yourself and your family by coming here tonight," Maximilian replied.

"The cartel wanted to make sure that all evidence is destroyed after you leave. I'm here at their request."

Maximilian shook his head and looked at Kazim. "You hear that? The cartel sent him."

Kazim glared, his dark features frozen except for the habitual movement of his lips, as if he were chewing tobacco.

"You have more men here than we agreed on," Julian said.

"I needed this many for things to succeed."

"Succeed? What in God's name are you talking about! You are to fail! That is the plan! You *know* this!"

Maximilian stepped to the side and windmilled a kick to Julian's face. A crack sounded as the heavy boot broke the Frenchman's jaw and sent him spinning to the floor.

Julian lay on his side, gurgling while holding his broken jaw and staring up with confused, fearful eyes.

Maximilian leaned in close. "We have new plans, which are supported by Dominik Kalmár."

Julian mumbled something unintelligible.

Maximilian lectured the suffering man. "This goes beyond your cartel friends and their network of organized crime. This is a revolution. This is the beginning of a realignment of world power. And it starts with the death of the American president. We will not hide the evidence that we were here. While my men move through the tunnels, I will leave clues to make sure future investigators can follow the path we traveled. The president will be dead within the hour, and weeks from now, when the investigators are here, they will find the connections to the cartel and to governments in the Middle East. And then the fire, already ignited, will grow faster than any politician or military leader can control."

Julian tried to slide away from Maximilian while still holding his broken jaw. Kazim pulled out one of his pistols and held it at his hip like a gunslinger, leveled at Julian's head.

"Why does no one understand what needs to be done?" Maximilian added. "Why does no one see how quickly we can solve so many of the world's problems?" He wiped away the few beads of sweat that had formed on his forehead. "Well, soon everyone will understand."

Turning, he walked toward the door. "Good-bye, my friend. Thank you for all your help. Your assistance will help change the world."

Then, as he walked out the door, he nodded, and Kazim fired a single shot from across the room and silenced Julian's mumbling forever.

Then Kazim followed Maximilian back up the metal stairs to the armed company that three years of planning had created. With their deep passion to right the world and level the field for future generations, they would now unleash hell.

When the two men arrived on the main floor of the factory, all the fighters were ready and waiting. Maximilian led them to the opposite end of the factory and down an old stone stairwell into the basement. There they proceeded to a narrow metal staircase, built in perhaps the 1930s, which descended yet deeper into the earth. It ended at a short landing in front of a steel door encrusted with small clumps of rust. Maximilian grabbed the round handle protruding like a steering wheel from the door and turned it counterclockwise a few rotations until he felt the latch release from the steel frame.

He pushed open the door and stared into the dark tunnel, which led into one of the many abandoned shelters that the Parisians had built in these ancient underground tunnel systems to protect themselves against German bombing raids. After Hitler decided to forgo bombing Paris in order to preserve the city for occupation, many French resistance fighters had used these same shelters and tunnels to hide from the Nazis.

Maximilian turned on his headlamp, which pierced the tunnel's darkness for perhaps fifty feet. Beyond stretched the pitch-black void. Here, near old war shelters, the tunnels were as tall and wide as most hotel corridors, with perfect ninety-degree angles cut into the bedrock. He knew that most of the tunnels beneath Paris were not nearly this wide or modern. But these shelters still hadn't been used since the war, though random spray-painted words and markings left indisputable signs of recent illegal exploring. His headlamp picked up a white stripe painted on the left wall, with orange and black line arrows pointing ominously back at him, opposite from the direction he planned to go.

Stepping through the doorway, he jogged down the tunnel with Kazim and their two guides right behind him, followed by his small but eager army. They would encounter a few concrete obstacles along the way, but eventually their path would take them to the basement wall of the American president's hotel. He could hardly believe that this night was finally here. The greatest fight of his life was about to start. One night to alter the course of history. Strength flowed through him at the thought that the future was now his to decide.

4

S PECIAL AGENT IN Charge John Alexander sat in the front passenger seat of the presidential limousine as it drove through the bright-lit streets of Paris. An agent from the Secret Service's transportation division sat beside him, driving the armored vehicle behind the black counter assault team Suburban in front of them. The follow-up vehicle, an identical limousine, was right behind them, with two more CAT Suburbans behind it. An ambulance and a dozen police motorcycles completed the eighteen-vehicle motorcade racing down the Champs-Élysées.

John's long, athletic build would make him look much younger than his forty-five years but for the bags under his eyes, and the prominent streaks of gray overtaking his brown hair. His twenty-year career in the Secret Service had taken its toll. The stress and nearly constant anxiety of working on the Presidential Protection Detail was more than most agents could handle for so many years. Thus, most agents assigned to PPD were usually reassigned to other sections of the Secret Service after four or five years, if not sooner. No one spent his entire career working protection—except, maybe, for John Alexander.

It was a week before Christmas, and a light snowfall was drifting down on the city. Armed officers from the Garde républicaine and the Préfecture de police de Paris were stationed at cross streets along the planned route from the World Economic Forum venue to the president's hotel. The vehicles in the motorcade had rapidly flashing red and blue lights, sirens off, but occasionally one of the flanking motorcycles would chirp out a *whoa-whoa*.

They approached the massive, brightly illuminated Arc de Triomphe. As they entered the broad roundabout, John glanced at the eternal flame at the head of the Tomb of the Unknown Soldier and let himself be briefly distracted with thoughts of his fallen brothers in arms from a lifetime ago.

It was a fleeting distraction. His alert mind turned from the past and processed everything happening around the limousine. The cold was keeping people indoors and off the Paris sidewalks, which was fine with him because it lessened the threat of a gunman hiding in a crowd. Not that there was much an assassin could do as long as President Clarke was inside the vehicle. The presidential limousine was so weighed down by its armor that it was slow off the line even if the driver should gun its powerful 450-cubic-inch engine. In addition to the heavy armor, the vehicle also had seven-layered bulletproof glass, run-flat tires, and a sealed interior with oxygen supply pumped into the inside cabin from tanks secured in the trunk, making the vehicle proof against even a chemical attack. The inside of the presidential limo was so protected and cut off from the outside that speakers inside the cabin were needed to pump in sounds from the small microphones on the vehicle's exterior so the president could hear the outside crowds.

They drove along the length of the Louvre Museum, catching only a brief glimpse of the giant glass pyramid in its courtyard. Crossing the Seine on one of the many bridges infested with small padlocks of love, he saw the illuminated towers of Notre-

Dame on the other side of the Palais de Justice. The upper half of the Eiffel Tower was visible much farther away to the right, lit in bright yellow, its two spotlight beams spinning across the night sky from its top level as if it were a lighthouse.

Once the motorcade rolled onto the Left Bank, low buildings blocked the view of the tower. They continued through St. Germain and the Latin Quarter. When they were only four blocks from the hotel, John raised his wrist to his mouth and spoke into the small microphone clipped to the cuff of his shirtsleeve. The encrypted radio was linked to all two hundred agents on PPD in Paris for the president's trip.

"Firefly approaching Shield One," John said into his wrist communicator. "Sixty seconds."

The motorcade was right on schedule, to the minute.

The small American flag and the presidential seal flag flapped from the front corners of the limousine. The black suburban in front of them had its backseat windows half lowered and the rear window flipped up. He could see the Secret Service CAT agents sitting hunched near the windows, in their black tactical gear with helmets and submachine guns, peering out and ready for anything. He needed CAT agents, the Secret Service equivalent of a SWAT unit, anytime he was transporting the president. They were so well trained and armed, they could take on a small army, and he would rely on them if there was an attack on the motorcade.

As they passed the next street, he caught another glimpse of the Eiffel Tower, less than two miles away now, through the falling snow. Looking at its ghostly outlines, he could tell that the snowfall was getting heavier. This, too, was good, because the low visibility would make it tougher for a sniper to get a shot at the president. Countersnipers from his team were paired with the watchers on the rooftop of the president's hotel and many of the surrounding buildings, and they were prepared to make precise shots in any kind of weather.

He was anxious to get back inside the hotel. The safest place for the president was either the White House or Air Force One. After that, it was Camp David and a few other of the president's favorite locations that the Secret Service had fortified after the election last year. Then came private meeting locations and small events with foreign diplomats, or large fund-raisers on US soil. Ground transportation was always riskier, and large events open to the public gave most special agents sleepless nights as their thoughts cycled through endless nightmare scenarios. But nothing was more complex and difficult than planning and coordinating a president's protection on foreign soil.

At least, the hotel gave them better odds for limiting the president's exposure. The advance team of a hundred special agents had been in Paris, working around the clock for two weeks with the police to ensure that nothing went wrong during the visit. They had covered every inch of the planned site visits, and every minute on the two-day itinerary. All routes and vantage points had been mapped and covered with ground teams. Agents had taken bomb-sniffing Belgian Malinois dogs through countless sweeps of every location where the president would be. Counter assault teams were stationed all around the hotel. Blood matching the president's type was stored in the limousine, and additional reserves had been sent in secured storage to all regional hospitals in Paris—each guarded by a shift agent from the Service. The HMX-1 White Hawk that would serve as Marine One was parked next to Air Force One and the other nineteen passenger and cargo jets and helicopters in their entourage at Charles de Gaulle Airport. And the Secret Service's cyber team back in Washington was electronically monitoring every aspect of the president's movements, and the location of each key member of the protection team.

The front four motorcycles split from the motorcade as it turned along the side of the massive twenty-seven-story hotel, which took up an entire city block. The streets around the hotel were closed to public vehicles, but sporadic clusters of pedestrians braved the cold to watch the procession from behind barracks guarded by a mix of French police and US Secret Service agents. Early in his career, John had spent many years working rope lines or standing post on the perimeter of the protection bubble. Even though it had been many years since those entry-level shifts, he still glanced toward the line of pedestrians and, out of habit, scanned their faces for any out-of-the-ordinary behavior or expression in the brief moment that the motorcade moved past them before turning into the underground garage.

As the vehicle sped through the hotel garage, which had been evacuated and secured by the Secret Service two days ago, John exhaled a sigh of relief. POTUS was now back within the safest area that the Service could control on foreign soil. Raising his wrist to his mouth, he communicated the status to the other agents stationed in and around the hotel. "Firefly is back at Shield One. I repeat, Firefly is home and secured for the evening. Initiate Night-watch. Good job, everyone. Over."

Although the possibility of threats to the president was always at the forefront of every Secret Service agent's thoughts, John allowed himself a few seconds of relief. This week, the agency's Intelligence Division at the Secret Service's headquarters in Washington had received over two thousand threats against the president, all of which were being thoroughly investigated by the agency's National Threat Assessment Center. And the CIA was reporting heightened terrorist chatter in its daily intelligence reports the past few days. So even though John had been on protection details for nearly fifty presidential foreign trips in his career, he couldn't help feeling relieved that the cares and worries of another day were now winding down.

5

THE SUBTERRANEAN MAZE had long, unobstructed passageways, as if it wanted to lull explorers into complacency before gradually disorienting them. Maximilian slowed so the men behind him could close the gaps that formed as they ran. The long line moved through the tunnels in a single file, like a column of ants. They were nearing the end of a shelter used by the French in the Second World War.

Passing an open doorway, he spied a long room with six metal desks lined against the walls. A bundle of dusty cables rose from a panel of forgotten gauges and snaked along the wall before branching off and disappearing into a hole. A rusted bicycle, welded to a stand, was connected to the base of an air duct with a gauge facing out—he assumed it was some early 1940s innovation for soldiers to generate electricity or create airflow while cut off from the outside world in the shelter complex. Though the desks were now abandoned, he could imagine the importance this room must have once had during the war. He could envision it filled with military officers sitting in metal chairs or standing over the desks, studying large, unrolled paper maps and engineering schematics. Now the room was stripped, forgotten after the war, abandoned in the darkness for all eternity by soldiers long since dead.

Mehmet, the older of the two guides spoke to him. "We are very near point Beta," he said, pointing at a map in a soft binder of pages in plastic sleeves. "The tunnels used by the Inspection Générale des Carrières are just ahead. We will be at the old aqueduct in less than five minutes."

"And we still believe going through the catacombs is the best route?" Maximilian asked.

"Yes," Mehmet said. "Fastest and safest. Won't get lost in them . . . won't have collapses."

These were advantages enough, but he also saw value in taking his men through the Empire of the Dead before assassinating the American president. It would put his men into a dark and sober mind-set before the attack. And days from now, when investigators started putting together the pieces of what had happened on this singular night, the added horror of the catacombs' part in the story would send chills down the spine of every American. The effect was too perfect to pass up, and it was exactly the sort of strategy that Hannibal would have taken.

The tunnel narrowed, and a pair of large rusted pipes stretched down the corridor only a foot above his head before curving right and disappearing down a branching corridor. The ceiling was lower now, and it was clear they were past the shelter area.

His heartbeat ramped up as the team hurried through the claustrophobia-inducing passageway. By attacking at night, they had the most flexible time schedule in case they should have trouble navigating the web of tunnels. In preparation for his plans, the guides had spent months walking and, where necessary, crawling through much of the two hundred miles of passageways that honeycombed the bedrock below Paris. They shouldn't get lost. But like Hannibal in the Alps, he must move his men with caution as well as speed, for over the centuries, the tunnels had been known to take the lives of lost visitors. But they had time. The president wouldn't leave the hotel tonight, and the US Secret Service would soon fall into a strong but predictable night watch.

The bricks lining the tunnel walls were now larger, which meant this part was older. Maximilian smiled, knowing they had just entered the concentrated network of IGC access tunnels west of the old Arcueil Aqueduct. The Rochefoucauld Hospital was somewhere on the streets far above them. He slowed to give the line of men another chance to close the gaps.

Red graffiti scarred the bricks near him, as if the walls were bleeding. This was the hell he must journey through to pay for failing to protect the man who would have brought peace to his country—a peace that would have protected Naomi and Eli. A peace that would have prevented him from becoming the monster he now saw every time his dark, dead eyes gazed for too long into the mirror.

His past haunted him now more than ever. But after tonight, his demons would leave him forever.

Now in the IGC tunnels, they often encountered diverging paths. Mehmet and his assistant led the way with spotlights glued to their plastic-covered maps. No more straight running, for they continually hit forks and were constantly turning, this path then that path, as if in a hedge maze with a low ceiling and stone walls. Maximilian was disoriented by the headlamp beams slicing through the enclosing shroud of darkness. The floor crunched as the men's boots trod the grains of rock that had fallen from the walls and ceiling over the centuries. Without the guides, he would have been lost.

Then, after moving through the IGC tunnels for what seemed an eternity, the tunnel came to a dead end. It was filled with gray concrete that reflected his light more brightly than the darker-gray rock walls and ceiling he had encountered so far.

"Is that it?" he asked excitedly.

"Yes," Mehmet said, looking from the wall to the plastic-sheaved map.

"The Empire of the Dead is on the other side?" Maximilian said, placing a hand on the cool concrete.

"Yes," Mehmet repeated, his voice more certain now.

"Twelve feet of concrete," he mused. "Hannibal's engineers had to build small bridges in the Alps where rock paths had fallen from the mountainside. I can certainly get around twelve feet of concrete." He turned to Kazim. "Ready for the demolition team."

Kazim smiled in his boss's narrow pool of light and motioned to one of the platoon leaders to escort the demolition team forward.

Two men wearing heavy backpacks moved easily through the thick, parting line of mercenaries. Behind them, a group of twelve men moved forward slowly, with great caution. Maximilian had selected these twelve for their steady, controlled body movements and their proven ability to stay calm under pressure. They had trained for their roles harder than any other men in the group, for at this moment, the entire mission could fail in its infancy if any made the slightest mistake.

Maximilian saw the eerie string of headlamps stretching back down the long, straight corridor. Like all the other soldiers, he held his breath as the group of twelve moved toward him, bearing three plastic cases. It was really the first case that held his attention. It was filled with a hundred red-orange sticks of ANFFO—ammonium nitrate fertilizer and fuel oil—an explosive compound that was more stable than dynamite but carried the same punch. To protect the explosive mix from contact with water, which would neutralize it, it had been mixed with plasticizer in special packaging that made each stick look like a single sausage link.

Maximilian motioned to Kazim, who pushed the line of soldiers back down the tunnel. The two guides followed the retreating group. If they couldn't get into the Empire of the Dead, he would need them alive more than anyone else.

The twelve men carefully set the cases down, four men to a case. They placed the case full of ANFFO fifty feet from the concrete wall, and the other two directly against the wall. Opening the tops, they lifted out a portable gas generator and a drill engine the size of a football. They then removed two yellow air-compressor hoses, an eight-foot-long drill bit, and a long metal pole with a rectangular steel plate roughly the size of a license plate on one end, and a spike on the other. Hurrying, they secured the plate to the base of the drill engine, connected the compressor hoses between the engine and the generator, and mounted the drill bit to the engine's nose.

Maximilian watched intently as his lead engineer, a stout Ukrainian named Mozgovoy, lifted the heavy drill and shuffled toward the wall. His assistant, a burn-scarred fellow who rarely spoke, started the generator, stood the drill up on the spiked pole, and pressed the bit against the limestone just right of the much harder concrete barrier. The generator's growl bounced continuously off the surrounding rock as Mozgovoy gently guided the bit with leather-gloved hands. It cut briefly at the limestone before spinning off target. The men repositioned it, and this time it held and burrowed violently into the rock.

Maximilian watched as the two men wrestled the drill against the stone. Three minutes later, they were sweating and panting, but they had drilled the length of the eight-foot bit into the limestone. Fifteen minutes later, they had drilled four more holes in a diamond formation around the first, center hole.

The engineers disassembled the drill, repacked it and the generator into their cases, and carried them back near the curve in the tunnel.

Maximilian glanced to Kazim and saw that the foremost men in the column had now moved all the way back around the distant curve, so they all were safely out of the blast zone.

But his focus returned to the two engineers as they opened up the case of ANFFO next to the five holes in the limestone face. First, they jammed a long wooden stick into a borehole, working it to knock down any loosened shards of rock and push them to the back of the hole. Then they slid two four-foot plastic pipes into each hole.

The demolition assistant opened his backpack and grabbed the first of many spools of braided red and blue wire. As he unraveled a few feet, Mozgovoy took out a stick of ANFFO, wrapped the end of the wire around the front end, and tied it securely with a loop. Then he slid the stick into the plastic pipe stabilizing the center hole and used the tamping bar to gently push the packaged explosive compound to the back of the hole, pulling the wire through with it. Seven more sticks, one at a time, followed the first, until the center hole was completely filled with ANFFO.

They repeated this process for the other four holes.

Maximilian glanced at his watch and noted they were still barely within the planned time frame. They needed to move a little faster to make sure they didn't fall too far behind schedule, but this was the one part of the mission that they couldn't afford to rush.

The engineers opened the other backpack and took out the yellow nonelectric detonator control. They had explained to Maximilian that electrical-current detonators could still be accidentally triggered by sparks, so mining demolition teams generally used non-els. The men taped together the five wires extending from the holes and made sure the blasting caps were properly connected. The non-els were a hollow tube containing a tiny bit of special powder that, once the Primacord set off the powder, would rush through the tube and set off the blasting cap, which, in turn, would detonate the explosive.

Mozgovoy was ready to light the three-foot safety fuse that would set off the Primacord and the near-instantaneous chain reaction of the detonation. Maximilian had made sure his men were at a safe distance from the blast zone and would now insert their earplugs and put on gas masks to protect them from the hazardous fumes and rock particles that would soon fill the air in the confined tunnel.

Once the ANFFO was set off inside the five holes, it would create a high-pressure area beyond the rock's ability to withstand, creating a zone of cracked rock within four feet of the lines of explosives. The explosion would also generate a shock wave, which would continue the cracking process. The explosive gases would expand quickly, forcing the cracks apart, shattering the limestone and ejecting it into the open parts of the tunnel.

The engineers had made the final connection with the non-els while the same four men who had carried in the ANFFO case now removed it from the blast zone. Only half the explosives brought into the tunnels had been used at the barrier.

"Make sure masks are on!" Maximilian yelled to the first men in the column who were within earshot. Their actions would push the message to all the men along the queue stretching back into the tunnel.

He moved toward them and stood by Kazim. Then he put on his face mask with air filter and looked through the plastic lens. The hollow sound of his breath through the device reminded him of a deep-sea diver.

The engineers moved toward him. Mozgovoy held in his hand the yellow ignition device connected to the wirelike non-el tube attached to the five wired blasting caps.

"We're ready, sir," he said through his mask. "Say the word."

"Do it," Maximilian ordered.

"Fire in the hole," Mozgovoy yelled. "Three . . . two . . . one . . ."

Maximilian barely noticed the man turn the two plastic knobs on the detonator. Then he heard a quick, two-part crack that sounded like lightning striking right beside him. The force blew rocks down the curve of the tunnel toward them. Then came a slow brown cloud of dusty limestone particles that sparkled in his headlamp beam as if he were shining it into a blizzard at night.

Maximilian made sure his men stayed back while the engineers did their follow-up inspection. He watched the two men walk back toward the blast zone, their headlamp beams lighting up billions of dust particles that floated in the air.

Staring in silence as their silhouettes vanished into the cloud of light, he waited for the all-clear signal. After they moved over the pile of rubble, the engineers would check for misfires and bootleg holes. Any misfires would be washed out with the small portable water spray. The water would also control some of the dust. Any bootleg holes could mean structural problems with the blast area and would be carefully examined.

Two minutes later, Mozgovoy came back through the dust cloud and nodded when he got close to the front of the group. (Maximilian had given orders for radio silence before the attack started, because the US Secret Service local command post would no doubt be scanning all radio channels for open or encrypted signals.)

"It's clear and secure?" Maximilian asked as the man reached him. He could hear the other engineer still spraying water inside the newly created hole in the rock.

"The muck pile needs clearing, but most of the rock blew out here or on the other side."

"So we're through?" Maximilian said. "You old devil. This tops your embassy bombing."

"Yes sir," Mozgovoy replied. "If we pull this off, it will be our magnum opus."

"I want to see it," Maximilian said. Turning to Kazim, he spoke loudly through his mask. "I'm going through. Send the guides in behind me. Have some men clear the biggest rocks from the muck pile on both sides. Then start moving everyone through. Keep the remaining explosives near the front."

Kazim nodded and began relaying orders to the platoon commanders.

Maximilian stepped away from them and moved toward the concentrated center of the dust cloud. He breathed slowly through the mask while carefully stepping over chunks of limestone the size of his head. The light was trapped in a small space around him within the cloud, as if he were bathing in particles of light and energy.

The blast had opened a new tunnel twelve feet long, paralleling the old pathway that the Paris IGC had filled with concrete to close off outside access to the catacomb tour path. Crouching, he entered the new tunnel, amazed at the power of explosives against rock. The concrete fill was exposed all along the left side of the new tunnel.

He stepped forward, and before he knew it, he was through to the other side. The space was now a narrow, four-foot-wide tunnel that extended as far to his right as he could see with his light. Just over six feet high, it was cut with almost perfect ninety-degree angles.

To his left lay most of the rubble blown out from the demolition. The blast had caused a small collapse in the reinforced stone walls, blocking most of the pathway to the left, and he planned to have his men barricade the rest of this left passage with rubble. He recognized both directions as the long access corridor near the entrance to the Paris Catacombs tour path. He looked up and confirmed this when his light revealed the broad black line painted on the ceiling. It was a guide to help Parisians avoid getting lost as they explored the catacombs by candlelight in the eighteenth and nineteenth centuries.

He was lucky that this was the direction mostly blocked by the rubble, and not to the right. Left went toward the tour's entrance, and right went into the catacombs. He looked down and saw a door-size metal gate, bent and blown away from the side tunnel. He would have some men clear the backfill rubble on the right, throwing it into the pile to further block the left path.

He stepped over a few more sizable rocks until he was again standing on the smooth, lightly graveled tunnel floor. Something on the wall caught his eye, and he shined his light on it. It was the famous plate with the chiseled-out fleur-de-lis. He had read about it in his studies of the city's underworld.

A smile broke out on his face as the excitement of this moment energized him. They had made it through. He was inside the Paris catacombs.

6

A S KAZIM STEPPED into the tunnel behind him, Maximilian turned and then laughed at the man's expression of awe. "And you didn't think it was worth it."

"To blow through twelve feet of rock just so that we might walk past the dead? No, I didn't. But you still think it's important?"

"Not important—*essential,*" Maximilian replied. "When the story of tonight is told, the conjured images of us approaching through the catacombs will be imprinted on the imaginations of all who hear it."

Four men worked fast to remove the rubble from the path near the explosion. They had needed only a minute to clear what remained on the path. Maximilian saw one throw the last piece of rubble onto the large pile of broken limestone, which now completely blocked access in the direction of the tour entrance.

"The men are ready?" he asked Kazim.

"Yes."

"Tell them."

Kazim ducked his head into the blasted tunnel and yelled, "We're ready! We're moving! March!"

Hearing the men start moving in the darkness, Maximilian turned from the demolition tunnel and began jogging down the long, narrow corridor. His head came close to hitting the rock ceiling as he ran. The tunnel was lined with limestone bricks on both sides. A plastic guard on the upper left wall ran the length of the tunnel, protecting cables for the wiring of the lights (which were turned off after tour hours), the emergency call boxes and speakers, of which there were perhaps a dozen, and the air conditioning system, which had been installed to help generate air flow in the catacombs after they were sealed off from the rest of the tunnel system in the 1990s.

Some dust was still in the air, but they had moved far enough from the blast zone that it was only barely noticeable. The rock path's surface was smooth from the traffic of a quarter-million tourists each year. The occasional plastic information plaques fixed to the walls gleamed like ice as his headlamp caught them in the darkness.

He jogged for over a minute in a mostly straight path, taking only a few turns in the single tunnel before reaching the Atelier—a "turned pillar" wider than a car, made up of a solid uncut mass of limestone, which the original quarry inspection unit had cut around. Left there three centuries ago to help prop the ceiling up, it looked like a giant redwood trunk that axmen had hewn at from all sides before giving up. He ran past on the right.

After another hundred meters, the walls turned from limestone brick to rough-cut solid limestone that looked like stucco in his light.

As he ran through winding catacombs, any sense of time and distance fell away. He felt like a modern Theseus in a labyrinth created centuries ago and now kept by the dead. It was like no earthly place, as if, at any moment, he might stumble onto a secret gateway to hell.

An iron gate blocking another tunnel forced him to the left.

The path became even narrower, and he worried that it would slow the men carrying the equipment. The tunnel was really curving left and right now. The dead could not be far away.

Rounding another right turn, his light sparkled off an eerie scene: the sculpted towers over a miniature seaport, carved long ago. This was indeed a place lost in time.

He loped along through some more turns and past a half-dozen more gates, installed to prevent tourists from straying off the path. The gates looked as if they held back a deeper darkness.

He ran on with Kazim and the two guides, and the crunching footsteps of his men behind them. He had to remind himself, as he ran through this vast subterranean boneyard, that he was on the righteous path. These were only tunnels in rock, dug by men, for the stone used to build Paris.

The path sloped downward and ran straight before rising again, and the ceiling rose higher, supported by archways of white limestone brick—the remnants of an ancient aqueduct.

Forced left at the top of the slope, he found an open room with two square pillars guarding a dark entrance blocked by a sheet-metal door. Engraved in the stone lintel above the opening were the words "*ARRÊTE! C'EST L'EMPIRE DE LA MORT.*"

Kazim stopped behind him. "What does it say?"

They could hear the line of men running on the gravel surface stretching through the many turns behind them.

"It says, 'Halt! This is the empire of death.'"

"Then we're getting close."

"Yes," he said. "Come on. The best is still ahead." And he kicked the door hard near the lock. The thin metal flopped away from the door frame and hung on one hinge.

Jogging through the entrance, he felt like a grave robber breaking into an ancient tomb. Square pillars of white stone brick were at first clustered on both sides of the low passageway. Again he had to be mindful not to bump his head on the low rock ceiling. A few more tour information boards glimmered in his light. Then he passed bones, stacked like cordwood on both sides of the path. A row of broken, toothless skulls stared at him from empty eye sockets. In some places, the bone piles didn't reach the ceiling, so that he could see how deeply they were packed into the tunnel recesses.

Another gate barred an off-limits tunnel, forcing him to continue on the tour path. His light flashed on a white stone cross surrounded by a hedge of stacked leg bones. Beyond it, another narrow passageway opened onto what had once been a fountain, in the center of the room. He popped a flare and dropped it in front of the fountain so his men would see its low barrier and move around it. It was only a few feet deep, but he didn't want men tripping over it, especially those carrying the cases.

Rounding a wide left turn, he found himself getting used to the way his jouncing headlamp splashed light against the moving shadows of the dead. The rough ceiling cast waving, illuminated reflections that looked like a stormy sea raging above him.

With more room now, he could run a little faster. Another long walkway was crowded with uneven piles of skulls and bones amid the bricked columns, cold chains, and barred gates.

He dropped another orange flare in front of a low bench along the left wall. Cutting around a large, square pillar in the center of the path, he saw a tomb the size of a casket, elevated and to the left of the corridor, with French inscriptions surrounding a white cross.

Somewhere behind him, he heard a man gasp, followed by the sound of bones clattering to the limestone floor. Someone cursed. Others laughed. But the train of soldiers kept moving forward at a good clip, and for now that was all that mattered.

He passed more square central pillars and more side gates. Then the walls became smooth, like the catwalk in a subway tunnel. He ran for a few more minutes, passing more monuments, erected like tombstones along the sides of the winding path. He was getting used to this hell. He threw down another flare where a monument's low concrete base protruded a few feet into the path.

Three strata of skulls stretched along both walls, with long bones filling in the spaces between them. Even though cracked and staved, the skulls held the weight above them.

Then he hit his longest stretch yet without a sharp turn, and he knew they were getting close. Skulls and bones were strewn everywhere. Even the curving scallops in the ceiling looked like skulls in his moving light.

The path sloped downward, sliding deeper into the earth.

He stopped and turned to Kazim. "Tell the men to wait here. We'll need the guides and the demolition team."

Within a minute, the line of men had stopped as far back as he could see, and Kazim had summoned the guides and demolition engineers forward. Maximilian led them around the turn. The ceiling got lower again, forcing him to hunker down.

Then he stopped when he saw the monument that he had been thinking of since entering the catacombs. The size of a large tombstone, the white slab was engraved with French verse of Delille's "The Visit to the Underworld."

"This is it," he said to Kazim and the two guides. "We are here, correct?"

"Yes," replied Mehmet, staring at a page in his binder as if it were a treasure map.

Maximilian put his hand on the brick-reinforced wall across the path from the monument. "Then this is where we go through?"

"Yes," Mehmet replied again. He looked at the younger guide, who nodded in return.

"*Exactly* here? You're both certain?"

They were.

He looked at the two demolition engineers. "This is just brick reinforcement wall. It shouldn't take long to get through. There's a short tunnel on the other side of this. Then there's ten feet of concrete seal. Drill and blast a new tunnel section around it, like before. How long to do everything?"

"Twenty minutes," Mozgovoy said.

"Do it."

Twenty minutes later, the final blast rumbled through the catacombs, sending a cloud of dust drifting slowly over staring skulls. Some men were assigned to clear the rubble, piling it up in the direction of the tour exit.

Soon all his men had left the catacombs, entering the larger IGC tunnel system in the Paris underground. Maximilian estimated they would be at the American president's hotel in fifteen minutes. He couldn't wait to add more skulls to the millions scattered throughout this vision of hell.

7

IT HADN'T TAKEN long for Special Agent in Charge John Alexander to recognize David Stone's potential as a special agent on his protection team. He had been monitoring the weekly training statistics from the academy instructors for months. It had been clear enough on paper which of the cadets consistently fell in the top 5 percent for aptitude, field strategic assessment, fitness, and marksmanship. But this had been only a starting point—an early filter in his evaluation process to find the right agents to assign to the protection and, from there, specifically to the Presidential Protection Detail. Agents would also be assigned to other branches of protection, such as the Vice Presidential Protection Detail or the Dignitary Protection Division, but ultimately, all agents working protection wanted to be placed on the PPD.

John didn't know Stone's reasons for choosing a career in the Secret Service. The file showed that he came from a well-to-do family in San Diego. He had surfed his whole life, even during law school, and back then his long, sun-bleached hair was much blonder than now. Most agents came to the Secret Service with a background in law enforcement, with only the best officers passing the initial application process. Other applicants, especially agents interested in joining the CAT division, had a military background. Most agents went into the investigation section, with fewer than half working protection. David Stone had never been in the military or law enforcement. He was athletic, though, had a law degree from UCLA, and was a top marksman, scoring in the top 1 percent of his academy class on the pistol range. John had personally selected him to stand post near the president on PPD a few months ago, even though it was rare for a new agent to work so closely to POTUS.

Closing the doors to the teleconference room as he left the president, John said to Stone and the other two agents in the antechamber, "The president has another two hours of conference calls. Then she's planning to return to the penthouse to review briefings for another hour before turning in. She'll be waking at five thirty tomorrow morning. That puts us at three hours green watch and four hours station watch before the next cycle shift." .

"Yes sir," the three men replied almost in unison.

"Agent Reid has informed me that the Threat Assessment Center in Washington is tracking a hundred and fifty investigations in Paris related to potential threats. Twenty-seven are considered viable threats. Right now none are classified as eminent threats. She'll give updates every half hour. Also, we've received notices from the CIA, NSA, and Mossad that there has been a spike in intelligence chatter on their second-tier channels, but a decrease on first-tier channels. This means more midlevel terrorism suspects are talking to each other, but fewer high-level suspects."

"Same pattern as before the attacks on Nine-eleven," Stone replied.

"That's right, although the channels are different. Mostly European and Asian origins. Little cross talk in Africa or the Middle East. CIA's still trying to conclude their analysis. Some of this is to be expected because of the summit. Regardless, we'll continue to remain on high alert the entire time we're in Paris."

The men nodded. Their tense, focused expressions continued to reassure him that he had surrounded the president with some of the smartest, most skilled protectors that could be recruited and trained from a country of over three hundred million.

He paused, glancing down the hallway as he tried to think of any minute detail that hadn't been covered. The red-and-white-checked wallpaper had pictures of Parisian cafés and city lights. He wondered if there was a better way to secure this antechamber from the hallway, but they had already locked down the floors above and below and posted agents everywhere.

"All right," John said, turning back to the men, "initiating phase two of Night-watch." Bringing his wrist up, he gave the command to all two hundred agents in and around the hotel. His routine command would create a flurry of activity. Countersnipers on the hotel's roof and surrounding rooftops would reposition themselves for the night traffic patterns the scout teams had mapped, patrol agents would move through the hotel floors where curfew had been imposed on other guests, and additional agents would move into the basement floors and any other potential entrance points, including all garage and sewer access points.

Within thirty seconds, all agents in and around the hotel were at their Night-watch protection posts. The president was as locked down and as safe as the Secret Service could make her for the night.

8

MAXIMILIAN WATCHED THE burly technician connect the air hose to the hydraulic chainsaw. Starting the powerful motor, the man cut a small opening into the concrete wall, making a deep plunge cut before guiding the diamond teeth down the wall in a long, straight cut.

The big man worked the heavy saw, cutting away sections of concrete until an open space revealed a row of black metal pipes, each six inches in diameter. Setting the chainsaw on the stone floor, he removed his goggles and looked at Maximilian.

"The hard part is done, sir. All I need now is to cut through the pipes and she'll burst. The computer at the water main will sense the pressure change and shut down the flow."

Maximilian looked at his watch. "Confirm time sync."

"Twenty-two forty thirty-seven . . . thirty-eight . . . thirty-nine . . ."

"Good," Maximilian replied. "Start cutting through at exactly twenty-two hundred fifty-eight. And whatever happens, make sure the water delivery system is destroyed in less than two minutes after when you begin. We are depending on you."

The man nodded, and Maximilian left him and a few other men by the exposed pipe. He jogged back through the tunnel system with one of the guides, feeling alive with the anticipation. He looked at his watch, then tapped Kazim's shoulder. "We have less than eighteen minutes."

Kazim's face tensed. "The scouts are ready with the demolitions, and your men are set up behind them. My team is also ready."

"They may have the president out in four minutes. Maybe less. There won't be much time."

"I swear to you, my team will make it!" Kazim said, his voice showing rare emotion.

Maximilian returned his pledge with a solemn nod. Then, looking at his watch again, he said, "My friend, you have my faith more than any other man alive. In seventeen minutes, our threat will tingle up the spine of our enemy. We've been on this journey for nearly five years. Once it starts, we may never see each other face-to-face again. If we do not both survive this battle, if we don't both escape on the other side, I want you to know, it has been an unexpected honor to know you."

They walked together through the group of armed men, who looked like soldiers readying for the battle of their lives. Maximilian couldn't help but think that even Hannibal would have been impressed with the surprise attack he was about to unleash.

9

SPECIAL AGENT REBECCA Reid stepped off the gilt-doored elevator into the large, elegantly appointed hotel lobby. A surprising number of other guests were moving through the lobby, but that was okay—security was airtight. The top three floors had been blocked off for the president and those who were part of her trip to France. And every guest in the hotel had gone through a thorough background screening a week ago, in addition to having their identities verified and their persons searched by Secret Service agents every time they entered the hotel.

Looking toward the front entrance, she saw the two agents in white button-down short-sleeve shirts with the blue Secret Service patch sewn to one sleeve, individually guiding hotel guests through the magnetometer that had been set up the day before. In addition to screening visitors for metals, the mags also provided a visible deterrent. What patrons didn't see, however, were the chemical receptors, covertly attached to the top of the mags, which could detect anthrax, countless toxins, explosive chemical residue, and even radiation.

Four agents were hidden in a side room that Rebecca had helped set up during the advance team's work. They were the command center for the Secret Service on site, responsible for monitoring the data feeds from the receptors, along with communications from the working shift of PPD agents around the hotel. If there were any problems, the thirty heavily armed CAT agents in another nearby room had the advanced training and weaponry to take on virtually any threat.

Most of these agents were men, she thought, feeling a little surge of annoyance. Within the Service's protection detail, it was still a man's world. She had hoped that after the election of America's first female president, the ratio of women agents around the president would improve. And it had, but not enough to satisfy her. Rebecca was one of the very few women assigned to the detail, but even so, her duties were not directly involved with the physical shield of agents moving around the president. Her skills and focus were directed elsewhere, removed from the president's immediate orbit but still vital to the vast team effort. She was the assistant lead on the advance team and was now the head communications agent, responsible for connecting the ground protection team with intelligence from the Joint Operations Center at Headquarters in Washington.

A voice in her earpiece said, "Firefly in Video Com. Night-watch Two. Thirty seconds."

She recognized the voice of the president's top guy, Special Agent in Charge John Alexander. It was a broadcast message to all two hundred agents in the area. Using basic Secret Service code words over the encrypted radio, it informed them that the president had been moved safely from the motorcade into the hotel and that she was now in the video command center set up on the twenty-sixth floor. In recent months, tensions between Russia and China had been increasing as evidence of cyber espionage emerged from both sides. And now China had threatened to cut off trade in rare earth elements to Russia. In hopes of resolving the conflict, the international community had pressed the US president to serve as a neutral moderator.

With the president back in the hotel, Rebecca needed an update from the Joint Operations Center, which she would then relay to the command center and the protection team on the ground. She walked across the beige marble floor and into the hotel's grand ballroom. Inside, a dozen men were setting up banquet tables with velvet cloth covers, and the dais for tomorrow night's speakers. The podium stood above everything, but it looked somehow naked with the empty space on its front where the seal of the president of the United States would be attached in the morning. Two white-uniformed men led bomb-sniffing Belgian shepherds through the room for the twentieth time this week, sniffing chair cushions and plant pots and anything else in the room that could possibly conceal an explosive device.

She stood in the center of the room, under the largest of the nine chandeliers, and called Headquarters on her encrypted satellite phone using GSM mode for indoor reception.

The JOC officer ran through the half-hourly update with her. At the moment, 8,463 open death threats against the president were being investigated. Of those, special agents had marked 92 as "highest priority," although over time, all would be thoroughly investigated. Only a hundred and fifty threats were focused on Paris—strangely few considering how highly publicized the trip was. The Service currently had ninety agents from the Paris field office moving throughout the city, investigating various leads on the threats, and half of the JOC's resources were concentrated on the many moving pieces involved in the president's trip.

The call lasted only two minutes, but in that time, Rebecca had learned everything critical for updating the special agent in charge of PPD.

Leaving the ballroom, she passed a half-dozen agents wearing suit jackets tailored to conceal their weapons. This being one of the largest luxury hotels in Paris, it took her a few minutes to move past the elevators leading to the lower conference rooms, past the ground-floor piano bar, the vast open greeting area of the front lounge, the library, and the business center, until she was back at the central elevator bay.

Rebecca was just one of a hundred components on the PPD, but she was proud to be a critical member of the team entrusted with protecting the single most important thing in America: not just the woman herself, but the office of the president of the United States. Ever since George Washington had humbly accepted the first office in front of a band of victorious rebels in Philadelphia, after a heroic, bloody war for their freedom, the president of the United States had become the personification of individual freedom. Which was why so much weight rested on the shoulders of her and every other member of the Secret Service. And that burden weighed heaviest on the protection detail team.

Her father and brothers had been so proud when her application to the Secret Service was accepted. That felt like a lifetime ago, and she could only imagine how amazed they would be if they saw the details of everything she had coordinated to prepare for the president's short stay in Paris.

The bell dinged, and the elevator doors opened on the twenty-sixth floor. Wide hallways with lush red carpeting branched in three directions. Walking down the corridor, Rebecca nodded to each of the half-dozen dark-suited agents standing at their intermittently spaced posts along the chestnut-paneled walls. Each man nodded in return, with a professionally serious expression. One greeted her by name.

This floor was reserved entirely for the president, as were the twenty-fifth and twenty-seventh. Rebecca nodded at the men as she strode halfway down the hallway to the right of the elevator and knocked on the double doors. When they opened, she saw David standing with three other men in the center of an entryway. Behind them were the doors to the conference room where the president was teleconferencing with her cabinet.

David flashed her a brief smile, which she returned with a subtle shake of the head. Turning, she walked over to John Alexander. He had been saying something to another agent, but seeing Rebecca, he paused to receive her report.

"Agent Reid," he said. "What's the latest from Washington?"

"Agent Alexander," she replied, "Washington is still tracking a few dozen high-priority investigations in Paris, but fifty-two have been resolved and cleared. Others are lower priority. I'll have an update report sent to you."

"Thank you," he said. Walking to the double-doors, he opened them and entered the large conference room.

Rebecca saw a woman sitting at the conference table alone, her back to the door, facing a large video monitor that sat on the table. Short brown hair hung evenly to her shoulders, and the dark suit seemed to camouflage her amid the dozen black leather chairs around her.

Rebecca didn't need to see the woman's face to recognize President Abigail Clarke. Though Rebecca wasn't on the direct shield detail, she had met the president on a few occasions. But despite the professional discipline and emotional detachment that agents were trained for, Rebecca couldn't help feeling pride in what President Clarke represented for all women—and, for that matter, for all Americans. She knew that every agent on the protection detail would take a bullet for this president without hesitation, but deep inside, she believed that she would move faster than any of the men to dive in between this president and any threat. And yet, she had been denied the opportunity to serve in that way. She had been told that men were better protectors around a president: they were more intimidating to potential assassins, and because their bodies were bigger, they made better human shields against bullets and shrapnel. It didn't seem to matter that she was an accomplished athlete or that her aptitude tests were in the top 5 percent of her highly qualified cadet class. But her marksmanship scores were below average, while most of the men directly surrounding the president had top marks at the Beltsville firing range. Still, it hurt being denied the opportunity to serve on the president's direct detail.

Turning to leave the room, she caught David's eye. He gave her a tight smile, and she replied with a subtle nod to let him know she had forgiven him. It wasn't completely true, but in the few seconds she had waited for John to enter the conference room, she realized that neither David nor she could afford any personal distraction when protecting the president. After they returned to Washington, where the president was scheduled to be at the White House next week for Christmas, she would have time to pull David aside and continue their discussion.

Leaving the room, she walked down the wide, luxurious hallway. A small noise disturbance had been reported on the twenty-second floor, so she had radioed for another agent to meet her at the staircase there. All guests and employees had undergone a thorough background check by local police a week in advance, and the Secret Service was screening and searching everyone entering the building, so there was little likelihood of this disturbance posing a threat to the president. But as always on this job, the stakes were so high that she had to make sure they were leaving as little as possible to chance.

She opened the metal door to the stairwell and ran down the concrete steps two at a time, her equipment rattling on her belt, her holstered P229 slapping against her ribs, and her long brown hair brushing her face as she whipped around the stair landings and descended through the building.

10

SINCE SHE FIRST stepped into the Oval Office eleven months ago, President Abigail Clarke rarely had a free moment. Of course, her husband would remind her that her nonstop schedule had begun two years earlier, when she first started campaigning for her party's nomination. Not that she had enjoyed much leisure time during her eight years as governor of Virginia before that, or the six years as a US senator before that, or as a state prosecutor for the decade before that. In some ways, her entire life had been a high-pressure race for as long as she could remember.

"No, Madame President," said the gray-haired attorney general through the speakers. "There's nothing else to add." The man was one of five cabinet members on the teleconference.

President Clarke's eyes shifted to each of the other cabinet members through the camera-monitor sync of the teleconference. "Anyone else have anything to add?"

"No, Madame President," the others said almost in unison.

"So we all agree, it's time for the United States to raise organized-crime syndicates to a threat level one—equal to terrorism."

The others nodded, though the conversation of the past fifteen minutes had left everyone visibly uncomfortable over the task ahead.

As the teleconference call ended, the screens went dark. The voice of the head secretary, back at the White House, announced over the phone's speakers that the next teleconference, with the prime minister of Israel, was scheduled to begin in ten minutes, though it could start earlier if she wanted.

"No, thank you, Stephanie," the president said. "I could use the ten minutes. Could you please connect me to Richard?"

"Yes ma'am."

It had been a long day, and Abigail wanted to hear her husband's voice, to be reminded that she wasn't alone. She had fought many political battles over the years, most of them on partisan issues. It always frustrated her that it should be so difficult to push through legislation on the issues she was most passionate about—the ones that had driven her to politics at a young age, managing local campaigns of national candidates. The Founding Fathers had specifically designed the government to be slow at passing new laws, to ensure a gradual evolution of America, without wild swings based on sudden trends. But she couldn't help feeling impatient at how long it took just to do what was *right*. Still, that was the plan all along. The founders had known that a complex and growing country, which would only grow larger and more complex over the centuries, must evolve either through slow change over time or—far more rarely—through sweeping change during moments when historic issues reached a boiling point. Boiling points such as the abolition of slavery, or the pernicious rise of ruthless corporate tycoons, which would have given Adams and Jefferson fits and which was eventually handicapped by Theodore Roosevelt, or FDR's use of government to save citizens from the continuing fallout of uncontrolled economic and financial freedom. And when the country reached one of those historic cruxes, pray that the president got it right.

The phone clicked back. "Madame President, I have the First Gentleman on the phone."

"Thank you," she said.

The phone clicked again. "Abby."

"Richard," she said, feeling soothed just to hear his voice.

"How's the trip going?"

She smiled. "It's okay. I just wanted to hear your voice while I'm in the City of Love, and this might be the only free moment I have. I was thinking about our honeymoon when I rode through St. Germain this evening. Did you know our old café is gone?"

"Oh, no," he said. "What happened to it?"

"I don't know. I'll have the CIA look into it."

Richard chuckled. "No doubt the Russians were involved."

Abby rolled her eyes. "You always did read too many spy novels. Do *all* history profs live in the past?"

"One of the job requirements, I'm afraid." There was a short pause. "So how'd the summit go today? You get the traction you hoped for?"

She glanced at her watch—four minutes before her next teleconference call.

"Does anyone ever really get traction on anything at an international summit?" she said. One of the reasons she always made time to talk to her husband while traveling was so she could briefly drop the usual diplomatic and political talk and have a candid discussion with the one person in the world she could completely trust.

"Abby, you're trying to rally the world to take on international crime syndicates. It's the global black market, honey—it'll be harder to fight than all the oil-rich dictators and belligerent leaders of the military-industrial complex combined."

"That's why it's so important for the future that I succeed at the summit."

"It'll take time, my love. It'll be like putting together a modern League of Nations—except, unlike Wilson, you won't fail to get Congress's approval. You'll succeed. I know you will. But don't put too much pressure on yourself. A change this big is gonna take time."

"Thanks, sweetheart."

"You still getting home Thursday? Christmas is less than a week away, and the kids were asking me more questions about Santa today. I don't know if I can hold 'em off much longer on my own. They're getting older now, and they're starting to get suspicious about all this Christmas magic stuff."

"Maybe the White House staff can help you tell them the truth," she joked.

"Oh, no. Only you are authorized to declassify top secret information like that."

Smiling, she was about to respond when her secretary broke into the call. "I'm sorry, Madame President. There's a developing situation in Nigeria. The Joint Chiefs and Sec Def are in the Situation Room and waiting for you to patch in."

Abigail stiffened. Only a serious crisis could have gotten that group together at the White House's Situation Room.

"Richard, something's come up, so I have to let you go. Tell Stacy and Jessica I love them."

"All right. I love you, honey."

"I love you, too."

She smiled and ended the call. Then, taking a long, slow breath, she pressed the button to bring up the screen teleconferencing her into the Situation Room. The call with the Israeli prime minister would have to be postponed.

On the screen were eight men. The secretary of defense, in a cool gray suit, sat in the center of the group. Flanking him were the seven Joint Chiefs of Staff, their uniforms decked with medals, ribbons, patches, and insignia in the military tradition of trying to display a lifetime of leadership and heroic sacrifice on the limited real estate of a man's chest and shoulders. When the president joined the call, the men were speaking among themselves, though she couldn't hear them.

Sec Def nodded toward the screen and pushed a button on their end to open audio. "Madam President," he said. The other seven greeted her in the same manner.

"Secretary Nelson, Generals, Admiral."

"Madam President," Nelson said, "we have a problem in Nigeria. Intel shows that a group of rebels are breaking through the outer perimeter of the Shlaikee Oil Refinery Plant outside Kaduna. Security is strong on the facility premises, but the rebels are over a hundred strong and well armed. Besides our financial and national security interests at the refinery, there are thirteen American engineers working there for Shlaikee's parent company. We're afraid they'll be taken hostage if the plant is besieged. The Nigerian government is insisting they can handle this and that we stay out of it, but our intel says the Nigerian forces are not qualified for a tactical rescue operation this complex."

The president's mind flashed through all the daily security briefings she had read over the past eleven months, recalling all the political tensions between the United States and Nigeria over oil rights. She had been a strong advocate of providing aid to help Nigeria maintain political stability, which was in the best interest of the United States. With so much in the balance, how much value should she place on the lives of thirteen Americans—Americans who must have been well aware of the risks of working in such a dangerous environment? She had the responsibility to do what was best for trade agreements and international diplomacy. But she also held herself responsible for the lives of Americans on foreign soil who needed her help.

"If the Nigerian government can't ensure the safety of the refinery with Americans in it, then it's our job to make sure they're safe," she said. "What are our tactical options?"

"We can get a drone in the area within twenty minutes," said the chief of staff of the Air Force.

"We can also get a SEAL team on the ground within two hours," said the chief of Naval Operations.

"All right," President Clarke said. "Let's patch in the secretary of state and the vice president. Put our embassy in Nigeria on high alert and send out alerts to other embassies in Africa. Send in two high-altitude drones as soon as possible and get the SEAL team ready to move in. I'll have a short phone call with President Okonko to mitigate international political tension while we respond with our forces."

The conversation with Richard about the children and Christmas was now forgotten as she raced through the crisis response with the Joint Chiefs. It was her job, not theirs, to understand the long-term implications this could have for diplomatic affairs in West Africa. But she understood the political issues perfectly, just as she understood the needs of her countrymen and -women in harm's way. And as their leader, she had silently vowed never to abandon an American in trouble on foreign soil. It was a principle she was willing to go to her grave to uphold.

11

T HE YOUNG MAN knelt on the thick blue carpet in his hotel room and prayed to God. For so many years during his youth, he had been adrift growing up in a Chicago suburb, unable to see the path he was meant to take. It wasn't his parents' fault. They hadn't failed him, but he had been born to serve a greater purpose than they could understand. God had promised to reveal his path to him only when he journeyed alone. He had needed to leave his parents. And so he had.

And God had indeed shown him the way, over time and through much despair, to his new family. A family that had eventually put him in the Tour Montparnasse Paris hotel, with ten yellow plastic bottles of lighter fluid. To avoid suspicion, he had bought each bottle at a different petrol station in Paris. Combining the purchases with other items and using only cash, it had taken him half the day to discreetly acquire enough flammable liquid for his task. It was a critical role to help purge the world of godless sin. He was honored that his new brothers had rewarded him with such an important role in the mission.

He glanced out the window at the Paris skyline, the low lights of the "short" city with its beautiful Eiffel Tower standing less than a kilometer away from his hotel room. In the distance, just above the twinkling city skyline, floodlighting illuminated the three imposing white domes of the Sacré-Cœur Basilica at the top of Montmartre. Gazing out at the church, he felt more certain than ever that God was watching him with approval. And as an omen of his coming eternity in heaven, light snowfall drifted down like small celestial feathers from the dark-orange clouds hovering over the city.

Zipping open his backpack, he took out the ten yellow bottles of lighter fluid and stood them in a circle around him like a miniature palisade. Then he removed his long-sleeved button shirt so that he was now barefoot and wearing only his jeans and white cotton T-shirt. Sitting cross-legged within the ring of bottles, he lowered his head, raised his hands, and said one last prayer while imagining the brilliant wonders of the next life, which would be far better than anything he had ever known in this one.

Then he snapped open one of the bottles and squeezed it so tightly that a thin stream of fluid shot across the room to the windowsill. Moving his arm, he sprayed the fluid all across the carpet in front of him, until the bottle was empty. After replacing the empty bottle back in the ring, he snapped open the next bottle. Still sitting, he sprayed fluid on the bed. When finished, he sprayed another bottle toward the hallway door, then another at the desk, and another toward the bathroom. Then three more at the ceiling. And finally, the last two—on himself.

When all ten bottles were emptied, he took the steel cigarette lighter from his jeans pocket. Then, looking out again through the falling snow, he took a few seconds to marvel at just how beautiful the world could be when the moment was right. Smiling, he flicked the lighter, closed his eyes, and turned the hotel room into a box of fire that would send him to heaven and justify his martyrdom on earth—but only after death silenced his screams of pain.

*   *   *

The siren screamed through the central firehouse of the Paris Fire Brigade on the north side of the Seine River. As the firefighters rushed through the building in their heavy, clanking gear and turquoise helmets, the announcement came over the speakers: *"Dépêchez-vous! Alarme d'incendie dans un hotel. Dépêchez-vous!"*

The men and women spilled into the garage, the large front doors opened, and the mid-size red fire engines roared off into the night.

12

REBECCA REID LEFT the room where three young GIs on leave had been partying noisily enough to attract the Secret Service. Beforehand she had grabbed Ferrara, one of the floor's three post agents. They had just finished checking the young men's identities and suggested they dial back the revelry a notch. They promised to quiet down and even asked if she could tell the president hello for them. She assured them that she would.

Just as the door closed and she was back in the hallway, the coded transmitter on her belt started beeping and flashing red. She held up her hand for Ferrara to hold position as she flipped the transmitter switch. "Reid here," she said into her sat phone, using the encrypted GSM mode for indoor reception. "Go ahead."

"Special Agent Reid, this is JOC. Be advised there are reports of a hotel fire at the Montparnasse Tower, one mile west of Shield One. Local fire crews are responding. The incident is beyond the outer perimeter of the protection bubble, so no threat to Firefly. The fire is containable and shouldn't spread. Will give a situation status every five until first responders give the all clear."

"Cause of fire?" Rebecca asked. Ferrara stepped closer after the question.

"Unknown," said the voice from the Joint Operations Center. "No reports of explosion or other suspicious sounds. Alarm box indicates single-room fire was triggered first. Other alarms on floor triggered afterwards. Probable cause is electrical problem or guest accident."

"Okay. Keep us updated. Over."

She looked at Agent Ferrara, who was plainly curious. "Hotel fire close by, but no current threat. They'll keep me informed." She switched from the sat phone to the small microphone clipped inside her sleeve, at the wrist. "Agent Alexander," she said, "this is Agent Reid. JOC just informed me of a developing situation in the area: hotel fire about a mile west of Shield One. No current threat to Firefly. Paris responders are at that site. Joint Ops will keep us informed of developments."

"Roger that," Alexander replied.

She didn't especially like the coincidence of the fire and the president's trip. Fires were real concerns for the Secret Service, and for many years it had been considered too risky for presidents ever to stay in a hotel anywhere above the eighth floor—the highest point a fire engine ladder could reach at the time. But over the past few decades, that policy had eased considerably because of the advances in fire suppression systems for large hotels. Still, a building only a mile away was now blazing, and that made her a little uncomfortable.

"Alexander doesn't think we should move POTUS to a lower floor?" Ferrara said, showing an eagerness to contribute more to the protection team other than just standing post.

"She's on a call with the Joint Chiefs. It could have national security implications."

Ferrara said, "I guess if we're monitoring the fire, we'll have plenty of time to move her if it gets more serious."

"Yeah," she said. "Just seems a little strange . . ."

A small fire a mile away wasn't justification for moving the president. But there was one precaution she could take.

On her wrist microphone, speaking into the encrypted radio connected to all agents and transportation units, she said, "Commander Robinson, this is Agent Reid from Command Center. What's the status of HMX-one?"

Two seconds later, Commander Robinson's flat, almost lazy-sounding voice came through her earpiece. "I have three White Tops with one escort resting next to Air Force One in our DL zone at de Gaulle. Pilots are on call and on-site. All active crew on standby."

Robinson was the HMX-1 White House Liaison Officer on-site, responsible for helping coordinate the four-helicopter lift package sitting at Charles de Gaulle: three HMX-1 White Hawks and one King Stallion. They had been flown in on Air Force C-17s from Quantico to Paris a week earlier with the president's entourage, as was done with all HMX-1 lift packages for presidential trips.

"Call the pilots in and have them prep one of the White Tops and the escort. Maintain on hot-evac standby for one hour. Contact the French military and request permission for possible flight activity for POTUS on Marine One over Paris."

"Roger. Marine One White Top and Secret Service escort King Stallion will be on hot-evac standby in four minutes. Over."

Ending the communication, Rebecca noted Agent Ferrara's intense look.

"You sense a threat?" he asked.

She shook her head. "Increased risk factors, but no threat. I just want to leave as little as possible to chance."

Ferrara nodded. "For a moment, I thought you were going to issue a Crash POTUS alert."

"Are you *serious*?" she said. "I analyze threat potential and maintain communication with Joint Ops to monitor and manage risk, but this situation is nowhere near a Crash POTUS."

He sighed. "Bad joke. Sorry."

She nodded, then said, "Want to hear a punch line to all this? I need you to head to the roof. I know we have countersnipers already up there and on surrounding buildings, but I'd like your assessment of the fire. Can you see it? Smell it? Will the snowfall help the firefighters? What does the city sound like? How many sirens and emergency vehicles are moving in the area. Give me the trained eyes and ears I need up there that the JOC updates can't provide."

"Yes ma'am. How long would you like me up there?"

"Twenty minutes. Things are quiet enough in the building anyway."

"Except for a few GIs on leave having a little too much fun," he said with a grin. "I loved the look on their faces when you said the president was asking if they could keep it down."

"If those guys are the biggest problem we have in this building tonight, we'll all feel like joining them. Now, go tell me what you see across the Paris skyline. And stay sharp."

While Agent Ferrara walked to the stairs, she turned down the hallway, wanting a better vantage point of the area between the hotel and the distant fire. She was missing something. Something wasn't right.

13

COL. JOSEPH MAZURSKY raced past Air Force One in the secured hangar at Charles de Gaulle. His fellow Marine HMX-1 copilot, Maj. Aaron Parker, in a leather flight jacket matching his, ran next to him. Bright lights gleamed off the buffed wax finish on the president's jet, which was surrounded by a dozen Air Force guards and Secret Service CAT agents.

The hangar doors were opened just wide enough for any of the dozens of Secret Service or Air Force security vehicles to pass through. Mazursky ran out into the snow flurries—his first true glimpse of the weather system he'd been monitoring on radar all evening.

"Be better if it were a clear night," he said.

"Yes sir," Parker replied, running at his side.

"The others coming?"

"Twenty seconds, sir."

He saw one of the most expensive helicopters in the world waiting thirty yards in front of him. The green and white fifteen-million-dollar custom Black Hawk—known, oddly, as a White Hawk—was a beautiful aircraft, with a long, sleek body like a shark's. Large and powerful in the front, with a long tail, it looked built for speed and agility. It was just one of over twenty helicopters in the Marine HMX-1 fleet used to fly the president, and he was proud to be its pilot. Inside the United States, the Marine Corps used either the old Sikorsky VH-3 Sea Kings or the newer Lockheed Martin VH-71s. But overseas, they used the White Hawks, which were slightly smaller and more easily transported on the Air Force C-17 cargo jets, yet had the same communications and defensive capabilities as the larger Sea Kings.

"Warm her up," Mazursky ordered. "I'll do the walk-around."

The White Hawk had been buttoned up in the hangar, but the support crew had pulled it back out after getting the call from the HMX-1 White House Liaison Officer.

He turned on his flashlight and began examining the exterior. The HMX-1 mechanics were the best in the world, and they kept the president's birds in perfect condition. There had never been an in-flight mechanical failure in the history of the HMX-1 fleet, dating all the way back to the Eisenhower administration, so he had no concerns about the White Hawk's readiness. It was by far the best-serviced helicopter he had ever flown. But a quick preflight walk-around was a safety precaution drilled into him since his first days of flying, decades ago.

The cold wind was picking up, and thick, wet snowflakes hit the side of his face. Ducking under the tail, he touched the smooth, moist metal. After examining the tail rotor, he moved down the right side and circled around the bubble nose. Seeing no imperfections, he pulled the door latch handle and climbed in the right side of the warm cockpit.

Parker was flipping through switches, lighting up the large instrument panels in an array of crimson-lit square buttons and soft-green glowing displays.

Mazursky pulled the dual shoulder strap over his head and snapped the harness buckle to secure him in the seat. Putting on his white helmet, he said, "Comm check." He punched in the radio code of the selected channel into the square keypad on the large instrument console between the seats.

Flipping through the small, four-inch-thick VH-60 operating manual to the proper page, he began running through the checklist items for the pre-engine start cockpit procedures. Once their harnesses were strapped, he continued through the long series of challenge-response steps. Reading through the checklist, he said, "Circuit breakers and switches—set."

"Back me up," the copilot replied.

Parker reached above his head and checked several indicator LEDs. Then he checked "CD ESS BUSES" on the aft portion of the overhead console, and "BATT/BATT UTILITY BUS" on the lower console.

Then they went through the avionics-off frequencies set. Mazursky verified each against the checklist as Parker performed the set actions with the COMM cont-transmitter, GPS/Doppler mode set, transponder master switch, and other settings. Finishing the routine, the copilot flipped another switch above his head and said, "Blade deice power switch, OFF." Then, checking a few more items, he said, "APU control switch, OFF. APU fire T-handle, IN."

"Fuel Pump Switch, APU boost," Mazursky said, still reading from the checklist.

"APU boost," Parker replied, moving the fuel pump switch.

"APU generator switch, on," Mazursky read.

"APU generator switch, ON," Parker responded.

They moved through the rest of the preflight and engine start checklists. Mazursky knew by heart the procedures that his co-pilot was going through, but he still read them off the sheet as Parker performed them. When he read off the last one, he said, "Engines on to idle."

He reached above him and grabbed the baseball-size knob at the tip of the throttle lever for engine two. Parker mirrored his movement, grabbing the throttle for engine 1 above him. They both pulled them down slightly to the white "IDLE" line between the levers. Each pilot's green RPM gauge rose slowly toward 70, just below the level that would give them lift.

With his left hand, Mazursky grabbed the collective next to his seat, which would control the pitch angle of the main rotor blades. With his right hand, he grabbed the cyclic stick between his legs, for controlling the pitch of the main rotor disk. He put his feet up against his left and right antitorque pedals, for controlling the pitch of the tail rotor blades. Parker had matching controls on his side, but the only things he would operate when Mazursky was piloting would be the engine 1 throttle and the comm and navigation equipment.

Mazursky patched into the control tower, where the White House Liaison Officer was already in contact with flight control. "Tower, this is United States Colonel Mazursky, requesting flight standby for Alpha Niner One Four Seven." Just as with the Boeing VC-25s used for Air Force One, the presidential transport helicopters used only the "Marine One" call sign when the president was on board.

"Request granted, Colonel Mazursky," an American-accented voice said through his headset. "Hot departure for POTUS exec lift granted at will. Advise when hot."

"Roger, tower," Mazursky replied.

A hundred feet away, he could see another pair of Marine pilots boarding the much larger Sikorsky CH-53K King Stallion support helicopter. A dozen Secret Service CAT agents rushed across the asphalt in their heavy tactical gear and jumped in behind them. The massive black escort helicopter could carry enough men to secure any emergency exec lift.

The main rotor blades were now spinning in a soothing purr, with barely any vibration in the cockpit.

"Sitting warm, sir," Parker said. "Ready and waiting for hot."

"Waiting for hot," Mazursky confirmed.

Snow flurries wafted and circled outside the large cockpit's windows, blurring the fluorescent glow of the surrounding ground lights in a bright wintry cloud. He sat in silence beside his copilot, waiting for the possible emergency call from the president's protection detail—a call that he prayed would never come.

14

MAXIMILIAN LOOKED AT his watch: only ninety seconds before the first explosion. By now his men in the other tunnel should already have started cutting into the pipe system, which would trigger the emergency cutoff protocol when the water utility's main computer detected the sudden drop in pressure. He stepped forward and addressed the crowd of headlamps and the ominous silhouettes of heads and shoulders and assault rifle barrels stretching back down the tunnel.

"Men!" he yelled. "When Hannibal finished crossing the Alps and entered northern Italy, the Romans still believed they could quickly destroy his army. They believed their enemy would fight them head-on in the open field, as armies of that time did. But Hannibal was a military genius, now considered the father of war strategy. And he used the Romans' arrogance against them. He used misdirection and deception to win battles in which he was heavily outnumbered. Now, the Americans are well trained and well equipped—much like the Roman soldier once was. But we will use surprise and deception and strategy to destroy them. They will not be prepared for our maneuvers!"

The tunnel filled with cheering.

Maximilian stepped up onto a large fallen stone from the underground ruins and placed a hand on the rock wall for balance. "You all know your roles. And like Hannibal, I will be right in the middle of the battle, fighting with you!"

The men cheered again.

He stepped back down and knelt behind the protruding rocks of the tunnel's right angle. He looked at his watch: ten seconds from detonation. He closed his eyes and smiled.

The exploding C-4 split the air like a thunderclap. A gust of stale, dusty air brushed past him through the tunnel. He could smell a trace of chlorine, and when he opened his eyes, a blue haze glowed in his headlamp beam.

"A perfect cut, General," Mozgovoy shouted at him out of the cloud of rock dust.

The shaped charge had blown through the building's outer concrete foundation.

His army had been well trained in what to do after the explosion. Before the cloud of concrete dust had settled, the line of men was already rushing through the breach, into the upper sewer tunnels. And these would lead them to the outer wall of the hotel's basement corridors.

15

S PECIAL AGENT IN Charge John Alexander raised a finger to his earpiece and said into his wristband, "Please repeat that."

"Sir," the voice said, "we've just received a vibration hit on the EK-one."

"What's the magnitude?"

"Zero point two. Lasted zero-point-four seconds."

John knew that any earthquake would be at least 0.6 in magnitude if the epicenter was within a few miles. But Paris had no known fault lines in or around the city. The closest subway station to the hotel was far away—one of the reasons the Secret Service had selected this hotel. It shouldn't put out even a 0.1-magnitude vibration unless a crash happened on the tracks. The advance team had scouted the tunnels under the hotel, and because of the sealed passageways, he had determined a low risk of unauthorized access near the hotel. Thus, they had installed EK-1 seismometers in a perimeter along the basement, to serve as an early-warning system beyond the hotel's secured area. John had agents in the basement, monitoring the devices.

Agent David Stone looked at him with raised eyebrows. The other agents would also have heard every word over the comms. John turned away and stood by the narrow floor-to-ceiling window at the edge of the antechamber. The snow was falling thicker than a half hour earlier. The clumped white flakes turned to slushy drops after hitting the glass pane. He looked out at the blurred city lights, studying the horizon as if he might discern a threat somewhere out there, coming this way.

The EK-1 readings didn't make much sense. Advance team agents with their bomb dogs had been sweeping every inch of the hotel, surrounding buildings, and sewer systems twice a day for the past week, and every four hours since the president arrived in Paris, so a bomb seemed unlikely.

"Agent Perez," John said into his wrist microphone. "I want you and the other agents down there to check out the northeast corner of the basement where the first EK-one hit registered. I'll have HQ analyze the magnitude data and give us a better idea what might have caused it."

"Yes sir. On our way to check out the area now."

John nodded as he thought about the possibilities. He had trained agents to trust their instincts because they were often subconscious reactions formed by past training and experience. He had never seen an EK-1 detection like this before, and it had him concerned. He flipped his radio to the wider U.S. military channel so he could talk to the HMX-1 White House Liaison Officer. "Please prep a White Top for possible exec lift of POTUS."

"A White Top is currently prepped, warmed, and ready for flight," the Marine attaché replied.

"She's already prepped?" John asked in surprise.

"Yes sir. Agent Reid called it in because of a building fire in the vicinity."

"Roger, copy." He was impressed that Reid had made the call. "Maintain readiness and stand by for further instructions."

"Yes sir," the HMX-1 WHLO replied.

Flipping back to the wrist microphone, he said, "Command Center, send five CAT agents to the twenty-fifth floor to form an additional perimeter blockade below Firefly. I'll meet them there in one minute for setup."

"We're sending them up," a voice replied in his earpiece.

He shot a serious glance at Stone. "I'll be back in two or three minutes. You've got POTUS."

"Yes sir," Stone replied a little too loudly, as if snapping to attention.

John walked fast toward the stairwell. So much of protecting the president was about decreasing the odds that something devastating could happen to her. That was why cooks and foods were flown on Air Force One, to prepare all meals for POTUS at travel destinations, even foreign diplomatic dinners. That was why every agent knew "ten-minute" first aid—how to stabilize the president in a medical emergency, until an ambulance could arrive. That was why agents went through monthly weapons training even after years of fieldwork, why the Service sent a hundred-person advance team to the location weeks before a planned trip, why they shut down highways for hours just for a five-minute drive in the motorcade, why they used bulletproof glass in front of podiums during speeches, and why they never let the president remain in one place for very long when in public—always moving POTUS to lessen the odds of an enemy finding an opportunity for an attack. An ever-changing calculus was always running in John's head, gauging whether changing factors were increasing or decreasing the risk to the president. And when something—even something small—increased the risk, he would try to counter with something that lowered it again. So even though a small but strange blip had registered on the EK-1, he now countered with a temporary increase in the protection force directly around the president.

Now he would just maintain his slightly elevated internal alert level until he heard back from his men in the basement.

16

REBECCA STOOD BY the elevators on the twenty-second floor, staring out the windows at the smoke plume from a small fire blazing a mile away, its flames occasionally reflecting back at her off the long glass-covered tour boats drifting under lighted stone bridges on the Seine. The orange flames stood out in a city lit only in white. Only the bright yellow lights of the Eiffel Tower competed with the liveliness of the distant fire.

The fire itself no longer concerned her; it was far enough away and wasn't spreading. There was no wind, and the snow was drifting down heavier now. What did concern her were all the flashing lights of fire trucks and emergency crews around the fire.

She spoke into her sat phone. "JOC, how many emergency responders were sent to the fire?"

After a short delay, the voice replied, "All available."

"The Paris dispatchers *are* aware of our requested protocols regarding local law enforcement around the president, correct?"

"Yes, ma'am. They have been briefed, and we've been monitoring their radios to make sure they comply with our requests. No Paris police officers have been pulled away from the outer perimeter of the protection bubble."

Rebecca exchanged a nod with her reflection while still trying to make out details around the distant fire. Then she felt a sudden chill. "What about firefighters?" she asked. "How many from the area were dispatched to the fire?"

Silence roared in her earpiece.

"How many?" she demanded with more urgency.

"Hold, please . . ." After ten long seconds, the voice returned. "All fire response from central Paris responded to the fire. I repeat, all in the area have responded."

"Oh, God . . . *all* of them!" Rebecca said, her mind flashing through the possible scenarios. "Get the White Top airborne. Now!"

She knew that this was quite possibly merely a coincidental fire and nothing more. But the risk level had increased for the second time in two minutes, and all her training and instincts told her to err on the side of overreacting to an increased risk. So there was no question in her mind what she needed to do. She switched from the sat phone to her wrist microphone.

"Alexander, this is Reid. Do you copy?"

"Go ahead," the SAIC's voice said in her earpiece.

"Joint Ops says all fire responder resources have been directed to the fire at the Montparnasse Tower. No one's on standby. I recommend we move Firefly to a lower floor until the emergency responder resources become available again."

"Roger, Reid. Can't move Firefly for five minutes. On a Nat Sec call with the JCs. I'm meeting a CAT group on twenty-five. Then we'll bring her down."

"Copy that," she said. Five minutes for POTUS to finish a National Security call with the Joint Chiefs. There hadn't been enough threat indications to move the president while on an important call, but the timing couldn't be worse. The risk level was now higher than Rebecca had ever experienced.

She looked at her watch. Five minutes couldn't go by fast enough.

17

MAXIMILIAN AND KAZIM ran through the tunnel that ran beside the hotel's foundation. During planning of the raid nine months ago, when the men who hired Maximilian had identified the sixteen hotels where the president might stay during the conference, the entry point to this one was determined to be the northeast corner of the third basement level. To support the garage and the weight of the twenty-seven-story hotel, the builders had laid a fifty-foot foundation of Iranian quartz-infused concrete. Not even a bunker-buster bomb dropped from the sky could break through that much concrete, so Maximilian's team sure as hell couldn't, either. But in their planning, they had found one vulnerability in this building's schematics: the water pipes coming through the northeast foundation wall of sublevel three.

Maximilian and Kazim stopped and knelt in the passageway. The cool limestone enclosing them made the stink of the men more noticeable than back in the warehouse. Metal clanked behind him as the men at the front knelt and rested the butts of their MP5s on the rock floor. He glanced back at the long procession of heads silhouetted in the beams of their mini headlamps. They looked like an army of miners frozen in the black subterranean void. His own light shone on the two men closest to him and Kazim. One, Tomas Lindqvist, had a pale face, blue eyes, straight blond hair, and a curly blond beard. The other, Asghar Maadi, had Mediterranean olive skin, a black goatee, and shining dark eyes. In the shadows of the tunnels, Tomas looked like a Viking, Asghar a Barbary pirate. Both had a background in arms dealing, and aside from Kazim, they were the most dangerous killers Maximilian had recruited. The first month in camp, the two men had bonded over their similar experiences selling illegal weapons in conflict zones. Now Tomas and Asghar were like brothers. The other men had nicknamed them the Merchants of Death. Maximilian was proud that his polyglot collection of terrorists and mercenaries resembled the mix of races in Hannibal's own hodgepodge armies.

Mozgovoy's assistant worked fast, his burned-pink hands deftly connecting a detonator to the shaped charges plastered over the outer concrete wall. After Mozgovoy attached the wires to the detonator box, he and his assistant darted back around the bend and crouched with the rest of the group, out of blast range. Reaching out a long, thin arm, the assistant handed the remote trigger to Maximilian.

Maximilian looked at the small black device that had the power to release a shock wave of death and suffering on America. If they succeeded, it would be one of the most brutal blows in history to the failed experiment in democracy known as the United States of America. The Civil War, the assassination of Abraham Lincoln, Pearl Harbor, the assassination of John F. Kennedy, the terrorist attacks on 9/11—these were the most iconic tragedies in American history. And now Maximilian and his men were about to add themselves to that infamous list of men who, individually or anonymously as a group, had struck a devastating blow to the pride and strength of America.

He moved his thumb to the small red button embedded in the center of the device. Then he turned to Kazim, still kneeling beside him.

"Are you ready to claim your revenge?" Maximilian asked.

Kazim looked at him with the intent expression of an attack dog waiting eagerly to be unleashed. "I am ready to send her to the hell she deserves."

Maximilian grinned and nodded. Then he looked forward again and pressed the button.

18

S PECIAL AGENT PEREZ moved down the steel-and-concrete stairs into the third sublevel of the hotel. With him were Agents Franklin and Silver. Agent Perez had gotten to know both men well during their time together in Beltsville and during their postings on PPD. They even played together on the same intramural softball team with other agents back in Washington. Now they were moving together to sweep the basement and check the positioning of the EK-1 that had registered the vibration one minute earlier. Perez wanted to report their findings back to SAIC Alexander as soon as possible.

Reaching the concrete floor of sublevel 3, he directed Franklin and Silver to sweep the northeast corner while he examined the EK-1. The fourth-generation seismometer was a cutting-edge device developed to detect slight movements and vibrations in the air and through solid matter. Three feet tall, it consisted of a metal cube the size of a small hatbox, with little holes drilled into the surface, mounted on a tripod.

As Franklin and Silver walked along the wall, Perez examined the device for anything suspicious. Its foundation was well set, and all the safeguards the advance team's technicians had put in place on and around the device were undisturbed. Barring an unlikely technical error from the device, the readings detected must be accurate.

Without warning, the north end of the east wall exploded inward. Shards of stone and concrete flew into the large basement, followed by a billowing cloud of dust. The deafening bang had set off a high-pitched ringing in Perez's inner ears. The blast had thrown him off his feet and back to the base of the stone stairs. The EK-1 was fallen and buried under loose rubble.

Blinking, he tried to focus, tried to see the room. In the brief moment of the explosion, he had registered seeing both Franklin and Silver blown back like rag dolls. They had been much closer to the wall than he, and the blast had undoubtedly killed them.

Then, through the cloud of dirt and concrete, he saw men come spilling out of the darkness. They were scrambling over the rubble, yelling to each other, their guns and equipment clattering with the sounds of a fast-moving army. Everything was moving so fast, his training now took over. He acted on instincts conditioned uniquely for protecting the president. As shocking as it was, he understood this threat. His training had developed a muscle memory that created a counterintuitive movement—one focused on saving someone else's life instead of his own. He had spent countless hours preparing himself for this moment in his career as an agent. As the man leading this army saw him and raised a gun toward him, Perez reacted in the way that his training had conditioned him. His life was over— this he knew—but the only thing that mattered was protecting the president. So, leaning against the stone stairway, he raised his left wrist to his mouth and, a half second before he saw the flash of the man's gun pointed at his head, Special Agent Perez yelled into his communicator, "Crash POTUS!"

19

S PECIAL AGENT DAVID Stone had stepped into the post position just outside the twenty-sixth-floor conference room. The president was still inside, video conferencing with the Joint Chiefs in Washington.

David had his back nearly touching one of the double doors so he could always have President Clarke in eyesight through the small crack left open in the doors. Secret Service agents on PPD often found themselves privy to sensitive and sometimes personal conversations that a president had with others, including private and even emotional moments with family members. This could be uncomfortable for the agent, but most of the time they were too focused on the job to pay any attention to the conversation. And all agents knew that one of the highest privileges of working on PPD was the conscious knowledge that at times, they were essentially standing next to history.

Because the protection bubble was so secure at the moment, David allowed himself to hear some of the president's conversation. It appeared that an international crisis had boiled up in Nigeria. But before he caught much of the conversation, he heard Perez in his earpiece, reporting to SAIC Alexander that he and two other agents were checking on the seismometer in basement sublevel three. He was still amazed at how much nonstop precautionary activity had gone on at every protection site he worked.

David had been trained and conditioned to be suspicious always, never to let his guard down. In training, he had reviewed and studied every known assassination attempt, not just of past US presidents, but all known assassination attempts on leaders or other influential people in history. If an assassination attempt had failed, he had studied what agents, security details, or circumstances contributed to the assassination's failure. If an assassination attempt succeeded, he had studied everything about it to determine where the protection had broken down, where safety and security compromises had led to an opportunity for the assassins.

He had studied the assassinations of William McKinley and James Garfield. He had studied the assassination of Lincoln. He had read the accounts of the assassination attempt against Andrew Jackson, studied the police photos of the scene of the attempt against Truman outside Blair House near the White House, watched the videos and dissected transcripts related to the two attempts against Ford. He had studied the complete lack of security planning that gave easy opportunities to the assassins of Mahatma Gandhi and Martin Luther King Jr. And he had watched slow-motion video of the attempt on Reagan, which illustrated how all agents on the scene reacted exactly as they had been trained: one agent throwing Reagan into the bulletproof limousine while another agent stood up tall and spread wide to take a bullet even as the surrounding police officers instinctively crouched down to locate the shooter. The agents had reacted exactly as they were trained. Only a few months into his first term, President Reagan might have died on the sidewalk if Special Agent Tim McCarthy hadn't taken a bullet for him. Or Reagan certainly would have died inside the limousine—from the one freak bullet that had ricocheted through the seam of the open door—if Special Agent in Charge Jerry Parr hadn't realized from his training that Reagan had suffered a lung injury and required immediate surgery at the nearest hospital.

David had studied the importance of controlling access even during back-of-the-building entrances, as during Bobby Kennedy's assassination. As a candidate in the presidential primaries in the sixties, he had only a single bodyguard and wasn't under the protection of the Secret Service—a policy that changed overnight after his assassination. And, of course, David had studied the single greatest failing in Secret Service history: the assassination of John F. Kennedy in Dallas.

According to the training that he and every agent now went through, the Secret Service had made one mistake after another by bending to the will of President Kennedy's staff—and possibly of the president himself—to compromise security procedures for the president's political image. The secure motorcade route was changed to a less secure one that gave the president more access to the crowds along the sidewalks, the metal roof that could shield the president was removed from the vehicle to give the president greater visibility, and agents were told not to stand on the running boards on the sides of the car, so that the crowds could more easily see the president. On all these points, the Secret Service should have refused to budge, but instead they had given in. And that had left open the window of opportunity for an assassination that shouldn't have been possible.

David nodded at the two agents across the hallway. The president was scheduled to spend maybe another hour on video conference calls; then she would retire for the night. All three perimeters were tightened and ready for the full Night-watch. The only activity in the area was a hotel fire too far away to be a threat, and a strange vibration blip from the EK-1.

It should be another quiet night of cautious tension.

Then his earpiece crackled, and a voice yelled, "Crash POTUS!"

Then silence.

David's eyes widened when the three spoken syllables reached his ear, but the silence that followed made the message feel even more urgent. His training had prepared him to act fast in every sort of situation, but never more so than in a crash alert.

His eyes darted to the closest agent to him, and he pointed toward the south staircase. Then he looked at the other agent and nodded toward the doors to the conference room. David pushed open the double doors and rushed toward the president, with the other agent on his heels. Startled, the president shot to her feet. The generals on the monitors watching through the video conference cameras gasped, helpless to do anything more than watch as the Secret Service burst into the room and rushed toward the president.

"David? What is—?"

But before the president could say another word, David and the other agent flanked her, lifted her by the underarms, and whisked her out of the room. Her feet scarcely touched the floor. Without speaking, they carried her down the hallway to the staircase, where the third agent had the door open. Then, lowering her so her feet could reach the floor, they half-carried her into the stairwell.

"What's happened?" President Clarke gasped as they started down the stairs, holding her tight.

"There may be a threat, ma'am," David said, conserving his speech so he could focus on the evacuation plan for a crash scenario.

"Can you please put me down?"

"No time, ma'am." Then, with his free hand, he spoke into his communicator. "Firefly in south stairwell, twenty-sixth floor, moving towards secure alley. Rendezvous with Stagecoach in two minutes, twenty seconds."

The response came through his earpiece, confirming the rush evacuation of POTUS. The presidential limousine would be raced from the garage to the back alley. Getting the president inside the vehicle was the quickest way to control security directly around her until any threat could be identified and neutralized. With the limousine's advanced communications equipment and a small army of PPD and CAT agents strategically posted all around the building, more agents ready for emergency response, and a few hundred French police within response range, the president would be safest inside the armored limo. It was one of the best protective bubbles the Secret Service had outside the White House and Air Force One.

But David knew he couldn't take the president all the way down the staircase until the location of the threat was identified and the CAT agents had secured a safe path to the alley. In his earpiece, he could hear the frantic calls of other agents throughout the hotel: some trying to locate and engage the threat, some trying to secure the president's escape path, others trying to get to the president, to increase the inner perimeter of the protection bubble.

David could hear John Alexander on the communicator, racing toward their location to intercept them on the twentieth-floor stairway landing. But that was still thirty seconds away. For now, David was the lead agent protecting the president.

Rushing down the steps, he heard Alexander giving sharp orders over the encrypted Secret Service radio. No one knew who had given the crash alert or even why, or where the threat was.

"Stone, stop on the twentieth floor. I'll rendezvous with you there."

David knew that other agents were escorting the president's personal physician down from the twenty-seventh floor, and a team of five agents was bringing down the military aide responsible for the football. The suitcase attached to the aide's wrist contained the controls and secure satellite links to confirm a launch order of the US nuclear arsenal.

Other agents were scrambling urgently all over the hotel, responding to the crash alert exactly as they had been trained to do.

As eager as David was to rush the president down the remaining twenty flights of stairs and get her inside the mobile protection of the limousine, he never hesitated to follow the SAIC's command. They had no idea where or even what the threat was, and they couldn't risk running blindly into it. They had been on the twenty-sixth of twenty-seven floors, and he needed to get them down to a more central floor and hold until they knew whether the threat was coming from the ground or the roof. Alexander had called for the limousine to circle around to the alley, and just before the crash alert, Rebecca had called for a White Top to get airborne and fly toward the hotel.

"Wait," David commanded the president and the two other agents as they reached the twentieth floor. "Hold here!" He held his hand up, then spoke into the encrypted radio. "Firefly on south twenty. Holding for thirty."

As he waited, he saw the terrified eyes of the president, staring at him as if she was trying to read his mind.

"What's happening, David?" she asked quietly.

But he had been trained not to answer her in situations like this. What she knew or thought or felt didn't matter when there was a possible immediate threat to her life. His job was to keep her alive at all costs. And that meant focusing only on the things that might save her life. Answering her questions could pull his focus from the many split-second decisions he might need to make over the next thirty seconds.

He pressed his hand to the center of the president's back, making sure the blazer she wore over her blue shirt was one that the Secret Service had provided her, with the bulletproof material sown into the inside fabric by one of the best tailors in

Washington. He felt the stiffness in the fabric and was a little relieved.

"Button up your jacket, ma'am," he said.

Then he stood in front of the president in the stairwell, with one agent a few steps above them and the other a few steps below. Then, as instructed, David held their position, waiting for reinforcement agents from the counter assault team and for information about the threat.

It was the longest half minute of his life.

20

JOHN ALEXANDER RAN as fast as he could down the hallway with the five CAT agents he had grabbed from a team briefing room. They all had been near the elevator bay a floor below the president when the Crash POTUS came through the radio. The cover-and-dash would use the south stairwell to evac POTUS. The command center reported an explosion somewhere on a basement level. A few gunshots had followed.

"Hold Firefly at twenty!" he yelled into his radio. If the threat was coming from the sublevels, there might not be a safe path to the armored limousine.

His team was desperately trying to locate and engage the threat while also securing the president. All it would take to kill her would be one well-placed bullet, one piece of shrapnel from an explosion, or a few toxic particles from a chemical weapon. Statistically, the most dangerous threat to any president—despite continued developments of new threats—was a lone gunman willing to sacrifice himself for a kill shot. Four US presidents had been assassinated, each by a lone gunman. John sprinted down the hallway. His greatest fear was that this unknown threat involving an explosion and gunfire and reports of missing agents could be the lone-gunman scenario multiplied exponentially by a strong number of attackers.

Nearing the end of the hallway, he drew his gun and opened the door by throwing his shoulder into it. The CAT agents were right behind him. Pelting down five flights, he saw Stone and the two other agents spaced around the midflight landing in the stairway. Then, in the corner, behind Stone, he saw a shaken President Clarke.

"What's going on, John?" she demanded.

"Ma'am, we think there's a threat from the basement. We need to move you to the car." Then, without another word to her, he turned away and said into his wrist communicator, "Alexander on twenty with Firefly! Evac to Stagecoach! Two minutes! All agents secure evac route White Sigma!"

Lowering the radio, he stepped toward the president and, together with David, lifted her under the arms just enough to keep her feet on the ground but with little weight for her to support. This allowed David and him to essentially half-carry her down the stairs, fast, without worrying about her tripping and falling. "No word on the exact location of the threat, but we need to keep moving. We need to get her to the limo."

As he and Stone raced the president down the stairs, they were protected in front and behind by the two PPD agents, in suits, and five CAT agents, in tactical gear. Other agents were giving situational status calls over the radio. Four more PPD agents entered the stairwell at the next floor and joined them.

John was relieved that the number of agents around POTUS had increased from three to thirteen in the minute since the crash call. They had dozens more agents scrambling on floors above and below them, and at any moment, the limousine should arrive in the alley, just two minutes from their current location.

Now that the added agents directly around the president had strengthened the protective bubble, they could fight off any terrorists in the race to the armored vehicle. Then they would rush POTUS across Paris to Air Force One, where, once they took off, she would be safe. The sound of the agents clomping down the concrete steps echoed like thunder in the narrow staircase that wound down the interior of the hotel. And in the center of this moving, clattering shield was the terrified president of the United States.

21

MAXIMILIAN RUSHED THROUGH the dust cloud and into the basement. An advance team of a dozen men was in front to protect him, but he was leading the rest of the 200 men behind him. They had less than a minute to seal the first floor.

He signaled Kazim to take his twelve men up the north stairway to the rooftop, twenty-eight floors up. Then he waved for the other men to follow him to the hotel lobby.

They entered a basement corridor of white-painted cinder block, used by the laundry and cleaning crews. He could hear the metallic hum of a roomful of industrial-size laundry machines, and the massive water-heating system.

Two maids in black-and-white uniforms came around the corner, screamed in terror, and fled behind a giant laundry machine. Unconcerned, Maximilian charged ahead. But as his men neared the short staircase at the end of the hallway, two Secret Service agents appeared. The agents stood square and fired six shots between them, killing four of his men with impressive efficiency before being riddled with submachine-gun fire.

Maximilian stopped at the base of the stairs and slapped his men on the shoulders as they ran past the two dead agents and pounded up the steps. As the first wave in his attack, many of these men would be killed in the next few minutes. But like Hannibal with his Numidians at the Battle of the Trebia, he was willing to sacrifice some of his men to lead his enemy into an ambush. And his men—aware of his plans and loyal to him and their cause—were eager to do their part.

He allowed the designated thirty men, armed with Kalashnikovs, to rush down the hallway at the top of the stairs. He could hear their brief firefights with some of the Secret Service men and women standing their posts in this part of the building. He understood the protocols and protective procedures of America's Secret Service. Any agents they encountered in the first thirty seconds, down in the basement stairways and first-floor hallways, far from the president, would be PPD agents instead of the deadlier counter assault team agents. PPD agents would be in dress suits and carried only SIG Sauer P229 semiautomatic pistols and the occasional shotgun. But the CAT and emergency response team agents wore full tactical gear and carried a number of powerful weapons, including the Knight's Armament SR-16 assault rifle. PPD agents would be stationed everywhere throughout the hotel at strategically chosen posts, while CAT agents would be in a few select locations, waiting in concentrated teams, ready to respond to any sudden threat identified by PPD.

Maximilian had ten to twenty more seconds before his first wave of men encountered CAT agents responding to the explosion. They would meet more PPD agents before that, but these they could push through without too many losses.

He had given careful instructions to all his men so that each knew exactly what he needed to do to fill his role. After watching the first thirty race away from the top of the stairs, he turned to the four waiting behind him. Each held in his hands a long brass nozzle connected to a black hose that ran from a metallic tank strapped to his back.

"Remember, on my signal," he told them.

Then he took from his pocket a small foghorn of the sort used by hooligans in soccer stadiums all over the world. He would use it to communicate to his small army, just as Hannibal had used signal flags to direct the movements of his men on the ancient battlefields across Italy, in a type of warfare now forever lost to time.

He raised the red and white horn, which was scarcely larger than a cigar, and pushed the plastic button to let out one short, bellowing shriek. It was loud enough to be heard by all the men in the hallway behind him. They roared in response. Raising an arm, he gave another blast of the foghorn before moving all his men into position on the wide stairway.

*   *   *

Special Agent Phil Abbott led the counter assault team stationed next to the Secret Service's command center, set up in a first-floor conference room usually reserved for hotel management. The instant the Crash POTUS alert went out, he and the twenty CAT agents on his team had jumped to their feet and rushed into the lobby. Every member on his team had joined the Secret Service after the military, and most had fought in combat zones. It occurred to him that after all the various hellholes these men had battled in during their military careers, it must seem strange to be running in full tactical gear through the sumptuously appointed lounge of this five-star Paris hotel.

As Abbott ran through the enormous lobby toward one of the many wide hallways branching out from the center, he heard a flurry of rapid commands and reports through his earpiece.

"This is Command Center. PPD agents encountered a group of attackers on the basement level."

"What level?" a voice demanded through the radio.

"B-two or B-."

"How many hostiles?"

"A dozen reported," the agent from the command center radioed.

"They're moving toward the lobby from north stairs by lower ballroom," a husky voice said, with loud snaps of gunfire in the background.

Abbott wanted to engage this enemy now before they could cause any more damage.

Another voice ripped through the encrypted frequency. "Firefly on south twenty. Holding for thirty."

"Abbott," the command center agent said, "we need confirmation of threat strength and locale before a lower evac of Firefly."

"CAT approaching threat! Stand by!" he replied.

His team dashed into the hallway leading to the basement entrance, still a half-minute away.

"Stagecoach moving!" another voice yelled through the communicators, referring to the president's armored limousine. "Leaving garage. Rendezvous at Pont Hoc in twenty seconds."

Abbott recognized the location code as the hotel's east alley entrance.

"Pevear to group," another agent announced. "Second CAT team's locking down evac route for Firefly. Cleared for Pont Hoc."

Halfway down the long, wide hallway to the lower ballrooms, he saw two PPD agents in dark suits firing at something around the corner. Seconds later, both agents fell in a fusillade of automatic fire. Then a few dozen men in black urban camouflage rushed around the corner, carrying what looked like old Soviet-era Kalashnikovs.

He and his men immediately knelt into firing position and hit the attackers hard with an array of overwhelming force from quick, well-placed shots from their SR-16 assault rifles.

They had cut down half the assailants within twenty seconds. The remaining men started falling back from the CAT team's onslaught, and another twenty PPD agents joined his men to help repel the assault.

Abbott led his men forward, stopping the attackers' advance and gradually pushing them back down the corridor. He had to secure the evac route for Agent Alexander within the next thirty seconds.

*   *   *

Maximilian led his men halfway down the first hallway before stopping and ordering most of them into several small conference rooms on the left and the large ballroom on the right. He kept back six to drag the bodies of fallen agents out of the hallway.

Then he rushed back to the top of the wide basement stairway with most of his entire remaining force, to lie in wait for the Americans. The trap was baited.

*   *   *

Seeing that the attackers were being pushed back down the hallway, Special Agent Abbott led his men forward, moving in a three-deep wave of CAT agents, with another twenty PPD agents behind them.

"There are no other warnings of breaches in the hotel," the agent from the command center announced through his earpiece. "The hostiles you're engaging are the only known threat."

"Copy that," Abbott replied. The hostiles were coming from the direction of the large staircase leading to the basement levels, where an explosion now appeared to have occurred. "We need to hit them hard!" he yelled to his team. "We can't let them retreat back into the basement, where they might find another way up into the hotel."

Yelling for his men to advance cautiously toward the retreating attackers, he counted only ten hostiles still standing. Four of his own men had been hit, but he had to neutralize the threat to the president before trying to get them first aid.

Two more attackers fell to the CAT agents' precision shooting.

They fired kill shots into the head of every fallen hostile as they rushed past, after the retreating men.

The wide corridor was lined with closed doors on the right, and large openings into the ballroom on the left. His men looked into the ballroom as they moved quickly past, to make sure none of the terrorists had run into it. When he glanced in, it looked empty. Small tables were positioned along the hallway walls to hold delicate vases and other decor, but everything was now getting shot to hell.

Then, to his surprise, the retreating hostiles suddenly stopped and held their ground at the top of the wide stairway down to the basement levels. Some even took a few steps down and lay against the top step, as if firing from a trench. It was as if they were now protecting something and wouldn't retreat any farther.

Abbott's men stopped and took position in the hallway. They still outnumbered the enemy and had better weapons and were almost certainly better trained. As they fired at the men, Abbott yelled into his helmet microphone, "Threat contained at north stairway to sublevel. Less than ten hostiles remain. We're holding them. Evac Firefly to east alley exit and Stagecoach. Cleared on first floor. Repeat, threat held. Evac Firefly to Stagecoach asap!"

Then, he heard the distinct sound of a handheld foghorn: two blasts, followed by a short pause, then two more quick blasts. He didn't know what it might mean—only that it came from down the stairway, out of sight.

Suddenly, all the doors to their right opened almost simultaneously. At the same time, he saw quick movement from the shadows in the ballroom to their left. Then, out of the darkness, gunfire from heavy, modern assault rifles roared, like a hundred jackhammers ripping into concrete.

Caught in the middle of this ambush, half his CAT agents were killed outright. Those still able returned fast, precision shots against both sides, but they had been lured into a kill zone impossible to fight out of. Abbott caught multiple rounds in his arms and legs and chest body armor. Falling to the floor, he watched with horror as most of the agents fell around him.

"Breach! Breach!" he yelled into his communicator. "Hold evac! Hold evac! Breach!"

And then something fast and hard hit his neck, and he knew that his life was over. The last thing he noticed before falling into eternity was the American flag shoulder patch on another CAT agent lying beside him.

22

MAXIMILIAN MOTIONED TOWARD the four men with the steel tanks strapped to their backs, who had been waiting at the bottom of the stairs, away from the ambush, for his command. Now they followed him, running down the hallway, hurdling the dead Secret Service agents.

He knew that this first victory was only the beginning of what he needed to accomplish. Like Hannibal after his army came down from the Dolomites and into northern Italy, Maximilian could not afford to make even one serious mistake—as the Americans had just done. If he hoped for any chance of success, his tactical strategy and execution must be far superior to theirs. The Secret Service was trained and equipped to fight off a small army, and they also had additional resources they could call in for support if given enough time. Any success he and his men had would be brief and, ultimately, pointless unless they managed to tip the scales completely in their favor.

He had sent fifty of his well-armed men down the hallway. Another fifty were spaced behind them in phalangeal order-of-reinforcement attack lines. On either side, twenty men flanked Maximilian and the four men with the tanks. This protection was necessary to prevent their being hit by surprise flanking fire as they moved out of the hallway and into the cavernous lounge area.

He could barely see the front rank of his men, but he could tell from the horrified screams that they had reached the lobby. More gunfire erupted. He thought his men might be making good progress, securing the area for him and possibly even overrunning the Secret Service's command center, but those hopes vanished when he saw them getting pushed back by a new wave of CAT agents—twice the number he had ambushed and killed. His men couldn't hold up in a head-to-head fight with these agents, and no doubt many more Secret Service resources were being funneled toward this location. He had to play his ace card now before the Americans wiped out his entire company.

He gave the order to the four men. Splitting off in separate directions, they raced through the lobby area that his front line had temporarily secured.

As they moved, Maximilian yelled into his radio, "Inferno! Inferno!"

The message was relayed to each soldier in his army. The ones engaging the Secret Service near the command center moved back toward the center of the lobby while still shooting at the agents. The soldiers still in the sublevels would be moving faster to make sure they got to ground level and the upper stairs in time.

But it was the four men with the tanks who made all the difference. Maximilian watched as they rushed through the lounge to their designated positions at the corners of the vast room. And he watched as the four men—each at least a hundred feet from the others—knelt and raised the thick black hoses attached to the tanks on their backs. Almost in unison, a stream of fire squirted thirty feet out from the nozzle of each hose. As the four men swiveled their flamethrowers about, everything around them on the hotel's ground level was blanketed in a living, growing fire. The flames rose greedily into the air and danced over furniture, and in mere seconds, dark smoke billowed up, indicating that the fire had also entered the hotel's walls. The entire lobby was aglow in firelight, and the air quickly filled with suffocating smoke.

Maximilian's smile widened as he watched the fire spread. With all the technology available to government security agents, it was important to him that the thing to defeat them be a weapon as primitive as fire. By now agents on the other side of the fire would be desperately relaying messages to their command center. They would wonder why the hotel's fire suppression system wasn't working. It would probably take investigators days to discover that the reason the sprinklers hadn't doused the hotel after heat broke the plastic holds on the sprinklers was because his team underground had ruptured the water main into the hotel just before igniting the fire. And thanks to the man who had martyred himself in the Montparnasse Tower only fifteen minutes ago, firefighters would be delayed getting to this hotel by just enough time to ensure that the fire spread beyond their ability to control it.

It was important to him that the world should visualize a great fire as the symbol of this night's reckoning. There was no weapon more powerful than fear for controlling the minds of others.

Then, without warning, one of the fire starters' tank exploded—hit by an agent's bullet. Maximilian tensed as he saw his man on the floor, writhing in flames from his own weapon. The shot must have come from a Secret Service agent. Wherever the hell they were amid the smoke and flames and heat, they would be as determined to protect the president as his men were to kill her. The protection detail had better training and equipment and outside support on their side, but the greatest surprise was yet to come. He prayed that Kazim would make it to the roof in time to secure their victory.

23

JOHN ALEXANDER MOTIONED for the agents to stop short in the stairwell at the sixteenth floor. Stone and the other two agents surrounded the president, each covering a different arc in case anyone came at them from above or below.

"Repeat that!" John said into his communicator. There was little time, but with all the commotion on the stairs, and the occasional sound of close gunfire coming through every agent's earpiece, he needed to be certain he had heard correctly.

"Sir, I repeat, we've lost control of the first floor."

"Where?" John asked. "Is any part of the evac route secure?" The words "lost control" cut through him like a knife.

"No sir. There's a massive fire spreading fast, gunmen are scattered everywhere, and the fire suppression system isn't working. Sir, this area is no longer secured for Firefly evac. I say again, we have lost control, sir."

John had to think, but he had only a few seconds to make the right decision. There were risks either way. Taking the president down was the fastest way to get her out of the building—a building being swarmed by terrorists and a growing fire. Taking her up moved her away from the immediate threat, but it would mean a more complex extraction from the roof, which could ultimately prove riskier. As the SAIC of PPD, it was his call. And his instincts told him to move POTUS away from the immediate threat.

He pointed to David, then up the stairs. Speaking into his communicator, he said, "Taking Firefly to Zenith. Extract with White Top. Two minutes."

And then, as if the ten seconds' pause had put them hours behind schedule, they rushed the president back up the stairs. John was in front, David and one agent here again half-carrying her, and the other agents were coming up the steps behind them, covering the rear.

"Zenith snipes, confirm secure," John said into his communicator.

"This is Agent Graves," a voice replied in his earpiece. "Confirmed. Zenith is secure."

John recognized the voice of the commanding agent posted on the hotel's rooftop with two other countersnipers and spotters. With the roof secured and the White Hawk on the way, his mind jumped through all the things that needed to happen in the next thirty seconds.

"Agent Payne, where's the military aide?"

"Twenty-third floor," another voice answered in his earpiece.

"Get him to Zenith now. Agent Billings, where's the doc?"

"Twenty-fifth floor, south side," another voice replied.

"Get him up top. I want him near Firefly asap."

"Agent Alexander, this is Command Center. We're gonna have to break down to keep links with HQ."

"Negative," John replied. "I need you to stay up."

"Sir, the fire's right on us. We're gonna lose comms either way. Encrypted radio will still work, but we need to break down now or we'll lose our equipment and won't have links with Washington for twenty minutes."

"Where's the White Top?"

"White Hawk is three minutes out. Supported by King Stallion."

"How long will you be dark?"

"Four minutes."

"Do it faster."

Looking back as he rounded up the next landing, he saw that the president was holding it together. The group was focused, moving up the stairwell as a unit. Every agent was doing exactly as he had been trained.

Into his wrist, he said, "All agents above six, go to Zenith. All on or below six, form block stops in stairwells and engage any hostiles."

"This is Zenith," reported a rooftop agent through the radio. "We have three countersnipers and three watchers. Zenith is secure."

"This is Reid. On twenty-two, north side. Night-watch has thirty station agents between floors one through six, forty between floors six through twenty-six, and now another forty from CAT caught in the first-floor blaze and firefight. Another hundred agents and French police officers are on the third perimeter outside the hotel, but the fire has kept them from entering the building."

On the past three floors, as they ascended, additional agents had met them, guarding the cracked doors from the hallways, announcing the Secret Service "white knight," "red knight" emergency code for quick identification. As the protection bubble rushed past, agents would then leave their posts to join it until, by now, some thirty agents surrounded the president.

The White Hawk and King Stallion helicopters should be at the roof in two minutes. The agents' footsteps pounding up the stairs clattered like hail on a tin roof. The command center had broken down and would be dark for three to four minutes, and he still couldn't get good intel on the threat.

24

MAXIMILIAN LED FIFTY men up the north stairwell. His group was far below Kazim's faster-moving team. Like Hannibal at the Battle of the Tagus in 220 BC, he knew that it was critical to control the flow of soldiers—both his and the enemy's. Hannibal had been a master at military maneuvers, rehearsing advances and flanks and false retreats with tens of thousands of men days before an engagement with the enemy— all to ensure that his army would execute his ingenious plans with perfection once the chaos of battle erupted. It was a strategy that Maximilian had mimicked while training his men during the past six months. Every motion and maneuver had been practiced in preparation for this critical moment in the attack.

Reaching the third floor, he found ten of his advance men stopped in the stairwell just ahead of him. Many more were crowded below him. "You men, secure four and five!" he commanded all those above him except the burly bearded man by the door. Those above turned and raced up toward the next flight. The door man grabbed the handle and yanked it open, and Maximilian stood aside while the others rushed past him and poured into the third floor hallway. Screams echoed, but no shots were fired.

Maximilian now jumped into the middle of the line of men and ran into the hallway. He saw Tomas and Asghar, the Merchants of Death, at the front. The group moved like a pack of wolves, loping past the doors that lined the long hallway. An older man stood in the open doorway of his hotel room, yelling desperately in French to someone still inside. Asghar smashed him in the forehead with a gun butt. A woman twenty yards ahead whimpered softly as she tried to swipe her key card in her door's electronic reader. Tomas shot her in the neck, spraying blood on the wall as the card reader turned green. She fell to the floor and jerked briefly while men rushed past her toward the midway bend in the corridor, by the elevator bay.

"Hurry!" Maximilian yelled. "The Americans will be fast! Move!"

He had a dozen men with portable fire extinguishers to suppress any fire that threatened to block their movements, and each man on his team had goggles and an oxygen mask for heavy smoke. The blaze was still too far below for much smoke to have reached their level, although the alarm had gone off and filled the hallway with its annoying electronic screech. Several people came out of their hotel rooms, only to be shot in their doorways. The hallway must remain clear for his men to maneuver, and he had no interest in taking hostages. The fire would kill everyone soon enough.

Four scouts had raced ahead of the pack and were already in the south stairwell, two going up and two going down. The main body of men was nearly to that end of the hallway, with five staying behind to keep it secured. Others should now have control of the north stairwell behind them from floors one through five.

In front of the pack, shots went off with a muffled echo, and blood spattered across the outside of the small window in the stairwell door. The door cracked open, and a bloodied scout fell back into the hallway.

"Aytek!" Maximilian called to the man. "Where are they?"

The scout, half dazed, glanced without a word, as if confused to see the rest of the men charging at him. His wide-eyed stare looked somehow puzzled, and blood covered most of his face.

"Where *are* they?" Maximilian yelled as the group neared the end of the hallway.

"Below," the scout replied.

"How many?"

"Three or four."

"Keep moving!" Maximilian yelled at his men. He looked at the Merchants of Death and could see their gleaming, eager eyes—one pair brown, the other blue—through the masks. "Fire wave, charge down. Overrun the Americans. Kill them all. They won't be able to hold the stairwell with just four agents. Charge! Charge to ground floor! Take it and secure it!"

As Tomas and Asghar went into the south stairwell to lead the downward assault, Maximilian held up his hand to stop the second half of the group. "Not too many," he said. "It's a bottleneck—could be a trap."

The dark face of the first man he had stopped stared intently at him. No true warrior ever wanted to be held back from a fight, and that was exactly why Maximilian had chosen these men. But it was also why he always needed to control them, to occasionally hold them back from rushing headlong to a needless death.

"Not yet!" he said to the man and those behind him.

Then he heard shouting and gunshots from the stairwell. It went on for half a minute before lapsing into an eerie silence.

"Scout it," he said to the man.

The man darted past him and into the stairwell. Maximilian could hear his boots clomping down the steps. Waiting for the report, he tipped his head sideways to make sure there were no problems back down the hallway. Other than the bodies of a dozen hotel guests, everything was open for his men to move through. He then stepped back through the doorway and looked up the south stairwell. The next landing was clear, and the other two scouts were calling down to him that it was clear to the fifth floor. He motioned for more men from the hallway to rush up the stairwell and help the scouts keep the next few levels secure.

Finally, the last man he had sent down rushed back up. "We lost half," he said, "but all the agents from here to the first floor are now dead. The stairs belong to us."

"Are Tomas and Asghar alive?"

The man's eyes smiled. "Nothing can kill the Merchants of Death."

Maximilian stepped past him into the stairwell and yelled down toward his men. Tomas appeared below, mask off and dangling around his neck. He looked as if killing Americans was great fun.

"How long can you hold the stairs?" Maximilian asked.

"As long as you wish!" Tomas boasted.

"You and Asghar hold this area with the men you have left. I'm sending twenty more down to raise hell on the first floor. Let them pass, but your group stays."

"We want to raise hell too!" Tomas said.

"You'll soon have plenty of opportunity," Maximilian promised. "But right now, keeping the stairs is most important." He turned back into the hallway and ordered a large group of fighters down to the first floor.

The flank was nearly complete. As he watched more of his men rush into the stairwell, he knew that he had taken control away from the Secret Service. He had the basement, the lower floors on the north side, and now the lower levels of both north and south stairwells. The fire had most of the lobby, with his men now carefully holding flanks on both sides of the spreading inferno. Any agents still alive on the ground floor were outside the ring of fire, pushed away from the critical access paths that could lead up into the building. And with the third floor now under control, he could easily maneuver his men between stairwells, giving them quick access to both sides of the hotel.

He did a call check into his radio. "Ground spot! Any eyes on Medusa?"

"No Medusa," a voice crackled through the radio. "Confirmed with other watchers. I repeat, no Medusa, no black carriage—nothing!"

Maximilian grinned. The president hadn't had time to escape the building and must still be somewhere above him, but she would undoubtedly have many Secret Service agents still protecting her. His bold strategic maneuvers had worked. He had systematically removed every path of escape for the president. He had trapped her and cut her off from the bulk of her protection resources, much as Hannibal had done to the Roman garrison at the citadel in Tarentum.

It was now up to Kazim and his special team to finish the mission. They were within minutes of their victory. And he could think of no man more motivated to give the American people a lasting visual nightmare that would break their hearts, crush their arrogance, and forever blind them with impotent rage.

25

KAZIM RACED BEHIND his men up the north stairwell, shouting, urging them to greater speed. He had twelve men with him, but four were carrying two large cases, which slowed the ascent of the entire team. If he could just get to the roof with at least seven men and the cases within the next two minutes, he could keep Maximilian's plan on track.

They had just passed the twenty-first floor—only seven more flights between them and their destiny. Maximilian had been brilliant in convincing the men that they would need to sacrifice their lives in order to hit the American government with a decapitation strike. It was a lie, but the other men needn't know the truth. The only thing that mattered was killing the president. It wasn't even guaranteed that the president would be taken to the roof, but Maximilian had been adamant: they must take the roof out of the equation either way if their plan was to have any chance for success.

But then, just as he was feeling that nothing could stop them, someone shouted something strange down at them. A faint shadow, cast down from the stairwell above, moved along the wall in front of him. The shout of "White knight!" came again, this time more audibly. It bounced and echoed off the hard concrete and sounded a little high pitched.

Another agent, hiding, waiting to ambush his group.

He motioned to one of his men, and together they darted up the last few steps to the midlevel landing and fired up toward the agent. The figure above had ducked down below the upper banister so fast that Kazim never got a look at them. And just as fast, the agent returned fire from a crouched position above.

Dropping to his chest on the hard concrete steps, Kazim cursed as bullets ricocheted off the steel banister and slammed into the walls. As he rolled to his back, he saw the agent's muzzle flashes light up the underside of the stairs above.

The agent was very close to him and his men—maybe eight feet away.

He waved for the rest of his men to crawl up toward him. Together, they would cut this agent to pieces in a hail of bullets.

26

REBECCA HEARD THE communication from SAIC Alexander that the direct PPD team couldn't get the president to the lower floors, because of the fire. He had alerted all agents that they were taking POTUS up twelve flights to the roof, where the White Top was en route to meet and extract her. Three Secret Service countersnipers were stationed on the roof, but most of the agents in the building had been directed to the lower floors during the first attempt to rush the president safely out to the armored limousine. Between the gunfights and the spreading fire on the first few floors, it was difficult to gauge how many agents would make it back up toward the new escape route for the president. Alexander and the bubble team were bringing POTUS up the south staircase, so Rebecca needed to help secure the north staircase until the team could get President Clarke on the roof for a Marine One exec lift.

With her SIG Sauer P229 drawn, she used her shoulder to push the handle, opening the twenty-second-floor stairway door. Almost immediately, a thundering of footsteps came around the stairs just one floor below.

"Stop!" she yelled. "White knight!" The response she needed to hear back was "red knight," but she wasn't hearing it.

"White knight!" she yelled again, stopping her descent and leveling her gun at the swarm of shadows coming into view. She raised her wrist microphone to warn the rest of the team of possible hostiles coming up the north staircase, but before she had a chance, the men appeared below and she had to fire shots. Bullets were soon coming at her and ricocheting all around the enclosed concrete stairwell. She returned more fire down at them while falling backward onto the top step of her floor. She fell hard, slapping the floor with her free arm to absorb some of the shock, and rolled back toward the door. All agents were trained to stand tall and advance toward gunfire because it was the best tactic for shielding a protectee. But despite the responses conditioned into her through training, she resisted the automatic reaction to engage the group of men. She could tell she was outnumbered and that this was a threat to the president, so her focus was on warning Alexander of the attackers' presence.

Rolling toward the door, she wanted only to avoid the bullets long enough to give a situational warning to the PPD team. But when she yelled into her wrist microphone, she couldn't hear her own relay in her earpiece. Feeling the ache in her lower back, she realized that the encrypted radio clipped to the back of her belt must have gotten crunched when she fell backward to the floor. Now she couldn't warn the team of this threat that was clearly heading for the roof.

She heard the men shouting to each other in a foreign language. They tried to move around the corner to ascend the stairs. She fired five more shots until her magazine emptied. Yanking her one standard-issue flash-bang grenade off her belt, she tossed it over the railing and covered her ears as she turned away with eyes closed. Hearing the loud pop and seeing the bright flash even through her eyelids, she then jumped to her feet. She heard men below, groaning from the noise and flash of the crowd-control grenade, but someone very strong was still on his feet, and shooting at her. A bullet whined off the steel banister near her. Knowing she couldn't risk being killed before she could warn the protection team around the president, she snapped one of the last twelve-round magazines into her gun, fired a few shots down the stairs, and then took off running up to the next floor. She had to reach the roof and warn John and the rest of the team.

One of the men behind her was moving very fast, and it felt like only a matter of time before she would be hit. She opened the hallway door to the twenty-third floor and closed it from inside just as bullets hit all around it. Pulling out her telescoping metal baton, she snapped her wrist down, opening the baton to its full eighteen-inch length. She then wedged it downward and lodged it into the door handle and outside frame. It would prevent the men from opening the door if they tried to follow her.

Then she turned and sprinted down the hallway. She had to warn the president's team before it was too late.

27

KAZIM SHOOK HIS head. He was rattled from the shock explosion. Rising to his knees, he took stock of the space around him. Two of his twelve men were dead of gunshots. The other ten were groggy from the flash grenade and getting up more slowly than he. Their weapons were scattered; some had fallen down the stairs to the floor below. But many of their weapons were still with them. And most importantly, they still had the two large black cases at the corner of the stairwell, and these looked unharmed.

He sprang to his feet while the other men were still trying to regain their wits and equilibrium. Having a good idea of what must have happened, he was grateful that the explosive device the agent had thrown down at them hadn't been a real fragmentation grenade, like those in the Iraq war. Raising his automatic rifle, he pointed it up the stairs where the agent had been, and fired a short burst. Everything had moved so fast, he had seen only a silhouette, but now it seemed to be gone. With his gun pointed at the landing above, he fired three more shots and then raced up to the next floor.

No one was there or at the next level up. And he couldn't hear any movement above on higher flights. Grabbing the door to the hallway, he pulled, but it wouldn't open. He pulled harder, but it was jammed by something on the other side. Looking through the small window in the door, he saw the agent moving away from him fast, down the hallway. He raised his gun and stepped back from the door a few feet so that the shattering glass wouldn't cut him when he fired. The glass would alter the first bullet's course, but then he would have a clear shot. The agent was moving fast, sprinting down the hallway, undoubtedly toward the far stairwell. He had put up an impressive fight against Kazim's superior numbers, but it wouldn't be enough to save him. A real soldier would have stayed and fought as long as he could before dying honorably in battle.

Narrowing his eyes, Kazim leveled the assault rifle at ninety degrees to the glass, to make sure of a direct shot. He would not miss. The agent was in a dark suit, running fast, arms pounding. He aimed at the center of his back. It was hard to see through the haze of the window, but he could still make the shot. He had it now. Target locked . . . finger on the trigger. A slight pull . . . then he stopped in astonishment at the sight of long dark hair swinging to either side as the agent ran. Everything had moved so fast in the stairway confrontation, he hadn't realized he was fighting a woman. A *woman* had just now killed two of his soldiers. A woman had met his group in a stairwell and been able to push them back enough to kill some and delay the others before escaping. She had even barricaded this door, and all in a few seconds. He watched her run, admiring her speed and strength and passion. And even though she was the enemy, his instincts made him pause. He couldn't shoot her in the back— not at a distance, not after the fight she had just put up.

He could hear his men staggering to their feet below. Lowering his gun slightly so that it was still pointing at the window but was now off target, he watched as the young woman

ran down the hall, hit the door hard on the other end, and
disappeared into the opposite stairwell.

He didn't understand what had just happened to him. He
should have killed her, but instead he had just watched her
disappear down the corridor. No matter, he told himself. She
couldn't make any difference to their plans. They would be on
the roof in less than a minute—a little later than planned,
perhaps, but still early enough.

Part of him believed it had been more surprise than empathy
that stayed his finger on the trigger. He wasn't sure that he could
have made the shot anyway. The glass complicated things, he
told himself. His shots would likely have missed, so it felt more
honorable to let her go. To choose to release her from death,
rather than risk a difficult shot. He could think of many reasons
why he hadn't taken the shot, but deep down, he knew the
disconcerting truth: for some mysterious reason, he hadn't
wanted to shoot. He had felt that she somehow deserved to live.
He hoped she had gone down in the stairwell, not up. Gone down
through the spreading fire, somehow gotten past Maximilian's
men and, miraculously, to the safety of the Paris streets. Gone
down to the rest of whatever life she had in front of her. For to
go up would be to find the death he had spared her. If they met
again, he couldn't grant her that kindness a second time. He
hoped she hadn't turned to go up the stairs. For he was going up.
And death was with him.

28

REBECCA DARTED THROUGH the hallway door into the far stairwell, pulled herself around the banister, and raced up the stairs. She tried her wrist communicator again.

"Reid to Alexander!" she yelled. "Do you copy?"

Nothing. She pulled the encrypted radio off her belt, yanked out the cord, and pressed it to her mouth with the talk button held hard.

"Alexander . . . E-comm. Do you copy?" she yelled, identifying her emergency communication message.

Again nothing.

As she feared, her radio was smashed and useless.

"Alexander! If you can hear me, there are hostiles ascending the north stairwell. They have heavy equipment—likely heavy weapons. They may be heading for the roof. I repeat, the roof may be compromised. Keep Firefly off the roof! Alexander, if you can hear me, keep Firefly off the roof!"

Still nothing.

She raced on, sprinting up the stairs two at a time, quads burning as she drove her body upward. Pulling around the metal banister post at each landing, pounding up the next flight. The president was up there somewhere, with Alexander and other PPD agents. And at any moment, the attackers from the other stairwell could reach the rooftop. With no way to warn the president other than in person, she continued her frantic climb.

*   *   *

David and another agent propelled President Clarke up the last flights. They had passed the twenty-seventh floor and were now climbing the service stairs to the roof. She was trying to run with them, but she felt her weight in her shoulders instead of her feet. She tried to catch the steps with the balls of her feet or even just her toes, but the two agents still had her clamped under the arms, carrying her even as they climbed the stairs.

John was in front of her with a dozen other agents, and others had joined them in the past thirty seconds. Behind her were her personal physician, the military aide with the football, and another nine PPD special agents. As their entourage gradually grew in size and strength, her fear lost a bit of its edge. They were only a few steps from the steel door leading to the hotel roof.

Everything had moved so fast, she barely had time to process what was happening. But she trusted the men around her, even though their complete physical dominance over her body terrified her. She had never seen the Secret Service move with such fierceness and speed, and she tried not to imagine what danger must be rushing up toward them.

29

COL. JOSEPH MAZURSKY glanced at the White Hawk's instruments to determine their distance from the landing zone on top of the hotel. Major Parker flipped through various controls on the cockpit dashboard, lit by dark green and red underlights as if this were a Christmas-themed flight. They should reach the hotel roof in less than two minutes.

Approaching from the north, Mazursky looked out the bubble windshield at the lights of Paris through the falling snow. The Eiffel Tower was faintly visible. The lights seemed dimmed, as if he were seeing a lantern-lit Paris of long ago.

Glancing back over his right shoulder, out the small side window, he saw the hulking King Stallion helicopter flying with them at four o'clock.

"Ninety seconds, sir," Parker said.

"Where are the backup White Tops?" Mazursky asked, knowing they might well need the two other HMX-1 White Hawks from the Paris lift package if the exec lift got hairy.

"Crew chief has 'em out," Parker said. "Pilots firing 'em up. At least twenty minutes behind us."

"Where's POTUS?"

"PPD's bringing her to the roof. She's there in sixty seconds."

"Okay. Let's not keep her waiting."

The White Hawk's great mass lowered a hundred feet, its pounding roar no doubt attracting the attention of anyone out on the streets. They were moving over the cluster of five-story apartment buildings and narrow streets of St. Germain and would soon pass the closed, darkened patch of Jardin du Luxembourg. It wasn't every day that Parisians saw a giant green and white helicopter with an American flag painted on its side, gliding low over their city, followed closely by an even bigger, all-black helicopter.

Mazursky knew that somewhere back at the Paris airport, a US military commander was talking fast with the Pentagon and in contact with the French government, getting authorization for the flight activity over Paris. But it was an approval that, in this emergency, no one was going to sit around and wait for.

"Touching down in forty-five seconds, gents," Mazursky said into his headset. "POTUS will be on the roof with a few dozen from the PPD. Ten seconds down and up! SS chop provides cover during evac! Building's on fire and hostiles reported on ground levels! Neither fire nor hostiles are near the rooftop, but we're not going to wait around for either. Ten seconds to save POTUS. Touching down in thirty seconds. Lights out, guns up. Let's get her safe, everyone."

Thirty seconds. With over ten thousand hours' flight time in military helicopters, this was the most important minute of his life.

30

S PECIAL AGENT IN Charge John Alexander stood in front of the group of men surrounding President Clarke on the roof. They were close to the south-side roof access door from the stairs they had just raced up. He had tried to get in touch with Rebecca about the arrival of Marine One, but he couldn't raise her on the comm channel.

In the past sixty seconds, an enormous amount of controlled information had come across the PPD encrypted channel. The fire had spread to nearly the entire ground floor of the hotel and was quickly climbing up through the building. There had been numerous explosions in the garage, with no explanation or contact from the agents protecting the backup motorcade. The president's limo had made it out but was now taking assault rifle fire from the third-floor windows. The command center had been broken down and would be dark for another few minutes.

Additional Secret Service CAT agents had crashed the building on all sides and were fighting the attackers, but the fire was making any counterassault difficult, and there were disturbing reports that the hostiles were much more numerous than initially thought. But John was confident of the CAT unit, which he saw as the missing link between SWAT and the Navy Seals. John had been rotated to PPD fifteen years ago, after spending his first five years in the CAT division, so he knew firsthand how good those agents were.

He did another quick check, glancing around to make sure everyone was in the best protection position. Tucked in close to the president were her personal physician and the military aide with the football. Then, in a tight two-ring huddle, were a dozen agents, including David Stone. Another dozen agents were spread across the roof. The three USSS countersnipers stationed on the roof were holding their positions on the far edges, to help cover the area. He had received reports that another two special agents were in the stairwell between the doorway and the next level down. He had relayed everyone's position into his wrist communicator so the half-dozen USSS countersnipers on surrounding rooftops could also help cover them.

He had the roof secured. The sky was dark, with thick snowflakes swirling in the unsteady rooftop air currents.

A crackling voice in his earpiece said, "This is Marine HMX-one-four-seven, inbound toward Zenith. ETA forty-five seconds. Do you copy?"

He couldn't resist the urge to do a little fist pump at the news. Marine HMX-1 pilots could do an emergency exec lift in less than sixty seconds on arrival. And once the president was inside one of the most technologically advanced helicopters in the world, flown by one of the best pilots, she would be safe and moving fast away from the threat.

He turned toward the president, who was staring at him with wide eyes from the center of her protective huddle. "Ma'am, your ride's on the way. We'll have you out of here in less than two minutes."

As he said this, a bright light beamed down on them from the gigantic White Hawk helicopter.

Bringing his wrist to his mouth, he said, "Copy that. Protection has Firefly ready for exec lift."

"Roger, White Knight," came the reply in his earpiece. "Wheels down in thirty seconds."

"Copy thirty seconds," John replied.

Back behind the approaching helicopter was another dark shape, and he recognized the enormous King Stallion support helicopter.

"Stay sharp," he yelled into his communicator. "Use visual signals."

The White Hawk emitted a steady roar as it lowered toward them. The tight area of the rooftop posed an additional challenge for the team as their comms were drowned out by the two GE-T700 turboshaft engines, each generating nearly two thousand shaft horsepower. The four main rotor blades created the illusion of a translucent disk fifty feet in diameter, fixed above the long green body.

"Reid reports ha—" The voice in his earpiece became lost in the noise. It was all but impossible to hear communications at this point. The White Hawk was now hovering twenty feet off the roof and slowly rotating to land between the large ventilation fans protruding from the building.

"What?" John yelled into his wrist communicator. "Repeat!" He covered his earpiece with his palm.

"Reid re—"

"You get that?" he yelled at Stone, only a few feet away.

"Something about Rebecca!" Stone shouted back while stepping closer. His tie whipped across his chest.

"Where is she?"

"Don't know! I think another agent said she saw something!"

"Saw *what*?"

"Don't know!"

"Doesn't matter!" John said. "We're out of time! Move POTUS the second the tires reach touchdown!"

Everything was blowing around them, whipping jackets and ties. John's eyes stung from the hard downdraft and biting snow. The command center was still down. He couldn't hear anything from Rebecca or any other agent not on the roof. He had no idea what was happening below him. They were pinned up here, and this was their last chance to get the president to safety.

This had to happen now, and perfectly. There was no time left, and no room for error.

31

L EGS BURNING, KAZIM raced up the stairs, exhorting his men to keep up.

As he rounded the north twenty-sixth-floor landing, two agents burst through the door up ahead of him. Their heads jerked toward him, but before they could get their guns around, he fired twice, and they died.

He reached the locked steel security door at the top of the stairs. Pulling the eighteen-inch crowbar from his pack, he stabbed the end between the door and the frame. He pulled backward, and the thin aluminum frame warped and bowed before a sharp pop told him the locked bolt had snapped away from the insert.

The door swung open.

He pushed through to the next level, and the men followed as he made a patting gesture with his hand, signaling them to move quietly. They were less than thirty seconds from action.

Up the final flight, now above the twenty-seventh-floor penthouse residence and any routinely known or visited portion of the hotel, he knelt on the large service landing just inside the final door—the door he had thought about for months after he and Maximilian began plotting the final movements in this operation of a lifetime. Years of strategizing, preparing for the moment when they could attack. A hundred scenarios discussed, five cities identified and scouted, narrowing down to Paris once the economic forum was announced. A dozen locations planned for, contingencies considered. And with the tunnels mapped, they had waited until their scouts marked the hotel that the Secret Service advance team had probed two weeks before the American president's arrival. And it all came down to this one door—and what he would find on the other side of it.

Because he was the youngest, his brothers hadn't lived to see the warrior he would grow into and the power he would command. They hadn't seen that his destiny would be greater than all of theirs had been in Iraq. But they were watching him now. He could feel their presence, and it gave him strength.

The other men now joined him and set the two heavy cases beside him on the top landing. Eleven men and one door. Snapping back the hard metal clamps, he opened both cases.

Pointing at the two men he had chosen as best qualified for the task, he gave the order. They were darker skinned than he, and he knew little about their personal lives other than they came from somewhere in North Africa, perhaps Libya. The army Maximilian had created seemed to be a hodgepodge of mercenaries from many parts of the world. It was not the sort of group Kazim was used to, having spent most of his warring days as an insurgent soldier against the invading American military in Iraq. But these men were strong fighters and technically proficient in their specialized skill sets. So as he watched the two men quickly assemble the weapons, he was confident that when the time came, they would not fail the mission.

He could hear the low, pulsing beat of at least one helicopter approaching on the other side of the door. Without actually opening the door, he turned the handle and moved it out a few centimeters, just to make sure it wasn't locked. Cracking the rooftop door made the sounds outside suddenly louder and more distinct, and he now believed he could hear two separate helicopters. One would be the green White Top that served as Marine One, and the other would be either a support helicopter or some military attack craft to provide cover for the American president.

His heart raced. The helicopters meant that Maximilian's plan had been right. The American president was either on or near the rooftop.

Looking back at the two men, he said, "Twenty seconds."

They both nodded without looking up from arming their two shoulder-mounted rocket launchers.

Kazim could hear one of the helicopters lowering toward the building while the other sounded as if it was hovering higher and to one side.

"Ten seconds," he said. He had been waiting more than ten years for this moment. "Five seconds. Are we ready?"

"Almost . . . yes."

They stood up, each with a shoulder-mounted rocket-propelled grenade launcher resting on his right shoulder. Two muscular men knelt beside them with a few extra rockets, preparing to load them as needed. Behind them were the rest of Kazim's men, each hugging his assault rifle and staring forward with fiery courage, eager to destroy the Americans.

His breathing deepened like that of a warrior staring at the enemy army across the field of battle. It felt as if the body needed the heart to pump harder, the blood to flow faster, so that the mind could comprehend the death and mayhem it was about to charge into.

"Remember," he said to the men, "what we do in the next few minutes, we do for our children and the children of all our brothers and sisters across the world. For those not yet born, and to honor those who have died over the years fighting this enemy."

And so Kazim pushed the door open to unleash the attack. But just as it opened a few more inches, bullets snapped and sparked off the metal frame.

32

REBECCA RACED UP the final flights of the south stairwell. She had to warn John about the attackers' position and movement. The feeling that the president's safety could rest solely on her slender shoulders spurred her to a level of effort she had never known. Her legs seemed to have grown stronger as she pounded up the staircase so fast that she was practically falling forward. Her right hand grasped the end of each level's metal banister, her arm whipping her around, launching her toward the next level up.

She could no long rely on her training to give her the emotionless reactions she needed to protect the president. Attacks never went on this long. In the history of the United States, no president had ever been under attack for anywhere near sixty seconds, let alone five straight minutes and counting. The value of the conditioned training was rapidly deteriorating because the moment of reaction had passed. The crucial first three to four seconds were long gone, and the chaos and fear had begun to settle in as the attack wore on with no end in sight. Her skills, also acquired through training, were as sharp as ever, but her emotions were becoming harder to control, so that she found herself once again digging deep for strength.

Pushing around the twenty-sixth-floor entrance, she saw the landing above, and the two agents in suits with their black P229s pointed at her.

"White knight!" she yelled. "It's Reid! Where's Alexander?"

"With POTUS!" one of the agents yelled back.

She took the steps up to them two at a time. "My radio's out. Tell him there's a breach on the north stairwell. At least a half-dozen men ascending fast, possibly to the roof. Heavily armed. Well trained."

The closest man raised his wrist communicator and relayed the message.

"They have the roof secured," the second agent said.

"These guys are going to hit them harder than they expect," Rebecca said. "They move like a military tactical team. We can't risk the exec lift on Marine One."

"The hawk's already here," the man said. "Landing right now."

"Oh, God," Rebecca said, racing past them.

She ran up the final flight to the open steel door twenty feet up. She could feel the icy air from outside and see snowflakes wafting in through the opened door. Counting the seconds, she knew how long it had taken her to run across the twenty-third floor, and how long it would take the attackers to recover from the flash grenade and continue their race to the top.

Reaching the top step, she raced out the doorway and onto the rooftop. The air was freezing, and she could hear the low, rhythmic rumble-*whop-whop-whop* of a big helicopter. A group of men had formed the inner layer of the protective bubble near the doorway, and there was the president, in the center of the huddle. Other agents were spread across the roof. She didn't see David, but there was Alexander, waving at the countersnipers on the far edge of the roof and radioing something in his wrist communicator.

"John!" she yelled, but the White Hawk's racket obliterated her voice. "John! North door!"

Several other agents turned to look at her, trying to understand what she was saying. She was now thirty feet from them. One of the countersnipers started toward the north door, probably because of the message she had gotten to John through the agent in the stairwell, perhaps for other reasons. But the countersniper carried a high-velocity, long-range rifle that wouldn't fire rapidly enough to stop more than one of the attackers before they killed him. Countersnipers weren't equipped for close combat.

The White Top was twenty feet off the deck and would be down in a few seconds. Once on the ground, it would be without its air defenses and completely vulnerable. The HMX-1 support King Stallion helicopter was hovering about a hundred feet diagonally above and right. Although Rebecca couldn't see clearly through the snowfall, she knew that at least three or four CAT agents would be strapped in the open door of their bird, with Knight's Armament SR-16 assault rifles, providing cover from the air.

"Gun right!" she yelled, but the noise from the helicopter drowned out her shout, and without a working radio she had no way of cutting through the White Top's noise.

There was no time. She went down on one knee, pulled her pistol, and aimed through the snow at the north door, across the roof. Snow was being blown violently in all directions by the White Hawk's powerful blades, and her hair whipped about her head as if in a blizzard. Narrowing her eyes, she thought she saw slight movement at the door—a subtle shift in the gap between door and frame.

Controlling her breath, she started firing.

Her shots sparked all around the door.

"Gun right! Gun right!" she yelled again, knowing that she now had the attention of everyone on the rooftop. The countersnipers each dropped to one knee and aimed at the doorway. The agents around the president had instinctively covered her at the sound of shots, while the agents on the outside ring of the protective bubble stood tall and squared their bodies toward the threat, pistols raised, in muscle memory drilled in from a thousand training exercises.

The White Top, which had been hovering just twenty feet above the roof while gradually turning to line its tail for landing, now seemed to hesitate. The HMX-1 support helo—the sixteen-ton King Stallion—tilted in the air to better align itself above the far corner of the roof. Rebecca's focus was on the door, which had remained half open without any more activity for perhaps five seconds. But out of the corner of her eye, she saw the center slide-bottom drop door open in the belly of the King Stallion. Then a fast rope fell out of the drop door, and a second later, the first CAT agents came sliding down it to the rooftop.

The Secret Service and Marine Corp position around the president was getting stronger. But the PPD agents seemed unsure, despite all their training, of the best course to take for protecting the president. Their training told them to cover and go with POTUS, but go where? The fire, which they had just escaped from, was still climbing up through the hotel. The only escape route now was on Marine One. So they held their position, even though every nerve and fiber of their being wanted to move POTUS to a position of greater safety.

Rebecca stared hard at the door.

Three CAT agents sprinted across the roof, toward the door, with their high-powered automatic assault rifles up. The White Hawk hovered motionless in the air until the landing site could be secured. The King Stallion hovered over the far corner.

The CAT agents were yelling commands into their headset microphones, which were linked into the comms with the Secret

Service, the Marine Corps, and the Pentagon. She wished desperately to know what everyone was saying to each other, and again cursed her broken radio.

The agents neared the north doorway. But before they could open it, a grenade bounced out. A frozen second cut through the air before the grenade exploded in a quick, sharp flash that killed the three CAT agents and blew the door off one of its hinges.

"COVER! COVER!" Alexander yelled.

More agents surrounded the president.

The PPD and remaining CAT agents unloaded a storm of bullets at the door, and the crackle and pop of gunfire resounded across the roof.

Then, to the horrified shock of everyone on the roof, a missile from a shoulder-mounted surface-to-air rocket launcher flew out of the blown doorway and hissed across the roof toward the White Hawk.

Immediately, fifty red heat flares shot out the sides of the White Top as the computer's defensive systems sensed laser lock and automatically dispersed its key antimissile defenses. But the system was designed for higher flight than the bird's current twenty-foot hover, so many of the hot flares fell onto the rooftop around the agents. The missile hit a flare and exploded only a few dozen feet from the White Hawk, hitting the side with shrapnel and pushing it sideways in the air until it was now hovering out over the edge of the roof and no longer in any position to land.

"RPG!" a number of the agents yelled simultaneously.

Rebecca had seen the missile blaze out of the darkened doorway, but she had no idea how far back into the stairs the man had been when firing it.

She fired more shots in through the doorway but quickly ran out of rounds. Standing on her feet to make herself part of the protective shield of agents crowded around the president—who was still held to the ground—she slapped a fresh magazine into her pistol. Two other CAT agents were laying down intensive fire on the doorway. If anyone had had a hand grenade, they would have thrown it into the doorway, but agents in the PPD and CAT didn't carry such explosive devices, because of potential risk to the president.

There was a pause in the firefight, and she heard John yell the command to cover-and-dash POTUS back toward their stairwell. The agents already standing and firing scrunched into an even tighter human wall, and those covering the president on the ground remained hunched over as they stood and lifted the president off the roof deck. Then they surged back toward the stairwell, shielding the president with two rows of interlaced agents: those on the outside firing at the opposite door while those on the inside pulled and pushed their tiptoeing protectee across the roof.

A second RPG hissed out of the doorway and across the roof at the White Hawk. And again the loud popping sound rattled in the night as hundreds of red deflector flares shot out from the side of the helicopter. The RPG exploded twenty feet from it, closer than the first rocket had. And again the helicopter was thrown sideways, farther still from the roof. Again some of the flares rained down on the agents, mixing with the snow. Rebecca could feel their heat all around her. Two agents fell to the ground, screaming from their burns. And through everything, she heard the president let out a sharp cry of panic.

"Stairs! Stairs! Stairs!" Alexander was yelling, though she couldn't see where he was.

The White Hawk's tail was smoking, but it continued to hover just to the side of the roof, as if refusing to leave the president no matter how much abuse it took. The King Stallion drew in closer. Rebecca saw two more CAT agents sliding down the fast rope toward the roof, when a third rocket shot out of the doorway and cut up into the air, exploding into the King Stallion's tail. Almost immediately, the giant bird fell into a slow, uncontrolled spin. The two CAT agents on the fast rope were thrown sideways and disappeared over the far edge of the roof. She didn't hear a scream from either man as they vanished from sight. The King Stallion began to lose altitude as it spun, drifting toward the roof.

"Stairs! Stairs! Stairs!" Alexander yelled again.

At that moment, Rebecca saw the attackers emerge from the far doorway. They screamed like savages, ready to die killing the president, just as the PPD agents were ready to die protecting her. Because there were already so many agents in the human sphere surrounding the president, Rebecca's training told her to focus on hitting the attackers as hard as she could. Again she stopped running and started firing. Half the agents still on the roof did the same, and several attackers fell. But as accurate as the PPD agents were with their pistols, the attackers had automatic weapons. All the CAT agents had been killed, and they were the only Secret Service people carrying assault rifles. The PPD agents had only their semiautomatic pistols. And because of this disparity in firepower, many of those agents now fell.

Rebecca fired at the attackers even as the King Stallion came closer to the roof in a flat, whirling spin. Smoke now blended with the snow flurries. She aimed and fired, aimed and fired, dropping a target with each shot. She knew it was only by luck or God's grace that she hadn't been hit in the storm of bullets flying past her.

While firing on the attackers, again she saw the man with shoulder-length hair she had seen in the stairwell. For a split second, their eyes met, and she thought that she saw in his expression a sense of surprise and recognition. She aimed at him and fired several rounds. Though she wasn't the best shot in the Service, she was good enough, and she had him in her sights, just as she had the last two men, who were now dead. But to her amazement, he ducked, like a fighter slipping a punch, and slid away from her sights just before she pulled the trigger, as if he had known the precise moment she would fire and where the bullet would go. It was an impossible, unnatural movement, with a speed and grace she had never seen before.

She steadied herself to fire again, but she had lost him in the melee. Just then something hard pushed into her from the side, grabbing her, almost pulling her toward the stairwell. Looking up, she saw David, herding her off the roof as he fired at the attackers with his free hand.

"Back inside!" he yelled over the gunfire and the roar of the incoming helicopter.

In that instant, she realized that only ten to twenty seconds had elapsed since the King Stallion was hit—five to ten seconds since POTUS was rushed off the roof and back into the stairwell. During those chaotic seconds, she had lost all sense of time. Everything had happened in slow motion. Only David, pulling her away from the rooftop bloodbath, had snapped her mind back into the reality of the moment.

The falling King Stallion was making a louder, much higher-pitched sound now as its pilots pushed the controls to their limits in the desperate attempt to avoid crashing on the roof.

"The other men!" she yelled at David, who was still pulling her toward the door.

"No time!"

He fired three shots, killing two more terrorists, before pulling her in tight to his chest as they both fell through the open stairwell doorway. A half second later, the King Stallion crashed onto the rooftop. It made a grinding metallic scream when it hit, followed by a sharp pop and a *whump!* as the fuel tanks exploded, spreading a marsh of flames across the rooftop.

After falling into the landing at the top of the stairwell, Rebecca pushed herself up to her knees, head still lowered.

She heard David ask, "Are you okay?"

"Where's POTUS?" she replied.

She felt his hands reach under her arms and across her chest to help lift her to her feet. Once on her feet, she looked back around the doorjamb, out at the roof. The King Stallion was in flames, along with nearly the entire roof. The White Hawk was smoking and hovering farther away than before. She didn't know its flying condition, but it didn't look good. Bodies of agents and terrorists were strewn all over the rooftop. Nothing moved except for the snow and the low blue and yellow flames from the helicopter crash.

"Where's POTUS?" she asked again. She pointed to her wrist and made a crossing motion to let him know that her comms were dead.

"Twenty-fourth floor," he said, touching his earpiece to listen. "Four floors below us, moving down fast."

"To where? There's fires on the ground floor and climbing up."

"Well, POTUS can't stay here!" David yelled. "The roof's an inferno like the ground floor. The White Top isn't safe anymore, and it would be impossible for an exec lift anyway."

"They'll never make it down the stairway!" she yelled. "I ran into them on the other stairway heading up. How long until you think they control both stairwells? POTUS will be trapped!" Stepping forward, she grabbed his wrist and brought it up. "This is Reid to Alexander! Do you copy?"

She watched David for any expression indicating he had heard a response from John in his earpiece. After a few seconds, he shook his head.

"Alexander! Do you copy?" she repeated. "Do not take Firefly down stairwell!"

"He's not replying," David said. "Command center is down. Our frequency may have been compromised."

"Oh, God," she said, taking a second to consider all the factors playing out simultaneously. "We've lost control of the lower floors. He'll never get her out that way."

"There's no choice now. He's gonna try."

"Come on!" she said. "Before it's too late!"

She turned and started down the stairs as fast as she could go. And soon she heard David's quick but heavier footfalls right behind her.

33

JOHN ALEXANDER RACED down the stairs with President Clarke, with the half-dozen remaining agents packed around her. Her short, straight hair hung mussed and wet from melting snow, and two buttons on her suit jacket had been ripped away, showing more of her blue dress blouse. While pulling her away from the White Hawk's antimissile flares and getting her off the rooftop, the team had been obliged to yank her around some. Her darkened eye sockets and wide-eyed gaze revealed to him how shaken she was, and he worried about shock setting in. Just when he thought they might get her to safety, the rooftop had turned into a holocaust. And now, as a thunderous explosion rocked and rattled the area somewhere above them, it was clear that they had been lucky even to get her back inside the building.

Colonel Marks, the military aide, was still with them, carrying the football. But the president's physician was dead. John couldn't believe that only six other agents had survived the chaos on the rooftop. They had lost the initiative. He could taste a thin flavor of smoke from the fire, which by now must have taken over most of the lower floors. As a former marine and former CAT agent, he would have literally run through fire for his country—but now, as special agent in charge of the PPD, his only responsibility was to keep the president as far from threats as possible.

The hotel's roof had just become one of the most dangerous places in the building. He had no idea how the attackers had reached it so fast—or how they had even anticipated a rushed exec lift with Marine One. In addition to investigation-and-prevention tactics, the Secret Service's training focused on the reality that most assassination attempts occurred in less than five seconds from start to finish. A single gunshot, a stabbing, an explosive device. Assassination attempts that lasted this long—ten minutes since the Crash POTUS alert—were basically unheard of. Many in the PPD were dead. Most of the CAT agents were separated from POTUS by the fire. And the blazing rooftop prevented them from getting POTUS onto Marine One. It was the ultimate nightmare scenario: no clear escape route and no safe zone in which to secure POTUS. The protective bubble was small and thin. With only a handful of agents, he had to assume they were now heavily outnumbered—something almost unthinkable in the meticulous planning and preparations conducted by the Secret Service.

It seemed as if his only course of action was to risk taking her down the stairway—toward attackers and the fire. The path terrified him, but he saw no other options.

But before he could go any farther, he needed to check that President Clarke hadn't been hurt during the rooftop attack. He ordered everyone to stop the descent. Pointing for the six PPD agents to cover any threats above or below them in the stairwell, he said, "Are you okay, ma'am? Are you hurt anywhere?"

"I'm okay," she said. Her voice quavered, and her hair was awry and her face streaked with soot, but she appeared unharmed.

"You didn't get burned?" he asked.

"I don't think so."

"You're not bleeding?"

"No."

He quickly looked at her head and neck and felt around her sides and stomach and back for any trace of bleeding that she may not have registered. It was risky pausing the escape for even ten seconds, but after what they had just been through, he had to check her before continuing. Everyone on the roof was likely dead, and they now had no way out without getting closer to the ground-level attackers and the fire.

After verifying that she had sustained no serious injuries, he pointed to the three agents a few steps up, indicating that they would continue evacuating the president down the remaining thirteen flights, toward the south-side exit, where they might find a way to get her near the limousine. If they could just get to the part of the first floor that wasn't being overrun by the attackers or the fire, then they could get support from CAT and the emergency response team, giving them at least a slight chance for a Stagecoach evac.

Eight minutes had elapsed since the command center stopped communicating with the entire protection team over the encrypted channel. This gave John the horrible feeling that the on-site command center had been compromised. The team should have reestablished communications by now.

A female voice yelled down at him, "John! Wait!"

Spinning to train his weapon on the unseen voice more than a flight above them, he yelled, "White knight!"

"Red knight!" the voice yelled down. "Red knight! Agents Reid and Stone!"

Rebecca and David! They had survived the rooftop attack. Relieved at having two of his best young agents back with the president, he said, "We're taking her all the way down the stairs. A two-agent rotating scout sweep of each floor's doorway in front of POTUS as we descend. Everyone else forms a tight-package protective bubble. If we're lucky, we can make it to Stagecoach. But we have to go now."

"You're taking her *down*?" Rebecca said.

"The rooftop is in flames," John said. "The White Top is damaged and can't do the exec lift. Backup White Tops can't be here for almost fifteen minutes, and we can't wait that long— especially if the roof keeps burning and the attackers keep climbing."

"But you're taking her down? *Toward* the hostiles and the fire?"

"We don't have a choice," John said. "And we don't have time!" He motioned for the other agents to enclose the president and start their final rush toward whatever chaos awaited below.

"Wait!" Rebecca yelled. "There's another way!"

"Where?"

"The cargo lift."

He shook his head. "All the elevators would have automatically gone to the first floor when the fire alarm went off."

"No," she said, "not so. The advance team shut down the cargo lift a few hours before the president arrived in Paris," she said. "We wanted to minimize entrance points to the top floors, so we locked it and limited access to the other service elevators."

"Tell me you froze it up here," John said.

"No, but we did lock it on the bottom level. Not on the first floor, like the other elevators after the fire alarm. It's on sublevel four—locked manually, so the fire alarm won't have moved it."

"Can we call it up here?"

"No, but we can climb down the shaft. Nothing will block our way until we reach it in the basement. From there, we can find a way out with the president. The fire's going to move up faster than it moves down. And the attackers will move up with it. We've already seen that from the men on the rooftop. They must have been planning to trap us with the fire and then hunt down the president. They wouldn't know about our locking down the cargo lift. They would never expect us to make it past them, unseen, into the basement levels. From there, we can find an exit from the hotel."

"We can't risk taking the president down a high ladder on the side of an elevator shaft," John said.

"Can we risk taking her through a firefight?" Rebecca asked. "We obviously can't keep track of all their men. The fire's spreading. The elevator shaft is concrete and will shield us from it as well as any place in this building. It's our only way out that might avoid the attackers and the fire."

"She could fall," John said. "One slip, and it's all over."

"I can do it," the president said.

They both turned and gave her an appraising look.

"Ma'am, it will be dark," John said. "It could be slippery, the metal ladder could heat up if the fire is close on any of the floors, and smoke could come into the shaft and blind us and choke us before we get halfway down."

"Right now I feel like we're playing into the terrorists' hands," President Clarke said. "Let's do something they don't expect. Let's take back the initiative."

John glanced at the faces around him. From David to Rebecca, to Colonel Marks with the football, to the other six PPD agents, and finally to President Clarke. He saw strength and determination in all of them.

They were just below the fourteenth-floor stairwell door, and the two agents providing the scouting motioned that it was clear. Since the president was only a few steps up, he didn't have the agents lift her.

"This way, ma'am," he said, motioning for the scout agents to hold open the hallway door. Then he gestured for Rebecca to lead the way onto the floor, with David and another agent, and take them to the cargo elevator shaft.

As they raced down the hallway, the other agents formed a tight cluster around the president. John made sure he was always directly to her right so that, if necessary, he could pull her to the ground with his left hand and fire his P229 with his right. He even asked the military aide to run behind them and do whatever he could to act as a human shield for the president if they should come under attack from the rear.

Everyone in the group seemed prepared to make whatever sacrifice necessary to protect the president. John only prayed that he had made the right decision on how to get the president to safety.

34

MAXIMILIAN HAD HEARD the sound of gunfire over the radio. While simultaneously coordinating the efforts of his men on the ground floor and his small band of fighters flanking down the south stairwell to surround the remaining Secret Service agents, he had also been monitoring Kazim's critical attack on the roof. If the president escaped on Marine One, all his plans would collapse.

He had radioed to his men to stay away from the windows for the past five minutes—except for the two small groups he had sent to the east and west sides on the seventh floor. He had instructed them to fire their automatic weapons frequently near the windows at various levels of the building. Hannibal was one of the first military generals in history to use deception as a key strategy in war, and it had been a powerful tactic against the Roman army. And like Hannibal, Maximilian knew how the enemy would respond to his maneuvers and deceptions. And part of his deception was to have these half-dozen men fire enough shots near the windows in the middle floors to give outside observers the impression of hundreds more men than he actually had in the building. By placing these men in sections where there was currently no fighting, he could also add another layer of confusion to any French or US emergency response teams trying to evaluate the situation from outside. It was a ruse inspired by Hannibal, who once tied torches to the horns of a herd of cattle and released them down a hill at night to mislead his distant enemy as his army marched another direction in darkness.

He had seen two helicopters approach from the distance. Kazim had radioed that he was near the rooftop and that he assumed the president was there, too, waiting for her military lift while protected by whatever Secret Service agents surrounded her. Maximilian had watched as those two enormous helicopters emerged through the snow flurries and slowed somewhere above the rooftop, out of his line of sight from the third-floor window. He had warned everyone to stay away from the windows; American countersnipers would have been positioned on surrounding rooftops before the night even began, and now their numbers had surely multiplied.

But he wanted to see where the helicopters hovered.

Creeping along the edge of the window, he stayed close to the wall and tried to look up at the best angle he could manage. He could hear the massive helicopters a few hundred feet above him, one of them the president's Marine One, and the other a powerful war bird: a King Stallion or a Sea Queen, or perhaps even a deadly Apache.

It had been impossible to hear any gunfire from the rooftop except over the radio, because of all the other shots going off throughout the building. But even though Maximilian couldn't hear the small-arms fire on the roof, he heard the RPGs exploding. One, then two, and then a third. Sparks flew past the window, looking like a hundred miniature flares. Then flames and large pieces of metal followed the flares. At least one helicopter must have been hit. Then another, bigger explosion sounded, and he thought he felt a shiver run through the building. He wasn't even sure he felt it the sound was immense, confusing him momentarily because he hadn't expected anything big to hit the building.

Putting his radio to his mouth, he said, "Kazim!" After a few seconds of silence, he repeated, "Kazim! Report!"

No sound came through the radio.

"Kazim!"

Nothing.

Then a large burning chunk of helicopter fell past the window. It was a ball of flames, plummeting fast, and even still, he felt the radiant heat through the window. And in that fleeting instant, he saw the US flag painted on the burning fuselage that fell past him.

Reports came through the radio that all the agents on the roof had been killed, that a helicopter had crashed onto the roof and broken apart, that the entire top of the hotel was now in flames, and that Kazim and his men were all dead. The president had also likely died in the explosive crash.

Was it really all over so quickly?

"Take a team of five to the roof," he said into his encrypted radio. "Check for survivors. And confirm that the president is dead."

Lowering the radio, he stared out at the sparks and burning debris still hurtling past the window. In the distance, he could see the Eiffel Tower rising above the low lights of Paris. A sense of awe washed over him at the sudden realization of how far he had come on the journey to this night. The whole world seemed showered in sparks. The memory came to him, unbidden, of a night five years ago.

* * *

Maximilian gazed at the sparks flying up from the train wheels. Mesmerized, he scarcely felt the frigid air blowing between the flimsy plastic flaps that gave the only protection from the elements. This was his third time standing outside during the night's journey, for he found sleeping difficult, even with the soothing rock and sway of the train. He was traveling to Istanbul, but he may as well have been voyaging through deep space. The world had become disgusting to him. Not the world as a whole, but the powerful, concentrated part that controlled all the rest. The injustice just went on and on for decades, with not so much as a breath of equality or fairness or empathy. The few turned a blind eye to the many, and no one, it seemed, could do anything to change this. Life was unfair. Nature knew this truth best and didn't bother trying to sugarcoat it. And for a long time, he had not cared, because he hadn't the energy to care, for he was powerless. He had been too busy fighting for his people before even they betrayed him. For a long time, he had dreamed of getting back at them. But then one day, he had found a book that opened his mind to the possibilities of living purely for a cause greater than himself. He had discovered a book about Hannibal Barca and his lifelong commitment to save Carthage from Rome. Hannibal had ultimately failed in his quest, but through no fault of his own. Rome had been too powerful for any army of that time. But Hannibal and his men had achieved astounding victories against superior forces, using tactics so brilliant that by the end, even though he had lost the war, he was forever remembered as one of the greatest military generals of ancient times. Of course he had to know that the odds were against him. And yet, Hannibal knew he had to fight. And reading that book had helped Maximilian come to know that he, too, must fight against the modern-day Rome—and its ally that had betrayed him. He must inspire the weak to defend themselves, and he must show the powerful that they could no longer act with impunity.

Looking out at the snow-laden stands of scattered evergreens that marked the crossing from the barren Mongolian plains into the endless wintry forests of Siberia, he felt the first real peace he could recall in months. In the pale moonlight, the patches of trees made dark islands on the vast, rolling sea of snow.

Hearing the door between the cars open, he turned from the austere landscape to see who was behind him. It was a man younger than he, perhaps in his late thirties. He had a short beard, and a hard strength in his expression that Maximilian often saw in this part of the world. But unlike so many Mongolians, who had a look of weathered tranquility, and a slow deliberateness in their movements, this man had yanked the door open and was moving toward the next car with a pent-up aggression that felt almost dangerous.

"Good evening," Maximilian said.

The man turned sharply with blazing dark eyes, obviously surprised to find someone standing outside on the small walkway between train cars. Maximilian was fascinated by his response: first the reaction to potential danger, then a wary stance, and finally, almost a hatred at the surprise. This man before him was like a snake: startled and immediately ready to strike at any possible threat. Not seeking company or conversation. Alone and wandering in the night.

"Is it *not* a good evening?" Maximilian asked.

"It's colder than Satan's bum out here," the man replied.

Maximilian nodded. "Hannibal and his men fought the frozen landscape of the Alps in the fall of 219 B.C. to invade Rome. He was a great man, in part because he could tolerate pain."

"I'm no expert on history, but didn't Rome defeat Hannibal?"

"Not really," Maximilian said. "He invaded Italy and terrified the Roman army for sixteen years, defeating them in battle after battle on their own ground—right up to the city gates of Rome itself. The very mention of his name struck fear into the heart of every Roman citizen. Eventually, his twenty thousand men—an army that he needed to replenish constantly with new recruits to replace the dead—did fall to the Roman war machine of a quarter-million soldiers. But can that really be called defeat? What man in the history of the world, other than Alexander the Great, could have achieved even a fraction of what Hannibal did? No, Rome didn't defeat Hannibal. Not really, not ever."

"You sound as though you worship him."

"No, not worship. But I respect him more than any other man who ever lived. Whom do you respect?"

"My brothers."

"All of them?"

"Yes."

"How many?"

"I had three."

"They're gone now."

"Yes."

"All of them."

"Yes."

"I'm sorry."

The man nodded.

"Would you like to join me inside for some tea?" Maximilian asked. "One of the great pleasures of traveling is meeting new and interesting people with interesting stories."

The man stared hard at him for a few seconds, then nodded.

They walked back to the dining car, where they could get late-night drinks. A few hundred souls traveling through the Siberian forest on a winter night, and Maximilian felt he had finally met someone with eyes darker and more dangerous even than his own. What kind of man could have survived a life more violent than his? If there was one thing that a man who had killed could do, it was to recognize the eyes of a killer.

"I'm Maximilian," he said as they sat down at a small table along the stretch of dark windows.

"I'm Kazim," the man replied, shaking the offered hand.

They were the only two in the dining car besides the barman, puttering about at the far end. Maximilian was ready to move past the pleasantries and start using the tactics he had learned as a case officer for the Shin Bet, recruiting Palestinian agents in Israel.

"You've been in prison," he said. Not a question, but an instinctive guess.

"Yes," Kazim replied.

"Where?"

"Istanbul."

"You're heading back there now?"

"Yes—to the city, not the prison. You?"

"Heading in that direction, but it's not my final destination."

"What is?"

"Paris."

The man behind the small bar stepped out onto the red rug that stretched down the aisle. Dressed in a white shirt, bow tie, and black slacks and vest, he moved gracefully down the quiet dining car. Maximilian watched him from the corner of his eye, looking up only at the last moment. The barman's bushy mustache outweighed all other features of his face.

"One Russian tea," Maximilian said. "And . . ." He looked at Kazim.

Kazim held up two fingers.

The barman took away the two tall glasses with standing cloth napkins inside and returned to the bar.

"How did you know I was in prison?" Kazim asked. "Not a guess, I'm guessing."

"No, I could tell."

"How?"

"I worked in a prison for years."

"Worked?"

"As an interrogator."

"Inside the prison?"

"Yes. In probably the worst prison in the world."

"A Russian prison, then—in the gulags?"

"Worse."

"A communist prison? China? North Korea?"

"Do I look Asian? No. It was much worse than any of those."

"What could be worse than a prison in Siberia or North Korea?" Kazim asked.

"The one in Jerusalem. There are no criminals there. No political dissidents. Only terrorists."

"You interrogated terrorists in the Jerusalem prison. You're Jewish."

"No, not anymore. I have abandoned my people."

"Why?"

"They betrayed me."

"I don't understand."

Maximilian smiled, then turned his eyes to the decorative wood paneling lining the sides and ceiling of the dining car. The wood was cut with curves and open sections that gave it the random botanical pattern of vines. His mind drifted back through time. How could he explain the world he had come from to this intense younger man sitting across the table?

"It was an old Turkish prison," Maximilian continued. "We took terrorists there for questioning. Inside, they would tell us everything they knew. We didn't want false confessions—only the truth of what they knew. We didn't bring anyone in there until we knew so much about them, we could torture them and know if they were telling the truth. We knew how to test for the truth. The Shin Bet was a well-oiled machine, and the men I worked with knew how to protect our country better than any other government on earth can protect theirs. Israel is surrounded by enemies, and because of the Palestinians, we have enemies living within our own borders. Our intelligence community is the best of them all. We don't make mistakes like America's CIA. Our counterterrorist groups give us better security. We spend a higher percentage of our country's GDP on the military than any other country on earth. We have nuclear weapons and a working antimissile system against short-range rockets from Lebanon and Syria."

"You do realize I am Muslim."

"So we can't be friends—because I was Jewish and you are Muslim?"

"I don't know," Kazim said.

"You're from Turkey?"

"Yes."

"So you are not an Arab."

"Correct."

Maximilian opened both hands and turned his palms upward, as if the supposition of their alliance had resolved itself. "Turkey has been a friend of Israel for many years now—not that I care anymore. Are you a religious fanatic—an Islamic fundamentalist?"

Kazim hesitated. "Why? Are you a spy?"

"For Israel?"

"For anyone."

"No, not anymore. Are you a religious extremist?"

Kazim smiled slightly. "No . . . not anymore."

Maximilian nodded, then tried to see out the window. But the light inside the dining car had cast their reflection on the black window, hiding the outside world.

"So we both are men who have lost their way," Maximilian said. "Men who have broken ties."

"We're on the Trans-Siberian Railroad in Mongolia in winter. I think that the only men on this train are those who have lost their way."

"We are in Russia now, in Siberia."

"Doesn't matter—it's all the far edge of the world out here."

The barman returned with two glasses of Russian tea in nickel-plated holders, with spoons sticking out. He set them on the table along with a tray of honey, sugar cubes, syrup, and jams.

"What changed your religion?" Maximilian asked, after the barman had left.

"I never said it changed. My interpretation of it changed. My intensity changed."

"How?"

"I became less intent on strictly following the ancient teachings of my religion, and instead focused on what had been taken from me."

"But Islam is based on strict behavioral adherence."

Kazim didn't respond.

"What was taken?" Maximilian continued before taking a sip of his tea, enjoying its distinct smoky flavor. He didn't want to seem as if he was forcing the question.

"My brothers—all three of them. I was the youngest. Now I'm the oldest—the only one left."

"You must be strong to have survived such a loss."

"What about you? Have you changed your religion?"

"In a way, I think I have. But Judaism is a birthright, so maybe my politics are what has truly changed. Unfortunately, politics has a strong role in religion, or vice versa. For so long, my faith was tied to the struggles of Israel. The connection was easy because the struggles were great. My father fought in the Six-Day War. I myself fought in the 1982 Lebanon war. War is common for citizens of Israel, and terrorism is even more common. Many in the world support Israel. Many have sympathy for its people, but they cannot truly know what it is like to be surrounded by a dozen nations wishing to wipe your family from the face of the earth. Israel has the strictest antiterrorism procedures in the world for a reason. They live with their enemies, surrounded by their enemies, and as I came to realize one day, they even have enemies among themselves."

"One day?"

"The day Yitzhak Rabin was assassinated."

"Did you know him?"

"I was on his security protection detail. His safety was my responsibility. We saw a rising tension in the streets after the Oslo Accord. Many Israelis hated him for giving Arafat so much in the negotiations. Many thought the Palestinians deserved much less than what he was offering, but he wanted peace. It was understandable. But tensions were growing. We asked him to start wearing a bulletproof vest, but he refused. He said he had been a soldier before becoming a politician. I admired him for that—for his courage. He was a truly extraordinary man. And one day, some punk with a gun just walked up behind him as we were moving toward the car, and shot him. He died within hours, just like America's President Kennedy. The nation—and most of the world—suddenly mourned. Then everything changed for the worse. The peace process stopped. The Shin Bet and all other security agencies in Israel came under fire for failing to protect Rabin. I was in the middle of it all. Something terrible had happened to Israel."

"So then you abandoned it?" Kazim asked.

Despite the warm tea, Maximilian felt a sudden chill. "Yes, I have abandoned Israel. I reject it and all its allies." He was not ready to reveal the full story of why he now hated his former home. He could not yet trust this man with the painful secrets of his past. "I have grown angry at the entire concept of powerful governments influencing foreign countries. And if I use this anger to attack a friend of Israel, I can show the world the folly of superpowers meddling in other countries' affairs. Ironically, I now fantasize about becoming like the madman who killed Bobby Kennedy, or the madman who killed Rabin."

"And who would you attack? Who would be the target?"

"It is a dangerous conversation—even more dangerous than what we have already said. So please, before I continue, I wish to hear your story." He paused, took a sip of his cooling tea, and said again, "Please tell me your story."

Kazim's features seemed to grow darker as he leaned away from the hanging light behind him. He stared silently at Maximilian. Then, standing up from the table, he said, "My story is too dangerous to tell. Thank you for the tea."

He started for the door.

"I know about Baghdad," Maximilian said.

Kazim stopped. He stood completely still, frozen in the aisle of the dining car. Then he turned sharply, like a startled animal reacting to a sudden danger.

"I know about Baghdad," Maximilian repeated, "but what I don't know is your story afterward."

Kazim looked at him without a word. His breath quickened.

"I'm a friend, Kazim."

"I don't know you."

"And yet, I'm still a friend." Maximilian gestured for him to rejoin him at the table.

He shook his head.

"I know Moqtada al-Hakim."

Kazim took a step closer. "How?"

"Through Abdul al-Sadr. I've been tracking you since Calcutta. Saw the mess you made in Bangkok. Lost you in Singapore. Found you again when you entered Hong Kong. Followed you to Vladivostok and have been with you on the train since there."

"You're tracking me? Who are you?"

"Don't worry, no one else is looking for you. You weren't on Interpol's radar, and the Americans have no idea who you are. MI-Six doesn't know. Mossad doesn't know. No one knows—no one except your friends."

"I have no friends."

"You have friends in the community."

"What community? Yours?"

"No. The type of operations you did were not a main concern for Israel. When Israel abandoned me, I abandoned it in return. But I still have channels with Palestine and Libya, and they have channels to Iran as well as to radical networks. I made some inquiries and was directed to a man who knew Hakim. We had a conversation in Kuala Lumpur. Your name came up. I was interested and made other inquiries. Saw you had spent some time in Dubai but had left for India. It wasn't easy, but I finally tracked you to Calcutta only a month after you left there. It was difficult catching up with you, but now we are here on this train, heading for Moscow. I hope that before we arrive at the end of this line, I will have convinced you to join my cause."

"The world is a big place, with a lot of people. Why are you so interested in me?"

"Because you have more motivation for my plan to succeed than anyone else on my team—perhaps even more than I."

"Your team?"

"I will need two hundred men for a special mission. I have many of them already, but I am in the process of obtaining more. I will need you to lead some of them. Hannibal was a brilliant general, but he had great generals below him who helped with his plans. Hasdrubal was his brother and his top general. I don't have a brother I can trust to be my top general. I am hoping you will be my Hasdrubal."

"You speak very dangerously," Kazim said, looking down the car to the barman, who was absorbed in a game of computer mahjongg.

"Only when I'm with dangerous people," Maximilian replied.

"I'm not the leader type."

"Of these men, you will be. On this operation, you will lead them with your fury."

"What kind of operation?"

Maximilian lost all the intensity he had allowed Kazim to witness up until that moment. "It is a decapitation strike on a major world power. There are five potential cities where it might happen in the next year or two. Maybe as long as five years. It will take immense planning and resources and caution, and the risks of early detection will be high—and the likelihood of surviving the operation is minimal even if it succeeds. And the unlikely event of survival will be followed by a lifetime of hiding and being hunted like a war criminal."

"What's the target?"

"I'm recruiting you because I know your past. I know what happened to you in Baghdad. Don't say it out loud, but think in your mind of the one person in the world you would most like to kill."

Kazim stared at him hard and silently.

"Do you have that person fixed in your mind?"

Kazim nodded.

"You're sure?"

He nodded again.

"That is the person we are going to kill."

"You can't possibly kill the person I'm thinking of," Kazim said. "It's not even a person, really. It's a position, a title . . . a symbol."

"Precisely."

"You can't kill that person."

"Yes. We can," Maximilian replied. "And we will. If our operation goes as planned, we will be able to kill them in five years or less. And you will have revenge for your brothers."

Kazim smiled. "Where would it happen?"

"There are events already planned that they will attend. World forums, et cetera. One is set for Tokyo, one for Rome, one for Dubai, one for Berlin, and one for Paris. We will plan for all five and will be in all five cities, ready to strike when they are there. We won't know the details of their trip until they are there, and we will never have any inside access to their plans or security measures other than what is public knowledge. But we will wait and we will be ready. And when we have the opportunity, we will strike."

Kazim's smile widened. And in that moment, Maximilian knew that after weeks of tracking this man, he had him. In the middle of a desolate winter landscape at what felt like the edge of the world, he had found the brother he never had before.

And together, they would change the course of history.

35

JOHN ALEXANDER OPENED the small square door to the service elevator shaft while the other agents stood behind him, protecting the president and Colonel Marks. Stepping through the low opening, he felt his stomach sink when he looked down into the dark abyss. They were on the fourteenth floor—a long way up from the basement's third sublevel. The elevator car was down there at the bottom, nearly two hundred feet below.

"All right," he said. "There's a ladder running down the shaft, without a shell. So it's open, meaning that if anyone slips or lets go, they're dead—along with anyone they knock loose on the way down. Madam President, we're going to figure out a way to tie you to the ladder so you can't fall."

"We don't have time," she said. "I can make the climb down just fine."

John shook his head. "I'm sorry, ma'am, but I can't take that chance. You'll be secured."

He sent Stone to look for a rope or cable to secure her to the ladder as they climbed down. Even under these desperate circumstances, he still must look ahead for the unseen threat, doing everything he could to minimize the probability of something going wrong enough to become that single mistake that cost them the president. He gave instructions for the two-minute protective formation in the hallway and prayed that Agent Stone find something that would work. If not, then they would have to risk the climb without securing POTUS. The thought made him queasy.

*   *   *

Rebecca was with the president in a small alcove of the hallway. John had sent David looking for a cable or rope, and he had also split the other six agents, sending three to each end of the hallway to establish a temporary perimeter. The military aide was helping John establish the best way to move everyone quickly and safely down the elevator shaft.

"You have family back home?" the president asked Rebecca.

"My parents are retired in Boulder, and I've got three brothers—detectives in the Denver Police Department."

"All three are older?"

"Yes ma'am."

President Clarke nodded. "We women need to keep the men in line. Growing up with three older brothers, it sounds like you have some experience with that."

"Yes ma'am, quite a bit."

Rebecca knew that in situations stressful for the protectee, it was sometimes helpful to engage in small talk—especially when waiting for others on the team to put the next transport plan in place. But she had never imagined having a few quiet words with the president amid such a terrifying situation.

She saw David come running down the hallway, empty handed. When he got close, she asked, "No rope yet?"

"No."

"Well, hurry," she snapped as he ran past.

"Right," he snapped back.

She watched as he kept running to look in the other rooms down the hallway.

"Are you two okay?" President Clarke asked her.

"How do you mean, ma'am?"

"I've suspected since the Chicago trip last month that you and David are in a relationship," she said. "In the walkway on Air Force One, during the flight back, I caught a glimpse of him being sweet to you, and you blushing back at him. I probably should have mentioned something to John, but I thought he would have to reassign one of you to another detail because of the relationship. I like both of you, and that wouldn't have felt right."

"Thank you, ma'am," Rebecca said, feeling her face grow warm.

"You shouldn't thank me. Maybe you wouldn't be here tonight if you had been the one reassigned. You could be with the vice president at Martha's Vineyard right now."

"I'm glad I'm here with you, ma'am. It's an honor."

"You're sure you two are okay? We really need everyone in the right state of mind if we're all going to get through this."

"We're fine," Rebecca said. "Thank you." After a short pause, she added, "It's only a small argument we had earlier. He gave me a present that actually offended me."

"What was it?"

"A gun, ma'am. A little two-shot Derringer thirty-eight Special, made in Italy."

"And that offended you?"

"A little bit."

"Why?"

"Forgive me, ma'am, but you don't seem like much of a gun person. Are you?"

"Never really fired one in my life," the president said. "My husband goes pheasant hunting, but I've never had any interest in personal firearms."

"Well, this is a small pistol the size of your palm. It looks like a lady's gun, even though it fires thirty-eight-caliber bullets—at close range, a decent concealed weapon. Designed for personal protection for a woman—that sort of thing."

"That doesn't sound so bad," the president said.

"Well, when I say for 'protection for women,' I mean it's a little like a floozy's gun, worn on the leg under a dress, in the old days. The only real difference is that the more modern pistols have a little more firepower."

"Oh, so a prostitute's gun."

"It sure looks the part."

"I'm guessing that's not what he meant to imply," President Clarke said.

"He gave it to me with one of those holsters designed to strap it to the inside of my thigh, just like hookers used to do."

"Oh, my. You're not wearing it now, are you?"

"No, ma'am," Rebecca said quickly. Then, after a brief hesitation, she repeated, "No ma'am. I returned the gun to him." She could hardly believe she was telling the president this. Then, for good measure, she added, "He knows he screwed up."

"Good for you," the president said. "Us girls gotta keep the men in line."

Rebecca smiled for a half second, then became dead serious. "Right now, ma'am, we just need to keep you safe."

Down the hallway, she saw David running toward the elevator shaft, waving his empty hands. Alexander motioned for everyone to come back toward the middle of the hallway.

"Okay, ma'am," Rebecca said. "Looks like we're going."

They rushed back toward the elevator shaft while the six perimeter agents continued to guard both ends of the corridor.

*   *   *

John and Colonel Marks examined the ladder bolted to the side of the shaft. It was wide and appeared properly welded. Agent Stone hadn't found anything that would work as a tether for the president, so John changed his strategy for the climb. He decided that the military aide should go down the ladder first, followed by Rebecca, then John, then the president, with David above them. The other six agents should be split: three remaining by the shaft entrance and three climbing above David. Once they safely reached the bottom, the three still on the fourteenth floor could quickly climb down to rejoin them. Marks seemed confident that he could climb down the ladder with the football.

John had the three agents stand post at the corner of the small alcove between the elevator and the hallway. An overwhelming force of the US military and Secret Service would eventually be able to overrun the hostiles and retake control of the hotel, but that could take twenty minutes, maybe longer. It was too risky to try to secure the president in a stationary location for that long when the enemy was already deep inside the middle protection perimeter. And the fire was quickly becoming as great a threat as the terrorists. They had to keep moving.

It was time to start their climb down.

Marks struggled from the beginning because he was forced to hold the football in his left hand while moving down the ladder. Rebecca moved nimbly down the ladder a few feet above the military aide. Seeing her in action, John realized she might actually be the best climber in the group. Her personnel file noted that she had gone to college on a swimming scholarship. That sort of full-body movement probably translated better for this work than all the miles he had run around the Washington Mall over the years.

Then it was his turn. After checking that his gun and other equipment were secure, he grabbed the cool steel sides of the ladder and stepped out onto the rung.

But before he started climbing down, he looked into the president's eyes. "Ma'am, move slowly. Look straight ahead as you move, so you can see exactly where your hands are grabbing. Don't look down. Feel with your foot where the next step is, but don't put any weight on it till you're solidly on it. And remember, three points of contact at all times. This is key. Only one hand or foot in motion at any one time. The other three stay on the ladder until you've completed that one move. All right?"

"Yes," President Clarke said.

"I'll be only a few feet below you the entire time. Wait for me to get set before you make each move. I'll call it out each time."

"Okay," she said. "But this is going to take forever."

"That's okay, ma'am. This is not a place we want to rush things."

"All right."

He could tell by her breathing that she was nervous about the climb. Some smoke was now coming from far below, and it wasn't unthinkable that the fire had moved close enough to the center of the hotel that the elevator shaft could quickly turn into a chimney.

John stepped out over the deep drop-off and briefly glanced down into the dark void. He knew that all people were born with three natural fears: loud noises, falling, and the dark. And as eerie loud pops and snaps came from somewhere in the distance within the hotel, he found himself looking into what should evoke instinctive fear: falling *into* the darkness. But whatever instinctive fears he once had were long ago trained out of him. He had only one great fear left in his life: losing the president.

Grasping the smooth, cool metal of the ladder, he swung out over the darkness. Marks and Rebecca were already near the next level, so he started down the ladder much slower than he needed to, wanting to set a cautious pace for the president.

He reached out his hand and took hers to help guide her onto the ladder. He held her by the wrist, allowing her the freedom to tighten her fingers around the first rung, while making sure he could tighten his own grip to catch her if she slipped. He would not let her fall.

"I've got you, ma'am," he said, guiding her as she stepped onto the ladder. "You're doing great."

She pulled forward and set her other foot on the ladder.

After making sure she had a stable stance and grip, he climbed down two rungs. Then, from that distance, he helped her climb slowly down as Stone moved out onto the rungs above her, and the three agents not standing post prepared to climb out onto the ladder above him.

It was torturously slow going. Five flights took about five minutes. At the beginning of each new floor was a small concrete ledge, where Marks and Rebecca would stop and wait for the others to move down closer to them before they continued downward.

Just as they got past the ninth floor the president's foot had trouble finding the next rung. John reached up and gently guided it down.

"Are you okay, ma'am?"

"Yes. Thank you."

"You ready to keep going?"

"Yes."

They moved even more slowly than before. If they went too fast, there might be a mistake and someone could fall. But the longer it took to move down the shaft, the likelier the attackers were to discover them. And John didn't even want to think of how difficult it would be to protect the president while boxed into the shaft and hanging on to an open ladder.

36

K AZIM'S EYES BURNED from the smoke drifting around him. Small fires burned in scattered, isolated sections on the hotel rooftop. Debris from the downed helicopter, much of it in flames, lay strewn over the deck. It was now impossible to land even a small helicopter on the roof, and more of Maximilian's men would soon arrive to make sure that none even tried to get close. But somehow, it still seemed that he had failed. He tried to remember, tried to recall what, exactly, had happened. Tried to understand why he felt as if he had failed.

And then he remembered: the American president had escaped. Her guards had pulled her back and shielded her just as his men sprang their attack. And the speed and skill of the American security response was beyond anything he had ever seen. Maximilian had been right to compare America to the Roman Empire. Each, at its moment in history, had reached a military sophistication and dominance over all other countries in the world. But as with the Roman Empire, America would no longer be able to sustain its dominance and was primed for a rapid decline and fall.

As he pushed himself up out of the ashes, Kazim tried desperately to fight against the pain he felt all over his body. Seeing the bodies of the other ten men he had led to the roof brought back memories of his many fellow fighters who had fallen in Iraq. And the bodies of the Secret Service agents reminded him of the dead American soldiers on his last day in Baghdad.

It was a time of death, sacrifice, and loss. And it was when he first learned to hate, when he first felt the need to seek revenge on America.

*   *   *

Kazim's life as a fighter had started in Iraq, during the US invasion and occupation. He had joined the insurgents against his father's wishes, and his mother and sister had begged him not to go. But Kazim knew his calling and what he had to do. He had to stand up for the people of Iraq. And he had to stand up to those imperialistic empires that would lie to the world and use their aggressive war machine to invade another people's country and steal their valuable energy resources.

He had fought with many comrades who died fighting courageously against a larger and better-equipped enemy. He and his fellow fighters had felt honored to be chosen to defend Iraq against this dangerous, domineering American enemy. But God had not given them the victory they deserved. Instead, the Americans had eventually won after years of fighting. Of course, those still fighting for his cause could still attack the Americans with small terrorist groups in Iraq, but that was losing popularity even with some of the most hardened insurgent leadership.

And Kazim, feeling which way the wind was blowing, had left Iraq to continue the fight in other parts of the world.

But his time in Iraq was burned into his memory. At times, he felt as if nothing else in his life would ever matter as much as those years had, fighting in the urban mazes of Baghdad at a time when the city's soul felt as unsettled as a shaken hornets' nest. But he wasn't Iraqi—he had been raised in a small town in southeastern Turkey, near the borders of Iraq and Iran. He and his three older brothers had been recruited by al-Qaeda in Afghanistan, before the September 11 attacks on America.

As expected, America had reacted to the attacks with panicked aggression, and al-Qaeda leadership had reacted to America's actions with what, to Kazim, seemed unusually rapid maneuvers. His two oldest brothers had been sent away, one to Yemen and the other to Pakistan, on assignments that he couldn't be told of. He had heard rumors that his oldest brother often traveled to Germany and other parts of Europe, but he never knew the details. All he did know was that less than six months after they left, both had been intercepted and captured by America's CIA. After they disappeared, there was no more information about them, no contact from them, no updates— nothing. The consensus was that they both were still alive, illegally detained somewhere at different CIA black sites and almost certainly being tortured and humiliated by the Americans.

Nothing in Kazim's life had made him as angry as the thought of his two oldest brothers helpless and being mistreated by Americans. So when he and his other brother had the opportunity to leave Afghanistan and enter Iraq through Turkey to join the growing insurgency against the American invasion, they had been eager for the chance to continue their older brothers' fight and honor them by killing any Americans they found in Iraq.

In Iraq, he and his last remaining brother, Haluk, had fought in dozens of major engagements against American soldiers. Most of their attacks had been in Baghdad, and many targeted Iraqi translators and Iraqis training to become police and security personnel to serve the American agenda for controlling Iraq through a puppet government. It hadn't taken Kazim long to learn that the Americans' greatest mistake after invading Iraq was to disband the military. This strategic error had given the insurgency a chance to thrive momentarily. But the Americans were a strong enemy. And what most surprised him about the American soldiers was their courage. Both sides fought hard.

And then one day, only a mile outside the Green Zone, during a chaotic firefight after an ambush on a patrol of two US Army Humvees, the worst thing imaginable happened: his remaining brother was hit by enemy fire.

Kazim had seen his brother fall and rushed to his aid despite his commander's shouts to stay down. The firefight had raged on as Kazim sprinted across the dirt-and-gravel road, bullets hissing past him, snapping as they hit rocks or stone building walls. When he slid to his brother's side, he found him on his back, gurgling blood in an effort to breathe. His brother's eyes, staring in panic and confusion at the bright sun, turned toward him at the last moment. And Kazim would never forget the helpless feeling as he held his brother's head in his arms and tried in vain to help him. But there was nothing he could do, and as his brother slipped away, Kazim had prayed to God to stop time. He could see the confusion in Haluk's eyes—the weakness, the fading away of life. Amid the bullets and explosions and yelling from the surrounding firefight, Kazim had sat by Haluk, held his head, and stared into his panicked eyes, telling him that everything would be all right and that he wouldn't leave him.

But Kazim's prayers went unanswered. Haluk slipped away and died in his arms, and suddenly, he was alone in the world. And the overwhelming pain turned to rage.

In that moment, he became lost to everything he had once known. He was lost to God, lost to his fellow al-Qaeda fighters. He no longer cared about the war or the insurgency or any of the fighting. Everything that mattered to him, everything that he cared about—his three brothers—had been taken from him.

So he just sat there in the dry dirt, not knowing what else to do with himself. Nothing seemed important anymore. And he probably would have continued sitting there in baffled silence for hours if the world had left him alone. But it hadn't. He was still sitting in the middle of a firefight. A bullet struck him just below the left shoulder. Then another bullet struck the chest of his dead brother, enraging him more.

He laid Haluk's head down with his good arm and—fighting the pain in his left shoulder—stood and raised his AK-47 toward the American soldiers scrambling around the two Humvees to help their own wounded. He flicked the selector to automatic and held down the trigger, channeling all his rage through the weapon, firing all thirty bullets into the American soldiers trying to help their wounded. Five seconds, all seven US soldiers lay dead or dying beside the tan Humvees. A thin cloud of dust drifted away from the bodies.

Suddenly, everything was quiet—except for his raging heart. Wind blew through the spaces between the squat stone buildings and the rock walls along the dirt road. No people were in the streets or looking out their windowsills or doorways, but he could sense that dozens were out there, hiding inside their homes, waiting for a prudent amount of time to pass after the last explosions and gunfire.

He dragged his brother's body into the shade of the nearest building. He had nowhere to take him. He was nothing now, and he was alone. He hated the entire world and didn't know what to do with that hate and rage. So he had left his last brother's dead body along the wall and hurried away when he heard the US helicopters approaching from the Green Zone.

That night, he abandoned his unit of al-Qaeda fighters. Leaving the building in Baghdad where they were housed, he walked down the dark street of their controlled city block, past the barking dogs, past the darkened checkpoints, never to return again. He walked the desert roads of Iraq between towns, catching rides on the backs of trucks when he could, until he arrived at the Turkish border. Because he was a nobody soldier in al-Qaeda, neither the government intelligence agency nor the military had any record or understanding of his terrorist connections. He was too young to be a leader or a courier or even a trusted midlevel operative for al-Qaeda, so he hadn't made it onto anyone's radar. But he still had his Turkish citizenship, so after presenting his passport and spending a few hours in an interrogation room explaining why he had been in Iraq—for which he pretended to be a failed business opportunist looking to capitalize on the millions the Americans were spending on private contractors and translators—the border patrol had let him return to Turkey.

And then Kazim began the long journey of discovery that would forever change his life—a journey that would eventually lead him to encounter Maximilian on the Trans-Siberian Railroad a lifetime after Iraq. A journey that would eventually lead him to Paris.

*   *   *

Kazim tried to wipe the smoky sting from his eyes. As he struggled to his feet, he seemed to will his strength to return. Death was all around him. He searched for the president's body, hopeful that his clouded memory of her escape was a phantom, frantic to find evidence that would end his long quest for revenge. But after he scoured the rooftop, his rage boiled. He had been through too much struggle over the years to let his quarry escape. He had suffered too long to fail now.

Turning from the destroyed rooftop, he rushed back into the hotel, driven by his hatred.

37

A T THE SIXTH floor, David stepped off the ladder onto the small shelf that rimmed the elevator shaft. There was one at each level, which helped with the climb. A small platform on the other side of the ladder gave him something to stand on as he removed his gun. Holding the side of the ladder, he leaned out and looked up past the shelf above him, to the blurred, dark movement of the three agents moving down toward him. He peered up toward the unseen heights where they had started, eight flights up. He watched and listened but sensed no threat.

Turning his gaze below, he saw the president moving slowly, carefully, down toward the fifth floor. Below her, Alexander moved easily, gently swinging his bulk from side to side, then waiting, always staying close to the president. Farther down, Rebecca swung along, graceful as a gibbon. Like David, she moved fast enough to leave no more than a few unguarded seconds before reaching a shelf to stand on and watch for threats. And below her, the military aide clambered along, the nuclear football briefcase attached to his wrist by a cable wrapped in leather.

Amid the ongoing chaos, David was at least relieved to have Rebecca still with the group. At Beltsville, no other agent from their cadet class was better than she when it came to intelligence and a knack for getting protectees safely through the most intense training drills.

From the floors below, streaks of red and yellow crept into the shaft; below that, the bluish-gray light faded into black.

Without warning, gunshots rang out above them. The sound cracked but didn't hiss or whine, which meant no bullets had been fired down at them. The shooting was from side to side several floors up, where they had entered the shaft. The agents they had left to guard the entrance must be under attack, and the three other agents on the ladder were now holding their position.

David's adrenaline surged.

"Cover! Cover! Cover!" Alexander yelled.

David swung out onto the ladder and leaned back out over the shaft to protect the president from any downward shots. Looking down over his shoulder, he made sure he was in position to shield her from above. Alexander had climbed up to where he could now have a hand on her back and was helping her move off the ladder onto the shelf. Once on the shelf, she would be better protected from above and less likely to fall.

"Reid! Colonel Marks!" Alexander yelled. "Take spread firing positions!"

David had holstered his pistol and hung out wide on the ladder with both hands. He watched below as Rebecca moved onto a lower shelf near the fourth floor, and the military aide joined her. It was difficult to see in the dark, but she appeared to be sliding out along the shelf toward the back of the shaft. Marks, the military aide, moved toward the front.

"She's secure," Alexander said, leaning out from the shelf and looking up at David. "Take position for counterstrike. Don't shoot unless we're engaged. Our men above might stop them."

The gunfire above continued to crackle, then ended with a sharp, inaudible cry from above. He heard voices; then everything went silent. The eerie quiet lasted for a dozen excruciating seconds before he heard the hiss of something large falling fast from above. A short yell followed. Then he felt a sharp jolt on the ladder, and he knew that something heavy must have fallen and hit at least one of the three agents above him on the ladder. Then a number of heavy objects flew passed. One fell straight down and cannonballed into Marks, knocking him off the shelf. His brief scream stopped as several heavy thuds sounded below. David didn't need to look up to know that all three agents above him had been knocked off the ladder, probably by the body of another agent thrown into the shaft by the attackers, many floors up.

Now gunfire came from above, and this time it hissed. The terrorists were firing down at them, and the bullets were pinging all around them, sparking off metal.

Below him, Rebecca fired her P229 up at the men. He could barely see her in the darkness, and he was pretty sure she couldn't see the men far above. But as she fired, the shots from above kept coming, so she must not be getting close to wherever the attackers were positioned.

It was the stuff of nightmares for any Secret Service agent. They couldn't whisk the president to safety, and from their disadvantaged position, they couldn't effectively engage the threat.

David had been the top shot in his recruitment class, and he was anxious to turn his lethal skills on the terrorists hiding in the darkness above. Wrapping his left leg around the back of the ladder, he locked his right leg into a straight and steady stance on a lower rung. He closed his eyes to focus on their position in his mind without the distractions of reflecting light from the gunfire. Then, knowing his position and imagining the position of the men, he fired.

He had imagined where the assailants might be firing from if they were near the shaft's entrance point on the fourteenth floor. And with that image in mind, he fired for a two-foot rotating spread by making slight adjustments to his aim. Controlling his breathing as he fired, he concentrated on counting each shot in his mind to match it with the imagined spread of the targets above. One shot . . . two . . . three, a scream . . . four . . . five, another scream . . . six, another scream.

He had concentrated hard to keep track of the shot locations and the screams from above, and he now had a good sense of where to focus his remaining shots. Squeezing the trigger faster, he unloaded the final six rounds, then loaded a fresh magazine and continued firing.

He heard another scream and more yelling. Then another body fell past him in the dark, making a short blowing sound as it rushed through the air before bouncing off a support beam below and crashing with a heavy thud into the top of the elevator, far below on the floor of the shaft—four levels below the first floor.

The gunfire slowed, making the angry shouts above more distinct. He could hear John speaking to the president. David was a marksman, and even though tonight was the first time in his life he had actually shot at anyone, he felt as if he had been preparing his entire life for this moment. The firing from above had paused, but he heard more men shouting than before. They were regrouping, maybe even calling others to join them. He felt certain that a larger, more concentrated attack would begin at any moment—that as soon as the men were ready above, they would unleash a hail of bullets on the team, making it impossible to protect the president.

"I'm going up!" he yelled to Alexander.

"What!" Alexander yelled.

"Up—I'm heading up!"

"No!" Rebecca yelled.

"I have to, or the president's dead! There's no other way!"

"Go!" John yelled.

David holstered the pistol and climbed. He pulled hard with his arms and pushed gently with the balls of his feet, conscious of climbing as fast as possible without making noise. Other than occasional slivers of light slicing through sections of the dark elevator shaft, almost nothing was visible beyond twenty feet. This was the one thing in this nightmare scene that he was actually thankful for. For while the men above couldn't be positive where his group was, he knew exactly where the open floor access door was above them.

He knew where they must be, and they had no idea that someone from the protection team was climbing up to meet them. The men attacking the president were about to get the surprise of a lifetime.

38

DAVID CLIMBED THROUGH the darkness, focused on stealth. He could hear the men above yelling to each other as they regrouped. Other than their voices, the shaft was quiet.

He could hear shuffling footsteps, as if they were stepping toward the edge. He had been climbing fast, swinging rhythmically upward as he felt his aggression build.

Locking his left leg to steady his stance, he wrapped his right foot around the ladder and leaned back onto a horizontal I-beam. He was practically invisible in the shadows. He slid an index finger into the center of the Velcro holster so he could pull it apart without much sound. Drawing the P229, he pointed it up at the point in the darkness where he heard the men. He had slapped in a new magazine before making the climb, so he had twelve hollow-point .357 SIG rounds ready to shoot. He had more magazines, but being this close without any real cover meant that if any hostiles were still alive when he ran out, they would easily kill him before he could reload—especially since he was balanced on the ladder in the open air of an elevator shaft.

He peered into the blackness, listening for any sound of the enemy.

Raising the pistol, he trained it on the flicker of light he had seen forty feet above. Something metal was moving and casting a strobelike sparkle from the red emergency light farther above. A gun or a wristwatch or a belt bucket—he didn't know. But it marked one of his enemies. And a few feet to the left of the flickering, he saw a small cloud of dust particles float down through a sliver of light from the elevator shaft. The dust was probably kicked over the edge by a boot sliding to the end of the shaft platform as another enemy leaned over to prepare the second assault on the group below.

He had these two locked in, and he was afraid that they were about to unleash another wave of gunfire on the president. He couldn't wait any longer. Even though he had only two of them identified, he had to attack the group now. He prayed there weren't too many, for once he fired even a few shots, his position would be compromised.

He took a breath and exhaled. Then, with his legs and feet braced on the ladder, and his back against the I-beam, he fired.

Men screamed. Then a spurt of flashes flickered in the darkness as shots came toward him in frenetic, misdirected lines. Bullets snapped and pinged off the metal around him. But none hit him. A man toppled into the shaft and slid down like a large bag falling down a laundry chute.

David relied on his instincts for where to shoot. The light coming from the door into the shaft was now enough to show him where the bulk of the group was. Shooting from a low angle, he aimed at waist level in case they should duck or step back. Having studied marksmanship in depth, he knew that from this angle, most missed shots would miss high, still hitting the torso.

Two more bodies fell into the darkness below—one screaming, the other silent.

David's back hurt, and his legs were weakening. He had been leaning out above the abyss while shooting, and he didn't know how much longer he could hold the position. But the men kept coming, so he kept firing. He had maybe five or six shots left before he must reload—five or six shots to kill them all.

He kept firing. Men screamed and hurried their shots, and fell and died.

The platform above him went silent. He stopped firing. There couldn't be more than one shot left in his gun. Steadying his breathing, he watched the dark platform above. Nothing moved. He listened for the faintest sound to tell him if anyone up there was still alive, still a threat. Nothing stirred. He waited, knowing that the greatest threats were the ones not seen. There had to be someone still alive up there. He couldn't possibly have killed them all.

As quietly as possible, he ejected the empty magazine, pocketed it, and inserted a full one. And he waited. Someone had to be up there still. Like a sniper or a leopard lying in ambush, he slowed his breathing and stood silently in the darkness over the elevator shaft—waiting.

And then he heard a soft rustle. It was the smallest sound, a bare whisper of cloth and rubber on concrete . . . the faintest click of metal. A muted rattle. It was above him now. One man still alive. One target.

He closed his eyes and raised his gun. Focusing on every slight sound, he adjusted his aim to it. Nothing else existed. Only this one shot mattered. Protecting the president was everything. A slight breath escaped the unseen target, making the last sound David needed for the final adjustment. He squeezed the trigger once. From above him came a sharp gasp, followed by the thud of a body and the clatter of a dropped weapon.

Opening his eyes, he listened for any further sounds from above. Nothing. At any minute, other men would likely arrive on the platform. The gunfight had made too much noise, and he assumed that the men had radioed to others in their group during the fighting. He had bought the team the time they needed. Now he must rejoin them as fast as he could and help them escape before more men descended on them.

39

THE GUNFIRE HAD stopped, but John didn't dare move. Standing on the shelf by the closed elevator shaft door to the fifth floor, he had one hand on the back of the ladder, the other holding the president against the concrete wall. Rebecca was a level below them. They waited in silence, hearts racing in the dark. He had heard Marks fall to his death. At least five or six bodies had fallen past them, one even clipping the shelf just above them.

"What should we do?" the president whispered.

"We wait."

"Where's David?"

He didn't answer. There was still no sound from above. They could wait thirty seconds more; staying any longer would be too risky. They had to keep moving.

A single pistol shot broke the silence, followed by a distant clank and clatter. For several seconds, no other sound followed.

"All clear!" David yelled from above.

John felt a wave of relief, but it passed—they had to keep moving.

"Okay, ma'am, back on the ladder. Slow and steady, like before. Three points of contact at all times. We're more than halfway down. Seven more floors down to sublevel three."

Staying two rungs below her, he focused on every step she took as they made their way down the remaining levels. Rebecca was back on the ladder, too, moving below them. And he could hear David climbing down from far above. It struck him for the first time that everyone else from the team was gone, but he didn't have time to dwell on it. They still had the president, and right now that was all that mattered.

He noticed some red emergency lights below that reflected off something metal. It could be the top of the elevator. If they were nearing the bottom of the shaft, he wanted to make sure there was nothing threatening.

"Ma'am, please hold," he said.

She stopped climbing down and leaned her head against the ladder as he pulled his Service-issue miniature Maglite from its case. He was in no hurry to turn it on, but he had to see what the roof was like before moving the president onto it. Shining the light downward, he saw, perhaps ten feet below, the top of the elevator—and the grisly mash of mangled bodies. Blood and viscera were spattered across the roof and several feet up onto the shaft walls.

Stepping down onto the roof, he found it slick but stable. Careful not to slip on the wet surface, he checked to make sure the bodies were all dead. It was a quick check. Then he dragged the bodies and parts to the other side of the attached cables, squeegeeing off as much gore as possible each time. After clearing the area, he opened the top hatch into the elevator car.

"Secure it," he said to Rebecca.

She had been waiting on the lower shelf, protecting the president while John cleared the roof. Stepping down over the pulped corpses, she holstered her gun and grabbed the sides of the hatch to lower herself into the cargo elevator.

As she climbed inside, John flashed his light onto the side of the shaft where the door led to the hallway. It was closed. He kicked the emergency release lever hard and pulled it back.

"Okay, it's ready to open," he said.

Rebecca grunted and heaved against the elevator door, pushing it open while John knelt by the hatch, gun trained above and past her, ready to cover her if they didn't like what they found on the other side. She slipped through the open door and out into the hallway.

Time felt frozen as John waited, praying he wouldn't hear gunfire.

She appeared again. "Clear," she said.

"Okay, ma'am," John said, looking up at the president. "Please step down onto the edge. Slowly. I'm going to lower you down."

The president moved away from the ladder and carefully picked the least bloody way toward him. He took both her hands and, spreading his legs over the opening—lowered her down into the elevator. Rebecca helped ease her safely down from inside the car.

"David's coming," he said to Rebecca. "Secure her in the hallway. We'll be right down."

"What are you doing?" she replied.

"The football is compromised. With Colonel Marks dead and no reason to believe this attack is from a sovereign nation, I'm not about to have one of us keep lugging this thing around. Not with just three of us left to protect her."

"How long do you need?"

"Not long."

As Rebecca took the president out of the elevator, he moved to the far corner of the roof and dug through the pile of corpses until he found the briefcase, still attached to Colonel Marks. Besides Marks, John was the only other person around the president who knew the combination to open it.

He knew the protocol intimately. On her first day in office, the president was given a plastic card that had on it instructions and her nuclear launch codes. It was essentially the only thing that she ever carried on her person. Even if someone else had the football and the codes, they still couldn't launch an attack. The briefcase was used to communicate with the US Military Launch Command Center, at NORAD headquarters in Cheyenne Mountain, Colorado Springs. The president's launch codes were only the first of many steps that an actual nuclear launch had to pass through. A number of generals and military commanders were involved in the tightly controlled process. It wasn't as if the briefcase had a missile launch button. It was more like a sophisticated, superencrypted communicator for the president to signal approval to Launch Command. If anyone else tried to signal with it, the US military at NORAD would use caution in case the device had been compromised—especially during an attack on the president's life.

But even though there was no threat of the attackers using the football, it still contained classified information that shouldn't fall into the wrong hands. He pulled the metallic Zero Halliburton briefcase out of its leather cover and opened it. Inside was the gray communication box with keyboard and display, four red break-plastic cards with sealed nuclear launch codes, a thin soft binder with eighty documents in plastic folders, and the Black Book. The first few pages of the binder were instructions on the communication protocol for using the football to link up with the nuclear launch command center at NORAD. The other documents were detailed inventory and locations of all top-secret nuclear site centers in the United States and Europe— all highly classified information for the US military. And the Black Book, roughly the size of the binder, contained over seventy pages of nuclear retaliatory options.

A clank came from above. He jerked his head up and saw David just one floor up, climbing down the ladder.

"The top's secure for now, sir," David said, stepping down onto the elevator roof. "But there could be others soon."

"Stay there," John said. Turning back to the football, he removed the plastic launch code cards and the paper manual with the printed classified nuclear site documents. He broke the plastic cards and removed the nuclear launch codes sealed inside them.

"Sir?" David said.

John ignored him, working fast. There wasn't much time. He set the open briefcase next to him as he cracked open the last two launch codes. Then he reached for the switch to the nuclear communication device.

"Sir! You're not authorized to do that!"

John looked back and saw that David had removed his gun from his holster but was still pointing it down at his side. John supposed that seeing any unauthorized person messing with a nuclear launch device would be unnerving, even if there was no way he could initiate a launch. Despite all the tensions and horror of this night, he still couldn't avoid a chuckle. "Relax, rookie. I'm disarming it. I don't know what this attack is, but I don't think the president's going to need to start a nuclear war tonight because of it. Since there's not many of us left and no clear escape route, I don't want to risk us getting caught by the attackers with this on the president."

He smashed the keyboard with the butt of his gun and slipped the leather-wrapped cable off Marks's wrist. Then, pulling a miniature flare from the military aide's belt, he popped the cap and lit it. A bright orange glow lit up the inside of the shaft. He used the heat from the flare to set the classified codebook on fire and burn the plastic launch codes into unrecognizable melted globs. Then he handed the football, now containing only the communication equipment with a smashed keyboard, over to David.

"Find a space along the shaft to slide this past the elevator. It'll land somewhere underneath. That way, they won't find it, and it's disarmed anyway. And we can keep moving without worrying about it."

"You want me to drop the nuclear football down to the bottom of an elevator shaft?" David asked.

"Do it."

"Holy crap, John! You're sure?"

John grimaced and nodded.

"Roger that."

David leaned back against the dark elevator shaft and dropped the briefcase into the dark gap between the wall and the roof of the elevator car. After a few clattering bangs, he heard it land with a clap on the floor below.

"I can't believe I just did that."

"Let's keep moving," John said, jumping down into the elevator.

40

PRESIDENT CLARKE WAS pushed against the cold concrete wall in the hotel basement. Agent Reid pressed her into a dark slot, shrouded in shadows and protected from both ends of the long hallway. She watched Reid glance right and left continuously, scanning for any approaching threat. She heard John's voice through the open elevator door, but he still hadn't jumped down into the car. The light from the elevator flickered in a jarring, strobe-like pattern, which distracted her more than anything now that the fighting had stopped. The flashing light seemed to be matching the pulse of her heart, or her breathing, or some other internal rhythm within her. She couldn't explain this bizarre fascination with the light, but she stared at it in what she vaguely supposed must be shock or madness or hallucination. It was a feeling of light-headed euphoria that she hadn't experienced in over a year. That past moment had marked one of the greatest nights of her life.

A time with her family.

Flash-flash-flash.

A time of celebration.

Flash-flash.

A time of hope for the future.
Flash.

*   *   *

The celebration had begun with a boom of music and the rampant flashing of the auditorium's elaborate lighting effects. Rainbow confetti and big, bright balloons floated down from the rafters.

"You did it!" her husband yelled at her over the cheering crowd.

"Mommy! Look!" her younger daughter, Jessica, shouted excitedly, pointing at the deluge of balloons about to engulf them.

Her older daughter, Stacy, just stared with moist eyes and an enormous smile, facing the sea of campaign staff and supporters stretching out from the stage.

President-elect Clarke smiled because the cameras were on her, and waved at the jubilant cheering crowd. She contained her desire to jump up and down and scream, because the world was watching and she must uphold the dignity of the office she had just won. She stood strong and composed, but the unfathomable prestige now being bestowed on her was something impossible to prepare for. Even now, in this historic moment, in the lights and under the microscope of the world and her own people, she thought about how her every action and gesture and expression would be perceived by others. Even in this moment, she wasn't allowed to be truly herself. She had to be calculating in her response: modest, intelligent, passionate—a stateswoman and a leader. But inside, she felt both excited and, to her surprise, terrified.

She had run for the office of president of the United States because she had witnessed the failures of other leaders and believed she could do the job better. But now she worried that the job was impossible for anyone to succeed at. How could any one person be expected to lead such a diverse, complex, powerful nation? She loved America deeply, and she suddenly felt terrified that its immediate future now depended more on her than on any other citizen. What if she couldn't do the things she had promised during her campaign? What if the system of government continued to be too difficult and divisive for her to lead? What if her political and economic ideas were wrong? What if she inadvertently hurt the country in her efforts to help? For the first time, she felt the weight of the power she had been given, and was astonished at just how heavy it was.

But she had to hide these fears. She waved at the crowd again, smiled, hugged her husband, and kissed both her children on the forehead.

Then she turned and walked toward the left side of the stage, to a group of supporters who had been cheering loudest. She wondered if they understood, amid their jubilation, that plenty of Americans out there would be disappointed, frustrated, even angry that she had won. She smiled and waved but was haunted by the knowledge that only slightly more than half of all Americans supported her.

Near the corner of the stage, standing in the shadows, was the Secret Service special agent in charge of her protection detail throughout the campaign. His cool gray eyes had been watching the crowd, but for a brief second she noticed him glance at her and smile when their eyes met.

Rock music was booming again, and the crowd seemed distracted by something on the image board behind the large stage. She seemed to have a moment until the crowd would settle down enough for her victory speech, so she took the opportunity to step over to Special Agent John Alexander, shake his hand, and thank him for his work. She knew it wasn't protocol, but in this moment of uncontrollable celebration, many protocols throughout the auditorium felt relaxed.

"Congratulations, Governor," John said with a smile. "I mean, Madam President-elect."

Abigail gave him a joyous grin. "I hope you'll stay on with me, John."

"It's the director's call, not mine," he said, "but I hope so, too. It would be my honor."

"How many presidents have you served protection for?"

"Three, ma'am."

"Any advice for me?"

"It's not my place to say, ma'am."

"Please. I'd like very much to hear it. Before they swallow me up."

"Agents aren't political, ma'am. We serve our country by keeping our protectees safe."

"Just this once, John. If that's against protocol, I won't ask for your thoughts again. But before I walk back out there, I'd like to hear some straight advice from someone not playing the political game. And you've probably been close to more presidents than anyone else here."

He nodded. "We'll, ma'am, if you're asking me to be frank—the way I see it, our country has been divided for a long time. Politicians always say they'll unite us, but they never do. Maybe it's impossible. But you've been given the honor to try to help, despite all our differences." He paused, stone faced and sincere. "I like to think of the American flag, ma'am. It's not one solid color—it's sliced up by stripes and dotted with stars—all those different pieces crammed together onto one flag. But it is one flag, all of it bound together. And it's *our* flag—yours, mine, all those who voted for you, and all those who voted against you. Those who have died before us, and those who will live on after us. You need to try to be like that flag, ma'am. Your presidency needs to be like that flag."

"Holding all those parts together," she said.

"Yes ma'am. We need you to hold us all together."

Behind her, a familiar patriotic rock song blared as it had at many campaign events over the past year. More colored confetti drifted down from the rafters like rainbow snowflakes. Balloons rolled and bounced along the stage like giant leaves at the end of autumn. People cheered and called out her name. Many blew into loud, fringed party horns. Large lenses of television cameras lined the room and followed the excitement of this latest historic moment. Her husband was back on stage with her children and the vice president-elect and his family. They all waved at the crowd. Then her younger daughter looked around, searching, found her with her eyes, and waved with a big smile for Abigail to come back to the stage.

"I should get back out there," she said to John.

"Yes ma'am," he said. "You've got a country to take care of now."

"And you've got a president-elect to take care of."

He laughed. "You protect our country, ma'am, and I'll protect you."

"Deal," she said, shaking his hand to seal their compact.

Then she turned and walked back out onto the stage, waving to the crowd and to the cameras broadcasting this moment to the world. Picking up Jessica, she kissed her on the side of the head and said, "Look at all those balloons, honey."

"It's like a big birthday party," Jessica squeaked excitedly.

"You're right."

"You have lots of friends, Mommy."

Abigail laughed. She loved the way her children saw the world. Despite the excitement of the victorious election night, it all would have felt hollow if her family weren't here to share in the celebration.

"Why isn't the dark-haired knight having any fun at your party?" Jessica asked.

"The knight?"

"Yeah, why isn't he having any fun?"

Abigail followed her gaze to the side of the stage, where John stood scanning the crowd.

"Is *that* the knight? Agent Alexander?"

"Yes," Jessica replied. "Stacy said you'll be like a queen now, and he's a knight to protect you from bad people."

Abigail smiled. "Well, your sister's right, and we're very lucky because he's one of the best knights in all America. But don't worry, he's having fun tonight. He just can't show it."

"Why?"

"Because he's here to keep us safe."

"From the bad people?" Jessica asked, her eyes widening.

"Yes, but it's okay because he's stronger than the bad people and he will always keep us safe."

"Okay."

"And you know what else? If I'm a queen, know what that makes you?"

"A princess!" Jessica said without hesitation, slightly embarrassed.

"Yes," Abigail said. "A very special princess. Both you and your sister are my little princesses."

Jessica burst into giggles. Abigail hugged her tight and then reached out an arm to wave at the celebrating crowd. She would need to start her acceptance speech soon. In it, she would pledge her devotion to helping the country past the divisive election season and toward a just and prosperous future—as all great presidents had done throughout the rich and turbulent history of the United States.

*   *   *

Flash—flash—flash. Her thoughts returned to Paris, and her eyes stared at the dancing light coming from inside the elevator. Agent Reid still had her pinned against the wall. She was tired and light-headed from the climb down and the adrenaline overload brought on by the constant danger. The darkness of the hallway only added to her confused state of mind.

It had been only a few days since she saw her family, but it felt like years. She wasn't accustomed to such violence, to such darkness.

But then, through the light of the elevator, John emerged into the hallway, followed by David.

And she felt Rebecca still at her side.

And with these three around her, the darkness became bearable.

41

JOHN AND DAVID jumped out of the elevator and moved into the hallway toward Rebecca and President Clarke.

"Clear?" John asked.

"Clear," Rebecca said.

John was familiar with all the details of the building's schematics, including the basement levels. They were now just below subbasement level three. Because of the collapsing attack and their frantic scramble down the elevator shaft, he had told the protection team to stay off communications until they knew where to move POTUS. Throughout the past few minutes, he had heard reports from other agents. The hostiles had stormed the hotel from somewhere in a sublevel, rising up into the building as the fire grew. The combination of armed men and fire had been a shock to the protection detail. The attackers were moving with the fire, as if it were a key element of their strategy. The hotel's fire suppression system had not worked, which couldn't be a coincidence. In hindsight, it might not have been too difficult for a team to cut the water supply to the building moments before the attack started.

But now he needed to open up communications with the other agents on-site. He raised his wrist and spoke into his communicator. "This is Eagle One with Firefly. I need perimeter status."

Almost immediately, a response came through his earpiece: a young man's voice, professional and steady, but speaking with urgency. Guns were firing in the background. "Sir, middle perimeter is lost. Zenith is lost. Command Center is lost. Most of Shield One is lost. Outer perimeter holds, and reinforcements are moving to retake middle perimeter."

"Where's the fire?" John asked.

"Spreading everywhere. The fire suppression system is out. Local fire trucks had been rerouted for another fire. They're a few minutes out, but it can't be stopped now. The building won't last an hour."

John swore under his breath. They couldn't go back up the elevator shaft, and they couldn't say here. Their only chance was to find the safest stairway up and pray that they could avoid the attackers and the fire.

They had to move fast.

John stepped into the dark hallway, illuminated only by the red glow of the exit signs. The president was still in the alcove, protected by Rebecca. David had moved thirty feet out in the hall to secure the section that branched into a delta of other corridors in the hotel basement.

"Are you okay to move, ma'am?" John asked.

"I'm okay," President Clarke said.

"Rebecca?" he asked.

"I'm okay."

"David?"

"Ready to go, sir."

John nodded. He knew that this had become a defining moment in the history of the United States. By now the entire world would be shocked and horrified, watching on television or listening on the radio. Some few would be celebrating. But as long as the president was alive, there was still hope of avoiding a catastrophic blow to his country.

He raised his gun and started jogging down the dark hallway. Rebecca ran with the president. David moved in the back of the group because he was best able to cover the president from either front or rear attack.

The four moved through the dark basement hallway. They could smell smoke and hear the fire and distant gunshots from somewhere above. John could only imagine what the rest of his men and women—those still alive—were going through. His fear was well concealed and controlled by his training. But no matter how much the Service had conditioned its agents to react with instinctive heroism, no training had ever been devised to last as long as this attack had already lasted. Over half an hour had elapsed since the Crash POTUS alert, and the president was still in danger. The stress was nearly unbearable. But he was digging deep for courage, and he would keep on digging deep as long as he needed to.

He would *not* lose the president.

42

KAZIM'S RAGE BURNED. So many of his men were dead! Most of the building was a blazing inferno. And yet, the American president was still alive.

He pelted down the stairs two at a time, his mind racing to adapt the team's strategy. Everything they had done was designed to kill the president on the rooftop. It had been their ultimate goal to decapitate her—throw her head off the roof while her body burned. It was that simple: send a message of horror to outrage the world and warn it that oppression had its consequences. And like the Romans in the empire's waning decades, the West misunderstood its foes to be savages. But the Germanic tribes and the Goths of France were not savages; they were a civilized foreign people. And like them, Kazim's and Maximilian's men represented that spirited group of people that refused to let the intruding American empire dominate their lives any longer. As with Rome, mighty America must fall to give the rest of the world the opportunity to forge its own destiny.

And Kazim would find immortal glory that would carry his name through the ages.

"The president is back in the building!" he yelled into his radio, no longer making any attempt to mask his thick Turkish accent.

"Is the rooftop secure?" Maximilian's voice erupted from the radio's small speaker.

"Negative," Kazim said. "We stopped the extraction and killed many American agents, but one helicopter went down, crashing on the rooftop, killing my men and destroying our heavy guns. Bodies and spot fires are everywhere. The landing area is destroyed, but the Americans could use ropes to land a team up there if they wanted."

"But they can't evacuate the president?"

"With ropes, maybe. But it would have been too dangerous to keep the president there. We have men that could get there before their next helicopters could. There would be another firefight. The president's security team wouldn't risk pinning her down on the roof for twenty minutes—they would want to keep her moving."

"There are reports of a team of armed agents moving down the service elevator shaft. Are you saying the president might be with them?"

"I'm saying the president isn't dead on the rooftop," Kazim yelled into the radio, his rage burning in him at the thought that his quarry was getting farther away and might escape.

"There have been no more reports of other Secret Service teams. Everyone else is dead or fighting on the ground level or trying to breach into the building from the outside. We thought it was just a team of agents lost from the pack. But they must be the ones with the president."

"Where, exactly?"

"Central service elevators. We had our last contact with our men on the fourteenth floor two minutes ago. Now nothing. They may be dead. I've sent another group."

"Send EVERYONE!" Kazim yelled. "They must be heading for the subbasement, to climb back up to an outside escape staircase—around the fire. Out of the building. Focus everything on the entrances out of the sublevels."

As he pounded down the stairs, he saw "19" painted in blood red, left of the stairwell door. Only five flights to go.

"We can't send everyone," Maximilian said. "We have other areas in the building to cover. And we need to fight off a possible breach. We don't know for sure that the president is with them."

"I'll find them," Kazim said. "And I'll kill them. Send as many as you can to block off the exit points from the sublevels. I'll be there in one minute. Once I get to them, I'll report when I have eyes on the president, to confirm she's with them. Then . . . send *everyone*."

He clicked the lightweight radio back to his hip and continued racing down the dimly lit staircase as fast as he could go.

43

JOHN RACED OUT in front down the dark hallway in the B-4 sublevel. Rebecca was directly behind him, jogging with the president, and David was running at the rear. They were approaching the northwest side of the building—the side they deemed most secure based on the information they had gotten over the radio.

As they neared the end of the hallway, John motioned for them to stop. Peeking around the corner, he saw another long hallway, but this one had an open right wall, with spaced divider support barriers that showed an opening to three large rooms. This must be the lower structure below the three giant ballrooms two flights above. There would be a wide stairway at the end of the hallway, leading up to level B-3. From there, they would have two options: head up a long, narrow staircase to the level near the lobby, or try to make their way to the lower garage level on the south end.

"Okay," he whispered, seeing that the area was clear. "Let's go."

They took off running down the long, broad hallway, with John leading the way.

As they raced past the rooms, he saw in the shadows hundreds of chairs stacked against the wall in preparation to being moved upstairs for the banquet ball tomorrow night. The advance team and frequent Secret Service security sweeps had been thorough and meticulous. They had left nothing unexamined. And the Secret Service Forensic and Investigative Division had been tracking and monitoring all available intelligence around Paris for weeks before the president's arrival. They had left nothing to chance, so he still didn't understand how an elite paramilitary attack force had made such an effective assault on the hotel.

Rounding the corner at the end of the last room, he threw up his hand at the three behind him. He heard Rebecca pull the president to a halt, and he knew that David would stop behind them and guard the rear. But John didn't look back at them, for he was focused on the stairwell. He motioned for the others to be silent while he closed his eyes to concentrate on the faint sound he had heard somewhere above. He heard air circulating and the fast, light panting of the president only a few feet behind him. Rebecca and David were silent. A soft ambient echo of sirens drifted around them like humidity in the air. But these things were not what John was searching for; they were not the danger he had sensed.

Then he heard the faint rattle and snap of distant gunfire. He could tell from the sound that it was at least three floors above them, maybe even higher. It was most likely on the ground level of the hotel, four floors up.

John was torn. In his twenty-year career, he had never faced a decision like this. He knew that the terrorists would sooner or later track them from behind, following the trail of bodies. And if they hadn't already realized that the president was in this group, they would soon figure it out.

So how could he stay here, knowing that men were likely tracking their movements and might attack them from the rear at any minute? He couldn't risk going back the way they had just come. Even with all this in mind, knowing that the only direction they could go was up, all the training he ever had warned him against taking the president in the direction of gunfire.

And yet, in this moment, John felt he had no choice but to do just that, the unthinkable: take the president up the staircase, closer to the line of fire.

Turning to the others, he said, "We'll try going up each floor. We may not make it all the way up to the ground level, but there are some exits on B-two and B-one that could be safe. Wait for me to get to the top of each flight of stairs first. If I see it's safe, I'll signal you up."

John moved lightly up the stairs, two at a time, and slowed near the top, pistol in both hands. The only sound was the distant random chatter of automatic gunfire. He slid out from the stairwell's corner, gun forward, eyes and ears searching. The long hallway was shadowy but seemed empty of threats. He didn't trust it, and his instincts told him not to let his guard down. He watched and waited, half expecting someone to jump out from any of the dark doorways spaced evenly along the hallway and falling into a distant vanishing point in the gloom.

After thirty seconds of motionless concentration, John's instincts calmed. There didn't seem to be any immediate threat in this hallway, and he was comfortable moving the president up to this level.

As the gunfire continued, it occurred to him that his men were still up there somewhere, fighting like hell against the terrorists. And even though the Secret Service had somehow failed to detect this threat in advance, to prevent the attack from ever happening—always the agency's primary goal—he couldn't help feeling pride in the way the Service had responded once the attack began. It was clear to him that the attackers had planned multiple opportunities for killing the president: the building fire, the small group of assassins on the rooftop, the group that attacked them in the elevator bay. In each case, the enemy must have hoped to kill the president. But in each case, the Secret Service had moved faster, with deadly force and heroic sacrifice, doing everything necessary to protect the president. And even though the Service had paid dearly in lives, they still had the president. It was terrifying to think of the force they were still up against with only three agents in the president's protection bubble, but they were close to getting her out of the building. They just needed a little luck.

He knelt and looked back around the corner and down the staircase to give Rebecca the signal to bring up the president. Then they proceeded up the staircase between B-3 and B-2, with John in the lead, Rebecca holding the president in the middle of the flight, and David at the bottom landing to watch the hallway on B-3.

At the top of the staircase, John repeated his cautious reconnaissance of the hallway. He sensed immediately that something on this level was different. The gunfire was much louder than he had expected. And he heard shouts in a foreign tongue. Something moved in the shadows up ahead.

He ducked his head back behind the corner. This wasn't going to work. They couldn't take the president any farther without getting too close to the attackers. He didn't know how big this group was, and shooting one or two terrorists down here could alert the rest to their location. They couldn't take that chance unless there was no other option. John motioned for Rebecca to move the president back down to B-3.

"It's too risky up there," he said once they were all back on B-3. "They're all over the place. We can't keep going up."

"Can we go back toward the elevator bay?" David asked.

"I don't like that, either. They might now have groups in that area looking for us."

"Well, we can't stay here," David said.

President Clarke hadn't said a word for several minutes. The commander in chief was hesitant to strategize with the Secret Service on protection matters, either because she had no experience in the area or, more likely, because she truly entrusted her life to John. But the hesitation shown by all three agents had seemed to encourage her to speak up.

"Can we work our way toward the parking garage?" she said. "There has to be a way into it from down here."

"Ma'am, it would be almost as risky," John said. "If they've secured the lobby, then they've most likely also secured the inside access to the garage—probably with a strong force since they would know it could be an entrance point for our emergency response teams."

"But what other choice do we have?" she asked.

"None," David said.

John nodded, although he felt terrified of the prospect of taking the president closer to the attackers—perhaps even into a situation that could make protecting her impossible.

"So how do we get to the garage?" President Clarke asked.

"We'll have to go back up to B-two and hope no one's on that floor on the north side."

"What are our chances?" the president asked.

"Not good," he answered.

"We have no other choice," David said.

"No—wait," Rebecca said, speaking for the first time after spending the past ten seconds in what looked to John like a deep, almost meditative reverie. "There might be another way."

The other three looked at her.

"What is it?" John asked, feeling a spark of hope. There were few opinions that he listened more carefully to than Rebecca's. Even though she wasn't a good enough marksman to earn an assignment on the direct PPD bubble around the president, she had proved over the past year that she was one of the best field agent analysts and investigators he had ever seen in the Service.

It was why he had requested her as assistant lead agent on the advance team for Paris, and the liaison between the PPD and Secret Service Headquarters in Washington.

"What is it?" he repeated.

"The threat—the attackers. How did they get into the building?" she asked. "The EK-one detected them underground just seconds before they breached the hotel, right?"

"Yes," John answered, growing more excited as he sensed where she was going.

"They must have found a way to use the tunnel systems below Paris. And if they used the tunnels to get into the building, couldn't we use them to get out?"

"The Paris Catacombs?" President Clarke asked, surprised at the suggestion.

"It's possible," John said, "but it's risky. We don't know the tunnels at all. We have no support in them. Our communicators probably wouldn't work down there. Most of the passageways are at least one level below any subway lines, and probably multiple levels below the Paris streets. It's an ancient, forgotten maze, a burial ground. We could easily get lost—easily get trapped and pinned in."

"But we wouldn't be walking directly into a fight," Rebecca said. "A fight where we could be outnumbered twenty to one or worse. A fight where we could lose all chance of protecting her."

"Wouldn't they just follow us?" the president asked.

"Maybe," Rebecca said. "Or maybe they won't realize we escaped the building."

"And if they did follow us?" David asked.

"Even then it could still be to our advantage," Rebecca said. "They might not be able to track us. And if they can, we're still better off fighting them in a narrow space, where their superior numbers won't matter as much. And they couldn't surround us; they would always be at our backs."

"Unless we get trapped," President Clarke said.

"Yes ma'am," Rebecca conceded. "Unless we get trapped."

"Do we even know how to get into them?" the president asked.

"Northeast side on level B-three, ma'am," Rebecca said. "This level. It's on the next wall of the building, around the corner and down that hallway. We know this from the report our perimeter agents communicated before the wall was breached and the Crash POTUS alert went out. We're very close."

"What if men are waiting there?" David asked.

"The men have swarmed the building, setting it on fire, and by our reports, they seem to have moved upwards in the building to force the president toward the roof—where they must have hoped to complete their mission. They may not have calculated that we might survive the rooftop assault and escape back into the building. The skirmish in the elevator shaft seemed random. I don't think they would have many men, if any, in the basement level near the tunnel entrance."

Rebecca looked at John. This was his decision to make.

John looked down, clenching and unclenching his jaw. "We set up the EK-ones to detect any underground movement or vibrations near the hotel, but otherwise, I don't know a lot about the tunnel system. What could we expect if we go into them?"

"I researched them during the advance trip," Rebecca said. "There are more than a hundred and eighty miles of old quarry tunnels that snake through the foundations of Paris. Nearly all of them are off limits, and most have been sealed off by city engineers. It's a huge underground labyrinth, with all the dangers you might expect. There have been collapses." She paused. "Most of the underground has been mapped by the Inspection Générale des Carrières, the government department responsible for monitoring them."

"So we don't know where to go once we're in them?" John asked.

"No," Rebecca said. "The main catacomb path, open to the public for tours, is well mapped. But even after nearly three hundred years, the IGC hasn't been able to map all the other tunnels, because of waterholes and multileveled passages, partial collapses, undiscovered entrances from ancient basements, et cetera. Some tunnels are flooded, some collapsed, some walled up with concrete by the IGC, some stacked floor to ceiling with bones of the dead."

"We can't be sure how to get out?" John asked.

"It's a dark maze," she said. "There are public exit points, unmarked shafts up to street manholes, and even access shafts built by the IGC—but there are also dead ends and passageways to quarries that have been walled up with concrete to prevent illegal exploring."

"Do you have any idea where we're at within the underground area?" the president asked.

"No ma'am."

"Well, we can't stay here," John said. "There's no way out going back the direction we came from, and I'm not taking you up any closer to the gunfight above. And it sounds like the fire is completely out of control and could even consume the building. Bottom line: we can't go up, can't go back, and can't stay here."

"It's your call, John," the president said.

He nodded. In situations where the president's safety was in question, his authority overruled everyone else's in her typically large entourage—even the most demanding White House staffers. He was the only one who could ever say no to the president, but this was the first time in his twenty years on presidential details that he had ever heard a president openly admit that he was in charge.

And he had already made his decision.

"The only entrance into the underground from the hotel is where the security breach occurred?" he asked Rebecca.

"Yes," she answered. "The reason there are not many buildings over five stories tall in this part of Paris is because, in much of the area south of the Seine, the tunnel system is right under the city streets. So large-weight-bearing foundations are out of the question. This hotel is the exception. They filled in the already sealed and off-limits tunnels directly below this site during construction. So all the hollow spaces under this building are now concrete. And the tunnels around the hotel's foundation should have been sealed by the IGC, but sometimes those barriers are just locked iron gates instead of proper concrete walls. The breach into the hotel basement will be our only access point into the tunnels."

"And you think we can find a way out once we get into them?" he asked.

"If we move far enough through the tunnels, we should eventually find an IGC access shaft to the surface. Maybe even one of the unauthorized chambers and sewer manhole entrance points used by the *cataphiles:* people who illegally explore and map the Paris underground for fun."

"*Cataphiles?*" he said. "Any chance we might run across any of them?"

"Yes. Once we go into the tunnels, it's quite possible. Sometimes they have underground parties. If we run into them, they could show us the way out."

"Okay," he said. "Let's move toward the EK-one and find our way into the tunnels as fast as possible. Even if we get lost in them, that might still make it hard for the terrorists to find us."

"If it makes you feel better, Madam President," Rebecca said, "the French Resistance used these tunnels to hide from the Nazis when Paris was occupied during the war."

President Clarke nodded approvingly. "If they helped the French against the Nazis, then I have faith they'll help us against these psychos."

John allowed himself a brief grin before turning his thoughts to the Stygian depths of the Paris underground. He couldn't think of another instance in the Service's seventy-odd years of protection when an agent had ever needed to rush a protectee into a blind maze with no known exit. But in this moment, it was their best option.

"All right," he said. "Let's go."

The four of them ran along the tiled hallway that seemed to stretch forever through level B-3. The emergency lighting offered only a feeble red glow that reflected off the tiles.

Rounding the corner, they went through a metal double door and down half a flight into the large furnace and water heater room. John stopped and raised a hand. He trained his gun on a man's body in a dark suit, lying on its back with the left wrist resting over his mouth.

John walked forward and knelt at the man's side, staring at the face as he placed two fingers on the throat to search for even the faintest pulse. After a few seconds, John snorted in frustration and anger. Then, realizing his lapse, he regained his normal dispassionate expression.

"One of your men?" the president asked. "Down here?"

John nodded. "Carlos Perez. Third-year field agent. He was a good agent, ma'am. He and two other agents were investigating the strange EK-one readings down here." John stood up, still looking at Perez's young face. "He's the one who gave the Crash POTUS alert after the attackers broke through, which gave us an extra thirty seconds to move you and our emergency response team. That may have been the slight difference that saved your life from their initial strike."

Looking back at the president, he pointed down the stairs. "I'm sorry, ma'am. I shouldn't have stopped. We need to keep moving."

With Rebecca helping the president, all four headed down the short, wide staircase into the lower level of the vast room.

Slipping past the burned and blasted remains of the other two agents, they rushed toward the concrete foundation wall and the jagged vertical rent that opened before them like a gateway into the netherworld.

Motioning Rebecca and the president to the opening, he stood on the left side and pointed at David to step through the underground portal. Gun up, David stepped into the darkness with the intensity and focus of a man expecting to walk into an ambush. As David stepped over concrete rubble and disappeared in the darkness, John pointed his pistol back in the direction they had come from, and listened, taking one last look at his fallen men.

David stepped back into the opening thirty seconds later and gave an all clear.

John nodded and raised his wrist microphone to speak. Then he paused.

"What's wrong?" Rebecca asked.

"Damn it!" he growled. "I can't tell anyone where we are."

"We'll need support in the tunnels," David said. "That place is a labyrinth. I only went a little ways and still almost got lost finding my way back here."

"And we don't know how, exactly, we're going to get out," John said.

"We'll *find* a way out," David said.

"But right now we *don't know how.* We might take a left and a right and hit a dead end. We might have to double back. We might go in circles. Every time we take the president into a building, we have set escape routes mapped and planned. But all our planned exits have been removed. And all we have left is this ancient underground maze seventy-five feet below the city. Our only advantage right now is that the attackers don't know where we are. And I can't risk informing them by trying to communicate anything to agents outside the building."

"But your communications are encrypted," the president said. "The terrorists can't possibly intercept the signal."

"They don't have to decrypt it to intercept it," Rebecca said, looking at John.

He nodded, impressed that she understood the reason for his concern. "Ma'am," he said, "all our agents use the same encoded frequency for lightning-fast communication and threat response across PPD. The Secret Service is designed to prevent threats, and when they do occur, we're designed to rush protectees to a secure location safe from the threat."

"What are you saying?" the president asked.

"Ma'am, we aren't set up for a long battle. A lot of our agents have fallen, and the attackers may have taken communicators from the dead and are listening for any message we send. We haven't heard anything from the command center. We can't risk revealing that we're going into the tunnels. The attackers could track us down before agents could locate someone from Paris's IGC to help find us."

"What about the Joint Operations Center in DC?" David asked Rebecca. "Can you have them relay rescue info?"

"The sat phone can't get a signal down here, even using GMS mode. We're already sixty feet below."

"Ma'am," John said, "we can't stay here any longer."

"So we're just going to jump down the rabbit hole without any support?" the president asked.

"I'm afraid so, ma'am. But no matter what we find in there, no matter what happens, we'll get you through it."

"Okay," she said. "I believe you."

David turned and stepped back through the opening, into the darkness. Rebecca took the president's arm and helped her over the scattered rubble. And John, giving one final glance at his fallen brothers behind him, stepped into the darkness beneath the City of Lights.

44

KAZIM HAMMERED DOWN the stairwell, his footfalls echoing off the concrete walls. Breathing hard, he grabbed the next metal banister and slingshotted himself around the corner and down the next level, then the next. As he descended toward the last known location of those survivors he believed were protecting the president, he was consumed by worry that he might miss his best chance of avenging his brothers.

Reaching the fourteenth floor, he met a group of twelve men, sent by Maximilian. He motioned them to follow as he raced to the service elevator shaft where armed resistance had been reported.

As he neared the small alcove in the corridor, he saw the cargo lift doors, wedged open by the bodies of four of his team. Any force deadly enough to take out these men had to number several Secret Service agents—and any agents still left in this part of the building must be with the president. It was clear they had used the shaft in an attempt to escape the building. And then he smelled it: the unmistakable scent of perfume, which no agent would wear. The president had recently been here.

"Exactly when did these men report this encounter?" he asked the craggy, shaved-headed man beside him.

"Eleven minutes ago, sir."

Kazim grabbed the metal edge of the doorframe and leaned out over the shaft to peer down into the darkness. He studied it for seconds, as if trying to see back into the events of eleven minutes ago. The shadows seemed to shift and reshape from the recent battle, and the cool wafting air to whisper the haunting cries of combat and death. He saw the ladder next to the elevator door. A steel I-beam led to it from along the wall. The president must have felt like someone walking the plank on a pirate ship as she edged out over the abyss. For a politician, a woman in her late forties, it must have been terrifying. And it would have been even more frightening for the Secret Service agents who were so careful not to put her at risk.

Still scanning the shaft and imagining how events had played out, he asked, "How many of us were here?"

"Maybe six or seven, according to our scout plans," his roughhewn lieutenant answered.

"And since I'm not hearing any gunshots down there, I'm assuming they're all dead. Four dead up here, so three must be lying on the bottom." Continuing to look around the shaft, he tried to imagine how the Secret Service could get the tactical advantage over his men from *below* them. "The Secret Service are all excellent marksmen, but it is too dark to be very good when shooting from below, especially with a pistol. Maybe one or two of our men could be hit with lucky shots, but not all of them." Then he saw the second ladder, across the shaft, barely visible in the gloom. "If one of the agents had climbed up that ladder," he said, "back into the fray, then they might get a better line of sight to take out our men."

But oh, the courage to climb up in the darkness, armed with a pistol, toward men with automatic weapons—and the skill it would take to kill them all with such limited firepower . . . He pondered for a moment, and despite the unlikeliness of such a feat, he could think of no other way that his men had lost this fight.

"These last agents are extremely good," Kazim said.

"They won't make it out," his lieutenant said. "We have all exit points covered, and the Secret Service's emergency response team has not been able to break through our lines, because of the fire and our own men's strength."

Kazim nodded, but he was still thinking about the type of agents he was tracking. They had gotten the president to the roof faster than he ever expected, but even then he still should have been able to end this up there. That they had managed to protect the president on the roof and escape through this elevator shaft had him concerned.

Stepping carefully out onto the iron beam, he swung his legs onto the first ladder. The agents had an eleven-minute head start plus the minute he had spent evaluating their skills. But there was nowhere for them to escape from this hotel. It was only a matter of tracking them down on a lower level. And then, after disposing of the agents, he would have the pleasure of killing the most powerful person in the world while his brothers cheered his victory from the other side of death.

45

MAXIMILIAN WOLFF CLENCHED the radio in his hand and repeated the question. "Status?"

It felt like an eternity before he heard Kazim's voice. "A force of Secret Service agents has broken past our midpoint cordon."

"The group in the service elevator shaft?" Maximilian snapped.

"Yes."

He felt his facial muscles twitch. Even though Kazim couldn't see his tightening expression, he was certain his friend could sense his disappointment from the long pause before his reply. Finally, he said, "Do you have eyes on?"

"No," Kazim replied. "We've moved down the ladder to the elevator locked down in the basement. There are a lot of bodies: theirs and ours. The top is open. So are the doors."

"Do you know where they went?"

"Hold on," Kazim said through the radio. "We're nearly at the bottom."

Maximilian waited in silence during the excruciating seconds it took for Kazim to finish the climb. As he stared at the radio, his mind ran through the memorized hotel schematics, trying to imagine how President Clarke's guardians hoped to escape from that location. Even though the position was likely safe from the fire for the moment, the president would be behind his army's front lines, with no way for any American response team to flank his men.

It would be much like when Marcellus, the great Roman general, scouting battle conditions near Venusia with a small group of soldiers, had stumbled into an ambush laid by Hannibal. Surrounded and trapped far from the Roman army, Marcellus was killed by Hannibal's Numidian soldiers. Now the American president herself had wandered too far from her army, not realizing she would be trapped in the basement. Once he got a better report on where she was, he would turn his men around to rush back into that specific part of the basement and crush her. But while Hannibal had given Marcellus an honorable burial afterward, Maximilian had no such plan for the leader of the United States.

Kazim's voice returned through the radio. "Sir, I'm in the hallway now, and I know the direction they headed: north."

"You're certain?" Maximilian asked.

"There is dirt and blood on the carpet, leading north. The top of the elevator car's roof was very dusty in the few parts not bloodied. My shoes make the same marks theirs did. They went north down the corridor."

"All right, go! I'll shift the other men to double the cordon to the basement. When you have a specific location, let me know and I'll tighten our line until we have her."

Lowering the radio to his side, he tried to imagine any scenario where the group of surviving Secret Service agents moving away from him might serve as a decoy for the president to escape by another route. But he knew from his years on the protection detail for the Israeli prime minister that this was not how protection worked. The men and women of the USSS were trained to surround the protectee in a bubble of security, and if the protection bubble was sufficiently formed, the extra agents would attack the threat head-on. It was unthinkable that any Secret Service agents would be running away unless they were the last remnant of the president's protection bubble.

He saw in his mind the building schematics that he had memorized six months ago along with those of the other Paris hotels most likely to host the American president. He knew exactly what Kazim had described. The service elevator shaft, the ends of the hallway—both had been strategically set afire to block potential entry points by the emergency response team outside the premises. Assuming that the agents had gone down to the basement levels with the president, they would still be trapped on level B-4 or B-3 because there was no way out. B-1 was too close to the fire, and B-2 was too close to his men holding off the emergency response team. There was no way the agents could get the president past his men without a terribly risky firefight. He had the northwest corner blocked; dozens of men with automatic assault rifles populated the southwest corner; fire was in the southeast, rubble in the northeast. There was no way out, unless . . .

"Kazim!" he shouted into his radio. "They could be heading for the furnace and boiler room on the northeast side, through the maintenance door. Level B-three. The room where we first broke through to enter the building."

"The room we came in through?" Kazim gasped.

Maximilian nodded to the radio as any lingering uncertainty evaporated. The hypothetical scenario now had his full attention. "They are completely trapped. We never imagined they could make it to the basement. There is no other way out of the building from their position except the tunnel system we came through. And they know the location of our breach."

"How would they know where we breached?"

"The agents we killed when we first broke through. They were there only because they must have heard something. That could be how they made it to the roof so fast."

"But the *tunnels*?" Kazim said.

"Sweep the basement and assess their options," Maximilian said. "Then examine the tunnel breach." He glanced at his watch. Kazim was a dozen minutes behind the agents protecting the president. "And hurry," he said, doing the math. "If they were heading for the tunnels, then they're already in them."

46

WITH THEIR FLASHLIGHT beams bouncing like headlights on a bumpy road, the three agents moved swiftly with the president through the dark, narrow, musty passages. They had switched positions again: David was now in front, with John at the rear, the president and Rebecca always in the middle. Rebecca kept one hand on the president at all times, ready to pull her down or behind her and making herself a human shield at any moment. Her small but powerful flashlight was in her other hand. And she had plenty of guns and ammunition now—they had taken as much as they could, including extra flashlights, off the three dead agents outside the tunnel entrance.

David was in front because he was the quickest and surest shot. It was the most likely place a sudden threat would appear. Both John and David had a pistol in one hand and a flashlight in the other. She had given one of the extra flashlights to the president, who was doing remarkably well at keeping their fast pace.

The tunnels were more claustrophobic than she had imagined. Growing up in Colorado, she had loved the few trips her family had taken into the great caves near Colorado Springs. Her brothers and she had so wanted to leave the tour group and duck under the restrictive ropes. They had dreamed of disappearing into the off-limits vaults and chambers of the vast system and exploring like the kids in the Mark Twain story. But between her parents and the tour guide, they had had no chance of wandering off the safe, marked path. Her childhood fascination with caves was one of the reasons she had studied the Paris underground so extensively when preparing for the president's trip. Now, in hindsight, she was angry at herself for not realizing that the concrete walls and motion sensors still left an opportunity for a determined, well-organized group of assassins to strike at the US president. She should have recommended that the president stay in a different hotel, or in a more controlled location outside the city. Or closer to the ground floor, which had been standard operating procedure in the past. Or, at the very least, she should have positioned a half-dozen CAT agents in the tunnels around the hotel's foundation.

This tunnel was narrow and of darker stone, giving off only a slight reflection from their flashlight beams. She could hear running water somewhere in the walls, below them or above them—she wasn't sure. She knew that the Médicis Aqueduct passed through some of the tunnels, even flooding some levels. Some of the limestone from the old quarry had been stacked in haphazard rubble pillars to support the tunnel ceilings as early diggers carved deep caverns and passageways hundreds of years ago. In other places, solid pillars of original limestone had been left intact by early quarriers excavating the surrounding stone. An old plaque on a wall read "I6 G I783," marking the reinforced quarry wall built by the inspector general's office in AD 1783. Water droplets had formed milky stalactites on the ceiling, which gleamed in the flashlight beams.

The ground was mud in some places: slick and mushy, but not deep enough to sink into. Then, a few yards later, dry gravel crunched beneath their feet. In some places the ceiling was barely six feet tall, forcing John and David to hunch over as they ran, the rectangular passage so narrow that even Rebecca could stretch her arms and touch both sides.

Occasionally, her light picked up designs on the walls—painted pictures and symbols left there centuries ago. One aging graffito was a crude red sketch of a Revolutionary-period guillotine, drawn perhaps by an eyewitness to Marie Antoinette's death.

They passed a small chamber where glass from a broken wine bottle flickered in the flashlight beam. She recalled that Parisians even today often hosted illegal underground parties in the tunnels. She pointed this out to John. Since this very spot had likely been the scene of recent revelry, they were likely close to an exit shaft, though seventy-five feet of limestone still lay between them and the city streets.

When they reached the first fork in the tunnel, David scanned both passageways. Once he felt that it was secured, he looked back at the others for direction. John deferred to Rebecca. She pointed right—north, toward the Seine and the central concentration of the tunnel system. The closer they got to the center, the more difficult the complex network would make it for anyone to follow them. And, she also hoped, they would be less likely to get cornered, and more likely to come across one of the IGC shafts leading to the surface.

As they moved down the next tunnel, the president tripped over a slight rise in the stone floor and pitched forward. But before she fell even halfway to the ground, Rebecca lifted her back up by the upper arm, which she had held since they started their underground flight.

With barely a break in stride, the little band kept moving.

"You okay, ma'am?" Rebecca asked.

"Yes. Thank you."

"It's dark and the terrain is uneven. Hit with your heels and roll through onto your toes with each step. Run in short, steady steps and keep your weight back. Grab me if you need to. And don't forget to breathe—deep breaths. Okay?"

"Got it."

Rebecca actually felt better having the president in the tunnels. There seemed a much smaller chance of coming across the attackers down here than in the hotel—no bullets flying, no fire burning. And with David in front, she felt confident that if they came across any hostiles, he could drop a half dozen before they got off a shot. And with John at the rear, she need only keep the president upright and moving. Her biggest worry was not finding an exit—getting lost, getting trapped. But right now all she knew was that each step they took got them farther from the group of fanatics dead set on killing the president.

Not on my watch, she thought to herself. *No way in hell.*

47

K AZIM RAN WITH his men down the long hallway on B-4, covering the ground quickly. With no sign of the president or any agents, he raced up the stairwell at the end of the hallway. Looking down the B-3 hallway, he continued up the stairs to B-2. But on B-2, it was clear that both fire and gunfights were very close.

"There is no way they took the president through that," he said to his men, looking toward the noise.

He turned and raced back down to B-3.

His men followed.

Landing hard on the bottom step of B-3, he slid a few feet before coming to a stop. He listened to every detail of the sounds around him, searching. With a predator's hunting instincts, his entire body and mind were melded and homing in on what he had come to kill. He moved to the northeast corner and down the wide staircase to the open room where they had blasted through the hotel foundation. He stepped over the bodies of the Secret Service agents they had killed there. Then his eyes narrowed. He stared at the jagged crack in the wall, and the loose rubble scattered around it.

Was it possible that the surviving agents had taken the president into the tunnels? It was not something he and Maximilian had even considered when planning the assault.

But even if the president had been taken into the Paris underground, Kazim and his men could find her before she escaped. No matter how good the remaining agents were, his men probably outnumbered them at least tenfold. And he and his men had memorized much of the intricate network within a few miles' radius of the hotel, which gave them a huge tactical advantage over the agents.

But what if the agents *hadn't* gone underground? He couldn't risk sending thirty to forty armed men if the president was still somewhere inside the hotel.

Then, almost as if it were a message from God, he saw the sign that told him exactly what to do.

48

MAXIMILIAN RAISED HIS radio to his face and yelled, "Repeat that!"

"You were right! The president has been taken into the tunnels," Kazim's voice said excitedly.

"You are positive?" Maximilian asked. He had to be certain before shifting and reallocating his men.

"The dead agents in here that are close to the tunnel entrance—the ones who died when we broke through," Kazim said. "They are missing their guns and ammo."

Maximilian exhaled. Kazim had to be correct. At least one or two agents were still alive with the president, and they had stripped what weapons they could find from their dead comrades before leading her on their desperate bid for escape. He had been monitoring a USSS radio taken from a killed agent, and there had been no communications on it regarding the president's location. These remaining agents with the president were stealthy. Not communicating their location to others was smart, but it also meant they were alone. It was perhaps the type of bold strategy that Hannibal might have used, and it had already given them a head start. He would need all his focus, all his cunning, to devise a strategy to find them. He must make sure the agents got no backup, that they remained alone in the tunnels until his men could trap and kill them.

Hannibal was renowned for devising creative strategies for every new military situation his army found itself in. When a massive Roman army surrounded and besieged his allied town of Capua in southern Italy in 211 B.C., Hannibal devised many clever and perfectly timed maneuvers to attack his enemy and free his trapped friends. But when the Roman army around Capua proved too large for his smaller army to break, Hannibal, with his keen sense of honor toward any ally, devised a completely new and creative strategy: he turned and marched straight on Rome, hoping to lure the enemy away from Capua. Hannibal knew that Rome's walls were too strong for him to breach, but he marched right up to its gates anyway and began pillaging the surrounding countryside. Even though the strategy ultimately failed, it was the first time in history that a general had attacked an enemy's capital just to lure the enemy away from another location.

It was that type of bold, creative genius in military affairs that had inspired Maximilian and had led him to admire Hannibal more than any other figure in history. And it inspired him now to focus on the enemy forces outside the fire barricade and to try to draw them toward the south side of the building— away from the tunnel entrance. In all the chaos, his soldiers had captured a dozen people on the president's floor, who appeared to be part of her staff. He would now have them brought down to the second-floor conference room on the south side, where they could be easily displayed in the windows facing the street. His men could also then fire their weapons out at the area surrounding the hotel. The resulting distraction might shift the outside response team's focus just enough for him to get half his fighters back into the tunnels while still maintaining a strong reserve in the hotel. And it just might pull some of the outside

Secret Service forces away from the side of the building he was
now most concerned with defending. It might keep their focus on
the hotel while his main force left the building and returned into
the Paris underground, just as Hannibal had tried to do by luring
his enemy away from Capua and toward the gates of Rome.

Maximilian knew that he could stay in the hotel no longer.
Moving toward the double doors, he jogged down the hallway
with a dozen of his fighters. Other men, at the staircase they had
secured, opened the metal door for him. He raced down the
stairs, his web belt jostling up and down with the weight of the
equipment it held. Pulling around each corner, he had to don his
portable oxygen mask, for the smoke was thick in the enclosed
stairwell. His men had given him updates on the fire every few
minutes, so he knew that despite the slow engulfment of the
entire hotel, this stairwell was still passable.

Hurrying down the stairs, he tried not to think of the
consequences of failing his mission. His team had worked too
hard for this opportunity. And the world desperately needed a
rebalancing of power. For too long, the great military powers of
history had prevented a true evolution and freedom of the world.
The Egyptians, the Macedonians, the Persians, the Romans, and
the Mongols conquered, subjugated, slaughtered, and enslaved
their weaker neighbors. Muslim tribes attacked Constantinople,
and in turn, Christian nations responded with unspeakable crimes
during the Crusades. European empires colonized African
countries and kidnapped men for the world's slave trade,
throwing that continent into a whirlwind of poverty, instability,
and violence that lasted to this day. The United States
dispossessed hundreds of Native American tribes, displacing
them or killing them outright. European powers sparked World
Wars, East and West faced off for decades, threatening
worldwide nuclear holocaust, and now global terrorism
threatened innocent lives everywhere.

Maximilian was no hypocrite. His actions tonight were not to conquer or exterminate a people, steal land, enslave a workforce, or murder innocents out of fear or hatred or religious fanaticism. His action was for world justice—to reset the scales and give mankind across the planet a chance to evolve freely the way they should have been able to evolve before the Romans conquered Alba, the Sabines, the Etruscans, Carthage, and Gaul, until mankind was forced to combine in groups, to kill or conquer other groups, for all eternity. He knew he couldn't stop or reverse the dark side of human nature in just one night, with just one death, but as with Romulus's murder of his brother, Tullus's dismemberment of Mettius, the assassination of Nero or Tiberius, or the senate's hundred stabbings of Julius Caesar, his actions tonight would weaken America and its meddling influences in the other countries of the world.

His body felt strong as he raced down the steps. The world didn't know it, but he was its best chance to bring it back to equilibrium. And if he failed, mankind's eternal conflict with itself would only continue until someone else found the courage to succeed where he might now fail. But as long as his lungs drew breath, he would pursue his goal of striking the colossus.

He reached the bottom steps to B-3 and sprinted through the stairwell door, held open by one of Kazim's men. Having memorized the layout months ago, he turned left, rounding the corner so fast, he had to push off the wall with his right hand before dashing down a hallway only dimly lit with the glowing red exit signs in French and English. As his mind worked through what the Secret Service was trying to do by taking the president into the tunnels, he began to realize that he had much more to worry about than he had first thought. Based on the maps he had studied of the labyrinthine tunnel systems and their current location in Paris, he realized with horror that there was actually one way the Secret Service might stumble upon, to get the president to safety. It was unlikely that they would know how to find the way even if they knew of its existence, but if they did find a way to get the president out of the tunnels and onto the streets of Paris, Maximilian would have lost all advantage of this trap that he had so meticulously designed and, until now, executed to perfection.

So he raced down the hallway with all the speed that his 50-year-old legs could manage. For the first time since this exciting, immortal night began, he was terrified of missing the historic triumph that he had been born to fulfill.

49

"JUST A LITTLE farther, ma'am," Rebecca said.

The three agents and the president were jogging through the dark tunnel system, their lights glinting off the sheen of the large, wet stones that walled in the narrow passage. Part of the passageway had walls of solid limestone; other parts had been bricked over centuries ago. The older brick walls were weaker—there were stories of them collapsing when people leaned against them. The stone, however, was as sturdy as steel.

Rebecca worried that the president was getting tired. Even though she had worked only on the advance teams, she had witnessed President Clarke's life up close on many occasions. And she had seen a side of the president that the public couldn't glimpse: the tender side of a loving mother trying to raise her two children in the harsh environment of Washington politics. She had seen the brief personal moments of a wife juggling a terribly complicated and stressful job while still trying to enjoy a private life with her husband of twenty-five years. And almost from the beginning, these intimate glimpses into the way the president managed her job while protecting and nurturing her private life had left Rebecca with more respect and admiration for the president than she could remember feeling for anyone outside her own family. As divisive as American politics could be—with strong rhetoric and powerful opposing views that were sold to the American people until they, too, were hating one side or the other—Rebecca had never seen another leader as widely loved and admired as this president. When Abigail Clarke stood before the American people, she seemed to speak for everyone. And somehow, she got most of them to see that she was in this to unite a diverse citizenry and keep the country strong. A Herculean task in this increasingly complicated and dangerous world, but she admired the president for giving it her best.

They had been in the tunnels just ten minutes, and already Rebecca feared that they had lost their sense of direction. The long passageways sometimes turned sharply, other times making long, gentle curves, and even when they seemed to chart a straight path through the darkness, she still felt that they were shifting left or right over time. Twice, they had hit dead-end caverns no bigger than the Oval Office and had to backtrack and find a different path. The air was thick and dank and cold. While their footfalls seemed to travel forever and echo back at them, nothing but silence followed—it was as if they were marooned in the caves beneath some distant world light-years from Earth.

The third dead end gave them pause. Brightly colored symbols and images like modern graffiti had been painted on the wall. Rainbows and skulls and a low sun with splintering rays of orange light, and an ocean of azure waves had turned this dark, abandoned room carved out of stone into a place of reflection and peaceful meditation—a place that had been touched by humanity not so very long ago.

"People have been here recently?" the president asked.

"Maybe," Rebecca answered. "But maybe not for weeks."

"So we must be close to a way out," John said.

"Probably, but sometimes they explore for miles using maps they've made themselves, or directions they got off online community discussions."

"Online community?" the president asked.

She nodded. "Yes ma'am. I had an agent in the New Orleans field office monitoring the Web discussions on a few Parisian sites as part of our advance work, but there was no unusual traffic on the discussion boards indicating any increased activity during your visit, or any interest or events in the areas around the hotel."

"So how do we get out of here?" David asked. "Any hidden doorways? Secret passageways?"

"This whole place is essentially the largest network of secret passageways on the planet," Rebecca said.

"We keep moving," John answered. "And we keep searching until we find a way out."

They moved back out of the painted cavern and hurried down another tunnel they hadn't tried yet. It ran mostly straight for the first few hundred feet before opening into a wider room with a central column of stacked limestone, which the IGC must have built ages ago to keep the ceiling from collapsing. They ran around the column and darted into the narrowing tunnel on the opposite end of the room.

A few seconds later, they hit a fork. John turned again to Rebecca.

"I think right goes toward the river," she said. "We're still a few miles south of the Seine, but the closer we get to it, the more likely we are to find older shafts that lead to the surface."

"Okay. David, you take point."

As they jogged into the right tunnel, Rebecca could tell that the president was feeling the pace. They had adjusted their speed to hers from the beginning, but she was tiring fast. The Secret Service knew all there was to know about her health: she was thin, 120 pounds, in her late forties, and had passed the two most recent annual physicals with no real concerns from her doctor. But Rebecca also recalled from the physician's report that President Clarke wasn't managing to get in as much physical exercise as many of her predecessors—just the usual twenty minutes each morning on the elliptical machine in the small White House gym installed in the residence.

She wasn't sure how much longer the president could continue under this level of physical strain.

Her flashlight cast a stylized shadow of David onto the uneven rock walls as they rushed through the tunnel. All their lights jounced and jostled as they ran, throwing flickering beams of transient luminosity into the pervading dark. In front of them, the view remained much the same: a perpetual black distance of unseen vastness, until the moment they reached a turn or dead end. Now, as before, a great solid object loomed out of the shadows some fifty feet away, but unlike the mottled, dark-brown rock they had crossed before, this barrier was uniform gray concrete.

"No!" David groaned. Running the lead, he had been the first to arrive at each of the last three dead ends before this, and he couldn't contain his frustration any longer. The group stopped behind him. Kicking a small rock on the blocked path, he watched it ricochet off the concrete wall and land in a small mound of rubble along the side. Turning to John, he said, "This was a mistake. We never should have entered the underground. There's no way out of this place!"

"Is it solid?" John asked. "Can we break through it?"

Rebecca said, "The IGC plugged a lot of passageways with concrete to prevent unauthorized exploring. Only certain parts are walled off like this. It's mostly to keep people from entering the unstable sections."

"What side are we on?" the president asked. "Stable or unstable?"

"I don't know, ma'am," Rebecca answered.

"What does it matter if we can't shake the attackers?" David said.

"Wonderful," the president whispered.

"All right," John said. "If we stay focused, we'll find a way out. We'll backtrack to the last fork and take the path going away from the river."

"We keep backtracking like this, and we're going to backtrack right into the attackers," David said. "You know they're going to figure out we came in here sooner or later."

"They won't know for sure," Rebecca said.

"They might not have to," John said. "It's occurred to me that these tunnels could be the perfect way for them to escape after completing their mission. The hotel was burning to the ground. It may have been their plan from the very beginning to exit back through these tunnels after they're done. They obviously know them better than we do."

They hurried back down the tunnel toward the fork. Reaching it, they turned right and continued their dogged run— even faster now after wasting so much time on dead ends. They had been in the tunnels for fifteen minutes, and Rebecca didn't feel that they had made it more than a half mile. David and John were right: once the assassins realized they were in the tunnels, it wouldn't take long at all to catch up to them.

Hunching over as they entered a low-ceilinged section, they slowed their pace. David splashed through a puddle on the rock floor, and Rebecca said, "Be careful! There are vertical shafts, filled with water, that go forty feet down in some places. Even if it looks like a surface puddle, it could be a water hole that runs down into the underground rivers or aqueducts. You step in the wrong puddle, and you might never be seen again."

"And even if it's just a little puddle, it could leave a temporary trail of wet stone for anyone following us," John added.

The tunnel finally opened like a delta into a larger cavern with five separate tunnels branching out in different directions, in addition to the one they had just come through. Five choices, each leading into unknown darkness. And if they had learned anything in their failed navigations so far, it was that this section of the underground had more dead ends than pass-through corridors.

"We can't waste any more time getting lost," John said. He turned to Rebecca. "You're the only one who looked at the map of the tunnel system south of the Latin Quarter, so you're the only one with any chance of picking the right path. I need you to tell us how to get out of here."

"I only looked at the map once, a few weeks ago," she said. "And only for a few minutes. I can't remember the details enough to know exactly where we are or how to get out."

"I need you to remember," John said.

"There are too many tunnels to know exactly," she said. He had to understand how impossible it was to do what he was asking.

"I need you to remember," he repeated.

"Come on, Rebecca," David said. "You can do it."

"Please," the president said. "You have to give us a chance to escape."

But Rebecca knew she couldn't. If she had only known how important it would be, she would have studied the complex map of the tunnel network and committed it to memory. The system had evolved a lot since the Romans dug their first quarry shafts in the limestone outcroppings, back when Paris was still just a small outpost of the empire. The limestone had been used to erect columns and forums and buildings, some of which still existed today. Then, when the Romans were forced to abandon Paris and their many other colonies as their empire split in two and eventually collapsed, the world slowly rebuilt itself during the Middle Ages. And during that time, the tunnels were forgotten. But when a cave-in swallowed buildings and people in 1774, Parisians got a shocking reminder of the extensive network of tunnels beneath their city. And King Louis XVI created the IGC department to map and manage the underground labyrinth.

She remembered the history she had learned two weeks ago, sitting in her hotel room late at night, preparing for the president's visit. Every detail of the trip had been rehearsed and planned for. Every site the president was visiting had been scouted and discussed by the advance team. And then, just ten minutes before heading to bed for a short night's sleep before another long and difficult day of advance work with the team, Rebecca had picked up a magazine on the nightstand and flipped past the history of the Paris underground to stare at its map.

She saw in her mind's eye the blue line that was the Médicis Aqueduct, running north-to-south across the map. She saw the yellow clusters scattered everywhere, showing the number of solid limestone pillars and structural rock beds. She saw the grid of tunnels running haphazardly as a rabbit warren—impossible for anyone to memorize in just a few idle minutes. Some tunnels had been filled with concrete; some were unfilled but still inaccessible; some were accessible only to engineers and government inspectors. She vaguely remembered the site of the deadly collapse of 1784, the Port Mahon Quarry, and the main catacombs. And then she faintly remembered the brown line on the map, representing the one public-access tunnel that ran north-south, across the aqueduct, and zigzagged through the main catacomb—a two-mile passageway open to the public for a limited tour of the Paris underground and the catacombs. It was their best chance for finding a way back up to street level.

"We're facing south, correct?" she asked the others.

"That's right," David said, checking the compass on his digital watch.

"I don't remember this specific room, but there were only a few large tunnel splits like this on the map." She paused. "We might actually be very close to the main catacombs."

"What's the main catacombs?" John asked.

"In the nineteenth century, Paris was becoming so overcrowded that the government exhumed many of the bones from the old cemeteries. They had been burying bodies on top of bodies for centuries, and no one remembered any of these dead anymore. So they exhumed them and threw them down into the sewers at night. Water washed them into what's now the catacombs."

"The six million dead people," David said.

Rebecca nodded. "It's been turned into a huge catacomb now, with bones stacked on other bones to form the inside walls. The Parisians call it the Empire of the Dead."

"And we're close to it?" John asked.

"I think so. I think it's down that way," she said, pointing to the tunnel leading away from them on the right.

"And why should we go in there?" he asked.

"We can't make it into the main catacombs: the part open to public tours. The IGC sealed it off, with concrete, from the rest of the tunnel network decades ago. But if we get close to the outer ring around it, we should be able to find one of the IGC shafts leading straight up to a street manhole."

"Fine," said John. "Then that's our best choice."

He had needed an answer, so she had come up with the best one she could find. She tried not to think of how significant her decision might prove for her country.

Leaving the large chamber room, they entered the tight tunnel on the right. Again their lights bounced off the wet, hard rock walls. Again they hunched over to avoid hitting their heads on the low ceiling that seemed ready to come down on them and grind them into nothing.

She thought she heard a small clink of stone somewhere behind them. Not loud enough to make her stop or look—in fact, barely enough to register. At any moment, they could come across hostiles in front of them or overtaking them from behind.

As they rounded another turn, she heard David swear under his breath. He was staring directly ahead of him.

She instinctively positioned herself in front of the president as they slowed, though she knew from his reaction that whatever had stopped him wasn't a direct threat.

Rebecca could see it now: a split gate of crisscrossing bars, mounted in concrete. The bars had three-inch gaps and a double-barred door with a chain and a heavy antique padlock.

"We can't get through," David said. "And we can't just keep hitting dead ends and backtracking until we come across the attackers."

John shook the gate, then examined the lock. Bigger than his hand, it looked like something from an ancient prison. There was little chance of breaking this monster with pistol rounds.

"It's okay, Madame President," he said. "We'll head back to the main chamber and start again. We'll take the tunnel closest to this one heading in the direction of the catacombs. Eventually, we'll make it."

The president responded with a tired nod.

"No, wait," Rebecca said, moving closer to the gate. "This is right." She touched the iron bars. "This gate is right. This *tunnel* is right." She looked at the concrete placements that had been poured to hold the thick iron bars in place. "The IGC did this to block off part of the tunnel." She moved her eyes across the pattern of iron squares, then shined her light through the bars to an engraving on the next tunnel wall. "Rue Dareau," she read. "That means we're below Rue Rémy Dumoncel. The street name was formally Rue Dareau. We must be very close to the catacombs tour. We have to go through here. There must be an IGC shaft somewhere along it. The other tunnels might not go near the main catacomb tunnel—and even if they did, they would all probably have gates."

"Can we break the lock?" the president asked.

John looked at it again. "It won't be easy. It will take time and make a lot of noise. But, Madam President, if this is our best chance to get you out of these tunnels to safety, I'll *chew* through it if I have to."

As John examined it more closely, David stepped back in the direction they had come from. He knelt by the inside curve of the tunnel and trained his eyes and ears on the darkness behind them. Rebecca led the president over against the limestone wall. Then, while David kept watch at the entrance, she turned to help John with the lock.

"Can you get it open?" she asked.

"No."

"Can we break it?"

"Maybe. I'll need a rock—a big one."

She looked for anything that had been knocked loose from the limestone wall. During the past fifteen minutes, they had run across countless chunks of stone, some the size of a blacksmith's anvil. But now she couldn't find anything bigger than a golf ball. Then, at the base of the gate, she spied a crack in the concrete footing. A large corner of the placement holding the bars had broken free from the rest. She squatted and picked up the heavy piece of concrete, roughly the size of a gallon jug, and lugged it over to John.

"Will this work?"

He looked at the heavy slab. "Good job! If *that* doesn't work, then nothing down here will."

He took it from her, lifted it high, and brought it down hard on the lock. A loud metallic pop echoed through the tunnel. In the dark silence, it sounded as loud as a gunshot.

The loud crack of concrete on iron made the president jump back against the limestone wall. Even Rebecca, who had watched John's movements and had every reason to expect the sharp bang, was startled by the noise.

He raised the heavy block again for another strike. This time, she covered her ears. She heard the muffled crash and saw the spark fly from the lock when it was hit.

And still it did not break.

50

MAXIMILIAN DARTED THROUGH the jagged crack in the hotel's basement wall, with two dozen men in tow, including Tomas and Asghar: the Merchants of Death. From the scramble radio, he knew that Kazim was already in the tunnels with another dozen men, pursuing the target. His soldiers still in the building had to fight off the Secret Service emergency response teams trying to push their way in. If the president was still somewhere inside, it would give his remaining men a chance to kill her. But if she had escaped into the tunnels, holding the perimeter would delay the response teams from realizing that the chase had moved underground.

He had hoped to burn the president alive in the hotel, so that the horrors of such a death would live forever in the collective American consciousness. But even if she had escaped into the Paris underground, she would never make it out alive. He and his men had studied the tunnel maps and knew them well; the president and her protectors did not. And the dark underground labyrinth would confound and trap them in its grasp until his men could close in and finish the job they had set out to do.

While tracking their target, Kazim had dropped mini flares in the tunnels for him to follow. And with each little hissing orange sparkler that he passed, he felt his eagerness quicken. Like Hannibal, he wanted to be with his men during the battle. Unafraid to take bold chances with his own life or those of his men, he could almost taste the sweet moment of conquest as he closed in on the smaller force cowardly fleeing the battlefield.

Rounding the third fork in the tunnel, he saw no flares indicating which direction to take. He stopped. Unsure which direction Kazim's team had gone, he sent two scout teams, one led by Tomas, the other by Asghar, out in different directions to find the next tracking flare. He rarely separated the Merchants of Death, but they were both smart on their feet and could maneuver through dangerous situations.

As Maximilian waited, he reached for the clasp under his shirt. Pulling it out, he held it with his thumb on the small latch. But he couldn't will himself to open it. He had thought he wanted to see Naomi's and Eli's faces one last time, but after all the violence of the past hour, he couldn't look into their eyes. Right now he didn't need to be reminded of the love lost by death. To finish his mission, he had to remain strong. He had to focus on hate. So he replaced the clasp under his shirt and turned his thoughts to Dominik Kalmár.

He recalled their first meeting, in a glass tower overlooking Hong Kong, and their second, the next evening, in a Macau casino. He had listened to Kalmár talk about a world that had lost its moral compass. Kalmár was a man on a personal mission so important, he was willing to break ties with the other syndicates. And he was a man of power, inviting others of superior skill and dedication to join his fight. Much of what Kalmár said made sense to Maximilian—especially the need to cut the United States out of the struggles in the Middle East and Northern Africa. Maximilian had spent his entire life surrounded by hate and violence and suffering. He had long ago given up on the notion of a peaceful world. Life was a constant bloody fight. The bold and visionary ideas that Dominik Kalmár had presented for changing the world were exactly what Maximilian needed to hear. And the strategy to realize those goals was as brilliant as any ruse ever devised by Hannibal.

The noise of a returning scout team brought him back to the present. Tomas appeared and shook his head.

A minute later, Asghar rushed out of the darkness. "We found the path," he gasped. His sharp voice bounced off the rock walls. "The next flare is this way."

Maximilian waved his men forward. He would soon catch up with Kazim, and together they would run down their fleeing prey.

51

JOHN LIFTED THE concrete slab again and swung it down, but the heavy iron lock held. "I need more force," he said. "Help me."

Rebecca helped him raise the slab to shoulder height, and together they slammed it down as hard as they could. Still it did not break.

"I hear something," David hissed back at them from his lookout around the corner.

Setting the slab down, John listened as Rebecca darted back to the president and drew her pistol. Then she heard it, too: whispers bouncing off the rock walls and carrying through the moist air. They were no longer alone.

John grabbed David's shoulder and pulled him back toward the gate. To Rebecca, he said, "You have to hold them off while we get this open. They're in this tunnel and coming at us. Our noise will only make them come faster, but we don't have a choice."

"How many?" she asked.

"It sounds like a lot."

Rebecca jumped up and lifted the president to her feet. "Madam President, I'm going to need your help!" Looking at David, she said, "Gun!"

David took his pistol by the barrel and handed it to Rebecca. With both guns in hand, she hurried back to the president and moved her to the left wall.

"Ma'am, you really haven't *ever* fired a gun before?"

The president looked at her with a horrified expression. "Once, on a hunting trip with my husband and some of his friends."

"Just once?"

"It was during the campaign—more of a photo op, really."

"I see . . . Well, that's okay. It's not hard at all." She held out David's extra pistol, keeping it pointed down the tunnel, in the direction they had come. "Bottom line is, keep it pointed away from you and any of us at all times. Fire two shots; then pause to make sure your aim is still level. You'll feel a slight kick, but that's natural and won't affect where the shot goes. I'm flipping the safety off. I'll do the shoot-to-kills. I don't want you to try to hit anything, but it will really help if they see shots coming at them from both sides of the tunnel. Stick your hand out only to this rock here so it's still protected, and fire at that side of the tunnel, just before where it gets too dark to see. It'll help keep them back, but your shooting hand will stay out of their line of fire. Do it with your arms out like this. Don't try to peek out at them or see where you're aiming. Just fire down the tunnel. I'll do the rest."

"What if one of my bullets hits someone?"

"Then that's a bonus."

"But what if these aren't hostile? What if it's just a group of Parisians exploring the tunnels, like you said?"

"Ma'am, we're being hunted. Men are trying to kill you. If anyone comes down that tunnel, I'm going to kill as many of them as I can. I just need you to help make them think we have a stronger force than we really have. They don't know how many we are. John and David will be trying to break through the gate, and I'm not sure I can hold them off on my own. I need your help with this, but I need you to make sure you stay behind these rocks the entire time." She pointed with her chin at the jagged wall where the tunnel began to curve.

The president gave a doubtful nod. "Yes . . . got it."

"You can do this, ma'am. We just need to buy enough time for John and David to break through the gate."

"What if they can't?"

"They have to, ma'am, and they know it."

The president took the gun. "You said the safety's off?"

"Yes, ma'am. Just point and pull the trigger. It'll go off. Don't waste ammo. Shoot twice; then pause. Stay calm and focused. I'll be on the other side, making sure they don't get close enough to have a shot at you. If I get hit and go down, fire two more shots and then run back to John and David. They'll protect you."

"Don't you dare get hit," the president said.

"I won't, ma'am. But just in case."

"Okay."

"And one last thing, ma'am."

"What's that?"

"Don't ever tell anyone I let you do this."

The president cracked the first subtle hint of a smile since the attack had started. "I won't. It's our secret."

"Thank you, ma'am. We're going to be fine."

Then Rebecca darted back across and knelt behind the jagged rocks protruding from the right wall. She glanced back to see John and David raising the concrete slab together and slamming it down onto the lock with all their combined strength. In the enclosed space, it sounded like a car crash. They did it again . . . then again.

The loud bang of concrete on iron rattled her nerves, making it difficult to focus on any sounds coming from the other direction. Glancing across, she was surprised to see the president looking alert and ready for a fight. Maybe the aggressive world of national politics had made her a scrapper after all.

Rebecca raised her pistol and pointed it into the darkness. The extra P229 she had kept was on the ground beside her. She breathed deeply and waited.

A sliver of pink light appeared on the ceiling far down the tunnel. It grew brighter, then turned orange.

Waiting until the shadows moved and coalesced into figures, she fired a few targeted shots at a small outcrop halfway between herself and the movement. There was still a chance that these were just some French *cataphiles* poking around. Then all doubt vanished in a spray of automatic gunfire.

She squeezed three quick shots at the muzzle flashes blazing like fireworks in the blackness. Men were shouting in a language she didn't know. John and David were still banging away at the lock. The president fired twice, paused a few seconds, then fired again, just as instructed. It was time for Rebecca to show these assassins some force before they made it too far down the tunnel.

She shot the last rounds in her magazine. The men still appeared as moving shadows, but now some of the shadows screamed in agony while new ones rushed forward to take their place. The attackers' submachine guns outmatched the PPD agents' pistols, though. She popped out the spent magazine and slapped in a fresh one from her belt, then started firing again.

The assailants returned with even more fire than before, as if their numbers were multiplying there in the darkness. A bullet sent limestone dust into her face, stinging her eyes.

She fell back to the ground, blind and terrified.

Rubbing her eyes and blinking to get back her sight, she hadn't fired a shot since going down. The attackers would soon sense that she was vulnerable. Still trying to clear her eyes, she crawled back toward the wall. Something hard smacked into her forehead.

Too much time was passing. She had to warn John and David that she couldn't hold back the shooters.

Suddenly, gunfire erupted from much closer. But these shots popped instead of hissed—they were not directed toward her; they were going away.

Blinking frantically and wiping her eyes on her jacket sleeve, she opened them, and the dark world came back into painful focus. Bullets were still smacking into the walls above and around her. Looking across the tunnel, she saw the president, still protected behind the rock edge, sticking her pistol around the corner and firing away.

"Ma'am! Pull your hand back!"

But the president seemed consumed by adrenaline and the desire to protect Rebecca and strike back at the men who had killed so many of her people.

"Ma'am!" Rebecca screamed. "PULL YOUR HAND BACK!"

The president kept firing. With only twelve .357 SIG hollow-points in the gun's magazine, she had to be close to empty.

A dozen headlamp beams sliced and jerked in the darkness ahead. In the three or four seconds since she fell, the gunmen had closed the distance by half. But apparently, the president's shots had kept them from overrunning the position. Now it was Rebecca's turn. Unlike David, she hadn't gotten a perfect score in the firearms training program in Beltsville, but 270 out of 300 on the P229 certification wasn't bad.

Moving her aim in a four-point spread count to cover multiple targets, she squeezed off four shots and saw four men fall. But almost immediately, others advanced to take their place in the crowded tunnel. Emptying a magazine, she ejected it, slapped in one of her nine remaining magazines, and fired in another four-point spread. She didn't know how much longer she could hold them off.

"Go back!" she yelled at the president.

The president, having emptied her magazine, didn't hesitate. She scampered back toward the gate, hunkering low as if a stray bullet might somehow find an impossible angle around the corner and hit her.

Rebecca burned through two more magazines, but the attackers were still closing, working their way forward before ducking behind supporting columns or protrusions from the walls.

With three rounds left in her fourth magazine and fearing that they might charge all the way on the next push, she saw a small, dark object fly past her from behind. Realizing what it was, she dropped her gun, closed her eyes, and covered both ears.

The sun-bright flash beamed through her closed eyelids, giving her a dreamlike glimpse of tiny branching blood vessels. After the deafening boom came screams and groans. The flash-bang grenade hadn't hurt anyone, but it would disorient them and hold their sight hostage for the moment.

A strong arm grabbed her shoulder and lifted her to her feet.

"We broke the lock," she heard John say. "Time to move."

With her sight slowly returning, she holstered her gun, picked up the spare from beside her, and rushed back to the gate with him. The grenade might buy them a couple of minutes. David was already leading the president into the next tunnel before stopping to wait for them. After passing through the gate, John stopped Rebecca and took the three plastic hand ties from her belt. Adding them to the six in his hand, he cinched each around the gate, where the lock had once been.

"Even assuming they have tactical knives, this will slow them down another minute," he said.

As they raced away from the gate, Rebecca sensed something wrong with the path they were taking. It felt unstable. A scent in the air reminded her of industrial cleaning chemicals, but she couldn't place it exactly. And a haze of limestone dust floated in the air, as if this place had been disturbed not so long ago.

David, in front, was the first to cough. John gave the president a handkerchief to cover her mouth. The others breathed through their sleeves as they moved through the dust sparkling in their light.

The tunnel never ran straight for more than thirty feet before curving left or right into the darkness before them. The passageway was mostly narrow, but occasionally it passed through larger quarry chambers. Crudely stacked rock pillars rose here and there, supporting the ceilings of the wider caverns, and brick reinforcement walls lined some sections. Every fifty feet or so, pitch-black passageways led off from the main tunnel, carved by stonecutters over the centuries.

The screams and shouts from the attackers were now muted in the distance behind them, but the tied gate wouldn't delay them for long.

They entered a much larger cavern than anything they had yet seen. Nearly the size of a basketball court, it had a low ceiling, and small stone monuments like tombstones scattered throughout. Remnants of melted wax candles splotched the rock floor like bird droppings. The debris from religious rituals, perhaps.

Baseball-size chunks of rock were strewn along the sides of the path. Her flashlight beam caught the thick haze of limestone particles drifting in the air. The area had been recently disturbed. Something was definitely wrong.

In another dozen paces, a concrete slab blocked the path. And just beyond the slab's edge was a narrow opening, wide enough for a person to sidle through. David shined his light into it, then disappeared inside.

After a few seconds, they heard him yell back, "It goes through to another tunnel."

Rebecca placed her hand on the president's shoulder and helped her through the gap. The rock on either side of the gap showed scrapes and fragmentation. And suddenly, it occurred to her where they now were. And when she saw David standing in a wider tunnel, beside a large slab like a tombstone, engraved with French verse, she had no doubt.

"We're inside the Empire of the Dead," she said.

"I thought you said it was sealed off from the tunnel system," John said.

"It was. Apparently, the terrorists unsealed it. They must have blown the hole we just passed through."

"My God. They did that just tonight?"

"Must have. It goes right into the tour path."

"So they came from this way?"

"Yeah," she said. "Using the catacomb tour path, they could cover a lot of ground without getting lost." She looked left and saw a thick pile of rock and rubble piled up to the ceiling, blocking the path. The right fork was still open. "Can we get through this way?" she asked David, gesturing toward the packed pile.

David holstered his gun and crawled up the pile of large limestone pieces. He tried to pull away a few chunks of rock where the pile touched the ceiling, but that only sent other rocks sliding toward him and filling in the part he had tried to clear.

"It's not very stable," he said, "but I think I can clear a way through in five or ten minutes."

"We don't have time," John said. "They'll be on us again any moment. We have to keep moving." He looked right. "Rebecca, will this way lead us out of the catacombs?"

She recalled the brown line running through the tunnel map, indicating the tour path. It was long and winding, but it was essentially a single path that didn't really branch out into side tunnels. So far, they had been like rats in a maze, hitting dead ends and being forced to backtrack, but this was their best chance yet of finding a way out. She nodded.

"You're sure?" he asked.

"Left takes us toward the exit," she said, "but it's blocked with debris from whatever they did to blow that gap behind us. Right takes us north, through the catacombs and toward the entrance on the other side. Maybe a little more than a mile through this tunnel."

"It's so far," John said. "If they follow us, they'll be moving a lot faster. We might not make it."

"What choice do we have?" David asked.

"I could stay here and try to hold them off," John suggested.

"No," the president said. "We stay together."

"Ma'am, it may be the only chance of getting you out of here."

"We should stay together for as long as possible," Rebecca said. "We don't know what we might face ahead."

David added, "We need to keep the protective bubble tight, sir."

John nodded. "Okay. For now, we stay together."

With David in the lead, they continued their mad dash into the Empire of the Dead.

Rebecca felt a shiver of revulsion. Sure, this was a well-traveled tourist path during the day, but right now it just felt like an ancient crypt, abandoned in time. The walls were lined with human skulls and long bones—all stacked neatly from floor to ceiling like so much cordwood. The most terrifying haunted house in the world couldn't come close to the eerie feeling of being surrounded by so many actual human remains. Running along, she felt as if the skeletal faces with their deep, empty eye sockets and flat nasal cavities were watching her, appraising her. Still, better these than the living, breathing demons now cutting and clawing their way through the tied gate not so far behind her.

52

MAXIMILIAN SAW FLASHES of light glinting off the moist limestone walls. Stopping, he held out his arms, halting the men behind him. "Hamilcar!" he yelled down the tunnel at the distant men, still unseen.

He waited, and someone in the darkness ahead called back, "Barca! Barca!"

Waving his men on, he charged ahead. The lights ahead grew brighter, illuminating the smaller group of men, pushed like flood debris up against an iron gate.

"She's on the other side?" Maximilian asked Kazim.

Kazim turned. "Yes! We were so close! She barely escaped!"

"You saw her?"

"No, not her. But her men. They were not many. Fewer than ten."

"I wish you had seen her," Maximilian said. "There is still the risk we're pursuing a false target."

"I'm certain they are Secret Service. And those people don't run from anything unless they are taking their president away from danger."

Maximilian nodded. He saw the bundle of plastic cuff ties wrapped through the bars and holding the gate shut. Kazim was cutting each tie individually with a small knife, and he had already gotten through half of them.

"Allow me," Maximilian said, pulling out a much larger tactical knife. Its heavy nine-inch blade was designed to do anything from gutting an animal to cutting through barbed wire. Putting the thick blade between the four remaining ties, he levered it against the iron bar, jimmied it back and forth a few times, and snapped it downward to cut the four remaining ties. Then he stepped back and kicked the rusty iron. The gate swung open with a long, groaning shriek.

"Which way did they go?" Maximilian asked.

"Toward the hole we blasted to get out of the catacombs." Kazim pointed left. "Right is the path we took from the catacombs to the hotel. We've circled around to here."

"They're going back the way we came," Maximilian said. "Into the catacombs."

"There is no quick way out of them," Kazim said. "Not anymore. Both the tour entrance and exit are blocked by demolition rubble."

"But they don't know that." Maximilian looked at Kazim as it dawned on both men that victory was all but certain. "They think they're going to make it out through the tour path. This is even better than burning her alive in the hotel. We're going to slaughter the American president inside the Empire of the Dead."

53

DAVID TRIED NOT to look too closely at his surroundings. The darkness of the ancient tunnels had been bad enough, but now that they had entered this vast boneyard, it was beyond creepy. His flashlight beam jittered across a wide, square pillar to his left. Moving past it, he glimpsed a dozen lines of engraved verse in French or Latin. Probably a warning to visitors: *fear this place.*

Seconds later, he ran past a giant sphere made up of skulls and arm and leg bones. It stood to the right of the path and reached from floor to ceiling. Empty eye sockets glared accusingly at him as he rounded a left bend in the tunnel. He nearly hit his head on the ceiling, as it ramped downward before rising suddenly.

The path was strange: loose gravel lined the edges, but the center was smooth, polished rock, worn down by millions of tourist feet over the years. Rounding a hard left bend, he skidded on the slick stones and nearly fell into a wide stone monument.

He flashed his light on a shiny red object, encased in glass, on the stone wall. It bore stenciled French words, ending in

"L'ALARME." Inside was a button, below the words "ALARME INCENDIE."

"There's a fire alarm or something here," he yelled at the others running in front of him. Maybe they hadn't seen it.

"It's an emergency incident alarm for the tour," Rebecca shouted back. "In case someone has a heart attack, or something. There should be dozens of them along the tour path."

"Should I trigger it?" he asked.

"No!" John said. "Don't. No one would get here in time, and it would only help the terrorists know how far ahead we are."

As they rounded more turns, the stone walls again gave way to walls of bones and skulls, stacked like firewood along the passageway. They rose about four feet high, like a crudely trimmed privet hedge. It was the most terrifying decor he had ever seen. He couldn't fathom how many human remains haunted these endless tunnels. Occasionally, the passageway appeared to branch in two different directions, but when he got closer he could see that any alternative passageway was always blocked with barred doors, as if from an old French prison or dungeon, keeping the adventuresome from veering off the designated path.

He splashed through a shallow puddle. Tipping his flashlight upward, he saw thousands of dark water droplets clinging to the wavy rock ceiling, each seemingly ready to fall from its miniature stalactite. The air in the tunnel had been cool and damp from their moment of entry, but this was the first real sign of water.

Their footfalls echoed less here, damped as they were by the surrounding walls of bones. They rounded more turns, passed more pillars reaching the six and a half feet to the ceiling, and followed the dark path unspooling forever in front of them. A crypt appeared on his left, followed by a tombstone with Latin inscriptions, then a stone altar, then a white-painted cross embedded in a block of skulls. He couldn't tell whether the intent of this place was to honor the dead, or to remind the living of what eventually awaited them. All he knew was that he needed to get the president the hell out of this house of horrors as soon as possible.

On they scrambled, through the Empire of the Dead. David kept hearing faint snaps and clomping behind him, but each time he whipped his head and gun around, he found nothing but shadows hiding behind bones and pillars. This place made it difficult to keep one's inner bearings. There was nothing to orient them to the outside world, and he had to wonder whether they might be running in a giant underground circle.

Then he saw something new: two wood panels, painted black, each with a white diamond shape, spaced like opened doors outside an entrance. A metal screen door had been kicked in from the other direction and hung bent on one hinge. They were moving along the tour path in reverse, so this was where tourists entered the Empire of the Dead along the larger catacomb tour path.

The walls of skulls, tibias, and femurs ended, and they entered a wider tunnel chamber. They had left the Empire of the Dead behind them, but they were still in the catacombs.

The chamber ended, and David followed the others into a narrow tunnel whose floor sloped downward as the ceiling rose high with Roman arches. Then it sloped up and entered a round room with a shallow pool of clear water surrounded by a stone wall, which he nearly tripped over.

They rounded a few abrupt turns, where he was surprised to see models of ancient city ports carved into the rock, like something found in a museum. Then they passed a fat stone pillar and turned into a long, narrow tunnel only three to four feet wide. Everything echoed here, and the ground changed yet again from slick, polished stone to crunching gravel. Numbers were engraved periodically on the limestone walls, followed by a wiring box at eye level along the right side, and a strange half-faded black line stretching along the center of the ceiling.

"The way out is just ahead," Rebecca called back. It was the first any of them had spoken since leaving the Empire of the Dead. "The tour entrance has a spiral stairwell that goes up to street level inside the tour office."

But just when David found his hopes rising, he heard the president say, "What's that?"

Then came Rebecca's irate "No! No!"

David was last to see the wall of rock rubble completely blocking the tunnel in front of them.

"This isn't possible," Rebecca said, stopping at the blockade.

"It is," John said. "They blew through here earlier tonight, just like the hole that first led us into this section. We're still on their path."

"What do we do?" the president asked.

"There still has to be a way out," John replied. "How did they get in the catacombs?"

"Here," said Rebecca, first to reach the rubble. "A small breach tunnel on the left wall, just in front of the blockade. It's more of a tall hole than a tunnel. You have to step up into it."

David stepped past them and tried to move the rubble. The first few rocks didn't budge, but he finally managed to dislodge a smaller one on the side. "It could take ten minutes to make an opening to get all the way through," he said. "I can't tell how thick it is."

"Judging from how much rock they had to clear away, it could be ten feet thick."

"We'll never get through that in time," David said. "They can't be far behind us."

"Then we have to keep moving," the president said. "If they used this hole to get in, we can use it to get out."

Rebecca nodded in the dim light. "It must lead into one of the IGC tunnels. They have to have occasional access shafts going up to the Paris streets."

"Okay," John said. "We don't have a choice. Head into the hole. But we have to move faster. If this passage was part of their planning, they know it well. David, you stay in the rear. I expect they'll catch up with us soon, and we have to be ready when they do."

David nodded.

They raced into the breach hole one at a time: first Rebecca, then the president, with John close behind her. And then David. Once they made it into the wider IGC tunnel on the other side, David ran twenty feet behind them, leaving enough room so he could hear and engage the enemy before they posed a direct threat to the president.

They had just left the catacombs, but the tunnels of the Paris underground continued to unwind into the darkness before them.

54

KAZIM HAD WANTED to lead the chase after the president, but his trust in Maximilian's intelligence held his impatient rage in check. He moved with Maximilian behind the half-dozen men serving as their shields while they advanced through the dark tunnels. Their headlamps only half illuminated the shadowy underworld, distorted by the kaleidoscopic effect from dozens of lights cutting through one another.

They entered the short blast tunnel that the demolition team had created earlier that night to get them from the Empire of the Dead to the president's hotel. Now, moving in the opposite direction, it would return them to the catacombs. He stopped when Maximilian raised a hand. All the men stood in silence.

"What are we doing?" Kazim murmured.

"We need to be careful we don't make a mistake," Maximilian said. "Careful we don't miss them."

"What do you mean?" Kazim questioned.

"One of the few times Hannibal was deceived during the Second Punic War was one night when Nero marched seven thousand men in secret, away from his army in front of Hannibal. While Hannibal thought Nero was still in the Roman camp, Nero marched those men a great distance, in quick time, to Metaurus. There he intercepted and destroyed the army of Hannibal's brother, Hasdrubal. Returning to camp, Nero threw Hasdrubal's severed head into the mud in front of Hannibal's camp. When Hannibal saw the head of his brother—his only hope for reinforcements in Italy—he knew he had lost the war. Nero's march was one of Rome's greatest moments in the sixteen-year war, and his deception to hold Hannibal in camp during the march was the key misdirection that sealed Rome's victory."

"You fear we are being deceived?" Kazim asked, wanting only to continue the chase. He could almost taste the moment of his revenge.

Maximilian turned his head left to cast light on the stacked rubble blocking the exit to the tour. The men had built it while clearing the blast tunnel, just as they had built the first blockage, near the tour entrance on the other side of the catacombs. "What if they escaped through there?"

"But it's blocked."

"What if they worked their way through it and replaced the stones to hide their escape?"

"They wouldn't have had time to clear enough of the rubble," Kazim said. "And even if they had, they wouldn't have taken the time to replace it."

"Unless they wanted to deceive us."

"They are not Nero. They're running scared."

"But what if they are more than that? They've already made two clever escapes tonight: first in the elevator shaft and then into these tunnels. The other side of this rubble is the shortest route to safety. They may have known that. The open direction into the catacombs goes for more than a mile, past the dead, and leads only to another blockade like this one."

"What are you saying we do?" Kazim asked.

"You take a dozen of your best men, clear through this rubble quickly, and make certain they didn't somehow go this way. I take the rest of the men into the Empire of the Dead and follow the passage toward the entrance. If you don't find traces of them, come back here and follow our path into the catacombs. There are places to hide in there. If we pass them, they may come out and double back, only to find you ten minutes behind us."

Kazim sent one of his men up the mound of rubble to start pulling out the broken rock for other men to stack along the left wall. Even ten protectors could not easily have climbed through here and rebuilt it so quickly, but someone had to check because this was the fastest way out. Still, as Kazim frantically helped his men clear an opening, he had the sickening feeling that Maximilian was moving toward the president while he wasted his time on a false trail.

55

JOHN RACED AHEAD, gun in ready position. He hated not having a deeper shield of bodies around POTUS. But the best he could do was an agent in front, one with the president, and one in back, and this left too many open shots for a gunman, especially considering the ricochet potential.

Along with not having textbook cover around the president, they also lacked speed. They weren't familiar with this area of the tunnels, which was a huge problem. The president never went anywhere that the Secret Service hadn't been at least a dozen times to scout, plan, and, if possible, lock down. But now they were in a place they had never dreamed of bringing the president. He had no idea what objective dangers they might encounter down here. There could be deep wells, pitfalls or even collapses, toxic levels of chemicals or methane from nearby sewer systems or gas lines. This had all the elements of a nightmare scenario for any Secret Service agent, especially the agent in charge of the PPD. Indeed, if he had had any better alternative than a burning building full of heavily armed attackers, he would never have brought the president here.

And John's instincts told him they wouldn't make it in time. The long tunnel felt like their best bet, but he could almost sense the pursuers catching up. They would never make it if they kept running along this main tunnel. Sooner or later, they would have to dig in and fight.

"Stop," John said to the others. "We won't make it."

"We *have* to make it," David said.

The president stared at him. "What's wrong?"

"Listen," John said, holding up his finger in the dim light.

They stood uncomfortably in the silent dark. They had been rushing frantically through the tunnels for so long that even a few seconds' pause felt dangerous. The meager illumination from their flashlights seemed to shrink under the weight of shadows, as if a cold, dark force were slowly drowning out their last flickering hope.

"Listen," he whispered.

Only silence hung in the air. And then, somewhere far beyond the reach of their lights, came a shuffling of loose rock on the path. Someone slipping . . . someone running . . . the sound growing louder.

"You're right," the president whispered. "They're coming. We won't make it."

"I can hold them back," David said. "Keep going."

"Not even that will give us enough time," John said.

"We don't have a choice."

"We could hide in a smaller side tunnel," Rebecca said. "They might pass right by."

"Isn't there a higher chance of getting trapped in a smaller tunnel?" David asked.

"Maybe," she replied, "but it could also buy us time."

"If we stay down here too long, they'll find us eventually," David hissed. "We have to keep running straight. The more distance we cover, the harder it'll be for them to keep choosing the right direction."

"I think they'll keep going straight," Rebecca said.

"I agree," John said. "We can't keep running this way. Not when they're gaining on us like this. They'll catch us, believe me."

"It's our only hope of escaping," David said.

"One of the side tunnels might have a way out," Rebecca offered. "Our chances are better now that we're around the main catacomb section."

"It's too risky," David insisted. "We can't even tell if the smaller tunnel goes anywhere."

"We can't tell if this main tunnel goes anywhere, either," John said, "but it's the one I think they'll follow." The sounds of pursuit were growing louder. The time for debate was over. "Rebecca, pick the next side tunnel you think gives us the best chance to hide until they pass."

"Okay," she said, jogging forward and pulling the president with her. John and David followed. "If we found a small tunnel near the aqueducts, we might just find a service shaft leading out."

"The water runs through the tunnels?" the president asked.

"In some places it runs waist deep. Some lower levels of the underground are completely submerged, which is why the IGC hasn't been able to map everything. *Cataphiles* sometimes explore them with diving gear."

"How will we know when we're close to them?" David asked.

"We'll hear 'em through the walls," she said. "They're big—and loud."

At times it was difficult for John to envision that Paris—the City of Lights—was humming along less than a hundred feet above them. Only a week before Christmas, he imagined the snowy streets would be filled with the nighttime holiday shoppers and people on the way to workplace Christmas parties and dinners with friends. Up there, life went merrily along, with no idea of the desperate struggle going on here below. If he could just somehow get word out above, the French would come to their aid. After all, the French had been the United States' first true ally. It had been the French who gave their support to America during the Revolutionary War, fighting the British at sea while the Americans fought them on land. Without the French to help them, the colonists would never have broken free of the British Empire. The Founding Fathers knew this, which was why Adams, Jefferson, and Franklin had spent so many months in Paris, getting France's support. Even to this day, the Statue of Liberty stood as a reminder of the great friendship between the two nations.

He could hear the terrorists surging through the tunnels. They must be less than a hundred yards away and closing fast. He kept looking back as he ran, expecting to see men emerge from the shadows at any moment. And this time, they would have no gate to slow them down. This time, if the attackers caught up, there was little more that he and David and Rebecca could do than to stand and fight.

"We have to get away from this tunnel," he hissed at Rebecca. "They'll be on us any minute! We have to find a place to hide—a place we can defend."

The next sharp turn revealed a side tunnel. Rebecca shined her flashlight down it and saw a dark rock wall that curved left near the end. "Let me take a look," she said.

"Quick!" John said. He turned to David. "Go back twenty feet and watch the rear."

"I think I hear water," the president said, leaning closer to the rock wall opposite the side tunnel entrance.

John watched Rebecca's flashlight beam bounce down the small, dark tunnel until a bright spot grew brighter and more concentrated, as if she was nearing a dead end. Then, without warning, her light blinked out.

John's danger receptors spiked, telling him to take off running with the president and call for David to catch up with them—never mind taking the time to investigate what had happened to Rebecca. Any of a number of possible dangers could have occurred: a deep pitfall, a plunge into an underground river of the aqueducts. Whatever it was, he didn't have time to save Rebecca and the president, too—not with their pursuers bearing down on them. But something in him told him to wait a moment.

Give her a chance, he thought. *Just a few more seconds.*

Then, just when he had nearly given up hope and was ready to start moving with the president, he saw Rebecca's light appear again. It cut back and forward, left and right, down the tunnel, rapidly bounding toward him. She was rushing back out of the darkness. She whistled, which brought David back from his dark hideaway around the corner.

"It goes far," Rebecca said, arriving back to the group.

"How far?" John asked.

"I don't know. Farther than I went."

"I thought I heard water," the president said again.

"Yes ma'am," Rebecca said. "It's even louder down there. We're definitely close to the aqueducts."

"Then it'll have to do," John said.

At that moment, David raised his hand to silence the others, then stepped back around the corner, into the darkness behind them.

He was out of sight for maybe two seconds. Then he came scrambling back. "Crunching gravel," he gasped. "They're very close!"

Without a word, John reached his arm around the president's back, hooking his hand under her arm, and pulled her to him as if she were a wayward toddler, into the side tunnel. Rebecca, already in front, sprinted forward with her flashlight pointed at the wall, to light the way for both her and John. David held back a few seconds, giving them time to rush the president ahead.

The growing racket of the pursuing force bounced off the hard walls. John's eyes were locked on the ground, searching for holes or large rocks that the president might trip over. His peripheral vision followed Rebecca's movements, and his ears kept track of David's running footsteps behind them.

Soon, they rounded a sharp corner, and he saw the reason for Rebecca's light vanishing a minute earlier. The tunnel curved back straight after a dozen feet, explaining how it had been so hard to see her light from the entrance. She had made the right call: this side tunnel was as perfect a concealment as they could hope to find in the short time they had.

"Slow down—stop," he said after they rounded the bend. "Lights off! Hurry—off! If we're lucky, they'll keep to the main tunnel."

As their lights blinked out, he felt as if he were standing on a rock while floating in a thick, dark void. President Clarke leaned hard against him as if she was fighting off vertigo. The sound of men shouting and rushing down the main tunnel echoed from somewhere in the surrounding void—impossible to tell whether they were coming closer or going away.

And the only nearby sounds were the breathing of those huddled with him in the darkness.

56

MAXIMILIAN RUSHED THROUGH the tunnels with the rest of his group behind him. He had begun the night letting his men lead the charge while he remained back to avoid the first onslaught of Secret Service resistance. But now, with the initial barrage over, he felt the rush of the moment. He thought of all the great generals he admired—their courage and their brilliant strategy. All those who had died fighting for love or hatred or desperation or ambition. And he thought once again of the one who stood above them all: Hannibal Barca.

Even though many powers in the world detested America, few had the courage to act on that hatred. Just as during Punic Wars, the world again needed to force the hands of great nations. For had it not been for Hannibal's provocation of Rome in Spain, and his siege of Saguntum, the two great world powers at that time in history might not have fought the Second Punic War—a war that, by all rights, Hannibal should have won against the Roman armies.

And so now, once again, the world needed someone to throw his weight into the teetering, unbalanced power of the international stage, beginning the bold shift against the dominant power. And so, like Hannibal, Maximilian charged ahead, leading his men to the one target that would make them all live forever in history.

The thrill of battle rushed through his veins as he ran past skeletons stacked in disjointed, unholy symmetry like the remains of an ancient plague. Although he had hoped to burn the president to death in the hotel inferno, he found some consolation that she would die in a place as dark and damned as this, where her soul would drift for all eternity, lost and confused, among six million others.

They moved past the last ricks of bones, and the walls were once again dark, gleaming with the flickering reflections of bouncing headlamp beams.

Nearing the last few turns before the long tunnel that would end at the first blockade his men had built, he slowed. Whatever agents were still protecting the president would likely be some of the best in the Secret Service. He sent a few men forward to check the rock barrier. Arriving behind them, he looked at the undisturbed rubble. He hadn't been able to track footprints at the other blockade, because it was along the tour path. And although this also lay along the hard path traveled by a thousand tourists each day, there was a way for him to verify that the president hadn't climbed through the rubble.

Shining his headlamp into the blast tunnel his demolition team had made, he smiled when the evidence appeared before his eyes. At least a few pairs of flat-soled shoes had made footprints heading in the opposite direction. And he knew for certain that all his men wore military boots with lugged soles. These prints were more recent and had been made by dress shoes.

"They followed our blast tunnel," he said to Tomas and Asghar.

Leaving the main catacombs, he found the passageway, extending in a seemingly infinite maze of twists and turns, with side tunnels jutting in uneven intervals from the main route. It all was familiar to him. He saw where the demolition team had set up the first blast zone and where he had waited during the explosion. Some of the columns were thick, solid limestone, carved from the original quarry centuries ago and sturdy enough to keep the ceiling from collapsing. Other columns were of roughly stacked rocks, broken away from some ancient dig and looking more like a child's construction than something designed by engineers.

Even though he believed that the president's protectors would keep her in the widest passageway, he couldn't ignore the many side tunnels splitting off into other areas of the underground. The Secret Service men may attempt to hide in them along the way, to ambush or distract his fighters. Kazim had said only a handful of men could have been with her by the gate, so Maximilian's small army surely outnumbered whatever agents remained with her.

"They may not have stayed on this path," he said. "We need to search and clear side tunnels as we move." Splitting the group in half with his hand, he pointed to those on his left. "Follow me, but break off as we advance. Two men go down each side tunnel. Asghar, Tomas, take the first side tunnel and catch back up with us once it's cleared. We need to spread out our search. Everyone use the code words, 'Hamilcar' and 'Barca,' to prevent friendly fire."

He paused to give weight to his next words. "If you find the agents, make sure to fire at least one shot. Even if you don't have a good shot, fire one anyway. A single gunshot will rip through these long, winding tunnels, sending a signal to the rest of us that you've found them. And then all of us will come crashing down onto the cowering American president!"

The soldiers fell into formation at once, ready to follow his lead. With his gun in both hands, he stepped around them and through the narrow opening.

57

ROUNDING THE LAST turn of the tunnel, Kazim stopped dead when he saw the grated metal door still sealed. This marked the end of the Empire of the Dead section of the catacombs tour, although the tour path continued on the other side of the door for a tenth a mile before reaching the narrow stone staircase that spiraled tightly upward to the surface exit nearly a hundred feet above. The tour staff closed and locked both ends of the Empire of the Dead each night, when the catacombs were closed. This was the same type of door that Maximilian had broken through earlier tonight, near the entrance. And no one had broken through this door. It was still locked and sturdy as ever. And there was no indication that the nearby emergency call box beside the door had been triggered.

No, the president had not come this way.

Kazim turned to the dozen men with him. "Back toward the catacomb entrance," he said. "They must have gone north from the breach. They'll be trapped. We'll have to hurry, or Maximilian may kill the president without us."

He took off at a fast lope, back the way they had come—a predator closing on his prey.

58

JOHN COULD SEE that the president's strength was fading fast. No one could have expected her to keep up the pace with conditioned agents—up and down the hotel stairs, through the firefight on the rooftop, down the ladder in the elevator shaft, racing around the hotel basement, and now running around half lost in the Paris underground. It was a miracle she had stood up to the intense exertion for this long.

He had an arm around her, his hand hooked under the armpit, half carrying her fatigued body.

"How are you holding up, ma'am?" he asked without breaking stride.

"I'm okay," she said weakly. "I can make it."

But he could tell from her voice that she wouldn't hold up much longer. Not moving at this pace.

He saw Rebecca rush around the next sharp curve in the tunnel. The moment she vanished from his light, he heard her hiss, "No . . ."

Alarmed, he pulled the president back behind him and motioned for David to stop. "Kneel down," he whispered. Then, with his gun drawn, he moved around the turn, leaving David to protect her. There, caught in his light, was Rebecca, facing away from him, staring with what must be utter frustration and despair at the solid limestone rock marking the end of the tunnel.

"My God," John whispered. "We're trapped."

"I'm sorry," Rebecca said. "We have to go back toward the larger tunnel."

"No. We've lost so much time now, they'll be all over it. We can't go back."

"There's nowhere else to go," she said.

"We have to stay here. Maybe they won't find us. Maybe we can hide here and protect the president until someone figures out we're in the tunnels, and comes to help."

"You know that won't happen," she said. "Not in time."

"It's too dangerous to go back," he said. "They were already on us. We'd be walking the president right into their hands. At least, hidden back here, we have a chance of protecting her."

"We won't have much chance if they find us," she said. "Not back here. Not with their numbers—and not against their submachine guns."

He knew that Rebecca was right. The tunnel curved sharply and had uneven, jagged walls in many places, making the terrain much easier to defend than elsewhere. So they would stay and defend the president as long as possible.

"David," he whispered, "go back down the tunnel. Slow and quiet, with your light out. Scout for any men coming down it. If you don't hear any, see if you can make it all the way back out into the larger tunnel. If you make it that far, listen and try to determine if anyone's around."

"What's happening?" the president asked.

"This is a dead end, ma'am," John said. "We can't get you out of the underground this way, but this is a good place to hide you, and we can protect it as well as anywhere down here." He paused, seeing the worried expression on the president's face. "I'm sending David back down the tunnel to see if it might be safer. It's possible they passed by this side tunnel and aren't in the area anymore. It's possible they missed us. Eventually, they could come back, but there are other side tunnels near the entrance, so if David thinks the attackers are gone, we can try to move all the way back out of this cul-de-sac and find another side tunnel—maybe one that has a way back up to the Paris streets—before they come back."

The president's concerned look turned to David.

"It's all right, ma'am," he said. "They can't touch me. I'll be back in a few minutes."

Then the president, in a complete breach of protocol, reached up and hugged David as if saying good-bye to a loved one. Releasing him, she put her hand on his shoulder. David looked surprised and unsure how to respond to such an unexpected gesture.

"You be careful, son," she said. "You've made me and your country proud—all three of you. This night will be remembered forever in American history, and it is my great honor to have been here with the three of you to witness firsthand the kind of heroism that can still exist in this world. And make no mistake, no matter what happens, all three of you are heroes." She paused, visibly choked up. With tears and strength showing in her eyes, she whispered again, "It has been my honor."

All three nodded to her without knowing what to say.

David then looked at John, who gestured with his eyes toward the dark corridor leading back from the dead end where they now stood.

John watched David look right past him, to Rebecca. "See you soon," he said.

"See you soon," she replied softly.

Then, without another word, he turned off his flashlight and started back, into the Stygian darkness.

59

ASGHAR AND TOMAS worked their way slowly down a dark rock-walled corridor. Both held Heckler & Koch MP5 submachine guns across the chests. They also wore hip-holstered Beretta M9 semiautomatic pistols, and a military-grade tactical knife strapped above the ankle. They were ready to fire at anything that moved in the darkness ahead of them. To keep their eyes adjusted to the darkness, they used a slender red light stick to see their way around the many turns while reflecting as little light as possible off the stone surfaces.

The Merchants of Death had trained in southern Turkey, near the mountain region that Alexander the Great had conquered nearly three thousand years earlier. They had trained in a copper mine, using the same red chemical tube lights to practice moving in darkness. And they had practiced firing their weapons at targets in low light. And Maximilian, ever the cunning perfectionist in military planning and tactics, had drilled them until they were ready for armed combat in pitch blackness.

As they moved cautiously around each turn, creeping through the darkness while casting a faint red glow across the rock walls and low ceiling, they felt a calm that seemed almost strange after the thunderous bedlam of the past hour. Each of them had killed several Secret Service agents in the hotel, along with various civilians who had been caught in the attack. They had answered Maximilian's call to battle with eagerness. Never before had they felt like part of something so important, so powerful. And they felt enormous pride serving their leader in this great campaign against the disease of powerful nations imposing their will on the less powerful. So each time they had seen an American Secret Service agent fall during the fast, chaotic fight, they had felt their excitement and jubilation grow. For these were the great, heroic actions that had been missing from their lives.

Rounding the next corner, they heard a faint noise. They knelt, staring into the darkness. Was something there? It was so hard to see anything in this blackness.

And then, as they peered into the black void, they saw two quick flashes of light, just before they fell.

60

A T THE SHARP, loud crack of two gunshots, John instinctively covered the president while drawing his gun. Shielding her against the limestone, he pointed his P229 out into the tunnel, prepared to fight whatever threat emerged.

After ten seconds of silence, he said to Rebecca, "Cover her while I check."

Rebecca had also drawn her pistol and crowded beside him to help shield the president. "David's down there," she said.

"I know."

"Two quick shots and silence. That's how agents shoot, not terrorists."

"I know. He's probably fine, but those gunshots will have carried to anyone within a mile of us. If they aren't already close by, they will be soon."

Turning toward the dark path, he caught President Clarke's terrified expression. The general rule was to conceal potential threats and dangers from the president, but his personal connection with her overrode the normal guidelines. So with as much confidence as he could muster, he said, "Ma'am, no matter what comes at us, we will protect you."

She nodded, in what was no doubt her best attempt to conceal her concern for all of them. He knew that she could accept death as a possible cost of leading their country on the world's stage, but it was his job to see that she never had to make that sacrifice.

Turning, he plunged into the darkness.

*   *   *

As Maximilian's men split off in pairs into the various side tunnels, the numbers around him shrank from twenty-four to fourteen. The risk of friendly fire rose, and so did his fear that they might not find the president in time. Eventually, American and French response teams would figure out that she had escaped into the tunnels.

Fifteen minutes had passed since he and his men left the catacombs. Running ahead of his fighters down the narrow passageway, he felt a surge of frustration at the way the president's team continued to evade defeat. The ancient tunnel system was too complex to guarantee him victory now, and even if he found the president, he would no longer enjoy an overwhelming advantage in a firefight against her protectors in these long, tight corridors.

Never mind the suicide mission he had promised his men; he had always planned to walk away from this night alive after the president was dead. He and Kazim had made special arrangements with a small elite group within their ranks to improve their odds of survival. But now, faced with the prospect of failing his mission, he found himself ignoring even the desire to live.

The muffled crack of a distant gunshot jolted him from his reverie. Immediately, a second shot followed. Then silence.

"That's it!" he said excitedly after pausing, hoping to hear more shots. "They're behind us. A branching tunnel we passed somewhere. Move! Hurry!"

As they ran back through the tunnels, Maximilian felt hope return. The president had failed to escape, and now she was trapped somewhere, completely surrounded by his men, waiting in terror until his little army descended on her and shot her to pieces.

61

MAXIMILIAN MET FOUR more of his men as they came trotting out of two side tunnels. Because he had separated his fighters into pairs searching the many branching tunnels, he could now cross off those branches as the men returned, and thus narrow down the possibilities for where the shots came from.

The gunfire had been loud, confirming that he and his men would be closer to the source than Kazim, who may already have reached the tour section of the catacombs. If Kazim and his men were now close enough to have heard the shots, they would also be running back this way.

As he kept moving back through the tunnels, the dark, curving path seemed strange and unfamiliar. He almost couldn't believe he had just come from this way only ten minutes earlier. The intertwined passages, dark and featureless in his headlamp, were like the ocean, with no memorable marks to navigate by. He felt as if he were in a forest blanketed in thick fog, or wandering through a desert of bright, vast nothingness.

He moved fast down the winding, narrow passages.

After he had heard from all but Tomas and Asghar, he motioned for the others to move into the branch where the missing Merchants of Death had gone. He was almost relieved when he realized just how close to the catacombs the president had turned off the main path. It showed how desperate she must be. How close he must have already come to catching her! And he knew from his study of the maps that all these branching tunnels were dead ends.

Maximilian had half his men race into the side tunnel, and the other half wait just outside it. He listened once more in the direction of the distant Catacomb breach that his demolition team had made earlier in the night. The closest Kazim could be was somewhere inside the Empire of the Dead, heading toward him. He could not be less than five minutes away.

And Maximilian couldn't risk waiting.

So he checked his pistol and tactical knife and adjusted his headlamp to cast a wider beam. Then, with his dozen best remaining men, he set off after the others, into the last refuge of his prey.

62

JOHN MOVED WITH quick, silent steps. After losing his suit jacket and tie in the elevator shaft, he had rolled up the sleeves of his once-white shirt at the gate to the Empire of the Dead. He held his pistol out and forward with a two-hand grip, elbows close to the ribs. Two shots had come from this tunnel, and he had no idea where David was. He moved cautiously. David could be dead, and an army of attackers could be creeping toward him, only yards away. The full magazine of hollow-point .357 SIG rounds gave him twelve quick shots, which could do serious damage, but he would have given his pension for an SR-16 assault rifle. Even a laser dazzler, one of the Secret Service's newer toys, would come in handy, allowing him to blind any attackers, stopping them in their tracks and disorienting them while he followed up with lethal force.

Moving around another turn, he smelled the warm discharge of gunfire. He must be only feet away from where the shots had gone off. He wouldn't normally have been able to smell burned powder so easily, but the scent hung in the close, still air. Flashlight off, he moved as silently as a cat, listening for any sound that might reveal another person. After creeping another ten feet through the darkness, he saw a faint glow coming from the wall of the next turn and heard a soft shuffling. Moving closer, he felt along the wall with his left hand while the right kept the pistol trained forward.

Then the sound stopped, and the light went out. Whoever it was had also heard something. Perhaps someone else was coming, or perhaps they had heard him despite his stealthy movements. He steadied his aim and remained motionless. The silence made him anxious. It was as if each party were hunting the other, waiting for the other guy to make the fatal first mistake by moving. For ten excruciating seconds, he waited, gun leveled at the darkness before him.

Then, just when he feared that his mind was playing tricks on him in the silence, he heard a voice whisper, "It's me."

John relaxed. David had held the tunnel against whatever threat entered it.

"What happened?" he said, flipping his flashlight back on. "Your shots?"

"Yeah," David answered, coming around the bend and into the light, gun down in ready position. "Two men. They were making their way down the tunnel."

John moved forward and saw two bodies on the floor of the tunnel. Their guns had been removed, and it looked as if David had been rifling their pockets for anything else of tactical use. He was holding the men's headlamps.

"Just these two," John muttered. "They must have split up their men to scour the branching tunnels. It's a good strategy. Down here, even one gunshot may as well be a signal flare to the others."

"I couldn't do it quietly," David said. "Not two of them."

"I know," John said. "But the others will be here soon."

"Do we fight them here?" David asked.

"No. Back closer to the president. We need to buy as much time and space as possible, and we'll be stronger if we're all together."

"We'll be trapped back there."

"We're trapped no matter what," John said. The words had a bitter taste.

Then he squeezed David's shoulder. "Son, we have nowhere else to go. But no matter what happens, we won't let these bastards get to the president. I don't care how bad it gets."

David nodded. Picking up the two submachine guns from the dead attackers, he crossed the slings over his head so the weapons would rest comfortably against his back.

Turning from the bodies, John motioned for David to follow as he ran back down the tunnel toward the president. Soon the enemy would find them, but his team was better armed now, and they had the favorable terrain of curved rock walls to hide behind.

63

MAXIMILIAN HADN'T MADE it far down the side tunnel when his light caught the cluster of men stopped at the bodies of Tomas and Asghar. A jolt of concern shot through him to see how easily the president's protectors had killed two of his most skilled fighters.

"The president must be very close," he said to the dozen soldiers crammed in front of him. More were rushing up from behind.

"Two shots and two bodies," he continued. "They didn't even get off a shot. They were taken out by surprise. At least one of her men must have waited in ambush. It means they don't think they can outrun us." He looked down at Tomas's body, coiled unnaturally after falling against the rock wall of the ancient quarry, his face pushed up against the hard limestone.

"They've trapped themselves," he mused. "And I think they know it."

"Then let's keep going and kill them," said a young soldier next to him.

Maximilian looked at the kid, whose name was Abdali. In those eager eyes, he saw the same passion for simple victory that

he himself had felt long ago. It was a time in his youth when he
had fought for Israel, before all his struggles and sacrifices had
driven him to the edge of madness after Rabin's assassination.
That madness had led him to revenge against the fanatic
nationalists who had ultimately turned Israel against him,
labeling him a criminal and forcing him to flee the country he
had once loved. But that love had died with his past life, replaced
by the hatred he now carried for the country that had turned its
back to him. They were not his people anymore, but the world
would see only the simple labels of his past without
understanding the complexity of his journey. After the president
was killed and they discovered the false evidence linked to
Israel—which was planted in their starting warehouse and tied to
the young man who had martyred himself in the hotel room fire
earlier this night—Americans would be enraged, and their
diplomatic ties with Israel would be severely damaged, if not
ruptured beyond repair. The Middle East would become even
more unstable, and the world would be without any strong
support from Western powers to mobilize in the region. Hannibal
had not invaded Italy to destroy the Roman army and sack the
great city. He had known that Rome was too powerful to be
conquered thus. Through all his maneuvering and battling across
Italy, Hannibal's true goal had always been to weaken and break
the alliances that Rome had made—usually by duress—with the
various tribes scattered across the Mediterranean peninsula of
antiquity. And so, too, would Maximilian use the American
president's assassination, and the false evidence against Israel, to
help break up the Western world's many alliances with the
Middle East and northern Africa. And then his leader, Dominik
Kalmár, could further advance their organization's initiatives
against Western governments.

His mind returned to the young soldier's face in front of him.
Abdali had a few scruffy hairs growing on his chin and cheeks,

as if he was trying desperately to become a man like all the bearded warriors on their team.

"We must proceed carefully," Maximilian said. "They could be waiting in ambush to kill more of us."

"But if we don't hurry, they might escape."

Maximilian smiled at Abdali. None of his other men would have spoken to him like this, but this inexperienced kid was more fired up from the chase than the others.

"Yes, but I can't risk so many lives only to discover we've all been led into a trap. I could send one man as a scout, though, and the rest could follow a little ways behind him. Only the bravest of the brave could take on such a task."

"I could do it," Abdali offered. "I'm fast and quiet. They will not ambush me."

Maximilian glanced at the other dark, bearded faces arrayed in the wide beam of his headlamp.

"Let him go," suggested a man with a patchwork of scars near his left eye.

A few others grunted in approval.

Maximilian looked back at the youth and nodded. "You are brave. A true warrior—like I was at your age."

The kid grinned.

"Remember," Maximilian continued, "I think they are trapped. Move fast. And make sure you fire your weapon when you encounter them. Do not let them take you by surprise. We will be right behind you, and we must know exactly when you reach them, so we can be ready. Now, go!"

Abdali turned and sprinted down the passageway.

Maximilian admired the kid's loyalty, but this was the same youthful fervor that got so many young men killed in battles throughout history. It was the same type of loyalty that he had held for his motherland for so long before his country's government had made him a criminal and an outcast—a betrayal that Israel was soon to regret.

The kid would die, he was sure of it. But it was a life he was willing to sacrifice to discover how far in front of them the president's men were hiding. He couldn't risk sending a large force into an ambush, as Caius Flaminius had foolishly done against Hannibal at Lake Trasimene. But he could tactically send one brave youth to his death. And to do so, he had been more than willing to use the same wiles, manipulating loyalty for his own ends—the same trick that had been used so successfully on him during his own vulnerable, idealistic youth.

But as his men began jogging carefully behind the kid, it occurred to Maximilian that he may have miscalculated. Abdali was much faster than he had imagined—perhaps from his eagerness to prove himself as a soldier. The courage of youth knew no bounds. And in just twenty seconds, the faded rim of light from the kid's headlamp had vanished into the dark, serpentine tunnel.

There was danger if Abdali should reach the president too far ahead of the main force, for it would damage the timing of his men's attack.

Yelling for his men to move faster, he cursed himself for neglecting to caution the boy not to get too far ahead of the group. It was the one thing that might give the Americans enough warning of his movement—a mistake that Hannibal would never have made. It was the one thing that could ruin his tactical surprise.

Desperate to maintain the element of surprise, he raced as fast as he could without stumbling. The president's death would set geopolitical events in motion and show all bullying nationalists what happened to people when their government placed its own interests above the basic needs of the rest of humanity.

His vision was only moments away from realization. One death to change the world, succeeding where even Hannibal had failed. He ran so hard that his light jounced this way and that, giving the illusion of shaking tunnel walls, as if he were at the epicenter of a great earthquake that would soon rattle the globe.

64

FEARING THAT REBECCA might shoot them, John made sure to announce himself loudly as he and David rounded the last turn before the small chamber in the cul-de-sac. And he was glad he did, because the first thing he saw in his light beam after rounding the last bend was Rebecca's gun muzzle, aimed at his forehead. She was in front of the president, who was tucked into a ball against the solid limestone bed at the end of the tunnel.

"David?" she yelled.

"Right here," he said. "I brought you something." He tossed her one of the attackers' headlamps.

"What's happening?" the president asked.

"I'm sorry, ma'am," John said, "We're trapped. Two men came down the tunnel. David took them out, but more will come. We're out of options. David and I will take position just outside this chamber to hold them off as long as we can. Rebecca will stay here to protect you if they break through us."

"How many?" she asked.

"Dozens."

"There are no other options?" the president asked. "We can't fight through them?"

"The tunnel's too long, ma'am. We're cut off. Back here, we at least have some protection from the bends in the passage to form a defense."

"We don't have long," David said.

"Can you hold them back?" the president asked.

John wanted to lie to her. He wanted to tell her that they would prevail, that their training alone was enough to make up for how outnumbered and outgunned they were. He wanted to tell her that he would protect her, just as every detail had protected every president since that tragic day in late November 1963. But he knew that in this dark hour, he should tell her the truth.

"Can you hold them back?" the president repeated.

"No, ma'am," he said, saddened by his admission of the truth. "Not with their numbers and weapons, not in a place like this. Eventually, they'll break through."

Neither David nor Rebecca said a word. They seemed to have already sensed what John had just described. It was the president who seemed surprised. Her unwavering faith in the Secret Service shone in her eyes as she looked back at John with the determination of an executive officer trying to exert control amid chaos.

"You have my faith to the end, John," she said. "You and Rebecca and David."

"Thank you, Madam President. We'll do everything we can to protect you."

Turning from her, he looked at David. "Take position over there," he said, nodding toward the right side of the chamber entrance. To Rebecca, he said, "Take her to the back wall on the left side. It should provide some cover if David and I can't hold the entrance. You'll be the last line of defense."

Rebecca nodded, then moved the president toward the back.

David stood behind jutting outcrop, just out of sight of the tunnel, submachine gun barrel all but hidden from the entrance. John stepped to the far side of the entrance and knelt.

"David?" he hissed.

"Yeah."

"Shoot at anything with a light. Any sound in the darkness. Don't hesitate."

"Roger that."

"Rebecca, get her covered," he said over his shoulder.

"She's covered."

He took a few deep breaths, trying to think of anything else they might do to increase their odds. But at this point, their options were limited. They were backed into a corner with the enemy approaching, and all they could do now was face their attackers and rely on training and luck and prayer to protect the president.

"Okay, everyone," he said. "We're going to have to fight them in the dark. So lights out."

The lights blinked out, and they waited.

65

REBECCA KNELT BESIDE the trembling president, worried that her charge was slipping into a state of shock. For nearly two hours now, ever since the Crash POTUS alert, they had been on the run and in constant peril—not something a chief of state was trained for. Anyone in the president's situation would be terrified of dying, of letting down her country, of never again seeing her loved ones.

Rebecca turned on her new headlamp to give the president something to focus on in the darkness and to help her, if she could, by looking into her eyes and saying a few calming words. To tell her that the three of them would somehow find a way to hold back these killers, that the US military and the remaining Secret Service units would soon discover that she wasn't in the fire, and would begin a thorough sweep of the tunnels. That even though they hadn't been able to see it, help was on the way.

"Turn the light off," John said.

"Just for a second," Rebecca replied. "The president's not doing well." She slid her light toward the president. "Ma'am, it's going to be okay. Just breathe slowly. We have the better position for a defensive hold. And David can shoot the wings off a fly in the dark just by the sound of its buzzing. We train for things like this all the time."

"Things like this?"

"Yes, ma'am. We've even got our own French tunnel system below our facilities in Beltsville, just for this type of drill."

"You're not supposed to lie to the president," Clarke said. But the weak joke seemed to help bring her back to a less shaken state of mind.

"I'm sorry to tell you this, ma'am, but we lie to you all the time. That's also part of our training."

The president smiled. "I always suspected it," she said, coughing. "It's the 'Secret' in 'Secret Service' that tipped me off."

"Yes, ma'am."

"We're not getting out of here, are we?"

"We're in a bit of a spot, ma'am. But we'll do everything we can to protect you."

"Need to give me a gun again?" the president asked.

Rebecca smiled somberly. "No, ma'am, you've done your shooting for the day. Now it's up to us to protect you from these bastards."

"I'm glad you're here, Agent Reid," the president said. "Your father's still a police captain?"

"Retired now."

"Well, he would be very proud of what you've done tonight."

Rebecca was moved. She had always wanted to believe that she could have even a slight personal effect on a protectee, but she was never sure how much they really knew about her. It seemed strange, hanging on to that thought at this moment, but she felt honored that the barriers between protectee and protector were lowered, even if only for a moment.

As she pulled the light away from the president and moved her hand to her forehead to turn it off, she noticed something strange on the wall.

"Turn the light off," John repeated.

Her mouth opened slightly as she focused on the details of the old stone bricks, firmly set in even courses and bonded with mortar. The stone wall was gray from centuries in these dark, damp tunnels. She looked around at the walls of this enclosed chamber at the end of the tunnel. At the sides, they were solid limestone, cut from the surrounding bedrock, but the far wall, the end of the cul-de-sac, was gray stone.

"Reid! Turn off the light!" John hissed.

"Wait," she said. "I think we were wrong."

"What do you mean, 'wrong'?"

She trained her light back on the gray square-cut stones. "I think this is one of the IGC walls built centuries ago."

"So?"

"So I don't think this chamber is a dead end. I don't even think it's a chamber. I think it's still part of a tunnel that keeps going."

"What?"

"The IGC built walls to seal off parts of the tunnel. I think it continues on the other side of this wall."

The president placed her hand on the rocks. "Can we break through it?"

"We don't have anything to break through it *with*," David said. "We have no explosives or tools."

"And no time," John hissed.

"These walls are centuries old," Rebecca said. "Many are decrepit and falling apart. There have been stories of people pushing through them and falling into hidden, forgotten sections of the underground." She looked at David. "You might even be able to use your flash grenade to collapse it."

"You think a flash grenade could knock it down?" he asked.

"If you blew it right at the center of the base, and the wall was weak enough, the small shock wave might be enough to vibrate it out of place—loosen it enough to make it collapse. These things are more than two hundred years old."

"No one's using a flash grenade," John said, standing up from his post against the wall. "It would be too loud and would only bring them to us faster. And it would blind and disorient us—not what we need." He examined the wall that, up until this moment, had seemed no different from any other part of the chamber. "Looks strong to me," he said.

"It's two hundred years old," Rebecca repeated.

The bright white center of the amber pool from his flashlight moved along the wall. "Is it a supporting structure?"

"No," Rebecca said. "Columns were erected for support structures. Reinforcement walls were built along the sides of some tunnels, but other walls were built merely to seal off sections."

"How do you know it's not just a reinforcement wall? What if there's nothing on the other side of this but unstable limestone that crumbles inward and crushes us?"

"Reinforcements were used mostly just for the sides. This is at the end of the passageway, so it seems more likely they were sealing off the rest of the tunnel."

John looked back at David. "Stay there and keep watch." Then he released the magazine from the submachine gun and set it on the floor. Then, raising the weapon, he slammed the butt into the mortar joint between two bricks in the wall. It made a loud clatter, but nothing moved. He did it again. Then again.

The clamor was loud, which lent their situation even more urgency than before. Now that they had decided on this course of action, they had to get through. Rebecca leaned into the wall and pushed as hard as she could, next to where John was pounding. The president followed her lead on the other side of John. As he kept pounding at the joint between the stones, the mortar began to flake away from the wall.

Rebecca felt the wall bend slightly as she pushed. "It's going to break through," she said.

"Push harder," John said, slamming harder and faster with the rifle butt.

Rebecca wedged her feet against a lip in the stone floor and pushed with all her strength. The president, too, was grunting from her exertions. The wall bent some more, but just when she thought it would fall and collapse outward, it seemed to tighten up again and held steady.

"We almost had it," she said.

John dropped the rifle and pushed with them. Again the wall bucked and bent, but it wouldn't break.

"We're right there," he said. "Push harder."

"We can't," Rebecca said.

"David," John called. "We need your help."

Slinging the automatic rifle over his shoulder, David wedged himself between John and Rebecca, and together all four pushed with all their might.

Finally, Rebecca felt it get a little easier. The wall had bent farther than before. And then, as if in answer to their grunts of exertion, it let out a groan of its own. And the wall gave way, falling away from them, into open space. And as it crumbled, Rebecca fell all the way through to the other side. Heavy stones landed around her. She heard John and the president gasp in relief, and then David yelped in pain.

66

JOHN HEAVED AGAINST the wall, encouraged by how it was starting to bow. He was desperate to give the president a chance to escape. Then, as if in answer to his prayers, a large area in the center of the wall folded as if hinged in the middle. Rebecca was closest to the breach and pitched forward through the wall, into the darkness on the other side. Large rocks fell from above, and for a second he was terrified that the ceiling was caving in. He stepped back and hauled the president away from the falling stones. David wasn't as quick and screamed out in pain when a large stone fell on his foot.

After a few seconds, John realized with relief that the ceiling was not going to fall in on them. The large fallen stones had been part of the wall. Rebecca had been right: they were in the middle of a solid limestone bed that would erode gradually over the millennia, perhaps even form a sinkhole, but knocking down the barrier wall wasn't going to collapse anything. Through the gaping hole, he could see Rebecca—standing up, so she was okay. David was gasping in pain, and from the protrusion near his shin, it looked as if he had broken the tibia.

But the wall had been broken through, revealing a long, dark passageway—a continuation of the tunnel, as Rebecca had predicted.

Turning to the president, he reached out to pull her toward the hole. But before he could reach her, a burst of automatic gunfire erupted behind him. The sound, echoing off the hard limestone walls, with the president so open and vulnerable, was the most terrifying thing he had ever heard in his life.

Bullets pinged off the rocks, moving in an uneven line toward the president. John lunged toward her, but not before bullets found her right arm and chest. With his back to the gunman, he managed to lunge between the president and the firing.

The president went reeling back against the rock wall with a stunned expression. Blood spattered across her and John. He tried to grab her and pull her to the ground, but his movement was stopped by the sudden stab of bullets now hitting him instead, cutting through muscle and organs and overwhelming the nervous system, making it impossible for the body to react, or the mind to comprehend exactly what was happening to it.

He couldn't return fire or even hope to fight the gunman. His back was to the attacker, and all he could do was pull the president down and do his best to shield her. Bullets continued to chip off the rock wall behind them, and they continued to cut into his body, but no more shots seemed to have hit the president since he intervened. He shook from the force of each bullet hitting him. The pain was strong, but the knowledge that his body was being irreparably damaged and destroyed was more painful still. Tears flooded his eyes as his jaw clenched from the sharp, endless pain. Now on his knees, he was staring into the president's horrified eyes, hoping that the blood spattered across her face was his.

Everything moved in slow motion. He felt pain everywhere, but all he could think of was the president's face. She was looking at him so deeply, as if shocked to find him here in front of her, doing what he could to protect her. But the bullets kept coming, kept bouncing around them, kept hitting him in the back. He fought as hard as he could to keep himself upright on his knees, to keep giving her cover. And just when he didn't think he could take any more, he heard another loud chatter of automatic fire, this time from beside him. In the corner of his eye, he saw the muzzle flashes from David, lying on the ground and firing bursts at whatever was behind John. A few seconds passed. David had stopped firing. And then John realized that the attacker, too, had stopped. Unable to turn and see behind him, he just had to assume that David had killed whoever was firing on them.

His body felt strange, and breathing was difficult. His first thought, after processing his unusual weakness and imposing some concentration on his cloudy mind, was for the president's safety. How many times had she been hit? Her eyes were wide open and gazing intently at him, and for the briefest instant he had the horrifying thought that she was dead. But then she opened her mouth and moved it slightly, as if trying to say something.

"Ma'am?" he whispered. He had a whole string of questions he wanted to ask. Procedural questions to establish where she had been shot, where she was hurting most—something to get an initial sense of her condition before checking her vitals. But he hadn't the strength to say more.

"John," she replied softly. "Oh, dear God . . . oh, no." She was now looking down at him, studying his injuries.

He couldn't see what she was seeing, because he felt too weak to move or even to look down, but the pain and sadness in her expression told him everything he needed to know. Nothing felt right, and he knew that he must be a terrible mess. But the thought of dying, if that was what this was, seemed strangely unimportant. It was exactly as he had always hoped: that death would be kind enough to find him in a moment of courage instead of fear and cowardice. There were times near the end of Desert Storm when he had felt the fear of dying before he could see his wife again, and times during the last stage of her cancer when he felt cowardly about facing life without her. But most of his life, he had been brave, proud of a life spent serving his country, honored to have been given the opportunity to protect the president, and blessed to have found his wife and lived ten wonderful years with her before death took her from him. And now, perhaps, the colder, lonelier existence since she was taken was now coming to an end. This time, death would take him and give him a chance to find her once again.

Mustering his strength, he forced himself to look down and examine the president, just as she had examined him. Her right arm was bleeding badly. The shots that had hit her in the torso all showed holes in the outer fabric. But her bulletproof jacket had covered her, so she probably hadn't been hit in any vital organs, for which he was grateful. But all that blood running down the inside of her arm worried him.

"John, can you hear me?" Rebecca asked as she crawled her way back through the hole in the wall.

He didn't understand why she was worried about him. The president was hurt bad. They needed to focus on *her*.

David grunted and hissed as he tried to prop himself up against the remaining section of wall. Putting all his weight on his left leg, he growled like a wounded animal and pointed his submachine gun in the direction of the attack.

"John?" Rebecca repeated.

"The president needs help," he said weakly.

"I'm fine," the president said. "Don't worry, John. We'll get you out of here."

"Damn it!" David hissed.

"Hold on, John," Rebecca said, reaching him. "We'll take care of you."

"Take care of the president," John whispered. He felt himself growing weaker by the second.

"We can get you out, too," Rebecca said.

"Her arm," John whispered.

Rebecca paused, then turned quickly to the president. The president had seemed numb to the pain, but John could tell that Rebecca was now seeing what he had seen. It was bleeding far too badly for a flesh wound.

Rebecca jolted upright and looked frantically around the room, then picked up the machine gun that John had broken while slamming it against the wall. Her fingers moved quickly, pinching and pulling at the shoulder sling. After unbuckling it, she scrambled back to the president and began cinching the strap high on the president's arm, close to the shoulder.

"What's wrong?" David asked.

"She's hit in the brachial artery," Rebecca said. "She could bleed out right here."

John hissed—the closest sound to a cry or moan that he could give in his worsening condition.

"We have to move," David said, hobbling toward them. "I can hear them coming."

Terrified, Rebecca looked at John. "I don't know what to do," she said.

"Well, I do," John whispered. "Go."

Her eyes were wet. "It can't end like this."

"This is exactly how it ends," he gasped. "Take the president and go. She has to live. She has to . . ." Pouring out all he had in one final command, he said, "Protect the president!"

The president had grown pale, and John knew that her blood loss was severe. David, with a broken leg, would be doing good just to support himself. Rebecca moved in to help lift the president, who didn't stand up to help her but listed sideways instead. Rebecca had to catch her and prop her up again before lifting her to her feet. John gave one last look at the president as she was moved away from him, and he saw her weak face and watering eyes looking back at him. He could tell that she had little strength left and, like him, was weakening by the minute. But he also knew that the bullets now in his body would have hit her had he not shielded her. And she knew it, too. He would never know how this insane night was to end. It was not his destiny to see any parade in his honor, any medal presented to him, or any smiles from grateful fellow citizens. He would die here, in darkness under foreign soil, as the screams of the enemy ripped through the silence.

And as he watched the president being half carried through the hole in the wall by Rebecca, he knew that she couldn't be in better hands. Just when he thought he had taken the last glimpse at his countrymen, David turned away from the wall and tucked the submachine gun behind him. He put a hand gently on John's shoulder.

"Sir, it has been the honor of my lifetime," he said, his voice catching.

"My . . . honor," John whispered, too weak to say more. There was so much he wanted to tell David, but the moment was rushed and he hadn't the strength. Yet it was enough. The young man turned and hobbled painfully through the wall to help Rebecca, and John knew that as long as the two of them were together, they would somehow find a way to protect the president.

And now, with what strength remained in him, he turned to face the enemy that would soon come crashing into the chamber. His P229 still lay at his lookout post across the chamber. Too weak to retrieve it, he got up onto his knees, eyes sharp from the pain. The only thing he wanted more than to stare his enemy in the face would be to have his pistol—better yet, a working submachine gun—as they came rushing forward to end what little life he had left.

67

R EBECCA WAS CARRYING half the president's weight as
David hopped behind her, gasping in pain at every step. She
couldn't believe they had lost John, but she had no time to dwell
on it. She was the special agent in charge now, and the only one
functioning at a hundred percent. She could tell that David
wouldn't make it far. He struggled to hop with his injured leg
dangling as he leaned against the rock wall for balance. And the
president was getting heavier by the moment, as if growing too
weak to support her own weight.

Rebecca had struggled for another fifty feet down the long,
dark passage when the president went limp and she found herself
suddenly carrying all her weight. The change was too much,
pulling Rebecca left, and she toppled to the rock floor with the
president. Tucking her knees under her, she sat up and tried to
lift the load off the ground. As she pulled up, she could see that
the president's neck was limp, so that the slight lift made her
head hang in an awkward position. Gently, Rebecca sat sideways
and pulled the president's shoulder onto her lap. Pulling the
lolling head to her chest, she realized that her charge was now
unconscious. She checked the carotid pulse, and it was still

strong. Then she carefully lifted the arm and examined the tourniquet to make sure it was still tight. No arterial bleeding. Shifting out from under the president, Rebecca lifted the dead weight up across her shoulders in a fireman's carry.

"How is she?" David said, finally catching up to them.

"She's lost consciousness, but her pulse feels okay. Not as strong as normal, but strong enough."

"Can you carry her?"

"Yes," she replied. Her strong swimmer's legs took a few steps, and she adjusted her hold.

David hopped and hobbled behind them, barely able to keep himself upright. The submachine gun strung over his shoulder made a thudding sound against his back with each jarring movement. He also had his pistol holstered on his hip, with a few extra magazines on hand. And she still had her P229, with three remaining magazines she had taken from the dead agents in the hotel basement. She hated leaving the spare P229, but it lay buried under the rubble of the fallen tunnel wall.

But none of that mattered. They had broken through the wall into the extended tunnel, but at great cost. And how could they hope to escape their pursuers when they couldn't move faster than fifty feet a minute?

Still, she had no choice. The president was now unconscious and completely helpless. They had lost John. David was still strong but not very mobile. Through good fortune, she was still unhurt and as strong as ever, but what good was that in this desperate situation? She could drag the president for as long as she needed to, but the enemy would catch them. David could fight them as long as possible, but they both would eventually run out of bullets.

They were lost in the dark, trapped in a stone labyrinth far below the city, their strength fading fast. And the president was in danger of dying from blood loss.

They had lost more than they could bear. In this moment, she found it almost impossible to have any real hope. But she dug deep and pushed ahead, moving as fast as she could with her precious burden, determined never to give up.

68

JOHN BRACED HIMSELF as a half-dozen men rushed screaming into the chamber. The moment they saw him, they raised their guns to shoot. He closed his eyes to die. But a single shout froze them all where they stood.

Opening his eyes, he saw a man move through the group, parting them as he advanced—obviously, their leader.

"Special Agent in Charge John Alexander?" the man said, looking astonished. "I am Maximilian Wolff, and I was hoping we would meet tonight. You look like a dead man. Where, oh, where did your president go?" Glancing at the gaping hole in the wall behind John, the man said, "Into the rabbit's hole? Deeper into this accursed maze from which there is no escape."

John said nothing but stared at the man, hating him.

The man turned to his men and pointed at the hole in the wall. "Go after her," he said. "Take her alive if you can. Kazim will kill all of you if he isn't the one to end this. It is his right more than yours. This man here was her strongest protector. Without him, her protection is weak. I'll stay here until Kazim arrives. Now, go."

The men loped past and through the hole like a pack of wild hunting dogs coursing after their prey. And there was nothing John could do to stop them as they rushed past him, one by one, until only their leader was left with him in the small rock chamber.

"I've been planning an attack like this on your country for longer than you could imagine," Maximilian Wolff said to him. "Like General Hannibal Barca, my entire life has bred me for war with the empire that seeks to dominate the world. The Roman Republic was endlessly hungry for growth in territory and people—both new citizens and slaves. They cared nothing for what their campaigns did to those cultures they conquered. And your United States does the same thing today. But instead of territory, your country hungers only for economic dominance—which you help guard, in part, with a massive military presence."

Wolff pulled a large tactical knife from the sheath on his belt. He turned it in the light, as if admiring its workmanship. Then he jabbed it at the hole that David and Rebecca had retreated through with the president.

"Only in the last year did I identify my target. Only then was I able to start devising my tactical plans for tonight, gathering and preparing the rest of my men. I learned that your president would likely attend the economic conference, if that's what you wish to call it. To me, it was more of a war tribunal." He waved the knife in a wide circle, nearly striking its sharp tip on the rock ceiling. "We had the tunnel systems under Paris mapped so that we could adjust our plans—there were only so many places the president would stay."

He then pointed the blade at John's nose.

"And in our preparations, I studied many on the Secret Service's presidential protection detail. You see, I began my career in the protection division for the Israeli prime minister—before he was killed by a fanatic in our own country. And in my studies of the PPD, I was particularly interested in *you,* an ex-Marine agent in charge who had lost his wife to cancer. What kind of man were you? I wondered. What kind of man gives so much to his country, then loses everything important to him, yet continues to serve. What kind of man, indeed?"

John Alexander sat slumped against the rock wall in the tunnels begun by ancient Rome. His broad shoulders slowly rose and fell with each difficult breath.

"You . . . will . . . fail," he said, finding the strength to look up into the man's gleaming, crazed eyes.

"But I have already succeeded," the man said. "America is dying, Mr. Alexander. It has been dying for decades now. Your country is morally repugnant. Your educational system is broken. Your workers cannot compete with those of other countries. Your advantages in manufacturing and innovation have vanished. China will soon surpass your country as an economic power. Your wars are ill advised, unpopular, and immoral. Your politics are destructively divisive. Your class separation is twisting your society into a frustrated, angry people."

John said nothing.

"America is a disease of the world! And it will be cured! Ancient Rome, too, *thought* it was a light to the world. It deluded itself for eight hundred years. It, too, had a time of glory at its pinnacle. And it, too, died."

"America . . . is not . . . Rome." John's eyes locked on Wolff's.

"If America is so strong, then why has this night happened? Like Hannibal, I will be remembered in history as a great man for daring to take on the colossus. Your president will die tonight." He stepped closer, grinning. "You pretend that America is strong, but you are so weak, you can't even stop me from killing you!"

Wolff plunged the blade into John's abdomen.

In reaction, John grabbed the man's wrist to prevent him from pulling the knife out and stabbing him repeatedly.

"Why can't you even save your own life?" Wolff taunted. "You will die here, alone in this dark place."

"America . . . will always triumph . . . over evil," John said, his voice raspy from the struggle to keep death at bay just a little longer.

"And you think I am evil?" Wolff asked.

"Oh, yes . . . evil," John groaned through the pain, his eyes holding his tormentor's gaze.

"Then evil wins," Wolff said, amused.

John squeezed hard and dug his thumb into the man's wrist, causing him to release the hold on the knife still stuck in John's belly. And in that same instant, John grabbed the knife with his other hand, pulled it from his body, and made a quick jab out and up, slicing into the inside of his enemy's wrist to make a long, deep diagonal cut.

Blood spurted from Wolff's wrist.

John dropped the knife and released the man, who stumbled backward in astonishment. Frantically Wolff squeezed the sliced wrist with his other hand, but it continued to spurt. He seemed to realize that he didn't have long to live.

John, still kneeling, still dying, whispered with his last bit of strength, "Not . . . Rome. We are . . . United States . . . of America!"

And he spent his last seconds praying for the president's safety.

69

K AZIM RACED THROUGH the Empire of the Dead while his men did their best to keep up. As he sprinted down the tunnel, his light caught the faint white glow of thousands of skulls staring out at him from the walls. Their wide eyes seemed startled by this intrusion into their silent domain.

He sprinted ahead, out of the black-framed entrance to the Empire of the Dead and down the high-ceilinged corridor below the ancient aqueducts. On he ran, past the overlook to the Quarrymen's Foot Bath and the Décure sculptures, up a sloping passage, cutting tight turns left and right and eventually arriving back at the stacked rubble and the hole leading into the demolition tunnel. He clambered through the narrow space, leaving the catacomb tour path behind him. Arriving back in the IGC tunnels, he raced past the place where the demolition team had first done its drilling and explosions. He followed the long main tunnel until he saw a new flare by a side tunnel. It had to be Maximilian's signal to follow. He darted in.

His headlamp sliced through the darkness, its narrow beam throwing a thousand shifting shadows on the limestone walls. Soon he raced into a small chamber, and the first thing he saw was Maximilian, lying motionless beside a Secret Service agent's body. The body of one of Maximilian's youngest soldiers lay slouched against the wall. Blood was everywhere.

"No!" he screamed as he ran to Maximilian's corpse. His explosive yell echoed in the chamber.

He felt his upper back rising and falling in deep, angry breaths. With Maximilian gone, he was now the leader of their dwindling army.

He pointed at the hole in the wall. "Go!" he commanded. "Follow the president. Kill any men still protecting her, but leave her alive. She is mine to slaughter. I will be right behind you. Now, GO!"

The men rushed past him and ducked into the hole, and seconds later, he was the only living soul in the chamber. He looked at the young soldier's body, then at the older agent lying dead next to Maximilian. He allowed himself a moment of weakness to kneel down beside his fallen friend. Turning Maximilian onto his back, Kazim studied his general's face: hard, pale, empty of life so soon after passing. This man he had met years ago on the Mongolian steppes was now gone. This man who had given renewed purpose to his life had been taken from him, just as his brothers had been taken.

"I will finish this," he swore to the body, as if its departed soul might still hear him. "I will complete our mission."

Still gazing at his fallen general, Kazim slowly stood up, like a boxer rising from a knockdown, battered but still with enough strength for one last round. His strength returning, he rushed forward through the hole in the wall. His men were a half minute in front of him, and whatever men had been with Maximilian must be a few minutes farther yet. All were racing toward the president and whatever remained of her protection detail. He was the last in the procession, but he must catch up, for he must be the one to slaughter the president—for his brothers and for Maximilian.

70

REBECCA THOUGHT SHE saw an opening in the distance as she carried the president down the tunnel. She could hear water rushing through aqueducts somewhere in the walls. She had the president's left arm over one shoulder, and left leg over the other. She felt strong; she could carry the president like this for as long as necessary. But they were moving too slowly to escape the assassins, who were somewhere back there and coming fast.

David was still hopping behind her. It was a miracle he hadn't passed out from the pain. She couldn't think of anyone, other than John, who could have fought through such torture.

Together, they pushed on.

"How you doing?" he asked through clenched teeth.

"I'm okay," she said, "but the president needs help soon. And we can't move fast enough to escape."

"I could stay back," he said. "I still have rounds in the H and K. And I have extra magazines from my SIG. I could hold them off—buy you time."

"No. We have to stay together as long as possible."

"We'll never make it out like this."

"Please," she said, "I can't do this alone. You have to stay with me."

As he managed to hobble closer to her, she felt how much her own pace was slowing. But she didn't feel tired. If anything, she felt stronger than at any other time tonight.

"We have to do what's necessary," he said.

"I can't do it alone," she repeated.

"You're going to have to. You protect the president, and I'll protect you."

"Not just yet," she insisted. "Stay with me as long as you can. Please."

Even though her body felt strong, she felt light-headed from the numbing bleakness of moving through these endless tunnels. It was getting to the point that she didn't know whether it was even possible to escape. John was gone. David was injured. The president was dying. And the attackers were only minutes behind them and closing fast.

They entered another chamber similar to the one where they had broken through the wall. She shined her light on the far wall and saw that it was another of the IGC walls built centuries ago. It had taken all four of them to knock down the last one, but this one had large cracks running between the stones and looked less sturdy.

"You still have your flash-bang?" she asked David.

"Yeah."

"If you throw it at the base of that wall in the center, I bet the concussion wave will loosen the wall for us. It might even make it collapse."

"Okay," he said.

But then, instead of removing the crowd control grenade and tossing it at the wall, he had pointed his headlamp away from the wall, as if noticing something else. "Wait," he said. "My God, look at that!"

She followed his light with her own, and there, in the corner of the cul-de-sac, was a steel ladder, mounted in the limestone and stretching from the floor up into a hole in the chamber's ceiling.

"Yes!" she said, lugging the president over and shining her light upward. The ladder rose up through a small roundish section cutting through the bedrock as far up as her light allowed her to see. "It's one of the IGC shafts used by the workers to get in and out of the tunnel system. This is what we've been looking for. It should go all the way up to the Paris streets—maybe eighty feet up."

She looked back at him. "This is our way out! It's our only hope! Can you climb?"

He shook his head. "I don't think I can make it with my leg," he said. "And I'll be useless at helping carry the president. We'll never make it up together. They must be close by now."

"I can't carry the president alone—not up the ladder," she said.

"You don't have a choice."

She could scarcely believe what he was suggesting. Her light beam froze on him. His face was contorted in pain, and he leaned against the side of the chamber, looking as if he might topple over at any moment.

"She's too heavy," she said.

"You're strong. Keep her close to your body. Just like when you saved that drowning guy when you were a lifeguard."

She knelt by the base of the ladder and carefully slid the president off one shoulder before gently lowering her to the rock floor.

"I'll drop her," she said.

"You won't. Use the ladder to take the weight off. Take short breaks. The shaft is small—you can use the sides to help prop her up."

With two fingers, she checked the president's pulse at the left wrist. It was strong enough.

"They'll kill you," she said without looking at him.

"Give me your gun," he said. "I'll hold them off while you get the president to safety."

"No."

"It's our best chance. It's what John would want us to do."

David stumbled and collapsed onto the rocky floor. Hearing him fall, she rushed over to him.

"You have to make it," she pleaded, her voice cracking.

"I can't," he rasped. In his momentarily lost stare, she could see that he was accepting in his mind the near certainty of approaching death. "I'm sorry, Becky."

"Please," she murmured.

But even as she said this, she knew he was right. The assassins were surely very close, and while climbing the ladder, she and the president would be sitting ducks. The smart move was for David to stay here and protect her as long as possible while she hauled the president to safety. But it was a devastating realization. It was hard to let go of him, to let go of everything they might have had together.

"I can hold them off for a while," he said. "Give you some extra time to make it up the ladder. There has to be an opening to the street up there somewhere. The ladder will take you there."

"I'm terrified . . . What if I drop her?"

"This is the only way. Keep the headlamp, but give me your flashlight. I can use it to confuse the attackers."

Rebecca felt an ache in her chest. The past few hours had been an adrenaline-fueled dream where half of what she had done and felt was conditioned in her from training. But nothing had prepared her for what was happening in this moment. David was ready to give his life, but she wasn't sure she could let him go.

"Becky, please. Now, or it'll be too late."

He was right. Throwing her arms around his neck, she gave him the most impassioned one-second kiss of her life.

"I'm so sorry," he said. "It's up to you now. I'll hold them off as long as I can. You're the last one left—protect the president!"

She pulled her Mini Maglite off her belt and handed it to him, then jumped up and hurried back to where President Clarke still lay unconscious.

Reaching under the uninjured arm, she tried to pin the president between her and the ladder. It was awkward trying to lift the body past the first few rungs with her. The president weighed 120 not counting clothes and Kevlar, and her dead weight felt like twice that.

The ladder went up through a dark hole in the eight-foot ceiling, and she couldn't gauge how much higher it went. She could only pray that it led up to another passageway or—she scarcely dared hope—up to a Paris street. She tried to slide the president's bottom against the ladder. By sandwiching the unconscious woman between her and the ladder, with her arms reaching under each arm to hold the rungs, she wriggled her knees in under the president's thighs and worked first one foot and then the other up to the next rung, then pushed till she could ease the president's buttocks back onto the next rung. It was awkward and difficult, and after struggling to climb up the first five rungs, she realized it was more than she could do.

"This isn't working," she said.

"You have to make it work," David said.

She tried something else—something she hadn't done in years. Sidling her body next to the president's, she reached her right arm across the neck and under the left arm, hooking her hand under the armpit and pulling her tightly to her side. It was the way she had been taught in lifesaving class when swimming in a sidestroke with an unconscious swimmer—the same stroke she had used when saving the drowning swimmer before she left for college. The lifeguard hold now kept her left arm completely free, but instead of swimming with an unconscious body buoyed up by the water, she had to haul it up a ladder.

But it seemed to work. She moved up one rung on the ladder. Then another. President Clarke's body felt heavy, but she had to tense up and lift up for only a few seconds, one rung at a time, then pause twice that time before lifting again. During the pauses, Rebecca could shove the president's backside onto the rung to take much of the weight off her arm. These brief pauses gave her arm just enough rest before she hauled them both up to the next rung.

She had just reached the ceiling and was about to continue up through the tunnel. During her final pause before rising up into the dark vertical shaft above the roof, she looked back at David. Through a panting breath, she said, "You find a way to stay alive, you hear me?"

He nodded but said nothing.

Then she continued the slow, painful slog upward. Pushing into the darkness above, she feared she would never see David again. Leaving him was the most painful thing she had ever done, but she had to bury her emotions and focus on the job.

And with each pull up to a new rung, she relived the agony of each desperate stroke from ten years ago on Lake Dillon. Back then, she had wanted so badly to give up, to let the heavy burden go so that she wouldn't also drown. But even back then she had sensed the responsibility to save a life. And no matter how heavy the victim or how tired she felt or how much the water tried to pull her under, she couldn't let them go.

She had been half delirious when fresh arms had grabbed her near the shore and lifted her and the swimmer from the cold water.

The dark, moist tunnel well was quiet except for the sound of dripping water and the soft *thunk* of her shoes hitting each rung. The president's legs and arms dangled free, gently bouncing against the ladder as she climbed. Her mind was a blur. Her burning muscles begged for relief. She had pulled the president up maybe twenty feet now, with no end in sight and no real hope of ever getting there. But she kept going. No matter how long this agony lasted, she couldn't let go.

71

DAVID WATCHED AS Rebecca's feet vanished up into the dark shaft. He felt the tears well in his eyes, knowing they would never see each other again.

He stood slowly up on his good leg and hobbled to the right corner of the chamber. Turning on one of the Mini Maglites, he set it on the ground and pointed it toward the entrance. Then he hobbled to the wall just inside the entrance, and placed Rebecca's Mini Mag on the ground, also pointing at the spot where the men would enter the chamber. Then he hopped back to the far side of the chamber, sat down on the ground with his guns around him, and turned off his headlamp.

There he waited for the enemy horde to enter the small chamber. The room gave no cover but that of the darkness. Sitting up with his legs stretched out in front of him on the rock floor, he awaited his death. He could hear it coming, its many voices now echoing down the stone passageway. It dawned on him that he was far from home, in a single giant tomb built by people long dead. He couldn't image a lonelier place to meet his end. His thoughts flashed briefly to his grandfather on his deathbed, weakened and dying and surrounded by family and friends until the very end, saying good-bye to everyone who arrived in time, before slipping peacefully into eternity. Eight-year-old David, unable to understand death, had cried for days after his grandfather was gone. But now, sitting injured and alone near the catacombs, somewhere far below the City of Lights and waiting for his enemy to rush out of the dark passageways and tear him to pieces, he realized that his grandfather had had the best possible death that anyone could hope for in this life.

He laid his pistol flat between his knees, then set Rebecca's gun next to it. She had given him her last three magazines, and he stacked them next to his remaining two. He turned his headlight on briefly to check the assault rifle and found that it had fewer rounds remaining than a single pistol magazine. He set it beside him. Two P229 pistols, fully loaded with .357 SIG hollow points, and five extra magazines. Eighty-six rounds, against an unknown number of men with fully automatic weapons. He would be lucky if he lasted ten seconds and killed more than a few.

He turned his headlight off again. Strangely, at this moment it felt supremely natural to do what he was about to do. He prayed—for speed and accuracy in his shots, and for a quick death after he was overrun. Then, opening his eyes, he focused on the spotlighted entrance and began preparing to kill as many as he possibly could. Nothing was going to make it through the chamber entrance as long as he had bullets to fire.

He would need to fire quickly and accurately, and he would need to load new magazines fast. It wouldn't be easy. His legs were stretched straight out in front of him, and he could feel his injured foot going numb. He was cold and tired and light-headed. But he had enough adrenaline firing through him to do what he soon must do.

The clomping and clattering was growing louder, and he could tell that the terrorists were only seconds away from reaching the chamber. His chest heaved from the anticipation. Everything that had happened to him in his life, it seemed, had been fate's way of preparing him for what was about to happen. This was his moment, the true purpose of his entire life, and he would give it all he had.

Two men rushed into the room. He fired two shots, dropping them both. Then five more rushed in right behind them. He fired the remaining eleven shots, killing all of them, then picked up the second pistol. The next man paused in the shadows of the entrance, peeked around the corner, and fired a shot, breaking one of the flashlights. David fired two shots. One hit the man's hand, the other the brain stem. The dead man spun around and fell out into the open.

David ejected the spent magazine and slapped a new one into the first pistol. Then he waited. Nearly a minute passed.

He heard the rumbling of many more men on the edge of darkness, just beyond the eight bodies that lay in a staggered pile near the chamber entrance. Then, with a sudden scream, a small crowd of men rushed into the room, spraying bullets everywhere as if they expected to encounter a half-dozen men. David's eyes widened. His odds of living another thirty seconds were slim. There were simply too many fighters, coming too fast. He felt neither terrified nor especially brave, as if his awareness had no room for emotions. Even thoughts of dying were gone from his mind except in the most abstract sense. All that existed for him were individual threats, to be neutralized as fast and economically as possible. Target—*pop.* New target—*pop.* Threat to the president—*pop.* He was dropping the men as fast as they rushed around the corner, each shot a kill.

But it didn't seem to matter how many men he killed. More kept coming.

The onslaught came faster now, as if each new man rushing into the chamber recognized the urgency required to avoid adding himself to the growing pile of corpses by the entrance. And each man was getting closer before dying.

Then a bullet hit David's left shoulder and knocked him back against the ground. His left arm no longer worked, and it hurt like hell. Sitting halfway up, he emptied the magazine, and more attackers went down, including the one who had shot him. And on they came. Unable to use his left arm, he released the empty magazine, set the pistol down, and reached for a fresh magazine. But with more men rushing around the corner, he had no time to reload. So he fell to his back, grabbed up the submachine gun beside him, and held the trigger, ripping the air with a jackhammer sound and hitting two more men before killing a third, who came at him from only ten feet away. Then it, too, clicked empty.

Sitting up, he put Rebecca's loaded pistol and the last magazine in his lap and, leaving his empty gun, scooted backward along the rock floor, toward the far wall of the ancient chamber. He was halfway there when two more men burst into the chamber. Forced to stop, he fired, killing both, but not before a bullet hit him in the side. Wheezing and blinking, he was determined to give Rebecca as much extra time as he could before he died.

He fired a few more shots at the next two men rushing through the opening, but then the pistol clicked empty. Ejecting the magazine, he wedged the gun upside down between his knees to slap in the last magazine. It slid into place as four more men rushed around the corner, firing. A bullet clipped his ear, another sliced into the side of his neck, and another shattered his left collarbone. Wincing from the sudden confusion of pain all over his body, he fell back to the dirt. The room felt smaller and louder as more men rushed in. Unable to look up and see them right away, he blindly fired the last magazine toward the sound.

He knew he had little time left. He had done everything possible to delay the men's entrance into the room, to give

Rebecca more time to get the president to safety. He tried to squeeze the trigger again, but it wouldn't budge. The action was open, ready to chamber a round that he didn't have. All his magazines were empty. He was finished.

A half-dozen men were now rushing into the room, coming at him like a horde of barbarians, eager to tear him to pieces. They were close now. He had only seconds left.

Then Rebecca's last words before leaving him here seemed to echo in his ears: "*You find a way to stay alive, you hear me?*"

And so, as the enemy force came on, their bullets pinging and whining off the rock floor and ceiling and the weak wall right behind him, David dropped the empty gun, pulled the flash grenade off his belt, and flicked it against the bullet-pocked wall behind him. Wrapping his good arm over his head to cover his right ear with the shoulder, and his left ear with his fingertip, he pushed with his good leg and rolled toward the wall just before the device went off.

A dazzling flash and deafening explosion blasted through the chamber. The weak wall beside him, its mortar pierced by bullets and eroded over the centuries, cracked and buckled and fell in on David.

As the stones from the wall fell, burying him in rubble, his world went from brighter than the sun to black silence.

His last thought, his last prayer, was that he had given Rebecca enough time.

72

WHEN THE SHOOTING started in the darkness far below, Rebecca never paused. By turns pushing and hauling her unconscious burden up the ladder, she hooked one leg between the president's legs and onto a lower rung to momentarily take the weight off her right arm. After taking a few deep breaths to gather her strength, she reached up with her left hand, grabbed the next rung, tightened her grip across the president's chest and underarm, and pulled up with her right arm while pushing up with her right knee.

Using this technique, she managed to lift the president up the ladder another two feet, just as she had done for perhaps forty feet so far. And as with each of the past dozen lifts, this one, too, ended with her desperately pinning the president to the ladder so she could grab a few seconds' respite. In her exhaustion, her head jerked forward and her headlamp hit the steel rung and went out. She tried to turn it back on, but it was useless. Now she was in utter darkness, her muscles weakening. Even holding the president against the ladder was draining what little strength she had left. She was terrified of how this might end.

The sound of gunfire filled the vertical shaft. It sounded as though David was giving them hell, but she knew there were too many for him to hold off very long. The ladder rose higher into seemingly infinite darkness. Thoughts of hopelessness wormed their way into her mind, and she fought them off. The streets of Paris were somewhere up there, just beyond her sight.

So she climbed on.

There was no part of her body that didn't scream in pain. She let out a whimper but immediately gathered her thoughts to move just one more rung upward. And then one more.

A staggering explosion eclipsed the gunfire below. Only a few gunshots followed, then complete silence. It was David's flash grenade, which he wouldn't have used unless he was out of bullets. But she couldn't imagine what he might use it for, other than a desperate attempt to stun a few men before the rest swarmed in and killed him. The details didn't matter, and she didn't want to visualize the scene anyway. All she knew was that the flash grenade meant that David's fight had ended. He was gone. She was alone.

Tears welled in her eyes as she fought to keep climbing. The president was growing unbearably heavy.

She heard shouts below. Someone shined a flashlight up the tunnel, but she had already pulled the president too far up to be seen from the bottom. Then someone fired a few shots up the shaft. She heard bullets ricochet off the lower ladder and metal ledges of the tight walls below. But since they couldn't see this far up, these may just have been tentative shots, on the off chance that she and the president were in the shaft.

After the shots, more yelling echoed off the hard concrete and stone. Then she heard footsteps coming up the ladder.

She couldn't climb at anywhere near the speed of the unencumbered men beneath her. Within a minute or two, they would reach her. The only advantage she had was that, for the moment, they didn't know whether she and the president were in this shaft. As long as she didn't make much noise, they might not fire any more shots until they got close enough to discover her. With no other options, she slogged on, pulling the president up rung by rung, resting briefly after each exhausting pull but growing steadily weaker.

With so much at stake, she felt on the verge of panic. The Service had trained her to react instinctively to threats, to keep focused even in the most extreme moments of intense pressure. But those conditioning exercises on the rope lines, and the mock attacks on the training motorcade or the one-third replica of Air Force One at the Beltsville facilities, had never lasted two exhausting hours.

Suddenly, it dawned on her that the steel rungs felt colder than they had only ten feet lower. And the air was cooler. The cold from the snowy Paris night must be sinking down the shaft toward her. The street must be right there, just above them— ten feet, maybe less. For so long, her eyes had been looking down or at the ladder or studying the president, that for the past half minute of climbing she hadn't found the extra strength to tilt her head back and look up.

Now, with the president pinned to the ladder, she turned her head sideways and looked up and through the darkness at the dot of faint blue light above. It was so small and round that it looked as if the opening to the shaft were still a hundred feet above her. She could never make it that far; she simply hadn't the strength.

She wanted to scream in anger, to cry and shriek at the unfairness. She wanted to curse the heavens and renounce her God for betraying her . . . and to beg her country's forgiveness and tell her unconscious president the shame she felt at having failed to protect her.

But just at that moment, when she had lost hope, she saw a snowflake. And another—big, fluffy flakes. Only a few seconds later, one landed on the tip of her nose—a fleeting pinprick of cold.

No snowflake could have fallen a hundred feet to reach her. And it couldn't have glimmered so, like a tiny falling flare. A simple snowflake had shown her that there was a world above to climb to. For what it had revealed was not the shaft's end a hundred feet above, but the small thumb-size hole in a manhole cover less than ten feet above.

Rejuvenated by hope and focused by fear, she lifted the president and climbed higher. The pain seemed to leave her muscles as if they, too, now understood the importance of what she was desperately trying to do. The metal was getting very cold. She could now hear sounds from the street: a honking horn, voices chattering, heels clicking across cobblestones. The blue spot of light flickered occasionally as feet shuffled over the hole, kicking puffs of snow down toward her.

She pinned the president to the ladder and locked her legs to take off some weight. By holding the side of the ladder with the same arm that crossed the president's chest and under the left armpit, she freed up her other arm and reached up to the manhole, now just a foot above her. She could hear traffic and shoes clomping along the sidewalk above, and people speaking fast in happy French voices as they strolled past.

The iron disk between her and Paris felt hard, cold, and impossibly heavy. She repositioned her hold on the president to give her a little more leverage with her legs and pushed with everything she had, but the heavy iron disk didn't budge a millimeter. Perhaps it was frozen to the metal rim that held it, perhaps even bolted down to the street. Or perhaps she was just too weak from the climb to continue holding the president while dangling from a ladder and pushing up against an eighty-pound slab of metal that people were walking on.

She wanted to cry out for help through the little rectangular hole in the center of the manhole, but she feared giving herself and the president away to the assassins blindly climbing up from below. Even if her cries made it through that little hole and were heard by someone on the noisy street above, they could never lift the heavy cover and pull the president up before her pursuers reached her.

So instead, without making a sound, she stuck her index and middle fingers through the hole in the cover. Those two fingers were the only hope she had left. Her arms and legs were now quivering from holding the unconscious president. The strain was becoming too much. Somehow, she had pulled the president up this high, but now there was nowhere else she could go. Stopped by a cursed inch-thick metal plate, which in this moment may as well be the marble slab above the Tomb of the Unknown Soldier on the Champs-Élysées. Tears welled in her eyes as she suppressed the urge to scream out for help and instead fluttered her fingers through the hole, feeling the soft, cold snowflakes on her fingertips.

She felt her muscles weakening. She didn't know how much longer she could hold the president. *Oh, please, God,* she begged, praying that someone on the sidewalk would see her two fingers sticking out of the little hole that so many were walking past.

Please, God.

But no one walking past noticed her minute, desperate plea for help. She could hear the clatter of the men below, feel the jarring vibrations, as they charged up the ladder

Tears welled in her burning eyes. *Please, God, just a little help. We've sacrificed so much. Just a little help . . .*

She closed her eyes, fighting against the last fading of her strength. No matter how weak she became, she would never let go of the president. She would hold on to the ladder for as long as she could before her strength gave out, but even then, even if she couldn't hang on to the ladder, she would not let go of the president. If it came to that, she would fall to her death while still clutching her protectee, but she would never let her die alone.

With her eyes still closed, she wiggled her two freed fingers again in the falling snow of Paris. Then, as her hope faded toward the certainty of death and failure, she half heard the foreign voice of a distant deity above the darkness. An astonished voice . . . then another. And another. Something soft touched her two fingers. Fur, like angora gloves. Then cold skin. She was light-headed and half drifting toward eternal dreams when she opened her heavy eyelids and saw strange wide eyes, peering at her with excited disbelief and fascination through the little hole in the iron slab.

She put her lips to the hole. "Help me," she whispered weakly. "Help me."

Frantic French voices spoke with excited urgency as a small crowd began to work at moving the manhole cover. Something pushed in through the hole—the end of a tire iron. Then came scraping and tugging at the heavy iron lid, struggling to jar it loose.

She could no longer focus on the men in the darkness below, crawling up toward her. Her focus was on holding the president tightly to her as random citizens of Paris fought to free the stubborn lid.

Then it moved a half inch. She felt a surge of anticipation, of hope. The circular metal slab rotated slightly. Then it stopped rotating, jostled subtly, and tipped up enough for half a hundred fingers to curl under the dark edge. And her eyes blurred with tears when, together, those fingers slid the heavy manhole cover away to reveal an orange night sky above the city, with fat white snowflakes falling through it. And concerned faces came forward from the crowd that now ringed the opening.

She shifted her weight to her left foot, which was one rung higher than her right. And with the last of her strength, she gave the president one final lift of a few feet.

"Take *her*," she commanded.

A dozen arms reached down like tentacles, instinctively feeling for something to grasp. Hands tightened and grabbed the president and lifted her up and away.

Seeing those gorgeous hands lift the president into the snowy Paris night, Rebecca felt an overwhelming relief. Her protectee was out of the nightmarish tunnels, but not yet out of danger. Rebecca could still hear the men thumping and banging their way up the ladder from below. She had done all she could, and now she hadn't the strength to climb an inch higher.

Her chin fell weakly to her slowly heaving chest, and her eyes caught faint movement in the darkness below. The men below her would be here in maybe twenty seconds, maybe sooner. She didn't have weapons to fight them, or the strength to run from them. Her grip on the ladder was beginning to slip, and she realized that if she fell, she would hit the top man on the ladder. The domino effect would send her and everyone below her down the shaft to the rock floor seventy feet below.

It was the only way she could protect the president.

Her consciousness drifted and seemed to float above her body. She had pushed herself to the limit to save the president, and now all she had to do to seal her country's victory was to let go of the ladder. Her face hardened, and her breathing calmed. Memories flashed through her mind like rapid lightning strikes: watching her father come home from work in his policeman's uniform when she was a little girl . . . hiking a mountain trail with her three older brothers . . . pulling an exhausted swimmer out of Lake Dillon . . . beholding the Rocky Mountains from the summit of Mount Evans.

With her feet still on the rung, she let go of the ladder and arched backward.

Then, just as her spent legs buckled enough for her feet to slip into the open air, something grabbed her. Hearing excited voices, she opened her eyes and saw three men, lying outstretched over the manhole, holding on to her with all six of their lowered arms.

"*Tout va bien, mademoiselle. Nous sommes là,*" one said. *It's okay. We are here.*

She tried to focus her half-open eyes.

The men had caught her as she fell back off the ladder, and now they lifted her closer to the rim of the manhole. As she rose, other arms grasped her and gently lifted her out of the darkness and onto a spread trench coat on the snow-covered sidewalk. Beside her, she saw the president, lying on the other half of the trench coat.

A man from the gathering crowd seemed to notice the US Secret Service pin on her shirt. Looking at her, then at the unconscious woman beside her, he murmured, "*Mon Dieu. Le président américain . . .*" His eyes widened. "*Le président américain!*" he repeated more loudly.

Others followed his stare and gasped in turn. A wave of shock and disbelief and excitement rippled out from the crowd's nucleus as, for a moment, all the faces stared in silence at the unconscious American president, lying bruised and bleeding, with frazzled hair, small cuts on her face, and a tourniquet on one arm. She was covered in a film of dirt, which was now growing wet from the soft, white snowflakes.

Rebecca's voice broke the silence. "Cover the manhole."

Only some in the crowd even acknowledged that she had spoken. Most were still stupefied to find they had hauled the US president out of a hole in the street. No one moved.

"Cover the manhole," she said again, louder now, pointing weakly. "Close it! *Ferme-le!*" she ordered. "*Ferme-le!*"

A woman in the crowd must have registered the concern on Rebecca's face, and repeated the frantic command to a group of men around the manhole. "*Ferme-le! Ferme-le!*"

The men, prodded into motion by the woman's tone, moved as if they, too, could suddenly sense the danger.

The men spoke to each other with decisiveness and urgency. *"Dépêchez-vous! Couvrez le trou! Vite!"*

Rebecca, lying only five feet from the hole, watched the men intently. The cold snow on her face was reviving her. Something about being on the sidewalks of Paris with the president . . . something about the uncontrollable factor of crowd control with no other agents to secure a rope line . . . It went against all her Secret Service training. Something about the men who were still climbing up the shaft with the sole objective of killing her president.

The men hunched over and dragged the heavy iron lid back toward the round black hole in the street. It grated across the concrete.

"Quickly!" she yelled. *"Vite!"*

As the men reached the manhole, they paused to adjust their grips on the thick iron disk. A careless move could cost a finger. As they fought it back into position, a flash and a loud bang erupted from below, and one of the men fell back onto the street, a piece of his head missing.

A wave of screams ran through the crowd. Many scurried away, tripping and crawling over each other in panic and fright. Some stepped back from the hole but then hesitated to run as they realized that the American president still lay unconscious on the sidewalk, with only one exhausted, unarmed Secret Service agent to protect her.

Rebecca had been trained to protect the president alone as well as with a team. In training, a crowd was always viewed as cover for a potential threat, and the crowd itself as a potential threat. So she was surprised when a number of Frenchmen rushed over to her aid and frantically asked her permission to lift and carry the president away.

She nodded.

Three men lifted the president. And three others lifted her, because she had been slow to sit up and hadn't shown them that she had even the strength to stand.

There couldn't be much time before the gunmen reached the street level.

The manhole cover had come so close to sealing the terrorists' only remaining path to the president. But she had come too far, suffered through too much, witnessed too many sacrifices by others, to fail now.

With only open sky above her now, the radio transmitter David had given her would work. As the men carried her and the president away, she spoke into the radio. "This is Special Agent Reid! I'm with POTUS! Located along an open street around pedestrians! Use the tracer to locate POTUS! Armed hostiles encroaching! Emergency secure POTUS! All ops! I repeat, POTUS is open and hit, with hostiles lighting up! I need an Em Sec now!"

Seconds went by, but support was out there somewhere. Then, finally, she heard a voice from the radio.

"Reid, this is Commander Jacobs. Trace confirmed! Interception in two minutes! Hold on! We're coming!"

The tears came again. She had known they would be out there, looking for them, listening.

But just as she felt relief wash over her, a gunshot cracked through the air. One of the three men carrying her fell and flopped spastically on the cobblestone street. With the man down, the others stopped carrying her. But the three carrying the president kept going, even faster now, until another shot rang out and one of those three fell.

People ran screaming, stumbling this way and that, scrambling for cover. She had been dropped near where the president now lay, and amid the confusion, she crawled the few feet that separated them. The men who had been carrying them stayed close, some to watch over them, others to check on their two countrymen who lay sprawled on the cobblestones.

More gunshots begat more screams. Still lying on the ground, Rebecca leaned up against the unconscious president to shield her from bullets as best she could. Looking through the scampering legs from her low vantage point, she saw a half-dozen other legs, moving purposefully toward her.

The three men were only seconds from reaching her and killing the president.

As the feet came closer, she was about to plead to the few men still around her for help. Then something strange happened. Several in the crowd stopped running away. She could scarcely believe her eyes when a dozen unarmed Frenchmen ran screaming at her attackers.

The three gunmen turned toward the men and fired, and half the Frenchmen fell. But the remaining six charged forward, as if aware that their chosen course was now irreversible. They lunged forward and tackled two of the three gunmen, sliding as they fell onto the snowy sidewalk. But the third attacker seemed faster, stronger, somehow more determined than his comrades. He shot a man dead in mid lunge, then whipped his arm around another man's neck and pivoted. The courageous Frenchman fell dead on the snow.

As Rebecca watched, the assassin turned from his kills and strode toward her and the president, not pausing to help his two colleagues who were now being pummeled. Others from the crowd had sneaked forward and sealed the manhole. And others were throwing whatever they had—keys, coins, a shoe—at the last attacker still moving toward her. It was the same tall, swarthy man with shoulder-length hair that she had first seen in the hotel stairway and, later, on the roof. After all that had happened on the rooftop, she had trouble believing he was still alive.

Rebecca rolled the president onto her side, with her back to the assassin. She heard sirens in the distance—not only the high-low claxons of the Paris police, but also the rampant chirp and scream of the presidential motorcade's Secret Service team. Help was on its way, but it would be too late.

She curled her body around the president, protecting every vital part of the woman against a distant shot from this last attacker. And she prayed. She prayed that somehow, the response team from the US Secret Service or the Paris police or the military would arrive in time. She prayed that someone from the crowd would break through and be able to stop the last attacker. And she prayed that no matter what happened in the next half minute, no matter the cost, the president would somehow survive.

*   *   *

Kazim's rage had consumed him. He hated America with a fury he could no longer control. As he moved down the snowy sidewalk toward the president and the last remnant of her protection team, he cut down those from the crowd who tried to interfere. Sirens wailed somewhere in the unseen maze of Paris's streets, but help would not arrive in time to save the American president from his wrath.

He quickened his pace to a jog. His chest heaved and the muscles in his back bulged as he parried a blow, hooked the Frenchman by the neck, and turned, letting the man's inertia break his own neck. Then he fired into the encroaching crowd, dropping two more people and pushing their line back a few yards.

He had left the two men who climbed up the ladder with him, for they had not successfully fought the crowd that charged them. He didn't need their help anymore—he could assassinate the president by himself, killing her just as her people had killed his three brothers.

Trotting through the snow, he locked his eyes on the last protection agent, who lay cocooned around the president in a gallant but useless attempt to keep her from her fate. Christmas lights lined the sidewalk, dangling between antique streetlamps, adding green and red to the yellow glow. It seemed the perfect setting to honor his lost brothers.

Only ten feet away from his quarry, he stopped. Seeing the way the Secret Service agent tried desperately to cover and protect the motionless body, he realized that the president wasn't even conscious. This angered him. It somehow diminished the justice of his actions if the last words the president heard were not his pronouncement that she was dying for America's crimes.

"Is she still alive?!" he yelled at the Secret Service agent, who lay with her back to him. She lay on her side, with her forehead pressed against the president's hair so that no bullet from the direction of the threat could hit the American leader's head without first going through her own.

The agent didn't answer him.

"Is she still alive!" he roared.

The female agent seemed to cower in fear, even lowering her head slightly and pulling her arms close to her chest.

"Answer me, witch!"

"Yes," the woman said, her voice muffled by the president's hair. "She's still alive." She seemed to understand the hopelessness of her situation, that all she had fought to protect was lost, for she gave up shielding the president and slowly rolled over to face him. It was as if she now accepted the price of her failure.

And despite his profound hatred for America and all who supported its ideals, he felt a grudging respect for this young woman who was passionate enough to kill and die for what she believed in. And out of respect, he would kill her first so that she need not endure the moment of shame between the death of the one she had sworn to protect, and her own.

He waited to meet her eyes before killing her.

But when she turned around, he felt a surge of confusion at the sight of the small silvery object in her right hand.

His rage exploded. He would not be denied the glory of avenging his brothers and destroying the personification of American tyranny. His arms were spread wide, with both guns pointed at the crowds lest anyone else try any heroics. Now he swung his arms forward to fire all his remaining bullets into the female agent and the president. But before he could bring his guns around, he saw a small flash from the agent's hand.

*   *   *

Rebecca's eyes darted about, looking for the next threat. She kept the little .38 derringer pointed at the corpse of the last terrorist, even though she had fired both its bullets into his brain.

"Mademoiselle! said a young man emerging from the huddle of men who had subdued the other two attackers. *"Vous allez bien, mademoiselle?"*

She didn't respond, but just stared at the dead man's motionless face. The terror she felt from how close he had come to killing the president now made it difficult for her to believe that he was really dead.

"Are you okay, *mademoiselle?"* the man said, switching to English.

She blinked.

"Mademoiselle?"

Looking at the young man, she said, "Carefully give me his guns."

He seemed startled by this, but then nodded vigorously. Leaning toward the dead man, he moved in slow motion with wide eyes, as if death were a contagion that one might catch by contact. Carefully reaching between the dead man's awkwardly folded arms, the young Parisian picked up the two black pistols. He saw the submachine gun strapped to the man's back, half tucked under his body.

"Do you want me to try to unstrap the big gun on his back?" he asked.

"No. Just give me the two pistols in your hands. Carefully. Point them toward the ground, away from the president. Hold them by the barrel, and let me take them from you."

He did exactly as she said.

The distant sirens were growing louder.

"Thank you! *Merci!*" she said, taking the pistols. "Now, I need more help from you."

"Yes, of course. Anything!"

She motioned toward the other two attackers, motionless amid the half-dozen Frenchmen who had beaten them down. "I need you to gather all the guns from those two men as well and bring them to me, just as you did with these."

"Even big guns?"

"Yes. Everything. And tell everyone to stand back and form a circle around this area—to create space to help protect the president."

"Yes."

"And find a few men to sit on the manhole cover in case other bad men try to come up. Have them stay off the hole at the center, in case someone tries to shoot up through it. If any are still down there, we can't let them come up here." She paused. "And find out if there is a doctor in the crowd."

"*Oui!* I will do this."

Then he stood up and ran back toward the group of men by the manhole. She heard him giving excited instructions in French, which no one seemed to question.

Finally, Rebecca had a moment to evaluate the president's condition. Keeping the two pistols on the ground beside her, she turned onto her side to check the president. Looking at her closely, she felt a jolt of fear.

"Ma'am! Can you hear me, ma'am?" she asked, her voice rising in concern.

She got no response from the president's motionless body. Pressing her fingers lightly against the president's throat, Rebecca felt no sign of life.

"No! Please, God," she said, staring up into the snow that fell gleaming past the overhanging Christmas lights. "Oh, please no," she whispered to the winter night.

She moved her fingers less than a half inch down, and a euphoric jolt shot through her. She had found a pulse—weak but steady.

A wide smile broke through tears of relief.

The sirens she had heard for the past minute grew suddenly loud before dying in an eruption of blue and red strobe flashes. The immediate threat was neutralized, help was here, and the president was still alive.

She placed her hand over one of the two black handguns, wrapping her fingers around its grip. But there was nothing to fire at. No threat to the president remained. She and John and David, along with many others, had succeeded in their job: they had protected the president.

Something caught in her throat as she thought of John and David and the other agents who had died tonight. She had been trained to react in the moment of an attack, but nothing had prepared her for the aftermath.

As she lay beside the president, hugging her close to give what warmth she could, with the cold gun gripped in her hand, she looked out at the Christmas lights of Paris in the falling snow. And her body shook as she cried.

But never once, even now, with French and American backup arriving, did she ever, for a moment, relax her vigil. Never once did she stop protecting the president.

EPILOGUE

DOMINIK KALMÁR STARED at the silent story unfolding before his eyes on the flat screen at the private resort's large, open-air dining lounge. For the past month, he had been at the luxury hideaway on this remote island five hundred miles southeast of Singapore in the Java Sea. It was the perfect place to hide from the Western world.

On the television was the view of a Paris street, taken, according to the news caption, via amateur video from a high floor in an apartment building. Fluffy clumps of snow glimmered in the flash of emergency lights as security vehicles rushed from the edges of the video's frame toward its center. His tired eyes glared at the focus of all the attention. In the center of the video, a young woman sat on the ground, holding a gun in one hand and cradling another woman's head with the other arm. A body lay directly in front of her, and a dozen other bodies lay scattered farther away. Pedestrians had formed a wide circle around the two women. The emergency vehicles arrived, and men in black tactical gear sprinted toward the women as the crowd parted. A second later, a black SUV raced up to them, and the men, after speaking hurriedly with the young woman, lifted the other woman into the backseat. Then the young woman was quickly helped inside, and the SUV jerked forward with a sharp turn and darted back through a gap in the crowd. The video followed the vehicle for as long as possible. As it raced away from the scene, a half-dozen other black SUVs followed, roaring through the Paris night. The video held on them until they vanished around a turn.

The breaking news caption said that the American president had survived a major assassination attempt in Paris.

It was all a colossal failure. Dominik couldn't understand the disturbing mix of anger and fear that he felt at this moment. So much work had gone into this night. And now, with nothing to show for it all, he was open to so many destructive repercussions. Maximilian had promised him victory but had failed in a way that could paint a very large target on Dominik's chest.

He focused one last time on the start of the video, which the news network was playing in a loop. The motionless American president again lay in the arms of the female Secret Service agent. And the agent was again pointing a gun forward with an outstretched arm, looking as if she had only barely survived the massacre that had claimed so many lives this night. Dominik stared hard at her, his blood boiling as he saw just how close he had come to success—just how close this woman and her president must have come to death. This should have been one of the most tragic nights in the history of the United States, but instead it would go down as one of its most heroic.

He felt sick.

Standing up with a jerking, awkward motion, he grabbed the silver lion's-head knob of his black Italian cane and moved with uneven strides toward the open terrace, away from the dining tables. It looked out over the rocky cliff and the crashing waves below. The warm air moved in a faint breeze laden with frangipani, and Java sparrows squabbled noisily in the jackfruit tree under a cloudless sky. The morning sun was still below the horizon, but its expanding line of orange light fired the ocean horizon.

Taking no pleasure from his tranquil surroundings, he turned his thoughts back to Paris, still in the dead of night five time zones behind his tropical island hideaway.

An hour ago, he had received a message that Ryurik Fyodorov, the Russian crime boss, had sent a man to talk to Maximilian just before the assault began. But the man hadn't contacted Fyodorov afterward, and it was now apparent to all the crime syndicate representatives on the Commission that Maximilian's actions had reached well beyond his orders.

Orders that Dominik had seen as too limited for dealing with the United States. And so he had developed a more aggressive plan for dealing a crushing blow to the American people—a plan that hinged on this president's assassination. A plan that Dominik would now have to find a way to execute on his own, without Maximilian's brilliant strategy and tactics, and without Kazim's powerful rage.

With one hand on the waist-high rock wall lining the terrace, he slid the expensive cane in his grip until he held it near the tip. Then, tightening his grip, he swung the heavier end with the silver lion's head against the rocks, then swung again, until the silver knob broke off and the cane cracked near the end. He flung the broken stick off the terrace and onto the rocks below.

Then he took a deep breath and began planning his next move.

*   *   *

Rebecca stood over the hospital bed at the Pitié-Salpêtrière Hospital in Paris. Her eyes welled anew with tears as she studied all the tubes and monitoring devices attached to David. She had been overcome with joy after hearing that the CAT rescue team sent down the shaft had found him buried under a pile of rubble, nonresponsive but still with a faint pulse. He was unconscious the entire time as they lifted off the rubble and hoisted him to the surface in a wire litter provided by rescue workers from the Paris IGC.

She touched his bare arm, gently moving her fingers along his skin. She hoped he could feel her, that somewhere deep inside his subconscious he might know that she was here next to him. She had never seen him so helpless. All these tubes and beeping, sighing, whirring medical devices . . . the casts on his other arm and his elevated leg . . . the relaxed features of his bruised face. She would have cried if she weren't so grateful he had survived.

The doctors had told her that David's left eardrum was ruptured and bones in his right leg shattered. Even if the surgeries went well, he would have a bad limp for the rest of his life. He had been shot four times, had a bad burn on his right arm, and had a dozen other broken bones and cracked ribs. But they had stopped the internal bleeding in time to save his life, and his heart was strong. The doctor said he should regain consciousness by tomorrow.

She heard footsteps stop in the doorway behind her.

"Special Agent Reid," a man's voice said.

"Yes," she replied without turning around.

"She's asking that you lead her out."

Rebecca turned to face Special Agent Chris Snyder, a tall, fit man with dark skin and a piercing intelligence. He had been in her and David's cadet class.

"You make sure you're here when he wakes up, okay?" she said.

"Wouldn't miss it."

"He'll need to see a familiar face."

"I'll be here," he said. "And I'll tell him you're with the president. He'll be happy to hear that."

She nodded. "Call me at once, Chris. Okay?"

He stepped into the room and put his hand on her shoulder. "I will. We have two more agents who'll stay here as well. No one's leaving him behind."

"I spoke with his parents," she said. "They're flying from California and should be here tomorrow morning."

"We'll have agents meet them at the airport."

She turned and gazed at David for a moment. Then she leaned over and whispered into his good ear, "You saved the president's life. And you saved mine. Now I need you to fight through this." She rose up and kissed him gently on the forehead, and with tears in her eyes, she turned and left the room.

Less than a minute later, she walked past the Secret Service's command center, manned by four agents. When the president had first arrived in Paris, only one agent was assigned to the hospital, to guard the president's blood supply and act as a quick-response emergency liaison. But now the medical facility was swarming with two hundred agents, most flown in from field offices across Europe.

The president had been in surgery for six hours in a secured operating room, to repair the damaged right brachial artery. The surgery had gone well, and she had spent the past ten hours resting in recovery. In that time, a team of top American surgeons had arrived from the Landstuhl Regional Medical Center, operated by the US Army in Germany. They had evaluated her and determined that—under constant medical supervision—she could fly back to Washington. And Rebecca knew that the Service was anxious to get the president back into the protective confines of Air Force One and, eventually, the White House.

She walked through the third security checkpoint and entered the restricted area in a recovery waiting room. She stood alone in the center of the room as other agents and military medical personnel moved around her. She had gotten a few hours' sleep in a chair by David's bed, so she wasn't especially tired. Waiting here gave her more time to reflect on the events of last night. Reports were coming out that a hundred hotel guests had died in the attack, most of them suffocating in the fire. And over a hundred agents from the Secret Service had been killed, many during the prolonged assault on the first floor. It had been the one area that she hadn't personally seen during their escape. They had made the right decision using the elevator shaft to avoid the ground floor. And they had made the right decision going into the tunnels.

At least, that was what she told herself. But she couldn't stop replaying everything over and over again in her mind. She couldn't stop wondering whether they might have done something different, something to avoid coming so close to losing the president. She couldn't stop replaying the nightmare.

A hush fell over the room. She turned around as President Clarke, in a wheelchair, was pushed through an open doorway. It was the first time Rebecca had seen her out of a bed since they arrived at the hospital sixteen hours earlier. She looked pale.

The agent brought her wheelchair to a stop in front of Rebecca.

"Madam President," Rebecca said.

"Rebecca, how are you holding up? They tell me David's getting great care and is going to make it."

"Yes, ma'am. I was just with him. He's still unconscious, but his surgeries have gone well and his vitals are pretty strong."

"I can't tell you how glad I am to hear that," she said. "I owe both of you everything . . . everything."

"Thank you, ma'am."

"They've cleared me to fly," President Clarke said. "I'm leaving in a few minutes."

"Yes, ma'am. The motorcade's waiting in the underground garage, the route to the airport has been cleared, and Air Force One is waiting on the tarmac." Technically, it was Air Force One only when the president was onboard, but at this moment, Rebecca didn't care about technicalities. It was the president's plane, and she would soon be back on it.

"And you are leading me out," Clarke said.

"Yes, ma'am. They told me you requested it to the director. I appreciate that, but I have to remind you that I work on the advance team—not technically a special agent in charge."

The president looked at her with a hint of a smile and said, "Under the circumstances, I think we can make an exception."

"Yes, ma'am—of course."

Rebecca raised her wrist microphone and said, "Stagecoach, this is Reid—acting SAIC. Bring Firefly down. ETA three minutes. All post agents elevate to code three. Command Center, alert Transport and Air Force command. Moving now."

A troop of agents led the way out the room, with Rebecca walking beside the agent pushing the president. As they moved down the hallway, hospital staff applauded from a secure distance. An elevator took them to the garage, where the shiny black presidential SUV limousine waited with red and blue lights flashing from inside its front grill. Two other stretch SUV's, four CAT SUVs, an ambulance, and a dozen police motorcycles completed the motorcade. The rest of the large parking garage level had been cleared.

As one agent helped the president into the backseat, Rebecca stood watch by the front passenger door. Her eyes scanned the empty distances of the garage, just as John had taught her. That was when she saw something move in the far shadows. Then nothing. She stared hard for a moment before deciding it couldn't be anything. They had the area secured. It had to be the product of her own hypervigilance.

Everything was ready. She closed the back door, then got in the front passenger seat and pulled her heavy door shut. Speaking into her wrist microphone, she said, "Firefly in Stagecoach. Eighteen minutes out from Bald Eagle." Then she nodded at the agent behind the wheel. The engine revved, and the presidential limousine moved forward with the line of other vehicles in the motorcade.

As they drove out of the garage, she was surprised to see the sunlight quickly fading from the short winter day. She had spent the past sixteen hours inside the hospital, mostly in rooms with no outside windows. It was still snowing. The streets had been cleared of traffic by French police blocking intersections along their route. The passing facades of buildings were gray in the vanishing light. Shop windows reflected the motorcade's flashing lights. As daylight faded, the streetlamps seemed to grow and expand like metallic flowers in incandescent bloom. They drove through the Left Bank, along the Seine, with a view of the Louvre across the river, and a last glimpse of the yellow-lit Eiffel Tower on the left, before the motorcade turned onto the highway flanking the twenty arrondissements.

"Any updates on the investigation?" President Clarke asked.

Rebecca turned her head enough to see her in her peripheral vision while still facing forward. "Yes, ma'am. They've tracked the source of the tunnel assault to a warehouse two miles from the hotel. Owned by a shell corporation based in the Caymans. We're still following the legal and financial trails. Not sure yet which terrorist group or organization was involved. No one is claiming responsibility for the attack. But a body found at the warehouse has been identified as a French organized-crime figure with ties to the Russian mob and terrorist factions in Yemen."

"But we don't know who is ultimately responsible?"

Rebecca looked back at President Clarke. "No, ma'am. Not yet. But we will find out. And when we do, we'll hunt them down and make them pay for their crimes."

"You're damn right we will," Clarke said. She looked out her side window, into the night. "No matter how long it takes."

"Yes, ma'am."

Rebecca knew that the president had already scheduled to be at Andrews Air Force Base in a few days, when the bodies of the fallen Americans arrived Stateside.

They pulled through the secured entrance at Charles de Gaulle, right on schedule. The motorcycle police slowed and fell in behind the group. The CAT SUVs closed in to tighten the bubble as they sped along the tarmac toward the enormous Boeing VC-25 known to the public as Air Force One. It was parked unbelievably close to other vehicles and security personnel by the hangars reserved for the US Air Force and the Marines HMX-1 division. The huge blue and white jet's many coats of wax gleamed in the surrounding lights, and Rebecca had little difficulty believing that this was the most technologically advanced aircraft in the world.

She couldn't help being proud to be a part of this. And she could never forget John and all the other men and women who had died to protect something greater than themselves.

"Are you ready, ma'am?" she asked as the limousine slowed to a stop.

"Yes."

Rebecca opened her door and stepped out into the falling snow. The air felt cold against her face as her sharp eyes scanned the faces along the rope line. Her team of PPD agents had everything covered. CAT agents were on standby, and at least one of their SUVs would race beside Air Force One on the runway during takeoff. The US military liaison was in the tower to ensure that air traffic control had cleared the surrounding airspace for miles before the departure.

But just then she again noticed something strange— something that stood out in her mind and worried her as the shadow in the hospital garage had done. It was someone in the crowd behind the rope line a hundred feet away. A man with slightly graying hair. It was difficult to make out his face through the falling snow, but he seemed to be smiling. And he was looking directly at her. His posture was too stiff, and he seemed to barely move within the vibrant group. And then she saw that the agents working the rope line had missed a critical warning sign: his hands were tucked deep into the dark coat that hung to his knees.

She raised her wrist to radio for one of the agents to have the man remove his hands from his pockets and keep them visible while they moved the president. But before a word left her mouth, he pulled his empty hands out and let his arms hang at his side. It was as if he had read her mind. It took her a few seconds to lower her wrist and move on with the rest of her visual sweep.

Seeing that everything was now safe and that all three layers of the protective bubble were sealed and secured, she pulled the coded switch on the president's door and opened it. She reached out her hand as the president carefully got out of the limousine. Then, with the crowd clapping and cheering, Rebecca slowly helped President Clarke through the falling snow, toward Air Force One.

THE END

About The Author

Bryan Devore was born and raised in Manhattan, Kansas, and received his Bachelor's and Master's in Accountancy from Kansas State University. He also completed an exchange semester at the Leipzig Graduate School of Management in Leipzig, Germany. He is a CPA and lives in Denver, Colorado. He welcomes comments and feedback, and can be contacted at bryan.devore@gmail.com.

Novels by Bryan Devore:
The Aspen Account
The Price of Innocence
The Paris Protection

www.bryandevorebooks.com

Made in the USA
San Bernardino, CA
20 December 2016